LOVE FROM
Greece

LOVE FROM *Greece*

THREE MODERN WOMEN
FIND LOVE IS AS PRICELESS
AS THEIR GRECIAN ROOTS

MELANIE KARIS
PANAGIOTOPOULOS

BARBOUR
PUBLISHING

Dear Readers,

The three stories in this collection (plus the historical novella *Olympic Dreams*, found in the collection *Olympic Memories*) are based on my experience while living in a Greek Mountain village.

As a young bride I accompanied my husband to the actual village of Louka, where he took part in the Rural Physician Service of Greece. Although the town of Kastro in *Love from Greece* is fictitious, the character of Papouli is based on the actual village priest of Louka, Theodore Papadopoulos (1901-1996).

When I first met Papouli, he was sitting at a café in the village square drinking a demitasse cup of Greek coffee surrounded by friends. Although 79 years of age, he didn't look a day over 59. My husband and I had scouted out other villages that were bigger and better situated, but we decided on Louka because of this very welcoming and special man of God. I have never met a more spiritual (and I mean in the Christian way!) nor a more fun-loving man than he! And his faith. . .it was a living one that shone forth daily and even more, when greatly pressed, at the tragic death of his eldest son.

I'm pleased, through the writing of these stories, to introduce such a special man—pastor, priest, father, husband, and friend—to you.

Please visit with me at my Web site, www.MelaniePanagiotopoulos. com, sign my guest book, and let me know something about you and what you thought about *Love from Greece*.

Melanie Karis Panagiotopoulos

With much love to my parents, Sara and Sayre Karis.
Thank you for your loving, encouraging, teaching, caring,
wonderful "Mom and Dad" ways!
But mostly, thank you for always loving each other.
Your more than fifty years of marriage (and still counting!)
is what romance is all about!
God bless you both always!

Happily
Ever After

In loving memory of Theodore Papadopoulos—
Papouli; *a true man of God,*
he made my year in a Greek mountain village extra special.
(1901–1996)

Chapter 1

The wide mountain valley shimmered and glowed in the heat of the summer day like wishes from her many dreams.

Beautiful, picture perfect, pastel and soft, timeless, and yet ever changing, it was also somehow familiar to Allie, even though she knew she had never visited it before. Her fingers smoothed down a section of peeling leather on the old bus's seat while she let her eyes, now narrowed against the strong glare of the sun, scan the landscape before her.

Ramrod cypress trees stood guard over ceramic-roofed peasants' sheds, while graceful groves of silver-clothed olive trees sat like a chorus of waiting ballerinas in the stillness of the day. Church-topped hills with whitewashed villages gleaming below in the strong summer sun—crinolines on a Victorian lady—dotted the landscape all the way to where tall, tranquil mountains formed a demarcation line with the rest of the world.

It was a world unto itself, a land of enchantment, of wonder. Allie's lips formed an amazed *O* as she realized that it didn't remind her of an actual place but rather of illustrations in her much-treasured volume, *Collection of Classic Fairy Tales*. The book had belonged to her mother and was even now making this remarkable journey with Allie in the luggage compartment of the ancient bus.

She settled deeper into the worn seat as a smile, a slow smile of satisfaction, of anticipation, lifted the corners of her lips. Allie Alexander, M.D., recognized that, for her, the Grecian countryside was the most enchanting place on earth. It was the Shangri-La she had been searching for, wanting, for as long as she could remember. At that moment she knew she had made the correct decision—was indeed following the path God had laid out for her—in becoming a country doctor here.

Born and raised in New York City, Allie had left America for the home of her father's birth to attend medical school and residency in Athens. But after having been falsely accused of ethical misconduct by a patient—a soccer star—Allie knew the time had come for her to seek the simpler, more basic lifestyle for which she had always yearned.

To hear the singing of the birds in the morning rather than the grinding and groaning of the trash collector's truck, to live where something new awaited her at every curve in the road, to work where her knowledge of medicine made a difference to individuals whose faces and names she knew—not just to unknown people who matched impersonal numbers on a form—was a way of living Allie had desired for as long as she could remember. Like one knowing she was moving in God's will, she clasped her hands together and thought how she had finally found it.

She had signed a year-long contract to become a member of Greece's Rural Physician Service. She was now on her way to her new home, Kastro, a remote village located high in the mystic mountains above her. With the clear, dry air softly bathing her face and with her nose savoring the complimentary fragrances of the heated earth and its trees—a delicate mix of rock and pine that reminded her of a man's expensive aftershave—Allie thought she just might like to stay forever.

The bus rounded a bend, and Allie spied a medieval castle atop a distant mountain. Excited, she sat up in her seat. She loved castles, and this one didn't disappoint. It seemed to float ethereally in the sky, as if it had been built on something other than the mountain beneath it. With turrets and parapets sharply defined, it was the artist's finishing touch on the actual canvas before her, and whimsically Allie thought the only thing missing from this land of delicate beauty and unparalleled charm was a prince on a white horse.

Allie wouldn't mind her very own prince. . . .

As long as he wasn't a patient of hers.

She would guard herself and her professionalism just as soundly as the walls of the fortress that loomed above had once protected the land surrounding it.

The bus rolled to a stop, but looking around, Allie couldn't understand why. A steep cliff fell to her left, while a dense forest was to her right. As far as she could tell, they were in the middle of nowhere, without even a sign to mark the spot as a bus stop.

But the only other passenger aboard, a man clutching two hens and wearing an old felt hat that had seen better days, recognized this no-man's-land as his own. He was disembarking, something the squiggling, squawking chickens were making difficult. With tough salt-and-pepper whiskers dotting his face and with skin leathery from spending much of his life outdoors, he more resembled a backwoodsman than a chicken farmer.

Cluck, cluck, cluck! The birds screamed with crescendo force, and the hitherto quiet man shouted back at them in a manner Allie thought similar to his fowl friends. Their wings flapped and their bodies twisted and turned in ways Allie wouldn't have believed possible if she hadn't been an eyewitness. She was reminded of the visiting Chinese acrobats her father had taken her to see at Madison Square Garden when she was a child. Those performers had been dressed up as chickens. Watching these real birds, Allie finally understood where their crazy choreography had come from.

But there hadn't been feathers floating around at that long-ago show as there were at this one. Soft and fluffy bits glided all around the bus like large snowflakes. The scene was different from anything Allie had experienced—something that might come from Lewis Carroll's crazy Wonderland. A cloud of downy fluff landed on Allie's wrist, tickling her sensitive skin. She could feel laughter ready to escape her.

But since the backwoodsman did not look like a man who would appreciate someone finding humor in the situation, Allie swallowed hard. She waved wayward feathers away from her nose and pointed her face in the direction of the staid safety of the castle, leaving the woodsman to a private, if inglorious, exit.

Her vision didn't reach the mighty bulwark on the summit, though.

It was blocked by the imposing form of a man outside her window.

A man who sat upon a horse.

Allie blinked.

A white horse.

Her gaze didn't spend more than half a moment on the beast. It went back to the man. And she was certain, absolutely sure, that Cinderella's prince could not have looked any better. With hair as dark as midnight and eyes that held the light of the stars in them, he was a perfect specimen of mankind.

When his lips curved into a smile, something inside of Allie jumped in response. She smiled back, and that age-old communication signaling a want, a desire to know someone better, passed between them like a fusion. His dark eyes reached out to hers, touched hers. Little shivers of pleasure ran up Allie's bare arms and down her spine, making her feel more womanly than she had felt in a very long time. She liked the sensation. She welcomed it.

That there was quick chemistry between them was evident to her scientific mind, although it didn't require her knowledge of science to figure that out. Science had nothing to do with what she was feeling. It was something basic, an impulse between a man and a woman, a feeling that probably went all the way back to Adam and Eve.

As the old bus ground into gear and slowly continued its journey up the mountain, their gaze remained connected until a turn in the road severed it.

Sighing, Allie sank back into the hot leather seat. She thoughtfully ran her hand over the length of her French braid as she wondered about him, who he was, what he believed. Slowly, her lips curved upward.

If her father had seen it, he would have looked at her with his love-filled eyes and told her that she was wearing her mysterious Mona Lisa smile. Actually, he would have told her that the one Leonardo da Vinci had painted on his portrait

11

of the woman named Mona Lisa had nothing on the actual smile that decorated her face.

It was a smile created by Allie's decision: For Allie knew then and there that she liked country life.

She glanced over her shoulder in the direction of the prince.

She liked it a lot.

Einai koukla—she's a doll." Petros spoke to his friend Stavros and nodded after the belching bus while struggling to keep his chickens from escaping his grip. Perspiration dripped from beneath his hat and down his chin, but he ignored it.

Stavros glanced away from the noisy vehicle to the woodsman. He'd enjoyed flirting with the beautiful stranger through the window, but he hadn't wanted anyone witnessing it. Although he knew that if anyone had to see him making a fool of himself over some unknown woman, Petros was the one to do so. Petros was a recluse, a man who minded his own business. He'd never spread rumors. Suspecting that the very personality trait he admired in the other man would most likely render his question unanswered, Stavros asked anyway. "Do you know who she is?" He clicked his tongue to control his prancing horse. Charger didn't like being idle.

Petros shrugged his bony shoulders, showing that it was no concern of his. "Most likely somebody's relative who has come from the city to make fun of us country yokels," he replied as expected and started walking toward a woodland path that was barely visible from the road, one squabbling hen now securely placed under each arm.

Stavros regarded his friend's straight back thoughtfully. Petros had a pride that was as hard as the oak forest in which he lived. Unfortunately, he had an anger that was equally rigid. When no one in the village had been able to save his wife and newborn baby on a snowbound winter day three years earlier, he'd packed up his brood of four children and moved up onto the mountain.

Stavros understood his motives. He'd done something similar himself at around the same time by leaving Georgetown outside of Washington, D.C., and moving to his father's ancestral home in Greece. But it was a move that had been positive for his family, and thanks to his computer and satellite hookup, he wasn't cut off from the rest of the world. He corresponded by e-mail with his mother and numerous friends and business associates in the United States practically every day.

Contrarily, Stavros wasn't so sure it was good for Petros's family to be up on the mountain totally packed away from civilization. His house—an old, stone structure from the nineteenth century—didn't even have electricity.

A chicken suddenly lunged out its neck and pecked Petros on his nose, almost making good her escape. "You scrawny creature!" Petros shouted, catching the loudly complaining hen by her thin legs. "I'll make you into soup!"

Stavros chuckled, a sound barely heard above the din. "Are you starting a chicken farm?"

Petros swung around, disgust making his weathered nose flare. "You know I'm not. Maria wants them," he snapped out, referring to his sixteen-year-old daughter.

Stavros frowned. Maria was Petros's oldest, and since Petros's wife had died, Stavros knew that she had been looking after her younger brothers and sister. "When are you going to move those children back to the village?"

"When I have a good enough reason to move them, I will," Petros shot out.

Frown lines cut across Stavros's face. "They need to be in school," he pressed.

"Maria teaches them."

"But who teaches Maria?" Stavros returned.

Petros swung away from Stavros. "Mind your own mind," he mumbled, just before disappearing into the dense pine forest. The trees closed in upon him within seconds, leaving no indication a man had just walked though.

Stavros blew out air through his teeth. He knew to "mind his own mind" was good advice—advice he himself often handed out.

He leaned forward and absently rubbed Charger's neck. He and Petros were a lot alike. He frowned and sat up straight. He wasn't so sure if that was a good thing.

The flash of the sun on the rusty chrome of the bus drew his attention up the mountain to where the moving metal contraption came into view on yet another curve as it snaked its way up the range. Squinting up at it, Stavros admitted how the woman aboard it had sparked something in him as no woman had for years. But, swinging his horse in the direction of the valley, Stavros also knew that if given the chance, he wouldn't do anything about it.

Or rather, he would.

He would steer clear of her.

Go in the opposite direction.

He didn't need a woman complicating his life, particularly not a woman who was obviously city born and bred. He'd been married to one of them.

He gently kicked his horse into a trot.

And she'd almost killed him.

Chapter 2

The village of Kastro sat gleaming in the sun like a necklace of rubies and pearls, and Allie didn't think the illustrator of *Collection of Classic Fairy Tales* had portrayed his fictitious mountain village to be nearly as charming as this one was. Not only was it topped by the castle she had already fallen in love with, but it came complete with a blue-domed Byzantine church and little streets and alleyways that climbed the steep mountainside with a grace that only very old towns can wear.

Entering the village, Allie glimpsed vine-covered verandas and rose-filled gardens with sweeping eucalyptus and modest citrus trees peeking out from behind old garden walls. It was spotless, and by the time the bus pulled up into the shaded village square, Allie had lost her heart to Kastro.

People gravitated to the bus like thirsty animals to a spring. Allie was surprised by how many people there were. Glancing at her watch, she saw it was almost siesta time, an institution in the villages of Greece. But still, men ambled out from the village *kafenion*—coffee shop—women wiping their hands on aprons appeared from kitchens, and children ran from hidden playing fields, flushed and excited. Chatting animatedly, they all wanted to greet the bus, which brought a little bit of the outside world to Kastro three times a week.

Allie let out a contented breath. These were to be her people—to care for, to get to know, to live with as neighbors. She had heard that villagers treated doctors who were a part of the Rural Physician Service as much-loved and respected members of the community. As she gathered her purse and medical bag, she knew that was yet another reason she had decided to become a country doctor. She wanted to be a member of a tight-knit, family-type community. Her fun-loving mother had died when she was only eight, and her dear but serious father ten years later. The only family Allie had now was a brother, Alex, and he lived on the other side of the world.

Anticipating a good welcome, she felt a smile touch her face as she alighted from the bus. But when the soles of her sandals touched the ground, all talking stopped with the finality of a TV being switched off, as everyone, from the oldest of men to the youngest of children, turned to stare at her.

Allie felt her skin suffuse with color. Certain, though, that once they knew who she was she would be welcomed, and grandly, Allie shifted her medical bag in front of her. Speaking in Greek, which had become, after her years in medical school, almost another native language, she introduced herself. "Hello. I'm Allie Alexander. Your new doctor."

From everything she had heard, that news should have been greeted enthusiastically.

But it wasn't.

If anything, it made the quiet even quieter. Now even the old men's *koboloie*—worry beads—stopped their rhythmic *click, click, click*, while the stare of many became as one.

Feeling confused, Allie asked, "This is the village of Kastro, isn't it?" But she was certain it was. The castle, *kastro*, sitting on the mountaintop above, proclaimed the village's name.

When the villagers remained silent, the bus driver looked up from pulling her suitcases out of the luggage compartment and answered her. "Sure is." Even he looked bewildered by their lack of welcome.

Allie nodded her thanks to him before further inquiring of the silent crowd, "Kastro is the seat of the medical clinic for this area, isn't it?"

After a very long pause, a giant of a man wearing a shirt that had matching sweat marks of huge diameter under each armpit, swaggered to the front. With eyes small and mean, he drawled out, "It is. But you're not welcome here."

Allie blinked. "I beg your pardon?"

"I said," he repeated as if she were dense, "you are not welcome here." From the gloating way his eyes met his cronies', she knew he was drawing strength from the embarrassment and confusion with which his words were meant to fill her. But Allie had seen his type before—a person who grew bigger as he hurt and oppressed others—and she had had it.

She might like fairy tales and dreams of a perfect land, and it might have been nice to have been welcomed, if not profusely then at least civilly. But more than anything else, Allie was a pragmatist. The events in her life had formed her into a person who could be as stubborn and as determined as the best of them.

Sending all fanciful thoughts back to storybooks where they belonged, and not giving the man or the people who hovered behind him like zombies from the *Twilight Zone* another glance, she left her luggage under the huge plane tree and marched into the kafenion that opened onto the square.

She was hot.

She was tired.

And she was thirsty.

Before she took another step or said another word, she was going to get an ice-cold cola.

The kafenion was dingy, but its thick stone walls kept it refreshingly cool.

A woman came out from behind a curtained-off area, the clicking of her dentures proclaiming her presence. Not even the fact that she was as sour-faced as a prune—and Allie knew she could expect no welcome from her, either—could deter Allie from getting that drink.

"One cola please," she ordered, and, reaching into her purse, she placed its cost upon the scarred wooden table.

Allie heard the shuffling sound of people following her in, and from the corner of her eye, she saw the ponderous bulk of the man whom she now thought of as the ogre leading the way. The woman behind the counter darted a nervous glance in his direction, not even trying to hide from Allie the tilt of her head as she silently asked his permission to serve the drink.

Allie's gaze swiveled to meet his as she dared him to say no.

He shrugged his bulky shoulders and nodded to the woman. Clicking her ill-fitting teeth loudly, the woman turned and went into the back area.

While Allie waited for the cola, she didn't look to the right or to the left. When the woman returned and plopped the drink in front of her, Allie drank it all down before she turned to face the villagers again.

The men, that is.

With the exception of the prune-faced woman, all the women and children had disappeared. A glance out the door revealed the square to be empty, too. Allie remembered hearing that in the more remote areas the village kafenion was a male stronghold. She just hadn't believed it. Until now.

Taking a deep breath, she addressed the "Men's Club." "Someone can either show me to the medical clinic—or I will find it myself."

When all their gazes shifted toward the ogre, Allie's did, too. Without flinching a muscle, she informed him, "I have the key." The Department of Health had given it to her in the city. She was glad that they had had such foresight.

There was a charged moment before the ogre commanded the woman behind the counter, "Ireni. Take her."

From the smirking stretch of his thick lips, Allie had the unsettled feeling he hid something, but with a confidence to her steps that held no hesitation or weakness, she followed the scowling woman out the door and across the square to a winding lane.

If circumstances had been different, Allie would have enjoyed the walk. Eucalyptus trees lined the way, with walnut, olive, and citrus groves appearing in the distance. Some houses were old, some were new, but they all had one thing in common: They were all kept in beautiful shape.

Except for one: the small whitewashed building with the official blue and white sign designating it as belonging to the Department of Health.

It wasn't that its paint was peeling or that its shutters were sagging, but rather, it had an unkempt, abandoned air about it. Like the overgrown rosebushes under its shuttered windows, it simply needed care. For the first time, Allie wondered how long Kastro had been without a doctor and why.

Smacking her dentures together, the woman named Ireni pushed open the door with a reverberating bang. With a surly look in her washed-out eyes, she stood back for Allie to be the first to enter the dark interior of the building.

Taking a deep breath, Allie reached for the light switch. But even before her fingers found it, her nose warned her that all was not going to be as it should. Mustiness and neglect clung to the air, as it would to a dungeon.

Allie flipped on the lone lightbulb and gasped.

The room, which Allie supposed was the waiting area, was a mess. It looked as though it hadn't seen a broom or a mop in at least a year. Papers littered the floor, while intricate spiderwebs hung like eerie wall hangings in the corners and in the niches around the windows. The sofa was turned on its side, and the wicker in the chairs had unraveled.

There was a closed door at the other end of the room, which Allie assumed led to her living quarters. But first, wanting to see the entire clinic, she crossed to the examining room, hoping she would find better conditions there.

But if anything, it was worse.

Medical equipment had been left lying around the room, with used wads of bloodstained cotton balls sitting in soiled trays and in the small metallic sink. The examining table was torn, and her desk had broken ampoules of medicine littering its stained wood, while the medicine cabinet's glass doors were too covered with grime to see through.

Allie reached for the handle and pulled it open. A scorpion—a little larger than an old silver dollar—ran from a length of unwound gauze and up the side of the peeling chest.

"Eek!" Allie yelled and dropped her hand, both instinctive gestures. She turned to the woman beside her, but when the woman only grunted, and in a pleased sort of way, Allie thought it best to ignore her.

Envisioning creepy crawly things running all over her skin, but striving not to show it, Allie left the medicine chest to the scorpion and walked over to a row of boxes that were, surprisingly, covered by a protective tarpaulin. They were the only things that seemed to be cared for in the building.

Pulling back the cover carefully so that the mice droppings that dotted the top would not fall on her, Allie was amazed to discover about twenty boxes of medical equipment and supplies stacked underneath.

She checked the transfer dates. They had arrived within the last month. For the first time since meeting the people of Kastro, Allie smiled. She knew that with these supplies, she could put together a decent medical station.

Pulling a tissue from her purse, she dusted off her hands and, turning to the woman, asked, "Who's in charge of cleaning the clinic?" Allie thought it was a reasonable question, a logical one. But the woman didn't seem to think so. Making a sound that resembled a pig snorting, she turned on her small feet and shuffled out of the building.

"Whew boy," Allie sighed out and watched the woman disappear down the walkway before she let her gaze wander again around the dusty, disheveled interior of the clinic. "Lord?" she asked of the only One who had never let her down. "It is Your will for me to be here, isn't it?"

Shaking her head, she went to the window behind the desk, and, to a rain of chipped paint and dust falling on and around her, she pulled it open. Coughing, she waved the dust away from her face while she reached for the shutters. She was amazed when they easily swung outward.

The view from the window made her forget the mess she had landed herself in. Red and yellow roses with an occasional pink one scented the air, while the green-and-golden patchwork valley shimmered far below. A scratching sound on the ground brought Allie's gaze downward.

She gasped in pleasure.

A tortoise, probably the largest Allie had ever seen, was sunning itself below the rosebush. Its head was tilted upward, and its beady little eyes, the friendliest ones Allie had encountered in the village thus far, were blinking up at her, while its tongue moved in and out of its mouth like a toothless old man trying to form his words.

Looking at that big, beautiful land turtle, Allie knew he was a direct sign from God, a sign telling her better than a million words ever could that in spite of her reception in the village, in spite of the disrepair of the clinic, she was right where she was supposed to be, right where God would have her. Because more than any other of God's creatures, turtles were Allie's love. Sea turtles, land turtles, even snapping turtles, Allie loved all members of the Testudinata family. She hadn't been allowed a dog or a cat in New York City, but her father had always allowed her a turtle. She had cried very sad tears when her little turtle had died a few years back.

But now, in her new home of Kastro, God had sent her a new one: a great big new one, and laughter, her mighty laughter, which her brother always said gave the word *delight* voice, rose from within her to spill out over the Hellenic countryside. "Hello, Mr. Tortoise," she greeted it after a moment. "Have you come to welcome me?"

The turtle blinked up at Allie again, and she was sure he was grinning at her. His presence made turning back to the unsightly disorder behind her easier.

But as her gaze traveled around the depressing room, she sighed. Never in her dreams—and Allie had had many of them—had she imagined that she would find such conditions in Kastro.

But with a firm flick of her braid, knowing that she had to get herself settled before she tackled the office, she walked over to the far door she had seen in the waiting room. She wondered in what sort of state she might find the doctor's quarters. Would it be asking too much to find a snug little apartment with a vine-laden veranda for the fragrant days of summer and a sturdy little fireplace to keep her warm in the winter?

Taking an anticipatory breath, she opened the door.

Not to the expected apartment, but rather, to the great outdoors and—to a donkey!

A donkey who seemed right at home in what Allie quickly realized was the backyard of the clinic. But even more, a donkey who seemed none too pleased at having her siesta interrupted!

Slamming the door shut, Allie leaned her back protectively against it while her gaze swiveled frantically around the room for another door. But there wasn't one, and she knew that there wasn't one in the examining room either.

Only the two rooms made up the clinic.

There wasn't even a bathroom.

Expelling a disappointed sigh, Allie Alexander, M.D., had no idea where she was supposed to live.

No idea at all.

Chapter 3

With a decisive motion, Allie reached for her purse and medical bag and set off back toward the kafenion. Determination and unshakable courage to face a situation, no matter how unpleasant, flowed through her, as adrenaline pumped through her system. It was a feeling with which not only her work but also her life had given her experience in coping.

Squaring her shoulders, she braved the "Men's Club" once again. She paused just inside the door as all the normal café noises—the shuffling of playing cards, the clicking of worry beads, the clattering of dice against wooden backgammon boards—ceased. That her presence in the kafenion disturbed the men was obvious. That she didn't care was readily apparent to them, as, with a slight, defensive tilt of her jaw—one she was very aware of—she walked to a table and, pulling out a wooden chair, sat down.

When the sour-faced woman poked her head out from behind the curtained-off area, Allie immediately ordered another cola. The woman quickly plopped the drink in front of her. Disregarding the proprietress, just as she did the men, Allie wrapped her fingers around the coolness of the bottle, placed her lips over the straw that danced around its opening, and slowly—very, very slowly this time—sipped the sweet, bubbly liquid.

The ticking of the 1950s Coca-Cola clock on the wall behind the cash register was the only noise in the room, and as the moments mounted one upon the other, it seemed to sound louder and more insistent, until the ogre finally slammed the front legs of his chair down onto the stone floor.

"We weren't expecting a woman doctor!" he fired out into the charged atmosphere. And as the men around him mumbled, like sheep bleating in a barnyard, that they hadn't been expecting a woman, either, Allie thought she just might have been given the reason for their antagonism.

Because she was a woman.

But she wasn't sure.

Nagging doubts made her think that there was more to it than simple gender prejudice.

Not even bothering to address his comment, Allie drew in another deep sip of soda before asking, "Where do Kastro's doctors normally live?"

"Well," the hulking man drawled out, "they normally live in the schoolteacher's house." He paused and smiled so broadly that Allie could see a couple of gold teeth in the back of his mouth. "But you can't."

Not a flicker of emotion showed in Allie's face as she asked, "And why is that?"

"Because you're a woman," he stated as if that explained everything.

Allie knew very well that she was a woman, and she was beginning to get a little tired of being reminded of it by this poor excuse of a man. Standing, she sipped the last drop of cola, placed the bottle back on the table, and said, "Well, I'll talk to the teacher and see what he has to say about it."

"Can't," the ogre returned smugly, and Allie knew from the way he shuffled the cards in his pawlike hands so confidently that the game he was playing with her wasn't over yet. "The teacher's not in town," he said, and fear that the teacher might not return until school started in four weeks' time radiated through Allie. If that was the case, she wasn't sure what she was going to do. Maybe start searching for a fairy godmother? The whimsical side of her answered the practical, and she was glad she could still have such frivolous thoughts while her immediate future seemed so uncertain.

"Then I'll talk to him when he returns," she stated, and nodding curtly to the men, she walked toward the exit.

"Nope. You can't live with him," the ogre's nasal voice followed her. "People will talk. You know. . .a single man. . .a single woman. . .living in the same house. . . ." He let the insinuation breed in the air, even as the words came out of his mouth. From her peripheral vision she saw the other men nod their heads as they agreed that people would certainly "talk."

But without breaking her pace, without letting a single muscle in her body convey that she had caught his ugly innuendo, she continued toward the door.

But she had caught it.

A perfect catch, in fact.

In light of what she had gone through a few months before with the soccer star, she inwardly cringed.

"Can't have no hanky-panky going on between our doctor and teacher, now can we?" Allie heard the ogre plant the seed of rumor deeper into the dirt of the village as her feet took her out into the now-empty square.

She was angry. She was disappointed. But more than anything, she was disgusted with herself and her fairy-tale notions. She knew the beauty of the land, the castle, and then seeing a man who could be any woman's idea of a prince had her forgetting the other ingredients that made up fairy tales.

Wicked stepmothers, witches, and ogres. . .

She sighed. In that case, didn't there have to be a fairy godmother around somewhere?

She shook her head as the verses from Psalm 37—real words of wisdom to live by—went through her head. *Trust in the Lord and do good; dwell in the land and enjoy safe pasture. Delight yourself in the Lord and he will give you the desires of your heart. Commit your way to the Lord; trust in him and he will do this: He will make your righteousness shine like the dawn, the justice of your cause like the noonday sun.*

Smiling as the verses of promise sank into her being, Allie swept her gaze over the still village and reminded herself that most of the villagers had not been about when she'd arrived. It was siesta time, the hottest time of the day, and most were quite wisely escaping the heat by sleeping. Surely when others appeared, a house or a room for her to rent could be found.

She sank onto the largest of her suitcases and rubbed her hand across her hot forehead. She wished that she could sleep, too. The emotions and physical work involved with making this move had caught up with her, and all she wanted was to lie down under the coolness of the reaching plane tree and let sleep overtake her.

With the cicadas seeming to serenade her, the broad trunk of the old tree welcoming her head, and the heated air surrounding her like a down comforter, she felt, in spite of the hostility she had encountered, safe in the arms of her Lord, and her eyes closed. She dozed. She didn't know for how long—it couldn't have been more than a minute or two—but when her lids slowly parted, she thought she was dreaming.

Before her, wearing a long robe with a matching black cap and with a long gray beard that had probably been only slightly trimmed in his entire life, stood a man with the kindest set of eyes Allie had ever seen.

"Well, well. . .could this Sleeping Beauty be Kastro's new doctor?" the man asked, his voice deep and gravelly and very, very friendly.

Allie smiled sheepishly, and he laughed, a good sound that brought all the fairy-tale wonder of the land back into Allie's heart, and she knew she must be looking at the village priest. But at the moment he seemed more like a fairy godfather.

Pulling herself away from the tree trunk, she stood. Just a little taller than her five feet five inches, the priest was thin and as spry as a young boy. Allie didn't think he could be a day over sixty, and yet, at the same time, he seemed ageless. She extended her hand to him. "I'm Allie Alexander, and I am Kastro's new doctor."

He took her hand in his, a callused one, Allie noticed, and she knew this was no idle priest. "And I'm Theodore Pappas. Welcome, *Yatrinna.*"

His use of the term *yatrinna* brought an unexpected burst of gratification to Allie. Meaning "lady doctor," it was used by country folk as a sign of respect for a female doctor's professional standing. After her lack of welcome, it was wonderful to be so addressed, and by the priest, the most respected person in village communities.

"Thank you, *Papouli.*" She returned the honor by calling him a "grand-fatherly" priest, and his smile widened, and she knew he liked it.

"But why are you sleeping here in the square?" His eyes danced in merriment behind his wire-framed glasses. "Why are you not in the apartment that has been made ready for you?"

Lines of puzzlement crisscrossed her brow. That there was a place prepared for her was news to her. "Papouli. . ." She paused and licked her lips, not sure how to continue. She was a stranger, and the people of this village were both his family and his flock. She didn't want to complain about people he had probably known all his life or want him to think she was a whining baby.

But Theodore Pappas was a priest who knew human character well, and his wise old eyes easily registered that something was amiss. "Please, feel free to tell me anything," he urged, and she saw him then as a man of God, in the truest and most unadulterated form.

So Allie told him. "I'm afraid the people, the men," she amended and motioned toward the kafenion, "have made it quite clear that there is nowhere for me to live in this village."

"Bah." The priest's deep, gravelly voice bayed in perfect synchronization with his eyebrows shooting up above the rim of his glasses. "Nowhere for you to live? But you will live where all the other doctors have lived—in the schoolteacher's house." He answered his own question as if it were a foregone conclusion.

"But they said that since I'm a woman—" She let the rest of the sentence trail off.

"Bah." He cut in authoritatively and guided her toward the kafenion door. "Come. I will set everything straight."

Chapter 4

And Papouli did.

Like a fairy godfather with a magic wand, he cast a spell of goodness, or at least one of compliance, over everyone in the kafenion. They all sat up a bit straighter when Papouli entered the room, and when Allie came in behind him in his respectful wake, their gazes shifted to meet one another, like children caught doing something wrong. Allie wasn't surprised to see that even the ogre held Papouli in esteem.

"Does anyone have any objections to our yatrinna living in the teacher's house?" he asked without preamble, and his sharp eyes, peering above the rims of his glasses, touched on everyone in the kafenion. When no one spoke up, not even the ogre, Papouli dismissed the subject with a slight "harrumph," and after instructing two of the men to carry Allie's luggage, he escorted her up through the winding lanes of the shuttered village to a beautiful white house—one of fairy-tale proportions—that sat in the shadow of the castle directly above it.

Trailing Papouli into a courtyard that had the fragrance of summer hanging softly over it, she forced her tired body to follow him up the marble stairs and around the wraparound veranda, past an opaque glass door and several windows to a large wooden door at the far end of the back of the house. He pushed it open, and Allie's eyes widened at the beautiful apartment. Like a Byzantine chalet, it was of deep rich wood with old stone walls, with cushions and needle-point pillows of bold colors highlighting it.

Allie stepped onto the polished, planked floor and felt as though she had walked into another era. Placing her medical bag by the antique desk that was to her left, her gaze ran over the wood-based sofa that sat in an L shape in front of a lovely *tzaki*—fireplace—the focal point of the traditional room. A breakfast bar backed the shorter part of the sofa, and a galley kitchen was behind it, the modern appliances all artfully hidden below. A brick wall with wooden shelves of the same dark wood as the shutters made up the other side of the kitchen. Ceramic jugs, bowls, and plates of earth tones, which she knew had to be antiques, lined the shelves.

She walked behind the brick wall and into the sleeping area. A huge wardrobe stood to the left, but it was the raised platform bed that drew the attention of her drooping eyes. It was covered with the same ecru fabric that was on the sofa, with colorful throw pillows on top, and she couldn't resist trying it out. She sat on the edge. The mattress was firm but soft—exactly as she liked it. Looking across the room, she watched in wonder as the priest directed the men to place her luggage next to the fireplace. So much had changed since meeting Papouli— that wonderful man of God. Both relief and amazement filled Allie.

The priest turned to her, and his brows rose above his glasses as a look of satisfaction covered his face. "Ah. . .Yatrinna. You like your new home?"

Sweeping her gaze up at the beamed ceiling and then out through the French doors at the fabulous view of the valley and of the tall mountains beyond, Allie felt tears prick the back of her eyes. After the way she had been treated, and after seeing the mess her office was in, the joy she felt over meeting the priest and being brought to this charming abode was almost overwhelming. She wondered at the extremes she had met in the village.

Fairy tale, indeed.

It had all the makings of a classical one.

She stood, then walked over to the desk and slid her fingers over the valuable Byzantine icons that hung to its side. "I love it, Papouli," she murmured.

"Good," he said and turned toward the door. "I will leave you to rest, and this evening you will come to dinner at my house. It's the house with blue shutters next to the church," he proclaimed in a way that brooked no arguments, and turning, he briskly strode out the door.

Allie ran after him, but she was only in time to see the hem of his robe as it followed him around the veranda's corner. She could hear his spry steps as he bounded down the stairs. Smiling warmly, she turned back to the apartment, and leaving the door open to create a crosscurrent, she went over to the sofa and folded herself into its welcoming comfort.

Leaning her head back, her gaze roamed over the huge tzaki, with its arched arms that extended out of the wall, before her eyes settled on the ceramic vase that was full to overflowing with wild, cut roses that decorated the summertime hearth. The roses filled the apartment with their welcoming bouquet. Allie closed her eyes and breathed in deeply of the soft, natural fragrance. It filled her senses, calmed her mind. That a man whom she had never met had gone to such trouble to have such a beautiful residence all ready for her arrival touched a deep part of her soul, a part that hadn't been touched in a very long time. Not since her father had been alive had anyone done kind little things for her. Somehow it made her feel safe.

Standing, she stretched her arms above her head, hoping to feed strength back into her blood. But it didn't do any good. She was exhausted. She needed sleep.

Of their own volition, her fingers nimbly undid her braid as she stumped on legs that were almost too heavy to carry her any farther over to the sleeping alcove. Lowering her weary body onto the inviting bed, she was asleep almost before her head fell against the softness of the pillow. Asleep in a land of castles and of fairy godfathers, where a prince with dark eyes sat on a horse of the most pure white, a horse that seemed to *clip-clop* around in her head. . .

⁂

"Who are you, and what are you doing in my house?" The demand punctured the sweetness of Allie's sleep like a bubble being popped. She willed her lids to lift their slumbering weights from her vision.

But when she did, she wondered if she were only dreaming of being awake.

She seemed to be floating, and everything seemed unreal and foggy. But more than that, the prince of her dreams, who had somehow acquired the same features as the man on the horse—whom she had seen while on the bus—was leaning over her.

Groggily, she gazed up his shirt to his strong chin and past his chiseled nose. When her gaze collided with his—hard and dark—he demanded again, "I asked who are you, and what are you doing in my house?" Allie felt less like a princess and more like Goldilocks of the Three Bears fame, with the man before her being the angry papa bear. She wished that she could get up and run away home like that heroine had. But she couldn't. She was at home.

"*Baba*. . . ," the girl-cub by his side, who was the image of him, admonished with preadolescent embarrassment. Her deep velvety brown eyes were trained on Allie, too, but unlike her father's, they held wonder and friendship in their remarkable depths.

Allie smiled at her, but when her fingertips ran across the fabric beneath her and she realized where she was—flat on her back in bed—she shot up, swung her feet to the side, and stood, ignoring the pounding in her head that was unprepared for such an abrupt change. "Hi," Allie addressed the girl, her friendly eyes preferable to those of her papa.

"Hi," the girl immediately returned, and Allie could see thrilled curiosity nearly ready to burst from her. "Are you the new doctor?" the girl asked with hope in her voice.

"I am." Allie couldn't help smiling at the excitement that was barely contained in the girl's compact body as she swiveled to her father.

"See, Baba. . .I told you," she squealed out her delight.

Allie saw lines of incredulity slash across the man's broad forehead as he looked at her above his daughter's head. "You are the new doctor?" It was more an accusation than a question.

Remembering their encounter on the bus, Allie understood his trepidation, and reluctantly, hesitantly, she nodded her head. The tightening of his jaw told her that he was remembering their first meeting, too. And with the same discomfort. She had liked the idea of romance with this man when he had been a stranger on a horse going in the opposite direction, but now that he was probably the man in whose house she was to live, well, it was a possibility she wouldn't even consider. Her professional integrity was too important to her for that.

"And you. . ." Her throat had gone totally dry. Clearing it, she started again. "I mean, you aren't by any chance the schoolteacher, are you?" But even as she asked, she knew he was. The ogre had led her to believe that the schoolteacher was going to be out of town for quite some time, not just hours. Obviously, he had meant to mislead her in the hopes that she would get on the next bus—or donkey—heading out of town.

"I am," he confirmed, his voice low, like the distant rumble of a dangerous thunderstorm.

"Oh," was all Allie said as attraction ricocheted between them. Something alive, something demanding, it rebounded between him and her, looking for a place to land. But that was not something she desired. She was thankful to get the same impression from him.

Trying to cover her reaction with a businesslike approach, she offered her hand to him and introduced herself. "I'm Allie Alexander."

With his deep eyes regarding her, measuring her, she lifted her chin and measured him back. Silently, communicating on a level that had no need for words, they agreed not to comment on the emotion that was between them. The pact was made in the narrowing of their eyes, in the flaring of their nostrils, in the beating of their hearts.

But putting her hand in his, she couldn't pretend not to feel the wonder of his touch. From the way his eyes widened and brightened, he couldn't, either. Charged with magic, the touch was potent, and they let go of one another as if zapped.

"I'm Stavros Andreas," he quickly replied, turning to the girl by his side. "And this is my daughter, Jeannie."

Allie smiled at the girl, glad that she was with them, especially glad that she lived in the same house. "Hi again, Jeannie."

"Wow!" Jeannie clapped her hands together. "You're the new doctor! You're going to live here!"

"No." Stavros's voice boomed, and both Allie and Jeannie turned to him. Allie knew that the features of their faces wore the same covering. Surprise. What amazed her, though, was that the schoolteacher's did, too. He seemed to be surprised by his own response even as he continued with, "I'm afraid that will be impossible."

"Excuse me?" Allie asked. After Papouli's assurances, this was the last thing she had expected.

"Baba. . . ?" his daughter asked, and Allie could tell that she was as confused by his declaration as was she.

"It won't work out," he said, and like a general having issued an unpopular command, he turned on his heels and walked purposefully into the living area.

Allie and Jeannie followed him. Jeannie turned beseeching, puppy-dog eyes to Allie, a look that told Allie that the girl wanted her to live in the house just as badly as she wanted to. It gave Allie courage. It was wonderful to feel wanted, if only by a young girl.

"Mr. Andreas," Allie began to his solid back, "Papouli brought me here. He said all the doctors have lived here."

"They have." Jeannie's dark-haired head bobbed up and down.

Stavros turned to face Allie. He didn't even try to deny it. "They have also all been men." His gaze swept over her face. "You're a woman."

Allie rolled her eyes and made an exasperated sound. "I have been of the female gender for all of my twenty-eight years. Why is it that everyone in this village feels as though they have to remind me of it?"

His brows cut an ambiguous line across his face. "What do you mean?"

Allie let out a vexed sound. "Let's just say the men in the kafenion weren't very pleased with the idea of Kastro having a female doctor."

His dark eyes narrowed, as though he was considering something. But he only said, "I wouldn't jump to conclusions, Doctor, if I were you."

"Jump to—" Allie stared at him, appalled by the idea. "Mr. Andreas, one thing I never do is 'jump to conclusions.' But when I'm told outright that I'm not wanted here and that the people weren't expecting a 'woman' doctor, what else am I to think?"

For a moment Allie thought he was going to say something, to shed some light on the unusual situation she had found waiting for her in Kastro. But he didn't, and when a deep breath came out instead of the words of enlightenment he might have spoken, Allie felt impotent to retrieve them.

Taking his daughter's hand, he crossed over to the front door, which was still as Allie had left it before she fell asleep—wide open. "I'm sorry," he tossed over his shoulder, "but you will have to find other accommodation."

"But, Baba." Jeannie pulled on his hand, forcing her father to stop and turn around. "Didn't you tell me yesterday, while we were picking the flowers"—she pointed to the summer bouquet that sat tellingly on the hearth—"that there is no place else for the doctor to live?"

"Jeannie." It was a command such as parents give to their children the world over. It meant "be quiet." Jeannie recognized it and obeyed.

"I'm sorry," the girl mumbled and lowered her eyes while her ears turned red with embarrassment. Allie's heart went out to her. Her father wasn't being fair to her.

Stavros sighed, and as he gazed at his daughter's bent head, Allie knew this was a parent who loved his daughter very much and would do almost anything for her. That he felt bad about his reaction was evident in the emotions that skipped across his face.

She watched as he placed his left hand in his pocket and jiggled some coins together for a few seconds. Allie couldn't help but feel as though he was weighing the possibility of her staying. But if that was the case, when he turned to her, she knew from his guarded expression that she had come up short on the scales.

"I'm really sorry. But I don't think Kastro's the place for you. It's remote, with problems a city person can't even imagine," he insisted.

But Allie wasn't about to give up. He might sound definite, but trained as she was in reading symptoms in patients, she saw the battle within, the hesitancy, even, in his stance. She knew how to use that knowledge. "Mr. Andreas, I signed a year-long contract with the Department of Health to be this village's doctor. I will complete the year even if I have to live in the clinic and sleep on the examining table to do so."

Jeannie's distraught brown-eyed gaze shot upward to her father's. "But she can't live there! It doesn't even have a tzaki for the winter. Baba. . . ," she implored, and Allie could tell the teacher was startled at how badly his daughter wanted her—the doctor—to live in their spare apartment. Allie couldn't help but wonder where the girl's mother was. The men at the kafenion had said that the schoolteacher was single. Did that mean he was divorced or a widower?

Allie watched as his eyes took on a soft light as he regarded his daughter, and seeing it, Allie knew that the girl was the most important person in his life. She knew because her own father used to look at her and her brother in the same way.

"Jeannie," he spoke gently, "please go to your room until I call you. I would like to speak with the doctor alone."

Shoulders slumped, Jeannie lowered her head, and walking over to the wooden door that was situated to the right of the desk, the girl turned the handle, opened it, and disappeared through it. Allie's eyes widened.

She looked at the girl's father in bewilderment, something she wasn't used to feeling. "I thought. . .I mean. . .I assumed. . .isn't that the bathroom?"

"It is," he answered, totally perplexing Allie.

She opened her mouth to asked what he meant, but closed it on the question. She wasn't sure she wanted to know.

"That's the reason you can't live here."

"What do you mean?"

He walked over and opened the door wide. "Our apartments are connected by this central hall," he said and pointed out the area.

Allie poked her head in to inspect it. He flipped on the antique wooden chandelier that hung from the center, and she saw the hall had three doors opening off it.

"We can lock our doors," Allie said, with what she thought was total logic. "It's just like living in an apartment complex."

"Except"—with the flourish of a real estate agent showing a room, he swung open the middle door—"we share the house's only bathroom."

Chapter 5

S o?" she asked. To her mind it was similar to sharing a bathroom in a coed dorm.

"So I just can't see myself sharing a bathroom."

"But why?"

He let out a deep breath and ran his hand through his hair, rumpling it. "Look. You might be from the city and think in very modern terms, but I just don't. I don't like the idea of sharing my bathroom with you, a woman."

Allie suspected that neither the fact that she was from the city nor that she was a woman was really the problem. The problem was the way the woman in her encountered the man in him to make them aware of one another in a way that scared them both.

She had seen fear in patients' faces enough times to recognize that was what Stavros Andreas was feeling. She felt it, too. As much as she would like a man in her life, she didn't want a relationship with a man in whose house she rented an apartment. She glanced toward the bathroom. Not even a complete apartment.

Trying to buy some time, she asked, "Umm, do you mind if I wash my hands? I haven't had a chance since arriving in the village."

He cleared his throat in an awkward way and took a step back. "Not at all."

"May we finish talking in a few moments?"

"I don't see that we have much more to say to one another."

"I believe we do."

He shrugged his shoulders. "Come on over to my apartment after you've freshened up." Turning, he opened the door she supposed his daughter had gone through a few moments before and went in, shutting it with a small click.

Allie sighed and walked into the bathroom. Of marble and wood, it was anything but traditional. It was modern and spotless and like those one might find in a penthouse on Park Avenue in New York City.

"The man likes his comforts," Allie mumbled to her reflection as she turned on the tap and washed her hands and face to the hum of a pump. But she had to admit that she was glad that he did. A nice bathroom was about the only thing Allie had dreaded not finding in a remote village. She had heard that in some villages the doctors still had to deal with no indoor water and, horrors of horrors, outhouses. . . .

She shuddered, and the thought that her clinic had only a sink, a very dirty, grimy one, and a donkey in the backyard where the outhouse was most likely located made her resolve to live in this house even stronger. Much stronger.

But the only thing Stavros had resolved as he stood staring out his kitchen window at the castle above was that Allie Alexander, M.D., couldn't live in his house.

When he had seen the open door of the spare apartment, the one which he and his daughter always referred to as "the doctor's apartment," the last thing he had expected to find was the beautiful woman who had occupied so much of his thoughts during the last few hours sleeping like a fairy princess on the bed.

It had thrown him.

The fact that she looked even more beautiful in repose, with her long dark hair gracefully settled around her head, brought a part of him to life that he thought he had successfully extinguished. All he had wanted to do was to lean over and kiss her full lips, to kiss her awake like he was Prince Charming himself.

He shook his head.

What was he thinking?

No, the lady could not live in his house. That was a definite.

Still, he wondered at how the first woman to really interest him since his wife was the very one who, by rights of her professional standing, should be allowed to live in the spare apartment. It had never even occurred to him that the woman he had seen through the open window of the bus could possibly be Kastro's new doctor.

He frowned. He couldn't ever remember any doctors he had ever visited being so beautiful. But he should have known who she was. Kastro was the terminus of the bus route. In the three years he had lived in the village, he had never seen her before. He had never even seen a picture of her as being a member of somebody's family.

He would have remembered if he had.

Something about her face, about her, did things to him. Things a man could never forget.

Because of that, he couldn't let her live in his house. If he had his way, she wouldn't even live in Kastro. He had worked too hard to make a life for his daughter and himself, and he didn't want any woman destroying it. Especially not a city woman, a woman who would be here for a few months—a year at the most, if she were conscientious—then leave, leaving him behind to pick up the pieces of his emotions, his daughter's emotions. No. He couldn't do that. Not again.

"Baba. . ." Jeannie's voice broke into his thoughts, and he turned to see her standing hesitantly in the doorway of her bedroom, her little Siamese cat held comfortingly against her shoulder. Even after nine years, it still amazed Stavros to think that he had had a part in making her and that she was his daughter. He loved being her baba, her father. She made being a father wonderful.

He smiled and held out his arms to her. "Come here."

Grinning broadly, Jeannie put down the cat, then ran across the wooden floor into her father's waiting arms. "Oh, Baba. . . I love you."

"And I love you, pumpkin." Jeannie was the most important person in the world to him. He would do almost anything to give her a good life.

He had.

He'd given up a prestigious position as a university professor in the States to become a village schoolteacher so that he could raise her himself and not leave her in the care of a babysitter day after day until she was all grown up. It was a decision he had never regretted.

Her mother had deserted her.

He never would.

"Baba. . ." She let go of him to scoot up onto the kitchen counter. It had been Jeannie's place since long before they had moved permanently into what had been Stavros's ancestral home. They had used the old home as a summer vacation home—as had his parents before him—before renovating it and turning it into their permanent place of residence. He had brought Jeannie here every summer. Except for the first time, he and his daughter had come alone. His wife hadn't wanted any part of the pastoral village way of life after that first summer.

"What is it, pumpkin?" he prompted, although he knew what was on her mind.

"Please. . .please. . ." She squeezed her eyes together, as she always did when she really wanted something, before opening them wide again to finish her request. "Let the doctor live next door."

Stavros smiled. That was one of the many things he loved about being a father and about working with kids. He could always count on them to say exactly what was on their minds. The problem was that he didn't know how he could explain his reasons for not wanting the doctor to live in their house. Except for how attracted he was to the woman, he couldn't explain it himself. And worse still, he knew that to use the bathroom as an excuse for the doctor not to live in the apartment was lame. Although the thought of her using the same bathtub as he did bothered him. It was just too evocative.

Jeannie continued, obviously taking hope from the fact that he hadn't immediately said no. "I overheard you talking," she said, admitting to eavesdropping. "And I know you think the bathroom will be a problem." His smile deepened over her innocence in really believing that was the issue. "But we can work out a signal or something so that we know when it's being used," she completed with a logic for which Stavros couldn't help but be proud.

Reaching out, he undid her ponytail to fix the wisps of dark hair that had escaped it since that morning. "Why do you want her to live here?" he asked, really wanting to know.

"Because I like her. She's beautiful," Jeannie answered quickly, stating two reasons Stavros certainly couldn't deny. "And it's the doctor's apartment. The doctors always live here."

"True," he conceded, but as he pulled his daughter's thick hair through the band, he thought how the other doctors had not been beautiful young women. More particularly, one whom he felt mightily attracted to.

"And it's my turn to have a girl living next door," she continued, catching Stavros by surprise.

He looked at her in question. "What do you mean?"

"The other doctors have all been men like you. It's my turn to have one who's a woman."

Stavros twisted his lips in a playful way as he tapped his daughter on her nose. "Like you, you mean?"

"Ba. . .ba. . .like I will be," she said, and he could tell she was slightly exasperated that she had to clarify the obvious to him. Reaching up, she put both small hands on either side of his face, something she did when she really wanted him to pay attention to her. It forced him to look into her eyes. Brown ones, a mirror of his own. "Please, Baba. Please let her live with us!"

"Let her live with us. . . ." Jeannie's words echoed in his brain, and Stavros thought again how innocent she was. He didn't know if he could give her what she wanted, but he was glad that, from all of this, he had learned how badly she wanted a woman around, wanted a mother around. It was a bittersweet knowledge, though, because a mother was the one thing Stavros didn't think he could give to her.

Not ever.

His wife's behavior had cut him deeply. Even after so much time, the emotional scar was still a red and oozing slash of bitterness and guilt across his cold heart—and it had only deepened when his wife had died recently while on a business trip, officially making him a widower. A true believer in the "until death do us part" section of the marriage ceremony, Stavros didn't think he could survive another relationship that might turn sour. Even more, he didn't want Jeannie to go through something like that. She had been too young to really understand that her mother hadn't wanted her, that the woman had deserted both of them upon the little girl's birth. At nine Jeannie could get hurt, really hurt. Something he couldn't, wouldn't, allow.

In spite of that totally male part of him that was urging him to get to know

Allie Alexander better, he had to remind himself that the woman already had too many strikes going against her. She was an M.D., a professional, just like his wife, the lawyer, had been. And she was a city woman, again like his wife.

"Ba. . .ba. . ." Jeannie impatiently broke into his thoughts.

Removing his daughter's slender hands from his face, he murmured, "We'll see." That was all he could promise her. He was thankful that, for the moment, it seemed to be enough.

"Okay." She jumped down off the counter and ran over to the front door.

"Where are you going?" he asked. One of the many things he liked about village life was that it was a child's utopia. Everyone in the village looked out for one another's children. It was safe.

"Eva and I want to pick figs for Papouli. He likes the ones from our tree up by the spring." She reached for the basket that was kept handily by the door. "Besides"—she threw back over her shoulder—"don't you want to talk to the doctor. . .alone?"

Stavros's lips twisted in an amazed sort of way over his daughter's first attempt at matchmaking. But as she ran out the door and he turned back to gaze unseeingly at the stonework of the castle above his house, he knew from past experience that she was trying her hand at a match that could never work. He and professional women just didn't go together.

⁓⚬⁓

Allie turned the corner of the veranda just in time to see Jeannie's ponytail follow her with a jaunty bounce down the stairs.

She grimaced.

She had hoped the little girl would be present when she talked to Stavros Andreas. It might have been a cowardly desire, but Jeannie was a friend, something in short supply in this village, and Allie really liked the idea of the little girl becoming a regular visitor. Allie and children had always gotten along well together, and she and Jeannie had clicked immediately.

Two swallows playing tag in the evening sky, with that same happy spirit that Allie loved in children, caught her attention. They led her gaze down to the blue-shuttered house that sat beside the Byzantine church midway down the village slope.

Papouli was another friend, and knowing he wanted her to live in the teacher's house made her resolve stronger. Nothing—not her racing heart, nor her fanciful thoughts, nor even the dark-eyed man who made her body react in a manner she never dreamed it could—was going to keep her from achieving her goals.

She would be cool and professional, and she would succeed.

Seeing that the door to the teacher's apartment was open, she took a deep controlling breath and poised her knuckles over the doorjamb to knock. But when she saw that Stavros Andreas was in the kitchen staring out the window, and that he hadn't seen her, her hand froze in midair even as her gaze roved over him.

He was tall, and every bit as princely as she had thought when she had seen him from the window of the bus. She decided she liked his hair and his hands the most. His hair was thick, falling recklessly across his cowlicked forehead as if he had just tamed a dragon, and his hands were long and broad and perfectly formed.

But spying on him made Allie feel anything but professional. She readied herself to knock again, but when the teacher whipped around quick as a sword flash to face her, Allie jumped back, startled.

The look plastered across his face made her feel as if she were a thief caught in the act of intruding. With sudden insight coming from years of dealing with people—people who had pains they could hardly explain—Allie knew he did consider her an intrusion in his life.

And that intrigued her.

～≈◎≈～

Even though Stavros had been expecting her, it was a shock to actually see her standing at his door.

She had changed into a flowery sundress and summer sandals, sandals that showed the pink of her pretty polished toes poking through their open front. Her hair was back in the same braid she had worn while on the bus, an elaborate concoction that he could never hope to achieve in Jeannie's hair. Braids were normally practical. This one wasn't. It was elegant and every bit as feminine as when her hair had been loose and mussed from sleeping. He liked the way it didn't hide her neck, her long, gently sloping neck. Her vulnerable neck.

That she was a stunning woman—at least to him—was obvious.

But it wasn't only that. Rather, it was that air she had about her, a grace, a class, and something else he couldn't quite place—an inner sort of peace—that mixed with the determination in her eyes, with their softness, to present a woman whom—

Whom he couldn't let live in his house.

For one of the few times in his daughter's life, Stavros didn't think he could give Jeannie what she'd asked for.

When she tilted her head upward and said in a formal and brisk take-charge manner, "Hello. May I come in?" it grated hard against Stavros's already taut nerves. It was the worst possible tone a woman could use with him. It smacked of his wife's snooty professional ways, and it not only irritated him but also brought all his apprehensions racing to the forefront of his mind. It made his resolve to prevent her from living in his house that much stronger. To get involved with another woman married to her career would be a big mistake.

One he couldn't make.

Walking around the kitchen bar, wanting only to conclude this interview as soon as possible, he motioned for her to enter and to be seated. "Please."

∼∼∽◦∽∼∼

Sitting, Allie crossed her legs and glanced back up at him. But she quickly slid her gaze away. There was something about him that made her feel like a blushing adolescent. She hadn't felt this way since high school and Dale.

Dear Dale. . .a boy whose framed pictures had sat in every home, dorm, and apartment in which she had ever lived. Forever young, Dale's pictures would sit in the house next door, too. If it became her home.

Her gaze wandered and finally settled on the huge fireplace's hearth, with its bouquet of wild roses identical to the welcoming ones in her apartment. She shifted her gaze to the medieval sword hanging over the mantle. Her lips curved slightly upward. But of course the prince had to have a sword. The whimsical part of her was never able to stay suppressed for long.

∼∼∽◦∽∼∼

"May I get you something to drink or maybe some grapes and cheese?" Stavros asked. He might not want her here upsetting his life, but she had had a hard day, and he knew she must be in need of refreshment. Amazingly, his desire to see her gone fought with his desire to care for her, a desire that was growing stronger in him by the second as he watched the daisies on her dress move up and down with each breath she took and as the soft scent of her seemed to fill his house, his senses.

"Mr. Andreas, I would very much like to live here," she said, patting the sofa on which she sat. She cringed when his gaze fell to her hand.

"Would you?" he inquired, raising his eyebrows.

She gestured quickly with her upturned palm toward the other apartment. "I mean—"

"I know what you mean." He smiled. He was glad her slip had succeeded, at the very least, in diminishing the tension, which had spun around them like electrons in an atom.

Feeling relaxed for the first time since meeting her, he took the bowl of grapes from the counter and placed it on the coffee table before her. But he couldn't help but wonder if her slip had been a Freudian one, telling of what she really desired. . . .

∼∼∽◦∽∼∼

Allie was wondering the same thing. She didn't normally make such bloopers. Relieved to do something with her hands, she reached for a grape. Her teeth bit into it, and its sweet, refreshing juice was like nectar to her parched mouth, reminding her that to go to the Lord about this situation here and now would be like nectar to her soul.

Dear Lord, please help me say the right words.

Immediately, she felt the Spirit of God hug her close, as He had so many times in the past.

Feeling fortified, she glanced up at the schoolteacher and reached for another grape. "Mmm. . .they're delicious," she murmured.

"They're from my own vines."

"Really." Allie slanted him a glance, and interpreting his comment as friendly small talk—something hitherto totally lacking in their relationship—she quickly reciprocated. "That's one of the things I know I'll love about living in the country. It's so close to the real things in life, the good things in the world that God gave to us—"

"Dr. Alexander." There was no missing the annoyance that flickered across his face. "I don't think you appreciate what living in a village entails. There's a lot more to it than pretty hillsides and"—he waved his hand toward the bowl of grapes— "freshly picked fruit."

"Mr. Andreas, believe me, I know that. There's sickness and disease and"—she paused and gave a hesitant half smile—"houses without bathrooms." She hoped that he might respond to her gentle humor.

He didn't.

"There's that and much more," he agreed with a steely quality to his voice, one that brooked no attempt at friendliness. "Things you can't even imagine until you've lived here."

She sighed, and standing, walked over to the window. She glanced up at the strong walls of the castle before turning back to him. "Mr. Andreas, nobody forced me to come to Kastro. I wanted to come. I know there are things about village life I probably won't like. But there are things about city life I don't like, either." She waved her hand in dismissal of the subject, not knowing how much the confident gesture antagonized the man before her. "But that's not the issue. As I told you before, I signed a year-long contract, and I won't leave before it's up. My only problem now is finding a place to live."

Stavros was almost certain that wasn't going to be her only problem. During the three years he had lived in the village, he had come to the conclusion that Kastro's population was a microcosm of the world, with all the emotions of people contained within a few square miles. Right now there were problems in town. Big ones. He suspected, too, that she knew it—her lack of welcome had to have alerted her to them.

In spite of himself, a grudging respect for her was growing. He suspected that if he didn't let her live in his spare apartment, she would live at the clinic. He knew that Jeannie would never forgive him for that.

He continued to regard her.

She continued to regard him.

It was a showdown.

Finally, he motioned for her to sit back on the sofa. She went to it and sat.

Reaching next to him, he picked up one of his daughter's fashion dolls, and holding it between his fingers, he spoke. "I didn't realize how much my daughter misses having a woman around until. . .we found you sleeping next door."

"I'm sorry about that. If we—I mean—if I am to live here. . .there"—she motioned toward the other side of the house—"I'll be certain to close my door in the future."

He waved her apology aside. "It's not the first time I've seen a woman sleeping." But he knew from the soft blush that touched her face that she wasn't accustomed to men finding her in that kind of situation. The knowledge somehow pleased him. Especially since she was a professional woman. A part of him wondered if perhaps she was different, if it could work having her live in the doctor's apartment. For Jeannie's sake. . .

Coming to a sudden decision, he tossed the doll back onto the sofa and spoke before giving the rational part of his mind time to rule the irrational. "As you know, Jeannie wants you to live next door."

"Yes," she acknowledged and waited, and Stavros couldn't help but compare her quickly shining eyes with those of his daughter's. The color was different, but in many ways they were similar. Two girls hoping for something special, like a sleepover.

But there the resemblance ended. His feelings for this woman scared him. Scared him badly. But for Jeannie's sake, and even for this woman who seemed to be very nice—a nice woman who had no idea what she was letting herself in for in coming to Kastro—he thought he might be able to ignore his desires.

School would be starting soon, and he would be busy. And she would be at the clinic most of the time. That fact would constantly remind him of what she was—a professional like his wife had been. A woman who had no room in her life for a family.

But this one would have to make room for Jeannie. He would make her living in the apartment contingent upon it. "Because of my daughter, we can try your living here." He waved his hand toward the other apartment, annoyed that he had made the same mistake as she. "I mean *there*. But I want Jeannie to be happy, to feel as though she has a friend in you." He paused. "Do I make myself clear?"

He watched as her eyes narrowed into a questioning frown. "Let me get this straight. What you're saying is that only if I am your daughter's friend will you let me live there?"

"That's right."

"Mr. Andreas, as I'm the one in need of friends here in Kastro, I'll be honored if your daughter counts me as one of hers."

"Good." That was all Stavros wanted to hear. He stood and held out his hand to her. "Then it's a deal." But when her hand touched his, he wasn't so sure if it was the right deal. Living with her under his roof and sharing the same bathroom might prove to be far more difficult in practice than in theory.

Stavros already regretted his moment of weakness.

~~∽∾∘∾∽~~

But not Allie. She silently breathed out a prayer of thanks to God for softening this man's heart toward her.

She now had a home in Kastro.

Chapter 6

The house with blue shutters by the church housed one of the nicest families Allie had ever met. And in Papouli's daughters, Martha and Natalia, Allie found two more friends in Kastro.

"You don't know how glad we are that you've come to live here," Martha quickly said, as she placed a demitasse of fragrant Greek coffee on the patio table in front of Allie, amazing Allie at how fast she could do so without slopping any. A small woman full of joyful energy, Martha was always in speedy motion, always doing something to make sure everyone around her was happy.

Her sister, Natalia, nodded in concurrence. "I don't feel so bad about leaving Baba"—the young woman's remarkable blue eyes glanced over at her father—"and Martha now that you're here."

Allie smiled at Natalia. She still couldn't help but be surprised by her appearance. When Papouli had first introduced his daughters, Allie had had to hide her shock at how different they were. Martha was the solid, salt-of-the-earth type, a handsome woman whom Allie figured to be about forty, who greatly resembled her father. Natalia, however, looked as though she had just stepped out of the pages of a fashion catalog. Tall and slender, she was stunning, and all the more so because she was completely oblivious to the rarity of her physical beauty, one Allie quickly realized was a mirror to that of her soul.

After taking a sip of her thick, sweet coffee, Allie inquired of Natalia, "Are you looking forward to moving to Athens?"

"I can't wait!" the young woman exclaimed, the adventure of her move in her expressive eyes.

"Natalia has always wanted to go out into the world," Martha explained from her perch on the edge of her chair as she smiled fondly at her younger sister. "Our mother knew this even when Natalia was a little girl, and before she died, she made us"—she motioned between her father and herself—"promise that when the time came, we would let our Natalia go."

"Don't worry," Natalia whispered and reached first for her sister's and then for her father's hands, and Allie could feel the love that flowed between them. "I'll be back."

"You will follow the path God has laid out for you, my dear." Papouli patted his daughter's hand. "That is all I want for you."

"Dear Baba. . ." The young woman rubbed her father's callused hand against her smooth face. "You are the best father a girl could ever ask for."

Allie took another sip of coffee, and as the sounds of the summer night played around them—the click of a backgammon board at a neighboring house, dogs barking in the distance, a cricket in a walnut tree—Allie knew that she was witnessing a family as God intended. A family made up of members who loved and cared for one another.

Allie wished for such a family again. She and her brother, Alex, loved one another and had been good friends as children, but it had been too many years since they had truly known one another. Their father's death, coming right on the heels of Dale's, had been too much for Alex. Dale had been his best friend, and Alex had left home, as had Allie, shortly afterward. Now they no longer even had a house to call home. Looking at the three people before her, Allie hoped that Natalia and Martha would never drift apart.

"Are you going to be renting an apartment or living in a dorm?" Allie quickly asked, wanting to escape her thoughts. The family had told her earlier that Natalia was going to be attending an art school in Athens. Allie couldn't imagine the girl in anything other than arts.

"Oh, no. I'll be staying with my other sister."

"Your other sister?" Allie turned to Papouli in surprise. "I didn't realize that you had other children."

The priest's eyes twinkled as his gravelly voice proudly proclaimed, "I have six children. Three girls and three boys."

"And six grandchildren," Martha piped in.

"And two great-grandchildren!" Natalia finished.

"Papouli!" Allie was amazed. "That's wonderful!"

The older man beamed. "I love children. My wife was quite a bit older than me; otherwise we would have had more after Martha. Thankfully, Natalia came to us."

Allie looked from one to the other sister, and then she understood the difference in their appearance. "You mean—?"

"Our Natalia was a direct gift from God." Martha confirmed that Natalia had been adopted, as she squeezed her sister's long slender hand in her own much smaller one.

"One that came to us in a basket," Papouli qualified, and Allie could tell from the way his eyes narrowed and crinkled at the corners that he was remembering back to when his daughter had first come to him. "My wife had just learned that she had a very serious disease."

With a physician's interest, Allie tilted her head in question.

Papouli whispered the illness, and at Allie's look of understanding, he continued. "We were at the bus station waiting to return to Kastro. We were very sad, but all the while I was praying for a miracle. I was praying for God to somehow heal my dear wife, my dear Talia. . . ." He looked over at Natalia and smiled with all the father's love a child could ever wish for shining in his wise eyes. "That was when I first heard Natalia cry. She was calling out to us."

"Someone had left her—a tiny little baby—in a basket at the bus station," Martha quickly explained, and Allie could hear the amazement in her voice, one that hadn't diminished with the years.

Papouli nodded. "No one came for her. We stayed in the town for a week looking for her parents—"

"But they couldn't find my parents," Natalia softly chimed in, finishing the story, one that almost seemed like a fairy tale to Allie. "Because my parents had just found me in that basket. No girl could ever ask to be part of a more wonderful family than this one."

Papouli smiled over at her. "God answered my prayer in our finding Natalia, too. The doctors thought that my wife wouldn't live more than a year or two. But because of Natalia, because Talia wanted to be a mother to her fair-haired child, she lived another ten years. Ten very wonderful years."

"So we don't feel as though we have the right to be sad in Natalia leaving us tomorrow." Martha finished the amazing story. "We look upon her being with us for the last eighteen years as a gift."

"And I believe"—Natalia reached across the circle of the wooden tabletop and tapped Allie on her arm—"that your coming to Kastro, Yatrinna, is a gift, too." At Allie's perplexed look, the blond beauty laughed, a laugh that sounded like crystal chiming in a gentle breeze, before she continued. "Even though I know that I have to go, I haven't liked the idea of leaving my sister and father. But now that you're here, I can leave knowing that Martha"—she looked over at her sister with a teasing glint in her eyes—"will have someone else to mother."

Allie turned estimating eyes to Martha. "I hardly think Martha is old enough to be my mother, Natalia," she murmured, feeling a bit uncomfortable for the older woman.

But she shouldn't have. Martha didn't mind in the least. "Oh, my dear, I most definitely am! I'm fifty!"

"Fifty!" Allie was genuinely shocked. Martha looked at least ten years younger.

Papouli sat forward and, with the excitement of a child playing a game, inquired, "How old do you think I am?"

Allie looked at him and gave a half laugh, sure that her first estimation of his age had to be way off base. She shook her head. "I don't know. When I first met you, I thought you were about sixty." Although she now knew that her other thought about him being ageless was probably closer to the truth. "You must be quite a bit older. Unless you adopted all your children."

"Ha!" Papouli laughed and, sitting back, slapped his hand against his skinny knee before proudly singing out, "I'm seventy-nine!"

"Papouli!" Allie loved the fact that he was a man who knew not to be afraid of the numbers going up on his biological clock, but rather to be proud and honored that he could live them. "Seventy-nine. What's in the water in this village that makes you all look so young, anyway?"

Proud as villagers are of their water, they all liked that, but Papouli, true to his calling, explained, "We do have very good springwater here in Kastro that reaches us from high in the mountains. But that's not what keeps us young. It's having faith that God will direct our steps correctly each day, and it's having people—whether they be family members or friends—who love and care for us and like each of us for what and who we are."

Allie shook her head. "Then I don't think I'll look young for long." But at their crestfallen faces she quickly explained. "Oh, after much prayer, I'm quite certain that God wants me here," she qualified, remembering who she was talking to. "But except for you three and little Jeannie Andreas, nobody else seems to."

"Bah!" Papouli rocked back in his chair. "Give them time, Yatrinna. The people of Kastro really are good. They just have some things to work out, things that have nothing to do with you," he admonished.

"But they're so unfriendly. Is it because I'm a woman?" She really didn't believe that was the problem, but she hoped that her question might lead to some answers.

Papouli smiled, showing a mouth full of nearly perfect teeth between his beard and his mustache. "No, Yatrinna, your being a woman has nothing to do with it. In fact, the problem has nothing to do with you at all. It's something that goes back many years." He knitted his gray brows together and pulled thoughtfully on his pointed beard. "So far back that not even *I* can remember—"

"Papouli!" A young girl's happy shout interrupted him, and they all swiveled around to watch as Jeannie Andreas came bounding up the stairs holding a basket full of what looked to Allie like large leaves.

But when Allie's gaze landed on the man following the girl, her smile froze. And her heart pounded harder in her chest. But whether it was a warning beat or a glad one, she wasn't sure.

When Jeannie's father noticed her, he paused in his climb. It was an infinitesimal hesitation that held his right foot suspended for a moment longer than necessary over the step, telling as clearly as any words might that he wasn't happy about finding her on Papouli's veranda.

Not at all.

Allie saw that his face was just as grim as it had been when he'd discovered her in his spare apartment's bedroom earlier. Wryly, she wondered if she were sitting in his chair this time, in his place on Papouli's veranda. Goldilocks revisited, perhaps?

"Welcome, welcome." Martha hopped up from the edge of her seat and held out welcoming hands to the newcomers.

"They're figs! From our tree by the fountain," Jeannie informed all excitedly as she gave the basket to Martha. "Eva and I picked them and packed them in their leaves to protect them—just as you taught us, Papouli," she practically sang out, inadvertently explaining to Allie why it looked as though she carried a basket full of leaves.

"From the tree by the fountain? My favorite!" Papouli exclaimed, knowing how to please a child.

"I know." Jeannie beamed at being able to give the grandfatherly priest she adored something he loved. But when she noticed Allie sitting across the table, her eyes widened and she danced over to her side. "Yatrinna! I didn't know that you were here! I thought you were sleeping again."

Like a magnet drawn to iron, Allie's gaze was pulled to the girl's father. A muscle jumped in his jaw, and Allie knew he remembered finding her asleep in his house, too. The current that passed between them crackled.

Blushing, she shifted her eyes back to Jeannie. "No, one nap is all I get in a day, if I'm lucky." She hoped that the covering of night hid the tell-all signs of her red face.

"Ah. . . ," Papouli commented prosaically, and Allie glanced sharply at him. From the twinkle that lit up his fine old eyes as he looked from her to the teacher, she knew that he had caught her blush—and worst of all, he knew the reason for it. What amazed Allie was how pleased he seemed by it. "You did get a chance to rest this afternoon, then?" his gravelly voice asked, and she was glad for his diplomacy.

She swallowed and nodded. "I fell asleep immediately—"

"And me and Baba found her sleeping on the bed just like Sleeping Beauty," Jeannie piped in. "And now she's going to live with us!"

"In the spare apartment," Stavros said quickly.

Papouli glanced above the rim of his glasses at the schoolteacher. "But where else would she live?"

Stavros looked sharply at the priest, as though Papouli had just told a joke that Stavros didn't find amusing.

"Sit—sit down and have fruit and coffee with us," Martha invited, and she and Natalia started to pull two more chairs up to the table.

"No, we won't stay," Stavros said, glancing at Allie.

"But Baba!" Jeannie said.

Ignoring her, he turned to Natalia and said, "You must have much to do to get ready for tomorrow. We just wanted to come and say good-bye and to wish you the very best." Jeannie opened her mouth again, and Stavros placed his hand on her shoulder and gently squeezed, quieting her. "You're leaving on the morning bus?"

Natalia nodded. "At 6:05 a.m."

That information seemed to distract Jeannie. "I don't want you to go," Jeannie whined, and leaving her father's side, she went over to Natalia and hugged her fiercely.

"I'll miss you, too, pumpkin." Natalia squeezed the girl close to her. "But at least you'll have the new doctor for company."

Jeannie stood back and looked over at Allie. A smile lit her face, replacing the sadness of before. "I know. And I'm sooo glad." She looked back at Natalia. "But you promise to come back. . .at least for visits?"

"I promise," Natalia said, with the solemnity young children appreciate. "But you have to promise to come and visit me someday, too."

Jeannie's eyes widened. "Really?"

Natalia nodded. "Really."

Stavros reached for his daughter's hand. "Come on, pumpkin."

Reluctantly, Jeannie went with him. From the dejected slump of her shoulders, it was obvious to all she didn't want to go. But as she thought of something, joy, with the quickness of a light being flipped on, suddenly filled her features, and turning to Allie, she exclaimed, "I know! Why don't you come with us, Yatrinna? You don't know the path too well, and we live in the same house, after all." She laughed, the delighted laugh of a child who was thrilled with a situation.

But her father apparently wasn't. "Jeannie. . ." He directed his words to his daughter, but his gaze swung over to Allie's as he sent her a strong nonverbal message not to accept the invitation. "Maybe Yatrinna wants to stay longer," he suggested pointedly.

Allie knew from the hard glint in his eye that he was warning her not to come with them.

And she bristled. If he had somehow asked her not to accept, she probably would have complied. But the warning was a challenge, and Allie rarely passed one up. Besides, wasn't he the one who had made her being a friend to Jeannie a condition to her living in the apartment?

And his daughter was right. It would be nice to walk the dark and unfamiliar path home with someone.

Toying with the strap of her purse, she answered Jeannie while looking at the man beside her. "Your father's right, Jeannie," she said. When she saw the look of relief that jumped into his eyes as he thought that she would decline the invitation, it almost kept her from her course.

Almost.

Not quite.

Using his own reasoning against him, she stood and continued, "I'm sure Natalia has much to do before leaving tomorrow. I should know after just moving, myself." His eyes flickered with something—guilt, anger? She wasn't sure which. But dropping her gaze to Jeannie's, she answered, "I would like very much to walk home with you."

"Hurray!" the girl shouted, but only the sound of coins being jiggled around in his pocket came from her father. Allie didn't look at him, but she could feel his glowering gaze on her, and for once, she wished she hadn't accepted a challenge. She knew that to back out now, though, would only worsen the situation and confuse Jeannie.

Turning to Natalia, she held out her hand. "I'm so glad we had the chance to meet."

"Me, too," Natalia agreed. "It would have been terrible had you arrived tomorrow and we missed each other. It really does make me feel good to know you are here to look after Martha and Baba."

Allie rolled her eyes. "I think it will be the other way around. They're going to be looking after me."

Natalia laughed her agreement. "They're good at that," she admitted.

"I hope you're happy in the city," Allie offered, and really meant it, even though she still couldn't imagine anyone wanting to trade Kastro for any metropolis, even Athens, which was one of her favorite places.

Natalia shrugged her graceful shoulders. "It's a great big, wonderful world out there. I'm looking forward to seeing it!"

That there was something very special about this young woman was obvious to Allie. Tilting her head speculatively to the side, she pronounced, "Natalia, I have a feeling that you're going to take it by storm."

Chapter 7

The smooth, silky threads of night hung like an antique tapestry around the man, the woman, and the child.

It was just as Allie had always thought nightfall in the countryside would be. Their feet trod upon the sun-baked soil of the earth until they reached the cobbled steps that ran beside the blue-domed Byzantine church. They then followed the stone walkway's meandering course up the mountainside toward their home.

With the setting of the sun, the cicadas had finally gone to sleep, the beam of the moon as it poked its face out from behind the ramparts of the castle being too cool to entice them to grind their legs in sound. But the summer song of the crickets now filled the warm air, along with the soft meow of two-month-old kittens and distant goat bells lightly flavoring the warm air with their tinkling notes.

It would have been perfect.

A glorious summer eve.

If. . .

The man walking on the other side of the little girl had been content.

But glancing over at Stavros Andreas, Allie knew he wasn't.

Not a bit.

And Allie knew it was because of her. She had come to his world, to his village, to his house, even, and had upset it. Allie could feel his unrest. It was palpable, hovering in the air around them, a discordant note, even as his daughter chattered on excitedly about her day.

Allie could see that his lips were a pale slash across his face and that his shoulders were held tensely at alert, like a man about to have an unpleasant medical procedure performed on him. Their afternoon conversation might have ended with his agreement to let her rent his apartment, but Allie was sure that the progressing hours of the day had only brought unease over that decision.

From the first, he hadn't wanted her in his house.

He still didn't.

She didn't have to be a mind reader to know that if he could come up with a way to get rid of her without upsetting his daughter, he would. But that was something Allie couldn't let happen. She needed to live in his spare apartment.

Other than the fact that there was nowhere else in the village suitable for her, the house already felt like home. She depended on its friendly walls to return to every day.

Again, she regretted challenging him at Papouli's house. She knew that he hadn't wanted her to accompany them. What she didn't know was what had made her push him.

Perhaps the warmth and friendship from the priest's house, combined with her romantic nature, signaled for something more with the teacher and had made her professional mantle slip.

It was a mistake she wouldn't make again.

She couldn't let herself forget that her professional standing and his daughter's needs were the only reasons he had finally relented and agreed to let her live in the apartment. To try for friendship or to contest his desires concerning their tenuous landlord-tenant relationship might provoke a problem. Remembering her lack of welcome that afternoon, Allie knew that she had enough predicaments to deal with in this village as it was.

From now on, she would treat him politely but formally. Nothing else.

She was Kastro's doctor.

A relationship with a man in such a small village would set her up for ethical problems again.

A relationship with her landlord would spell disaster. She wouldn't let it happen. She wouldn't let her physician's persona slip again. She would be cool and professional.

She looked down at the little girl who chattered on about her escapades in picking figs, and she smiled.

And she would be Jeannie's good friend.

What most upset Stavros was not the fact that he had to share his house with her, but rather, with her coming, he had learned just how badly his daughter missed having a mother. Up to that inauspicious moment when Jeannie had begged him to let the doctor live in the other apartment, Stavros had convinced himself that he had succeeded in being both father and mother to her. He had, in fact, prided himself on thinking that he had filled both roles as well as any two parents ever could.

But looking at his daughter as she talked animatedly to the doctor, a different lilting sound to her voice from that which she normally had, he now knew differently.

And it bothered him.

A lot.

He didn't want to involve anybody else in their lives. As long as he and

Jeannie were self-sufficient, he felt secure. Pain could be avoided; it could be prevented.

He knew very well that having Allie Alexander living in the apartment next door would spell involvement. It was inevitable.

His fingers jingled the coins sitting in his pocket.

With her living anywhere in the village, it would happen.

In spite of what he might want, even in spite of what she might want, this attraction between them was too strong.

He glanced over Jeannie's head toward the woman. Her head was tilted to the side and slightly lowered, that elegant braid falling over her right shoulder as she paid attention to what Jeannie had to say as if it was the most important thing in the world.

When her gaze suddenly lifted and touched upon his, it happened again.

That spark. That fusion.

But this time there was something different. A cover seemed to slide over the quicksilver in her eyes as a cool, professional quality came into them. It made him feel as though he had just been shut out on a cold winter's day.

He frowned.

She didn't challenge him but simply dropped her gaze back to Jeannie as if he was of no more concern to her than a distant relative of a patient.

But Stavros had been a man long enough to know when a woman was attracted to him. She might have him believe that she couldn't care less about what was between them. But he knew she did. She cared.

But like him, she didn't seem to want to do anything about it.

It made his mind glad.

But not his heart, which had remained dormant until he had seen her, talked to her. Now it was beating in want of more out of life. His heart had nearly broken when he didn't find that right relationship with Jeannie's mother.

He moved the coins in his pocket around with more force.

No. He didn't want a relationship now.

He didn't want involvement with any woman. It would be unwise to mess with the stability he had created in his life, in Jeannie's life.

Jeannie's laughter rang out, and it occurred to Stavros that maybe having Jeannie around could protect the doctor and himself from an entanglement neither he nor she seemed to want. It might not be all that difficult with his daughter to run buffer for them.

That was his bright idea until. . .

His daughter suddenly turned traitor. Taking ahold of first his hand then the doctor's, it was as if they were all connected somehow. It was suddenly too familiar, too—

"It's like we're a family!" Jeannie sang out, clutching each adult hand proudly out in front of her.

And Stavros knew that was it.

It was like they were a family.

A nice normal family.

And he learned then that having a child around was not a cushion against involvement. Jeannie would not make a good chaperone at all.

"We even live in the same house!" Jeannie continued blithely along, and Stavros would have liked to have taken masking tape and taped his daughter's cute, little, big mouth shut.

The doctor's gaze shot over to his, and Stavros was sure he saw amusement in the silver bits of light that danced in their cool green depths.

He was surprised when she opened her mouth to answer Jeannie, but relieved, too. It was nice not to have to be the one to think up a response to an embarrassing statement made by his daughter.

"We might be in the same house, Jeannie"—her soft voice was tuned toward Jeannie, but Stavros could have sworn that she was actually talking to him—"but we're in different apartments. So it's like we're in an apartment building."

"Except for the bathroom," Jeannie pointed out, as if that made all the difference.

"Except for the bathroom," Allie agreed, and Stavros was certain he hadn't imagined the resigned note in her voice. He suspected then that she wasn't as easy with the sharing of the house's only bathroom as she had earlier let on. The thought somehow pleased him.

"Oh!" Jeannie sang out as she remembered something. Letting go of their hands, she skipped ahead of them and walked backward, facing them both. "I've come up with the perfect signal so we know when the bathroom is in use."

Allie's gaze bounced over to Stavros.

He saw it coming his way, but he didn't catch it.

He let her gaze rebound off him and looked away.

Knowing from now on exactly when she was using the bathroom—the bathtub, in particular—didn't seem like a very good solution to him.

"I drew a sign on a piece of cardboard that says IN USE and put it on the hall table," Jeannie went on, the innocence of childhood hiding from her the undercurrent of tension that ran between the adults. "It fits perfectly under both of our doors."

"Great, pumpkin," Stavros mumbled, but all he could really think about was the next year. He could plainly see his future, sitting on the sofa correcting test papers and having the sign pushed under the hall door. It would be a viable reminder of the beautiful woman who was a part of his world, while not being a part of it.

It was going to drive him crazy. It already was. Knowing she was so close and yet not in the way his heart was crying for her to be. . .

He decided that he would have to start correcting all tests at school.

But what about when he was making supper, helping Jeannie with her homework, or writing on the computer? He couldn't leave his own house. Maybe he would spend more time down in the stable with Charger.

"What a smart girl you are." Stavros heard Allie commend Jeannie, but from the way she stumbled over her words, he was absolutely certain that she was uncomfortable with the whole idea. It softened his own trepidation and, in a crooked sort of way, satisfied him.

"Thank you." Jeannie gave a little bow and beamed up at the grown-ups, blessedly oblivious to the feelings of apprehension that swarmed around them like hornets ready to bite.

And about half an hour later, Allie wished that she had been as smart as Jeannie when, after a soak in the elegant bathtub, one that had her feeling like visiting royalty, she opened the bathroom door just in time to see Stavros—in the central hall—pushing the IN USE sign under her apartment door.

Realizing too late that she had forgotten to put the signal under his door when she went in for her bath, and wanting only to disappear, she took a sudden and very guilty step back into the bathroom. She might have made it unnoticed if her flip-flop hadn't met with a puddle of bathwater, which had effectively transformed the floor into a skating rink and her into a moving mass on a bull's-eye course for Stavros's broad back.

"Oh no!" she yelled out a split second before she slammed into him.

"What the—?" he grunted and swung around to face her, his hands automatically reaching out to steady her.

"I'm sorry," Allie gasped, her fingers clutching his shirt sleeves as she regained her balance.

She was panting.

He was holding her close.

Their eyes met.

She felt Stavros draw in his breath before disgust exploded from him. "Don't you know that wet marble and flip-flops are a lethal combination?" he croaked out.

"Yes, I. . ." She looked down at the floor and kicked off the offending shoes, knowing that it was much safer to walk barefoot on wet marble than to wear rubber footwear. "I wasn't thinking."

"Obviously," he ground out and swung his eyes to the sign, which he had just planted partway under her door. "What happened to the In Use signal?"

His tone made Allie feel like a teenager caught sneaking into her bedroom after curfew. She didn't like it, and a quick retort rose in her throat. But in fairness, she knew she should have remembered the sign. In the name of their tenuous landlord-tenant relationship, she swallowed her sharp words and let a simple apology come out instead. "I'm sorry. I forgot."

"Since we have agreed to use the sign, at least don't forget to use it."

Clutching her dressing gown tighter against her, she said, "It won't happen again."

"Make sure that it doesn't," he commanded, and his tone chafed against Allie's mind like sandpaper against her skin, and a quick retort wouldn't be held down this time. "Look, I said I was sorry. But couldn't you hear the water running?" That seemed logical enough to Allie. Water running through pipes was not soundproof, and, too, there was the noise of the water pump.

"If I had been in my apartment, I would have. But I was with Charger."

She blinked. "Charger?"

"My horse," he explained.

"Oh." She remembered his horse—the white horse. The horse he had been riding when she had thought he was a prince in a fairy tale. . .

A heavy settling sigh, like the last blast in a windstorm, rumbled from his chest, reminding Allie of how much had changed since that first meeting. "Look," he said, running his hand distractedly through his already tousled hair. Only his cowlick—a permanent rumple—remained in place. "I would appreciate it if you would try not to forget to put the sign out," he said, a definite request this time, with a vulnerable quality to his voice that reminded Allie of a patient in pain, begging for whatever relief she might have to give. It was something she knew how to respond to.

"I won't forget." Her voice was soft, much softer than she had intended it to be, and confused by her own reaction, she lowered her lids and brushed past him to push open the door to her apartment.

But as Allie slowly backed in, once again their gazes found one another, and Allie saw what this encounter was costing him. He had the look of a man who was confused about what he wanted, what he needed. His features were tainted with a grim sadness that was one of the most vulnerable looks she had ever seen. As her door clicked shut, she wondered what dreams and hopes had to have died in his life to have colored his face with such a naked and world-weary pain.

And she knew then that her first impression of him had been correct: He was a prince of a man, one who was definitely hurting, one who had things to overcome, but a prince nonetheless.

And one whom Allie liked. A lot.

An hour later she reclined in bed, gazing in the soft moon glow at the picture of Dale that she had placed on her bedside table. Dale's blond hair and laughing blue eyes slowly seemed to fade away as her eyes drifted shut, to be replaced by those of a man with dark brown hair and even darker eyes. Troubled eyes, they seemed to be asking something of her.

But what? She wasn't sure.

It was, however, something Allie was determined to discover.

And soon.

Chapter 8

A rooster crowed, a horse neighed, and Allie reveled in the feeling of the sun as its morning-time fingers of welcome gently washed her face.

She stretched out across the comfortable bed and smiled, a slow smile of contentment and peace.

Not a motor could be heard running, nor a horn blowing, nor even a garbage truck moaning. The sounds that surrounded her were all a part of the wonderful world of nature, real and balanced.

With exuberance for the new day, she hopped out of bed, and reaching for her dressing gown, she padded on bare feet across the wooden floor to the window.

Throwing the French doors wide, she stepped out onto the sunlit balcony and breathed in the fresh, pine-scented mountain air. She knew the heat wave had no intentions of abating for several more days. By the afternoon it would be another scorcher in a long line of them. So she relished the night-cooled air that tenaciously clung to the mountainside. The famous Hellenic haze, suffusing the landscape and making it look like an impressionist painting of the purest school, already covered the valley. But it hadn't reached the mountain heights yet, and it wouldn't until noon. Not even the cicadas had started grinding their legs yet, something they had been doing at least two hours earlier the day before in Athens.

The regal steps of a horse prancing below her balcony drew her gaze downward. Her breath caught at the sight of the schoolteacher sitting tall and elegant upon the same white stallion she had seen him astride the previous day.

The horse was arrogant and impressive.

So was the man.

As if sensing her gaze on him, the man looked up, and for a split moment, it was as the previous day when they had been strangers traveling in opposite directions. There was interest and wonder and romance in his deep-set eyes, not even a hint of the vulnerable man Allie had caught sight of the night before. That man was well hidden behind this man's solidly composed features, and the one before her now was once again a storybook prince wearing assurance that everything would turn out perfectly in his land. It had to. Nobody would want to read about his exploits if it didn't.

Allie shook her head.

It wasn't the previous day.

And they were no longer strangers.

They were real people who had to deal with the real world and real emotions. She knew now, as he slightly inclined his head toward her in greeting and clip-clopped off, that he was much more than a storybook prince. He was a man who was trying the best he knew how to handle the situations that life had thrown at him. She breathed out an automatic prayer for him while watching his straight back disappear down the lane. She wondered just what those situations had been—in particular, how it was that his daughter was motherless.

But with an office to get in order, Allie knew that she couldn't let anything or any emotions get in the way of what she had come to Kastro to do. Stepping back into her room, she drew the cream-colored curtains together, and pushing all thoughts of her handsome landlord to a far corner of her brain, she went to the central hall, pushed the In Use sign under the schoolteacher's door, and was happy to use the bathroom knowing that the apartment next door was currently empty of its male occupant. Back in her bedroom alcove, she donned a pair of jeans and a T-shirt. Then she padded over to the kitchen area and put as many cleaning supplies as she found under the sink into a plastic pail, and taking her medical bag—just in case of an emergency—she left her home and started the short walk down the narrow, cobbled street to her office. Since the good people of Kastro didn't seem to care that the clinic was in shambles, she knew that it was up to her to clean it and ready it for use.

She met several of Kastro's citizens along the way. Half of them totally ignored her, while the other half smiled shyly, mumbled a good-morning, and quickly went on their way. But Allie's knowing eyes didn't miss how they all looked over their shoulders, as if to check out who might be watching them speak to her.

She shook her head after each such encounter and continued down the cobbled lane. A few minutes later, she stepped into the courtyard of the clinic, greeted the friendly tortoise of the day before, and swung open the office door. Casting her gaze around its dismal interior, she sighed. It needed even more work than she had remembered.

Not wasting time thinking about it, she opened all the windows and shutters—but not the back door where she supposed the donkey still to be—then, taking a pair of surgical gloves from her bag, she collected all the trash that had been left around the rooms. That completed, she was standing in the examining room contemplating tackling the medicine cabinet—and the scorpion within—when she heard laughter coming from the waiting room.

"Allie. . . ?" Martha's friendly voice called out, and Allie's soul rejoiced at the warmhearted greeting.

"In here," she sang out and turned gladly away from the grimy doors of the cabinet. But it wasn't Martha who came bounding into the examining room, it was Jeannie.

"Hi, Yatrinna!"

"Jeannie!" Allie exclaimed and smiled over at Martha as she trailed behind the bubbly girl. "How wonderful to see you. But"—she motioned down to the cleaning supplies each held and shook her head in question—"what's this?"

Holding a feather duster up in front of her, Jeannie shouted out their reason for coming. "We've come to help clean the office!"

"What?" Allie looked from the child to the adult. "How did you know that was what I was doing?"

"I saw you leave the house with that stuff." Jeannie pointed over to where Allie's cleaning things sat in a corner. "And I told Miss Martha."

"A good thing you did, too." Martha commended Jeannie while casting her gaze quickly and thoroughly around the room. "I knew that it was in need of some cleaning, but this"—she made a disgusted sound—"this is terrible." She turned to Allie. "It's not fitting that you should have to clean the office at all, much less alone."

"I don't mind," Allie murmured, but she was touched by Martha's concern.

"Well, I do," Martha spoke firmly. "Anybody in this village is capable of cleaning, but not one other person can do the job you've been hired to do."

"Martha, thanks, but"—Allie shrugged her shoulders—"it's not your problem."

"The bad behavior of my neighbors," Martha said as she pulled a brightly colored kerchief out of her skirt pocket and tied back her hair, "is most definitely my problem." But seeing that Allie felt uncomfortable with her cleaning, Martha paused and gave another reason, one that was just as truthful. A gentle, hurting softness touched the older woman's voice. "Besides, I promised Natalia that I would look after you. She knows that I. . .need to keep busy."

For all of Martha's assurances of the night before, Allie knew that Martha was in pain over her sister's leaving. She missed Natalia, pure and simple, just as people the world over miss loved ones who have to go out and make their way in life.

"Did she get off all right this morning?" Allie asked quietly.

Martha nodded. "She was as excited and as high-strung as a thoroughbred ready to run the race of her life." She paused and sighed. "But she was ready."

Allie's smile deepened. "She'll be fine."

"I know, but I do miss her. Please let me help you. I need to do something," she admitted on a near desperate whisper.

Allie pursed her lips and remembered how she'd felt when her brother,

Alex, had left home for good. It had felt like the ending of a good book she had borrowed from the library, meaning that she couldn't even take it off the shelf and read it again whenever she wanted. Nodding, she admitted, "I would be very grateful for your help."

"I miss Natalia, too!" Jeannie sang out. "I want to help, too."

Allie and Martha turned to the girl and laughed. "You may!" Allie flicked the girl's ponytail. She grimaced toward the cabinet. "But please be careful. I saw a scorpion run up its side yesterday."

By way of answer, Martha leaned over and, pulling a can of bug spray from her pail, loudly proclaimed, "Lead the way. I'm an expert on getting rid of scorpions."

Jeannie giggled. "She's not a ghostbuster—she's a bugbuster! You should have seen the scorpions that were living in our house when Daddy and I first moved in for good."

Allie looked sharply at Jeannie. "In your house. . . ?" she echoed. Jeannie's house meant her house. Had she slept where scorpions slept? Allie hugged herself and rubbed her hands up and down her goose-bumped arms.

Jeannie giggled again and took ahold of Allie's hand. "Don't worry, Yatrinna. We don't have them anymore."

"That's right," Martha quickly piped in and, holding the can of spray up like a banner, proclaimed, "I annihilated them!"

The three worked diligently, and by two o'clock, when it was much too warm to work any longer, they had accomplished what Allie was sure would have taken her at least two days had she been alone.

Martha was out finding a new home for the donkey, and Jeannie was out getting rid of the trash, while Allie mopped the floor for the final time. She had been amazed to discover that under all the grime was a beautiful marble floor of golden white. Finished, she was smiling over the transformation cleaning had wrought to the two rooms when the shadow of a very large man fell across the still-wet section in front of her.

A bit surprised that someone would walk in without calling out a greeting, Allie nonetheless turned with a welcoming smile on her lips. But when she saw who it was, the mop slipped out of her hand and crashed with a loud clatter onto the hard floor.

The ogre stood before her, and his expression wasn't any friendlier than it had been the previous day. Even worse, he was looking around the office as if he were the proprietor.

"May I help you?" Allie asked, but the fingers of apprehension that crawled across her sweat-dampened back alerted her to the fact that his visit was not going to be a friendly one.

He stared down at her, the line of his mouth becoming long and thin before his whiny voice sounded out between it. "No. I just came by to see what you were doing."

That, Allie thought, was obvious. What was equally apparent was that he was up to no good. She was about to say something scathing when Martha walked in from the backyard.

"I took the donkey to the field behind the church. . . . Tasos." She paused when she saw him and greeted him with a familiar smile. "How nice to see you."

Nice? *Nice* was not a word Allie would have used to describe the man's visit.

"What are you doing here, Martha?" the man called Tasos, but the one Allie still thought of as the ogre, snapped out. For the first time, Allie realized that Martha might have stepped over a line, a picket line of sorts, in coming to help her. It concerned her.

But it shouldn't have.

Martha was a woman of faith whom no one could browbeat. Plus, being the priest's daughter put her in a neutral position in village politics, something she was about to show Allie she knew how to use wisely.

"I'm doing what every other man, woman, and child in this village should be doing. Cleaning this disreputable clinic." She turned to Allie and asked, "Have you met?" But not waiting for a reply, she quickly introduced them. "Dr. Allie Alexander, this is Tasos Drakopoulos."

Allie's lips quirked at the mention of the man's name, and she thought that if she had known it before, she would have dubbed him "Dracula" rather than "ogre."

True to her quick way of talking and moving, Martha admonished, "Honestly, Tasos, you were in charge of this clinic—"

Allie looked sharply over at the man. He was in charge of the clinic? So he had known precisely the condition in which she had found it the previous day.

"How could you let the new doctor come into such a dirty, unsightly place?" Martha continued voicing Allie's very question, but with a tone that Allie was sure she had probably used when they had been children growing up together and Tasos had tormented a cat or a dog. "It's embarrassing to the good name of our village," Martha finished.

But Martha was wasting her breath. Tasos Drakopoulos showed no remorse. Motioning with his thick thumb toward the boxes that Allie had discovered contained equipment far in excess to that which was normally supplied to rural doctors' offices—an EKG machine, a miniature ICU case, and all the equipment needed to perform emergency surgery—he snorted out, "I got all those things brought here, didn't I?" And not waiting for or wanting a reply, he turned on his big feet and stomped off through the door.

Allie turned to Martha. "He had all these supplies brought here? Yet he has obviously been the one to turn many villagers against me."

Moving quickly around the room, Martha gathered cleaning supplies while answering. "As my father told you last night, it's their problem, not yours. When the people of Kastro need a doctor, they'll come to you." For all Martha's talking—and while they had been working, she proved just how much and how fast she talked—Allie had quickly come to learn that Martha took the admonishments about the taming of the tongue, found in the third chapter of James, seriously. She would never gossip about her neighbors. It was a trait Allie couldn't help but admire in the other woman.

"I hope so," Allie murmured, but she wasn't so sure any longer. Something deep and ugly was going on in Kastro, and she didn't like not knowing what it was.

Martha paused in her work and touched Allie's arm in a comforting way before motioning to the spotless room. "I think we've done very well. This evening we'll whitewash it."

Jeannie rushed into the office and, hearing the last of Martha words, shouted out, "Me, too! I love whitewashing!"

"You, too!" Martha agreed. "You've been a big help. But for now," Martha spoke as she rinsed off her hands in the now sparkling sink, "it's lunchtime and siesta time." She looked at Allie. "My father asked that you come and eat with us."

"No!" Jeannie interjected, causing the two women to look at her in surprise. "Come eat with Baba and me! I know Baba would like for you to come. All the doctors have practically lived at our house!" Looking at her, Allie was sure that the girl spoke the truth about the other doctors. But she was also sure that such an invitation wouldn't apply to her.

"Thank you, Jeannie." She looked over at Martha and smiled. "Thank you both. But I think I'd like to go and pick up a few things from the store and just go back to my apartment, eat something light, and take a little rest." At the fallen look that crossed Jeannie's face, Allie quickly went on, "But you and I can walk down here together this evening. All right?"

Allie was glad to see that the suggestion brought the shine back to Jeannie's eyes. "All right."

They closed up the office that now smelled of disinfectant and bug spray, and after Martha directed Allie to one of the shops in the village that was just up the road from the clinic, the three split up, promising to meet again that evening.

Chapter 9

Allie found the store. And she was impressed.

It was located on the bottom floor of a home that was of the same period as the schoolteacher's. When she pushed aside the beads that admitted air, not flies, Allie felt as though she had stepped through a portal in time.

It could have been a mercantile shop of a hundred years earlier, with lovingly arranged displays set attractively on shelves made of the finest mahogany. A large antique counter, with flowers carved into its rich wood, was the focal point of the room. Allie walked over to it and lightly tapped her fingers against the shining silver bell that sat next to a masterfully gilded cash register.

She had to wait only a moment before a very pregnant older woman emerged from behind the curtain. She looked like a Victorian mother, and Allie was sure that the child she was carrying had to be the latest of many.

"Oh," the woman exclaimed in a voice that was hardly louder than a whisper, while she self-consciously glanced over her shoulder toward the curtained-off area of the shop. Allie wanted to feel irritated by the gesture, one she had experienced too many times that morning while walking to the clinic. But she wasn't, especially when the woman readily extended her one hand in welcome while resting the other protectively against her protruding tummy. "You must be the new doctor."

Allie took the woman's small hand in her own and wondered at the nervous way she again looked behind her. That someone in the back room probably held the views of the ogre, of Tasos Drakopoulos, was obvious. But the sparkle in the woman's eyes made it equally apparent that she did not.

Allie nodded, then said, "I'm Allie Alexander."

"Welcome to Kastro, Yatrinna." Allie was pleasantly surprised by the proprietress's use of her title. Even more so when the woman whispered her name. "I'm Sophia Drakopoulos."

Allie's fingers let go of the woman's hand as if it had suddenly turned into a scorpion. Could this sweet woman possibly be the ogre's wife? "Are you by any chance related to Tasos Drakopoulos?" Allie found herself asking.

The light left the woman's eyes as, with a quick glance over her shoulder, she whispered, "By marriage I am."

"Oh." Allie didn't know what else to say. How could she tell the woman that she couldn't stand her ogre of a husband? But more than anything, Allie was amazed that Martha had instructed her to come to this shop. Martha had to have understood how she felt about Tasos Drakopoulos.

Allie's gaze fell to the woman's tummy.

Tasos Drakopoulos's baby?

It seemed an ironic twist that her first patient would probably be the wife of the person she least liked in the village. "When is your baby due?" Allie finally asked, her professionalism holding her in good stead.

"Soon," the woman answered, and Allie's trained ears heard a wistfulness behind the word.

"How many children do you have?"

The woman's shoulders sagged, and she looked—with what Allie could only describe as hope—down at her growing child. "This baby. . .she's all I have."

Allie was troubled by the woman's reply. The doctor in her wanted to ask several questions. But she knew that now was neither the time nor the place. "I should have the clinic opened by tomorrow evening. Please come, and we'll talk." Tasos Drakopoulos's family or not, Allie worked according to the Hippocratic oath. Besides, in spite of the man this woman was married to, Allie knew that she liked Sophia Drakopoulos. Even after a few moments, Allie recognized the woman as one of the world's human "angels."

With joy lines painting her face—one that reminded Allie of a porcelain doll she used to have—Sophia looked up from the baby, whose face she had yet to see, to Allie's, and she spoke in a voice that Allie thought might have belonged to a mouse, if one could talk. "When I found out that the new doctor was a woman. . .well"—she lowered her shy eyes again—"I was very glad, and I thought. . .that maybe. . .maybe. . .this baby might be born safely. . .since you're here."

Allie was certain now that the woman had had trouble having children. Her medical curiosity wouldn't be held down any longer. "Mrs. Drakopoulos—"

"Sophia." She stopped Allie with a hesitant smile. "Please," she quietly suggested, "call me Sophia."

"Sophia." Allie smiled her thanks before continuing. "You have had other pregnancies?"

Sophia nodded, and Allie didn't miss the tears that highlighted her eyes. "Several. My husband and I have wanted a child for many years but—" At the sound of the beads in the doorway being shoved impatiently aside, Sophia clamped down on her words, and Allie could feel tension radiating from her as she looked at the woman who had just barged into the shop. Nodding toward the newcomer, Sophia softly said, "I'll be right with you, Elani."

Curious, Allie turned to the woman, but when she saw a replica of the sour-faced, Ireni from the kafenion, Allie wished that she had checked her interest. The venom that radiated from this woman, though, made Ireni, in comparison, seem like a saint. Her eyes held a fever, a fever of hate, while her lips held all the cold of an arctic winter. No smile lines marked her middle-aged face; rather, lines of discontent and enmity radiated from her lips like ill-placed spiderwebs.

Nodding, Allie turned back to Sophia and, as was the custom in villages, she handed the proprietress her shopping list. As Sophia gathered the things from the various shelves, Allie would have gladly ignored the other customer if the woman's hard voice hadn't broken the heavy silence with the force of a sledgehammer against stone.

"So, you must be the new doctor," she crackled out, and as Allie turned to face her again, she couldn't help but be reminded of the wicked witch in *The Wizard of Oz*. This woman would not have needed makeup to play the role, nor even to modify her voice. She was positively perfect for the part.

Allie nodded. "And you are—?"

The little woman's lips pursed together, showing how the sour lines had been etched into her face, as she boastfully replied, "Elani Drakopoulos, wife of Tasos Drakopoulos, the mayor of this village."

Allie's gaze flew over to Sophia, and relief coursed through her as she realized that she had been mistaken in assuming that "being related by marriage" meant that Sophia was married to Tasos Drakopoulos. Sophia was too nice to be married to the ogre.

Allie looked back at the little woman with the pointy chin. This woman, on the other hand, was the perfect match for him. "Well, *Kyria* Drakopoulos, the clinic should be open by tomorrow evening." Allie wasn't going to waste the opportunity to let Drakopoulos know that she was in charge of her job, regardless of his attempts to dissuade her. "Please let your friends—and family—know."

The woman's sharp face rose higher still, as if she were a cat sniffing the air. "If I or my family"—she looked toward Sophia, and Allie could tell that she was sending her kinsman a strong hint—"should require the services of a physician, then we shall send for a cab and have it take us down to the city so that we may visit a specialist," she proclaimed, and turning her back on Allie, she demanded of Sophia, "Do hurry, Sophia. I'm a busy woman, and I haven't got all day."

With a soft grace Allie was coming to expect from her, Sophia gave a slight nod toward Elani but continued to gather Allie's supplies without being harried or bothered by her relative.

Allie decided she wouldn't be, either. She refrained from telling Kyria Drakopoulos that she was herself a specialist, specializing in family medicine, and instead watched as Sophia put her purchases into two plastic bags. She paid for them. But when she noticed some things in the bags that she hadn't written on her list and for which she was sure she hadn't paid, she was about to point them out to Sophia when her new friend subtly shook her head, warning her not to say anything. With her sweet smile, she gently placed her hand over Allie's and mouthed the words, "Welcome, Yatrinna."

Allie understood that Sophia was welcoming her with gifts of homemade rose-petal jam, fresh-picked oregano, and mountain tea. Smiling her thanks, Allie pushed the beads aside and walked out into the heat of the day. She didn't even mind that Elani Drakopoulos had prudishly turned her back on her again. Sophia's kindness had more than made up for the other woman's pettiness, and best of all, Allie knew that in Sophia, she had another friend in Kastro.

⁓⊱◈⊰⁓

"Baba," Jeannie questioned her father when he sat down at the table across from her, "may I say grace?"

Stavros looked sharply at her. He knew that something important was going on in her little head. Normally he had to encourage her to say grace. Not having a mother to confide in, she had fallen into the habit of using grace as a means of telling him about things that were important to her little girl's heart but she was too shy to come right out and say.

Smiling, he nodded his head, glad that she had found this outlet. He wanted her to always feel as though she could tell him what was on her mind, even if she felt it necessary to tell God at the same time.

Looking like the classic picture of a child praying, Jeannie very primly and solemnly clasped her hands together and, lowering her head, ran through her normal prayer. "Thank You, God, for this food, for rest and home and all things good. For wind and rain, and sun above, but most of all for those we love!"

Stavros waited with his own head bowed. He knew that grace wasn't over until she said "Amen." Finally, with added warmth to her words, she continued, "And God. . .thank You for bringing Yatrinna to our house." She took a deep breath before sighing out, "She's one of those. . .I love."

Stavros's gazed lifted again to the bent head of his daughter. He knew she liked the new doctor, but loved?

"And, God," Jeannie continued to speak, totally confident that God was listening, "please help Daddy to like her more. . . and. . .to trust You more, too." Startled and convicted, Stavros widened his eyes until the little girl closed her prayer. He quickly lowered his head again, not wanting her to catch him looking at her.

When he finally raised it, Jeannie was eating her French fries and fish sticks. She wore the trust that only children seem able to don comfortably. She believed totally that her prayer had been heard and would be answered in exactly the right way. She didn't have to concern herself with it any longer. Stavros wished he had a portion of that trust. He knew that he had had such a trust and faith. . .once upon a time. . . . Even in his adult life. But that had been long, long ago.

He watched her for a moment before reaching for his own fork. He had to clarify a few things. "Jeannie, I don't dislike the new doctor," he said carefully.

"But you don't like her as much as you liked the other doctors," Jeannie pointed out and dipped a fry into ketchup.

"I like her," he said, defending himself. "Just. . .in a different way." *A very different way.*

"Then why haven't you invited her over to eat with us or to watch TV or anything?" she protested.

The *anything* was the problem. The *anything* was what worried him, and what, he suspected, worried the doctor, too. But he couldn't tell his daughter that. "Well. . ." He fished around for a reason, any reason but the real one. "Don't forget, she just came yesterday."

Jeannie's face brightened. "Then we can invite her to eat dinner with us tonight!"

Stavros felt his lips quirk. His daughter could deliberate a cause just like— his blood ran cold as he realized what he was thinking. That his daughter could deliberate a cause just like—a lawyer. Just like her mother could.

"Can we, Baba?"

Stavros shook himself and looked into his daughter's imploring eyes, eyes that were the mirror of his own in a face that was the female version of his. But that didn't mean Jeannie hadn't inherited something from her mother. His jaw tensed as he admitted to himself that she might have her mother's ability to reason through an argument, but he would make good and sure that she would use her ability correctly, not just for her own professional glory and monetary attainment.

"Can we, Baba?" Jeannie prompted again, bringing him back to the problem at hand. Two other things he had learned from Jeannie's prayer were that he had to start acting more normally toward the doctor—and toward God.

He knew his faith had been severely weakened by his wife's desertion of them—he just hadn't realized until that moment that Jeannie had realized it, too. He had always taken her to church on Sundays and other holy days such as Christmas and Easter and had taught her how to say her prayers. It had never even occurred to him that his daughter had noticed his own lack.

He had prayed so hard that his wife would decide she wanted the child with whom she had mistakenly become pregnant. Somehow, Stavros had kept her from aborting their unborn child, prevented her from killing Jeannie. . . . A shudder passed through him. He couldn't even think about that time without breaking out into a cold sweat.

But his wife had never wanted the baby, never wanted Jeannie. Stavros had thought that when she saw the little life they had made together, she would change. He had prayed so hard for it to be so. But his wife never even held Jeannie. Not once. She had only wanted her career.

What good had all his praying, all his imploring to God done? Nothing. Not only had his wife deserted their baby and him years earlier, but then, six months ago, she had had to go and die, too. While on a business trip, of course.

"Ba. . .ba. . . ," Jeannie impatiently called out and put her fork down on her plate with a loud clatter, effectively cutting into his reflections. He looked at her—the most dear being in the world to him—and knew she would refuse to eat another bite until he answered her.

"Yes, pumpkin." He came to a sudden decision—at least about the physician—one that made him feel good in a way he hadn't felt in a very long time. "I think it would be very nice to invite the doctor to dinner. We'll see if she's free tonight."

"Yippee!" Jeannie exclaimed, and picking up her fork, she stabbed a carrot. All was right in her world again.

There was a moment of thoughtful silence before Stavros spoke again. "I'm very proud of you for helping out at the clinic today."

His daughter beamed up at him, and while dipping a piece of bread into the olive oil dressing Stavros had poured over the tomato salad, she said, "We killed three scorpions, too!"

It was obvious to him that Jeannie thought that was the best part of the cleaning expedition. But it wasn't to Stavros. A frown, a father's instinct to be concerned for his child, sliced across his face. "Be careful," he admonished. "Their sting can really hurt."

"Don't worry. Yatrinna has medicine for bug bites, and if I got stung—" She stopped speaking at the sound of someone's light footsteps coming up the stairs. Leaning toward her father, she whispered, "That's Yatrinna." As the sound of the steps passed the door, Jeannie swiveled around in her chair to watch as the doctor passed by the open window.

When Jeannie waved to her, Allie waved back.

Stavros watched his daughter. She was so happy about the new doctor being a woman. But at that moment Stavros knew that it wasn't just that Allie was a woman. Rather, it was the woman Allie Alexander was. She had affected both Jeannie and him with her way of being.

Allie was good for Jeannie—very good. And anyone who was good for Jeannie made him glad.

Plus, the talk about scorpions had him admitting to himself that he liked having a doctor in the house again, even if the doctor was a woman who made him feel things he didn't want to feel.

"I like her," Jeannie said as she continued to watch the window where Allie had just passed. "She's so pretty and nice and—"

"Eek—" A bloodcurdling scream rent the air. A scream that both Stavros and Jeannie knew had come from the subject of their discussion. The doctor.

Chapter 10

S tay put!" Stavros ordered his frightened daughter, and in a flash he was out the door and running toward the now silent doctor. In that split instant of time before he turned the corner of the veranda, he would have preferred to have still heard her screaming. With the quiet, he didn't know what he would find, and fear, like a searing blade, sliced through him.

He found her leaning against the railing, motionless, her hands covering her eyes. Dread moved in to keep the fear within him company. Had something happened to her eyes, those beautiful eyes that could darken like velvet and yet flash like quicksilver?

"Allie!" Her given name rolled naturally from his lips, and when her hands left her face and he saw that she was physically uninjured, his knees almost buckled with relief. But the haunted look that glazed her normally clear expression told of another type of injury, one that was perhaps just as scary. "Allie." He pulled her into his arms. She was trembling. "What is it?" he demanded, concern making his voice gruff.

Allie motioned, but didn't look, toward her front door.

Stavros turned to it, grimaced at what he saw, then pulled the woman named Allie Alexander closer to him. He wanted somehow to shield her, to protect her, from a situation that was proving to be much worse than even he had thought it might become.

Someone, and Stavros suspected who, had taken two dead snakes, wrapped them around a pole, and stuck it on her door. Done in the exact manner as the medical emblem—a caduceus—the snakes' eyes had been grotesquely gouged out, turning them into something belonging only in a Halloween house of horrors.

Stavros wondered if Allie had seen the resemblance to her profession's insignia.

He hoped that she hadn't.

But as he held her close to him, it was the weight of his own lack of welcome toward her that was heaviest on his heart. She gave the impression of courage and strength, but at the moment, she felt so slight in his arms, so fragile. She was one woman, one slender woman, up against so much.

He knew there was a strength in her that was much greater than brawn. But that aside, he also knew it was time for him to get his emotions under control and to offer her the friendship that even Jeannie had noticed lacking in him: the friendship Allie needed in order to survive in this village.

But first, as a friend, he would try one more time to make her understand why Kastro wasn't the community she should make her home.

"Allie," he whispered her name again, and she seemed to relax. "I'm sorry, but I tried to warn you," he continued. "This village isn't the place for you. There's so much going on that you just can't understand—"

She stiffened against him, and he stopped speaking. She lifted her face from his chest and met his gaze straight on.

"Then tell me," she ground out. "When fighting a disease, a physician has to know the history of the patient. It's the same thing with this village. If I know what the root of this problem is, I can combat it." She looked deeply into his eyes. "Please, Stavros, tell me what's going on."

As he held her body close and gazed over her form, he knew, if he were honest with himself, that at that moment he admired everything about her. She was vulnerable and yet strong; she was proud and yet humble; she was professional and yet woman.

One woman.

One beautiful, smart woman who had asked for his help.

He knew then he would give it to her.

Besides, he was almost certain that once she knew the truth, she would leave Kastro of her own accord, then he—well, he could get his feelings, as well as his well-planned life, back on track. But a small, nagging part of him wondered if it would even be possible for him to go back to before.

Cocking his head in the direction of the grisly display on the door, he said, "Let me get this cleaned up. Then we'll talk."

Relief seemed to fill her at his words, and on a shuddering sigh she admitted, "My fear of snakes rivals Indiana Jones's, from the Spielberg movies," she said, a forced smile curving her lips. "Even when they're just slithering across the ground, I'm pretty scared of them. But this"—she jutted her chin toward the welcome gift—"this was just too much for. . ." She paused, and he could tell she was wondering if she should continue. He was glad when she did. "This city girl."

Stavros squeezed her shoulders, and feeling as if their relationship was moving onto a different level, he motioned in the direction of the snakes and grimly admitted, "This would be too much for anybody." She blinked her eyes in obvious appreciation of his honesty, and he was glad he had spoken truthfully.

Then, with a bleakness, a sadness, in her voice that made his muscles bunch beneath his shoulders, she pronounced, "It's the caduceus—the physician's emblem."

He should have known that its symbolism wouldn't get by her. "I know," he replied and again felt that need, that desire, to protect her. Especially when he saw worry flicker through her eyes.

"What bothers me the most, though," she continued, "is the human snake who put it there."

That was what worried Stavros, too.

"Baba!" Jeannie's frightened voice called out from the kitchen window. "Is Yatrinna okay?"

"She's fine," he called over his left shoulder, and letting go of Allie, he bent down to collect her fallen groceries, trying to ignore how empty he felt no longer holding her. He nodded in the direction of his house. "Go sit with Jeannie while I get this cleaned up. We'll talk when I finish."

Her lips moved into a smile. It was one of thanks, flavored with relief. Stavros knew that was all she wanted to hear.

He saw a slight tremor behind the smile, but as she held out her hands to take the bags, he also noticed that her long, slender, healing fingers were steady.

Iron will, cotton-soft personality. That seemed to sum up Allie Alexander.

Inadvertently, a few minutes later, while in his kitchen, Stavros repeated Papouli's words of the previous day almost verbatim to Allie. "It's not that the villagers have anything against you personally."

But Allie wasn't buying it. Not today. Not after the snake attack. She slung her arm in the direction of her apartment door. "No? Well, it certainly seems as though somebody does," she shot out.

Stavros's chest lifted on a deep breath, and he shook his head slightly as he added ice to the *frappés*—iced coffees—which he had just poured for them. "No," he denied and turned to her. "It goes much deeper than that and," he said, pausing, his dark eyes nearly boring holes into her own, "it's much more dangerous."

"Dangerous?"

He nodded toward the door through which his daughter had just exited. "I sent Jeannie to her friend's house because I don't want her alarmed by what I have to tell you."

She dipped her chin in response, and he was surprised that for a change he wasn't bothered by that professional quality in her. She was cool, waiting, and rational. All characteristics—he realized with a start—that were needed to deal with the situation.

He drew a deep breath and, crossing over to the table, handed her a glass of frothy frappé before taking the seat opposite her. After a moment he asked, "Have you met Tasos Drakopoulos?"

When her mouth quirked distastefully downward, he had his answer. "Oh, yes. He and his wife have been most"—she paused, seeming to him to test different descriptions in her mind before settling on—"shall we say, hospitable."

"I'll bet they have," he answered with equal sarcasm, while wondering what sort of run-in she had had with the good mayor and his wife. "I believe that Drakopoulos is behind all this."

"I suspected as much. But why? Why does he seem to hate me so much?"

"It's not you he hates," Stavros said and picked up the saltshaker from the center of the table, "but the fact that you hold the position he wanted for his son." With a small thump, he placed the ceramic shaker next to its mate filled with pepper.

"His son?" Allie sat back, as though, Stavros thought, she were trying to get a better angle on an X-ray. "A case of jealousy is the last thing I expected to hear."

Stavros stood, picked up his frappé, and walked over to the mantel. Turning back to Allie, he said, "Quite simply, Dimitri—Drakopoulos's son—is a recent medical school graduate, and Tasos wanted your job to go to him."

Allie shrugged her shoulders. "Then why didn't Dimitri put in for it? Depending upon availability, doctors can apply for whichever village or town they desire."

"I think that he did. But he did so too late or something." Taking a sip of his coffee, he continued, "Anyway, the way I understand it, the position had already been given to you."

"But how can I"—she lightly touched her hand to her chest—"be held responsible for Drakopoulos's son applying too late? And why is the entire village against me because of it?"

"It's not you they're against."

"Then who?"

"One another."

Frown lines appeared across the smoothness of her brow. "What?"

Stavros sat back down across from her and, after expelling a deep breath, asked, "Allie Alexander, haven't you realized yet that you've landed yourself in the middle of a feud?"

"A feud?" Allie's first thought was that it was a ridiculous notion. "I don't believe it!" Feuds didn't exist anymore except in far-off places that were away from the rest of the world—

She stopped her thought.

What was Kastro if not a far-off place away from the rest of the world?

There was a sardonic look in Stavros's eyes, which, for once, Allie knew she deserved. "I think, Doctor, that you have romanticized living in a village."

That was exactly what she had done, but there was no way she was going to admit it. With a throat that had suddenly gone dry, she stated, "Please explain about this feud." A feud wasn't something she wanted to deal with. But if she had to, she would, as long as she knew all the facts that had led up to it and where she stood in its history.

He picked up the pepper shaker and seemed to contemplate it for a moment before turning back to her. "Its origins are probably as old as the foundations of this village, going back deep into ancient times when one man ran off with another man's wife or some such equally romantic notion. The village has been divided into two camps made up of two main families for centuries." He held up the saltshaker. "The Drakopoulos family. And"—he held out the pepper shaker—"the Angelopoulos family." He knocked the tops of the shakers together, then set them on the table, a few inches between them.

Allie reached out and wiped the tip of her finger across the pepper that was stuck to the top of its container. Of their own accord her lips twitched. "Do their names by any chance imply their characters? The Draculas versus the Angels, maybe?"

Stavros chuckled, and Allie liked the twin dimples that appeared when he smiled. They matched the flash of sparkle in his eyes. "It might seem that way to you at the moment," Stavros wryly continued, "but even the Angelopouloses seem to be fallen angels on some occasions."

"Oh." She rolled her eyes and waited for him to continue. One thing the snakes on the pole had done was to bring them closer together as friends. Allie liked the feeling—a lot.

"Where you landed in this feud is really quite simple," he continued. "The only one in the village who had the connections with the Department of Health to ensure that the position would be reserved for Drakopoulos's son happened to be a member of the Angelopoulos family—"

"And he refused to help," Allie interjected.

Stavros nodded. "I'm impressed at how quickly you pick up on village politics."

"Why didn't he help?"

Stavros sighed. "This is the stickler. The Angelopouloses claimed that he did."

"You don't believe it?"

He shrugged his shoulders. "I don't know."

"Is there anything else that you can tell me about this situation?"

Stavros clicked his tongue against the inside of his cheek. "Just the same thing that I've said before. I don't think this is something you should settle into. You don't know how long it could go on or, for that matter, what they might do."

"Are you trying to scare me away?" she asked, but in spite of his words, she still felt as though they were on the same side.

"I'm not," he stated. "But somebody is."

"Mr. Andreas—"

"Stavros," he corrected her. "It seems a little redundant to go back to formalities after the crisis has passed."

She nodded. She wanted to be on a first-name basis with him. "Stavros, I've got one thing going for me that most rural doctors don't have."

He waited silently for her to finish.

"I want to be here."

"I'm glad," he said, surprising her. From the way his eyes widened, she suspected that his pronouncement surprised even him a bit. "The villages around here are remote, and they do need a doctor."

Allie squinted. "I"—she paused and licked her lips—"I mean, I was under the impression that you wanted me gone from here."

"I don't think Kastro is a place for a young woman on her own," he said, but she got the impression that there was much more to it than that. She was almost certain it had more to do with the feelings that bounced around them whenever they were together, feelings that were ready to take over even this conversation. "Especially with the feud."

She lifted her chin in challenge. "Isn't that a bit chauvinistic?"

"Maybe," he conceded, his tone clipped. "Look—life is tough enough in the city, but up here in the wilds"—he shrugged his shoulders—"it's wild."

She regarded him in silence for a moment as she thought about Dale—the forever-young boy in the framed pictures in her apartment, the boy on the threshold of manhood who had been caught in the cross fire of a supermarket holdup. "Believe me, Stavros, there are more animals in the city—in any city—than you will ever find in the country."

The faraway look in her eye told him she was speaking from experience rather than mouthing a cliché, and he wondered about it. But he still felt he had to try to convince her one more time to leave before things became any dirtier. "Allie, be realistic. We're talking about a feud. A real dispute. Not something Hollywood has dreamed up for modern man's enjoyment. But a dispute that reaches centuries back into the very fabric of this village." He paused and spoke each word deliberately. "And you are caught in the middle of it."

By way of answer, she gathered all her purchases, arose from her chair, and crossed over to the door. There she paused, and turning back to him, she lifted her chin a fraction and replied in the same measured tone he had used with her, "Then I will just have to figure out how to break free."

And she left.

As the door closed behind her, Stavros wondered if he would ever break free of the hold she had on him.

Or—he took a thoughtful sip of his coffee—if he even wanted to.

Chapter 11

An insistent knocking pounded within Allie's sleep-drugged brain, and as she willed her heavy lids to open, she realized the sound was knuckles hitting against the wooden door.

"Yatrinna? Are you in there?" The muffled sound of Jeannie's voice came to Allie above the racket of cicadas in the pine trees outside.

Fighting the gravity that seemed to be in cahoots with her weary limbs to keep her in bed, Allie pulled herself up and walked on leaden feet to the kitchen for a glass of well water. "Come on in," she croaked out after the first sip. "It's open."

Jeannie pushed the door wide, and Allie smiled when she saw how the girl was dressed. She had on white coveralls and a white T-shirt, while her hair was tied back in a painter's kerchief. A whitewasher's brush slung over her shoulder completed the ensemble.

Allie lifted the glass away from her lips. "My, don't you look like a professional painter," she commented with a twinkle in her eye.

Jeannie's lips quirked, a kid's combination smile of both pride and shyness. "It was the only way Baba would allow me to whitewash," she explained, motioning down at her clothes. "He said it wouldn't matter if he couldn't get it out since it was the same color."

Allie lifted her eyebrows at that. Stavros had learned how to think like a mother concerned with the laundry, but with an added flare. Allie seriously doubted that most mothers would think to color coordinate the paint with the clothes. "What a smart baba you have," she commented, and splashing her face with water from the kitchen basin, she padded over to the antique mirror that hung above the dresser to brush out her hair.

Leaning the whitewasher's brush in the corner by the door, Jeannie walked up next to her as she styled her hair in a French braid. "How can you do that by yourself?" She was in awe of Allie's skillful fingers as they flew over her head.

"Well," Allie paused, "since my mother died when I was just a little girl—"

"My mother died, too," Jeannie interrupted, and Allie's fingers stilled as she looked at the girl in the mirror. She had been under the impression that Jeannie's parents had been divorced. Thinking back, though, she realized that had never been said. "But it was like she was dead even when she was alive,"

Jeannie continued, as if she were talking about the weather. "I mean, she never lived with Baba and me, and I never saw her." Allie understood then why she had had the impression of divorce. But she also realized now that Stavros Andreas's life was much more complicated than she had thought.

"I'm sorry. . .about your mother."

"It's not your fault," Jeannie said with total logic. But Allie understood that even though Jeannie had experienced two of the most devastating things a child could go through—the breakup of her parents' marriage, plus the death of her mother—Stavros had brought his daughter through them both unscathed. She was coming to admire him more with each thing she learned about him.

But Jeannie was only interested in Allie's hair. Pointing to it, she asked, "Did your father teach you to do that?"

Allie resumed braiding and smiled at the thought of her dear father and his thick fingers trying to fix her hair. "No. He didn't even know how to fix it in a ponytail."

"He didn't?" Jeannie touched the tip of her ponytail, which peeked out from under the kerchief. "My baba fixes my hair."

Allie smiled. "He does a great job."

"But not even he can do it like that." She motioned to the way Allie took small clumps of hair from the side and added them to those at the back. "But I don't think anyone in the village can. Maybe Natalia, but she's gone now." Jeannie was quick to defend her father.

"Well, I'll fix your hair like this whenever you want me to," Allie offered and was rewarded with a smile almost as wide as the valley outside the window.

"Really?"

"Sure!" She tied the end of the braid with a piece of ribbon, slid her feet into her flip-flops, and, squeezing Jeannie close to her, said, "Now, come on. We've got a clinic to paint!"

Martha was waiting for them with all the necessary paraphernalia. Among the three of them, they managed to whitewash the interior of the office and waiting room within a little more than two hours. It smelled fresh and clean, and Allie had the deep satisfaction of knowing that she would be able to set up her medical supplies in the morning and open the clinic for patients by the following evening.

Even after all the years of working and living in Greece, she still had a hard time getting used to the working hours. But remembering the afternoon heat, she thought it brilliant. People left their offices at about half past one, went home for lunch and a snooze, and then returned to work in the cool of the evening. Allie hadn't been surprised to learn that the custom stretched back to ancient days.

"It hardly seems like the same place as this morning," Allie commented to Martha. They watched together as Jeannie finished the final section of the last wall.

Martha laughed and pointed to Allie's hair, arms, and face. "And neither do you!"

Allie looked down at her body and touched her cheek where her skin felt pulled by the whitewash that had landed there. One glance at Martha showed her to be spotless. Even Jeannie had less paint on her than Allie had gotten on herself. "How do you two manage to do it so neatly?"

Martha laughed again while, in the quick manner Allie was becoming accustomed to in the small woman, she hurriedly folded the sheet that had been protecting the desk. "Years of practice. We whitewash our homes every spring. Now"—she speedily moved on to another subject—"Kyria Maria will come in the morning and fix the wicker in the chairs, and *Kyrios* Pavlos will fix the broken furniture, and whatever upholstery can't be fixed, I will cover with pillows and material."

Allie would have told Martha how much she appreciated all her help if Martha had allowed her to get a word in. But Martha continued to speak with the speed of an Indy 500 racer. "And it will all look beautiful!" Standing in the connecting doorway, she surveyed the rooms as if seeing them completed already. "I will come in the morning and make sure everything is done properly, but I must be going home now—"

"I'm done!" Jeannie interrupted, standing back to look at the wall she had painted.

Martha took a quick moment to glance at it. "It's beautiful, Jeannie." Then, turning, she practically ran out of the office. "See you both tomorrow!"

"Bye, and thanks again," Allie called after her, but Martha was already on the road heading toward her house. Allie walked over to stand next to Jeannie as the girl continued to admire her work. There was pride in what she had accomplished, a good and healthy pride for something real and visible.

"It looks terrific!" Allie commended her, but when she would have pulled Jeannie into a congratulatory hug, the girl caught a glimpse of her paint-smeared body and stepped away laughing.

"Yatrinna! You're a mess!"

Allie looked down at herself and laughed, too. "I am, aren't I?"

Jeannie rolled her eyes. "Boy! Am I glad I don't look like that. My father wouldn't like it." As her parent chose that moment to walk into the office, she shouted out, "Baba!" Taking his hand, Jeannie drew him up to face her masterpiece. "Look! I did this wall all by myself!"

Stavros put his hand on her shoulder and glanced over at Allie. But seeing her appearance, his eyes widened, and Allie was sure she saw something like amused admiration flash into them, definitely not the aversion Jeannie had said he would feel, before he turned back to his waiting daughter to comment on her paint job.

"It's beautiful." His gaze danced merrily toward Allie. "But are you responsible for putting the white in our new doctor's hair?"

The girl's dark eyes widened like shiny marbles. "No! I didn't—"

Allie pulled her paint-speckled braid in front of her eyes to see just how bad it was. It looked like the trunk of a polka-dotted, stuffed elephant. "No." Allie laughed, as she slung the braid back behind her. "I managed to do it all by myself." As Stavros regarded her, the deep brown coloring of his eyes turned soft and glossy, and something in Allie's heart did a flip-flop.

"I think it's very becoming," he finally said.

Allie glanced over at Jeannie and smiled the smile of a female sure that another, no matter how young, would understand. "Well, becoming or not, I must admit that I can't wait to soak all the sweat and paint of this day away in a nice long bath," she admitted, thinking with longing about the elegant bathtub that awaited her. She wouldn't forget to put the IN USE sign under the Andreas's door this time, either.

But when Stavros turned back to her, she immediately saw that friendship was gone. In its light and happy place was once again the opaqueness of doubt and challenge. Allie cringed.

"Well, I'm afraid you're going to have to do without that bath," he stated sharply.

Her brows came together in a questioning frown. She had the uncanny feeling he was testing her somehow. "What do you mean?"

"The water pump is broken."

"Oh, no!" Jeannie wailed out, swiveling her face up to her father. "Not again."

"Yes, again," he answered his daughter. "And this time I've had to order a part from Athens in order to fix it." He glanced back at Allie. "It will be at least a week, maybe even more, before it's repaired."

"Until then?" Allie asked, as sweat trickled down her back, reminding her of just how in need she was of a bath. "What do we do?"

He shrugged his shoulders. "Either we do without or"—he paused, and there was no doubt in Allie's mind that there was challenge in the timbre of his voice now—"we lug the water up from the faucet in the garden and fill up the bathtub. I have an immersion heater that will warm the water just fine."

"Ugh," Allie groaned. Soaking in that marble bathtub at the end of the day had kept her aching arm moving the brush back and forth, especially during the last hour. Absently, she rubbed her shoulders. "How many pails does it require?"

"About twenty."

"Twenty!" she gasped.

"I'll help you, Yatrinna," Jeannie offered.

Allie glanced at the girl and smiled. "You've been the biggest helper in this village. Thanks, but I'll manage."

"I don't mind," Jeannie insisted.

"I do. I know you have plans with Eva, and I won't let you break them."

"Okay, but will you come to dinner tonight?" Jeannie asked and looked up at her father expectantly.

Jeannie had asked Allie earlier, but Allie had been vague in answering, not knowing if the invitation had really come from the girl's father as well. She turned her gaze to his.

"I've made *yemistes*." He surprised her by encouraging her to come and share a stuffed tomato dinner with them. But she knew the reason why. Jeannie. Jeannie was his Achilles' heel. He would do almost anything for his daughter.

"Mmm. . .sounds delicious." A lot better than the cheese, bread, and olives that was to be dinner at her house. "But I can't. Not tonight." At the disappointed sigh that came from Jeannie, Allie quickly suggested to the girl, "Maybe tomorrow night?"

"But why?" Jeannie persisted.

"Jeannie," Stavros admonished her.

But Allie didn't mind explaining. "I'm exhausted, Jeannie. And I must have a bath." She looked over at the girl's father. "So I'm afraid I'll be rather busy."

⁓⁓⊙⁓⁓

Half an hour later, Stavros heard Allie lug the last two pails of water up the seventeen stairs. He had counted every time she had carried the sloshing buckets past his door. Twenty pails of water, carrying two pails at a time, meant she had made ten trips. On trip numbers three, seven, and nine, he had almost gone out to help her, but he had stopped himself each time. The last time, his hand had been on the doorknob, his knuckles white from tension.

It wasn't that he was lazy or that he didn't want to help her, because he did. It would have been a whole lot easier if he had filled up the tub. But he had convinced himself that to do so would be to do her a disservice.

She had to learn how hard life in a remote village could be now, while she could still get away. Under the best of circumstances, living in Kastro would be hard for a city dweller, and she wasn't even there under good conditions. The feud made sure of that. A broken water pump was the least on a long list of problems that could occur.

He sighed with relief when he heard her leave the empty pails outside her front door. He hadn't expected her to carry the water from the garden up to the bathroom. He had thought for sure she would balk at the idea. Then, during trip number five, he had been sure she would opt for a partial bath instead of the real thing.

She hadn't. Even when her footsteps had faltered with exhaustion. He had never admired such iron will in a person when she continued.

And a few moments later, when the IN USE sign was shoved under his door and he heard the bathroom door click shut, he grabbed an apple from the bowl and strode across the room to his door.

While Allie splashed around in the tub he would go and visit Charger.

Maybe he'd even stay there all night.

Chapter 12

*C*rash! Allie's eyes flew open, and she shot up in bed. In the soft light of the street lamp, her focusing eyes saw that one of the French windows was gone. In the place of the smooth glass were knives of crystal sticking out from its edges, looking like a computer game's torture zone.

A storm was raging outside, not the normal kind that brought rain and wet but, rather, the dry, windy kind. One that pushed its way though the broken glass like a vortex—but of air, not water—and whipped her long, silky hair around her face in a wild and savage abandonment.

She reached for the bedside lamp. *Click.* Nothing happened. All remained dark. *Click, click, click,* she frantically tried the lamp again, her eyes opening wide in fear. But nothing. There was no electricity.

"Allie!" She heard Stavros call out, and relief washed through her. She wasn't alone. Stavros was in the central hall.

"Stavros!" she called back, glad that she managed to keep the terror that had begun to seep into her system out of her voice. "It's unlocked." Thankfully, she had forgotten to lock it the last time she had used the bathroom. "Come in, but be careful. There's broken glass."

"I'll put some shoes on and be right back."

He was gone for only a moment. When he entered, a beam of light, blessed light, preceded him into the room, and nothing, and no one, had ever looked so good to her.

Wearing untied hiking boots, he crunched across the floor toward her. With his bare chest and cut-off jeans, he resembled a road worker—a super good-looking one—during the heat of a summer day. "What happened?" he demanded, his voice husky from sleep.

She shrugged her shoulders and pointed at the broken window. "I'm not sure. . . ." A gust of wind slammed a shutter in his part of the house, and glancing toward the sound, she offered, "Maybe a branch broke it?"

In the dim light of the battery-operated torch, she saw his mouth angle into a frown. "There aren't any trees up front." His answer was clipped as he sent the light around the glass-littered room. "Where are your shoes?" he asked when she remained quiet.

She grimaced and motioned toward the broken window. "I put them over there last night."

The beam of light located her yellow flip-flops, summer sandals, and running shoes. They were as she'd left them, all in a neat row under the window— now, however, with shards of glass glimmering in and all around them. "Do you have others?"

"I have hiking boots." She motioned toward a large suitcase in the far corner of the living room. "But I haven't unpacked them yet."

Before she knew what was happening, he bent down and put one arm around her back while the other easily went beneath her knees. "What are you doing?" she asked and frantically smoothed her nightgown down.

"I learned years ago never to go through a woman's suitcase," he explained as her arms instinctively found their way around his neck, while her face settled against his shoulder. He smelled good, like summer sun and honey, but he felt even better, sinewy and strong, with muscles that easily held her weight.

He looked down at her, and their eyes met. His head slowly descended toward hers; hers slowly ascended to his. Their mouths touched in a sweet kiss that was wondrous and lovely because both wonder and, amazingly, love were in it.

Allie had only loved the boy in the picture who stared smiling up at them from a decade past on her bedside table. But he had only been a boy, and she an even younger girl. Although she had dated sporadically, as much as medical school and residency permitted, she had never felt this way with a man before. Stavros awakened feelings in her that she had thought were only to be found in fiction, in fairy tales.

After the sweet kiss ended, he gently, softly carried her into the living area. There, as if she were the most precious woman in the world, he lowered her to the floor.

He smiled.

She smiled.

When his dimples flashed in his cheeks, she knew he was going to speak. "You're quite a woman, Dr. Allie Alexander."

Suddenly feeling shy, she stepped away from him to open her suitcase. Stavros looked uncomfortable, as well, and he turned and walked back toward the sleeping alcove.

Allie found her hiking boots and put them on. Crunching her way toward Stavros, who was standing at the base of her bed, she saw he was examining something in his hand. He turned and held up a tennis ball–sized rock. "Now we know what broke the window."

She reached out for the rock and felt its weight in her hand, while he glanced over to where her head had been on her pillow, just a scant five feet from where the rock had landed. "It could have hurt you badly had it hit you."

"It could have," she conceded and grimaced. "But it didn't," she reminded him. "And I don't think the purpose of throwing the rock was to hurt me. Just to scare me."

"I agree. But I still don't think this is a good situation for you to be in."

"I'm not leaving," she returned.

They regarded one another, adversaries, and yet not.

Letting out a deep breath, Stavros turned and moved over to the desk. He lit the lantern he had brought when he entered the apartment. He picked up the book she had left on the desk and snorted. "*Collection of Classic Fairy Tales*? Do you read this stuff?"

She stiffened. "I like fairy tales."

"I don't even think fairy tales are good for children," he stated and glanced back up at her before dropping the book, none too gently, onto the desk. Even with the wind blowing hard and loud, the thump it made hitting the wood of the desk could be heard. "But at least now I understand why you aren't realistic in your expectations."

Her eyebrows shot up. "I'm not realistic? Stavros, if there is one thing being a physician does, it's to make realists out of people."

He glanced toward the collection of stories again. A Bible and a *Physicians' Desk Reference* were stacked beside it. He shook his head, then motioned toward the broken window and the rock she still held in her hand. "I suspect you're going to need a fairy godmother to get you out of this mess."

She remembered thinking about Papouli in that way—as her fairy godfather. But even more than that wonderful man, she needed her faith. "Actually, Stavros," she said, and walking over to the desk, she put down the rock and picked up her Bible. "I think all I need is the confidence that I am right where God wants me to be. That's a faith that enables me to commit my way to the Lord and to trust in Him even when men"—she pointed to the rock—"carry out their wicked schemes."

A sound, something more a close cousin to a snicker than to a laugh, emanated from him as he glanced down at the Bible in her hands. "Do you really believe that God cares about you?"

"Absolutely." She didn't allow even a moment's hesitation in her response. " 'In all things God works for the good of those who love him,' " she said, reciting part of Romans 8:28. "I love Him, so it follows that He cares for me—very much."

"Now that's a fairy tale," he huffed out.

She picked up her book of fairy tales. "No, these are fairy tales." She raised the Bible in her right hand higher. "What's written in here"—she paused for emphasis—"is truth." She pointed to the array of icons on the wall above the desk that depicted some of the greatest Christians who had ever lived. St. Nikolaos and St. Paul were two of them. "It's what they believed, too."

"You are as they were—idealist."

Allie didn't challenge him. What she did was scrutinize him, just as she might a patient when she was endeavoring to put together all the symptoms for a diagnosis. "You know what I think, Stavros? I think that in actual fact you are the idealist; an idealist of the most dangerous kind. You are one whose ideals have been shattered."

He waved his hand in front of him as if he were swatting away the notion like a fly. "That's ridiculous."

"Is it?" He didn't respond, so she continued. "You know, it's not an uncommon ailment. Many people, most people, actually," she qualified, "tend to blame God when things don't go their way, when life throws them a curve ball." She smiled wryly and looked down. "Or a rock. The thing is, most people quite quickly understand the fallacy of their thinking."

His upper lip twisted in a sardonic smile. "You know, Dr. Alexander, I find this a rather amazing topic, particularly since you're the one who was just attacked."

"Why is it amazing? It just proves that I'm not an idealist. I know human nature well. I'll admit that it would have been pleasant to have been welcomed to Kastro nicely and that it was a bit of a shock when I wasn't." She shrugged her shoulders. "But I've lived through worse things. I'll get through this." She placed the Bible back on her desk, lovingly running her fingertips over its cover before training her gaze on Stavros. "Particularly with God's Word to guide me."

He held up his hands in a halting gesture. "I tell you what, Allie, I'll live life my way, and you live life your way."

She smiled. "Not my way, Stavros. God's way. If I were living life my way, well, let's just say I never would have made it to Kastro. Not as its doctor, anyway."

He motioned toward the lantern, effectively stopping their discussion. "I'll leave that for you." Then he nodded his head toward the street lamp. "The rest of the village has lights."

She swiveled her head toward the streetlight that cut through the dark of the country night. "You mean—"

He finished for her. "We're the only house without power."

"They cut the wire?"

Stavros shrugged his shoulders. "That would be my guess."

Allie sighed, then collapsed onto the edge of the sofa. "Should I call the police?" she asked after a moment.

"If you want to, but this is a village feud with a jurisdiction all its own. Unless someone gets hurt, the police aren't normally involved."

"Do people normally get hurt?"

"No," he said. "In this day and age it's more psychological."

She sighed. "I thought as much."

A gust of wind rattled the loose daggers of crystal that stuck out of the window frame in the bedroom. Motioning back toward it, he said, "Let me help you clean up—"

"No." She patted the sofa. "I'll sleep the rest of the night here and pick it up in the morning."

"I don't mind."

She held up her hand. "I do. I'm too tired to clean it now." Her gaze went to Dale's photo.

"Who is he?" Stavros's voice sounded sharp.

She glanced back up at him before returning her attention to the picture. Leaning over, she gently ran her fingertips across the smooth image of the boy, the boy who was almost a man. "We were childhood sweethearts. I was going to marry him. We were going to go to medical school together, set up a practice in rural America, and live. . .happily ever after."

"What happened?"

Allie turned. "About ten years ago he was a casualty of the wild city." She paused and explained. "He was caught in the cross fire of a supermarket holdup."

Stavros's face softened. "I'm sorry," he murmured.

Allie sighed, a sound heavy with the evening's event and memories of Dale's death. "Thanks again for your help," she said, hoping he would understand she needed to be alone.

But he didn't. Stavros ran the light beam back toward the broken glass. "Let me clean it up. You don't have to do anything."

"I'll do it in the morning."

The muscles around his mouth tightened. "Allie—"

She held up her hand to stop him. "I'm not leaving," she lashed out, but blinked when all he did was smile.

"I was just going to say, there are good people in Kastro and people who need the care you have to offer. Just give it a little bit of time."

"Does that mean you don't want me to leave?" she ventured to ask.

"I still don't think Kastro is the place for you." He pointed in the direction of the broken glass. "This proves it." He paused. "I just want you to know, though, that since you aren't going to leave, you can count on me to help you in any way you need."

Relieved, she smiled. "Thanks. That means a lot to me."

Stavros smiled back, as if to say it meant a lot to him, as well.

Chapter 13

Allie awoke in the morning to a wind that was, if anything, even stronger, hotter, and drier than it had been throughout the eventful night.

But it wasn't the wind she was thinking about as she ran her fingers over her lips. It was the kiss she had shared with Stavros, a kiss that she knew must not be repeated. She couldn't, wouldn't, do anything to jeopardize her professional integrity.

She had already gone through that once. And it had been a false charge.

She might be able to handle gossip if she knew for a fact that there was nothing to it, that they had no more affection for one another than just simple friendship. But—she let out a deep breath of resignation, a breath she hadn't even realized she'd been holding—they were already past that point.

She slid her fingertips over her lips.

The midnight rock thrower had seen to that. He'd done much more than throw a rock through her window; he'd thrown the two of them together, as well.

Shoving her feet into her boots, she clomped over to the refrigerator for a glass of cold orange juice. The power was still off, so it was only slightly chilled, but it was refreshing. As the liquid relieved her parched throat and its natural sugar filled her veins with energy, she knew what she had to do, or rather, could not do.

She couldn't allow herself to be anything more than friends with Stavros.

Nothing else.

No more kissing, no more touching.

Friends.

Platonic friends.

Period.

She took a deep breath.

Period.

With that problem intellectually solved, she quickly swept up the broken glass and dressed in a summer dress of pale lemon for her day at the clinic.

But when, a little while later, she stepped out her front door and saw Stavros balancing high above her head on a ladder, she recognized how irrational intellectual decrees were in the face of the emotionalism that surrounded the two of them.

He was fixing the cut power cable.

She wished he could cut the emotional one that sang to life between them every time they looked at one another—sever it in two, and in turn sever the halves in two. But she doubted it was possible. They were conductors of a kind of power that would always zap to life when they were in the same room together. Charged atmosphere.

Highly dangerous.

But nice.

Like a romantic thriller.

She grimaced.

She liked inspirational romances more. Especially when referring to her own life. If her real-life adventure in Kastro had to be a thriller, though, she only wished that it might be one with a happy ending. But she had her doubts.

Stavros's gaze found hers. He held up the two ends of the neatly sliced cable. She knew that he was warning her to be careful.

Squaring her shoulders, she nodded and walked toward the stairs. She was aware of his gaze following her, as though her skin could feel it.

When she turned the corner and knew he could no longer see her, she paused and scanned the red-tiled roofs of the village. She knew now that its apparent peacefulness was false. There was no peace in the world, and there was no peace in the remote village of Kastro, either. She looked up at the castle. With it sitting high above the town, guarding it, she should have known better. Castles weren't built for romance; they were built for protection.

She sighed and looked back down over the village. Her gaze settled on the gaily painted blue shutters of the priest's home. The word *peace* entered her mind, but this time in a positive way. His home was a haven of warmth, friendship, and godly love. She smiled, gladdened by what she had found there. Her fairy godfather. But no, Papouli was much better. Her gaze shifted over to the ceramic tiles of the old Byzantine chapel next to his home. He was the real thing. A true agent of God.

Allie's lips moved a moment before words formed and came out. "Lord, I ask You in Your precious Son Jesus' name to please help me," she finally whispered. It was a simple prayer, not unlike millions prayed to the Lord of glory during the previous two millennia. But because she believed so strongly in God's loving care, it was powerful, too—probably fourteen of the most powerful words humans could ever speak. Like so many believers before her, both in this village and around the world, Allie was confident God would indeed come to her aid. With footsteps now lighter after casting her cares on her heavenly Father, Allie walked down the stairs and into the heart of the village.

When Allie turned into the clinic's walkway a few minutes later and saw the tortoise on his back—his short legs flailing in a futile effort to right himself—and the door to the clinic pounding in the strong wind, she knew her prayer for God's help was one she would repeat again and again. She righted the tortoise, taking a moment to place it in a protective corner next to a bowl of water, and turned to face the ominous black that was behind the unlatched door. She had left it closed and locked the previous evening. Someone with a key must have paid it a visit.

Allie thought she knew who.

She reached out her hand, tentatively pushed back the door, flipped the light switch, and gasped.

The office had been trashed, ruined, vandalized. It looked like the very people who had given the word meaning, the Vandals of the early Middle Ages, had swept through, leaving malicious destruction and chaos in their wake. The walls that Martha, Jeannie, and she had so painstakingly whitewashed the previous evening were smeared with graffiti, reminding Allie of an uncared for section of a city.

Allie got mad. Really mad.

Not taking the time to even turn off the light, she left the office as she had found it, with the door pounding in the wind, and strode purposefully through the village toward the kafenion.

She had had enough.

She might have unwittingly landed herself in the middle of an archaic feud, but that didn't mean she had to remain a passive player.

If they wanted to play hard, she would, too.

The courtyards and homes were buzzing with villagers battening down their belongings against the high winds. They saw Allie—and her demeanor—as she passed, and with innate village curiosity, many followed, or in the case of several *yiayias*—grandmothers—sent grandchildren after her to see what was happening.

The sour-faced Ireni's gasp registered in Allie's mind as she went into the kafenion, but she didn't have the patience to give the pathetic woman more than a glance. Marching right up to Tasos Drakopoulos's table, Allie slammed the palm of her hand upon it. She didn't care in the least that she caused the three demitasses of coffee to slosh their brown liquid over their rims.

"I'm not leaving," she said without preamble, her voice hard.

Drakopoulos smiled a slow, smirking smile, which confirmed Allie's suspicions. He was behind everything—the snakes on her door, the rock throwing, and the clinic being trashed. There was no doubt in her mind.

"You're not wanted here," he said, repeating his very first words to her on the day she arrived in Kastro. But now Allie had a history of the disease that had infiltrated this village, and she knew how to fight it.

"The clinic had better be cleaned and painted before noon and in the shape it was before you vandalized it, or I'll contact the Department of Health and let them know what's going on here." Allie had the satisfaction of seeing Drakopoulos blanch. From her peripheral vision, she saw all the men in the kafenion swivel their heads around as they looked at one another. She had their attention—100 percent. Feeling more like a lawyer in a courtroom than a doctor, she continued. "If not, the Department of Health will withdraw the honor and privilege Kastro has in being the seat of the Rural Physician Clinic for this area. It will go to one of your neighboring villages."

There was a gasp from her audience, a sound that echoed out the cafe's doors as her words were repeated to the waiting ears of the villagers beyond. Allie knew she had hit a soft spot in village politics. She had been counting on the notorious rivalry of Greeks, one that had its roots in the ancient Hellenic city-states, when neighboring cities fought each other over everything and anything. She had thought there must be a village in the area that was coveting Kastro's medical clinic.

Now she was certain.

Without another word, without a muscle moving in her face, she turned and walked out the door.

At noon, when she checked in at the clinic, she would be certain.

Until then. . .

She would go to her apartment, get down on her knees, and pray.

Chapter 14

When Allie returned to the clinic at noon, refreshed by her prayer time and ensuing nap—one that helped her recapture some of the sleep she had lost during the night—she knew her diagnosis of the situation had been correct. The people of Kastro didn't want to lose the Rural Physician Clinic—even if it meant she was the one to run it. They had been frightened into action.

She found the clinic spotless, if possible even better than Martha, Jeannie, and she had left it the previous night.

The walls had been scrubbed of the graffiti and beautifully rewhitewashed, and the floor, polished by a professional machine this time, was so shiny it looked as though it belonged in the marble halls of a stately mansion, not in a lowly medical clinic in the middle of nowhere. About ten women were busy finishing up, but when Allie saw who was overseeing the entire operation, lines of displeasure formed on her forehead and part of her wished she hadn't challenged the Men's Club.

Out of the examining room, supporting her tummy with one hand, holding a bucketful of some sort of blue solution with the other while instructing a woman in how to clean the stain out of the sink, waddled dear, sweet Sophia Drakopoulos. In that unguarded moment, the sagging of her eyelids spoke clearly as to just how exhausted Sophia actually was. Allie was dismayed to think that Sophia had been working since early morning. This hot office was the last place any pregnant woman should be. Allie needed to examine her to be certain, but she suspected that Sophia was suffering from a combination of exhaustion and the heat. She hoped there wasn't anything else.

"Sophia," Allie called out, and the other woman's china doll face lit up when she turned and saw Allie.

"Yatrinna." Sophia held out her right hand in greeting. "I was so sorry when I heard what happened." She looked around the room with a satisfied expression in her blue eyes. "But I think"—her voice was barely above a breathless whisper—"you must agree that the women have put everything right once again."

Allie glanced around the room, and her eyes took in all the extras that had been added. Potted plants, a rubber tree and a palm, the upholstery all mended, two new chairs, paintings on the walls, and even a new cabinet in the examining room—something Allie was relieved to discover, because she had wondered where she was going to store her multitude of supplies. The latest editions of various magazines were on the coffee table in the waiting room, and she'd noticed when she walked in that even the garden had been spruced up. The rosebushes had been trimmed, the soil beneath them tilled, while reaching bougainvillea had been planted elegantly beside the door in perfect Mediterranean balance. The air of neglect had been totally erased from the little building, and the office was, in essence, as it should have been the day Allie arrived.

But she didn't say that to Sophia. She didn't want the dear lady to feel bad. "It's perfect." Then, looking over Sophia with a doctor's eye, she admonished, "But you have no business being here."

Sophia waved her concern aside. "I just heard today about how terrible the office was when you first arrived. I'm sorry, Yatrinna. I would have cleaned it had I known."

"Then I'm glad that you didn't know," Allie said without pause, because she was sure that without her threat Sophia would have been the only one doing the cleaning. "You must go home and rest. This heat is too much for all of us, but for you—and that child you're carrying—"

Allie's voice trailed off as Sophia made a circular, dismissing motion with her hand and sweetly cut in. "We village women are made of hardy stock, Yatrinna."

Allie frowned. It was her opinion that village women were strong, but to the detriment of their health, most walked in their early forties with what she'd labeled the "village waddle." Too many winter days out in the rain tending animals, washing clothes, cooking in wood-burning ovens, and a multitude of other things had sent arthritis to their hips at young ages. Allie took the bucket of solution from Sophia's hand and, with a smile, handed it to a passing woman, while guiding Sophia toward the door. "Hardy or not, you're going home now and to bed. Doctor's orders."

Sophia held her face up for the air to touch it. "Even with this wind, it is hot," she admitted and turned to Allie with a tired smile. "A nap does sound good," she further acknowledged, rubbing her hand across the bottom of her protruding tummy.

Allie knew that the only reason she conceded to rest was for the sake of the baby she so badly desired. "I want to examine you tomorrow," she pressed while Sophia seemed to be in the right mood.

Sophia smiled and wearily nodded. "Tomorrow," she agreed. Allie watched as Sophia waved to the rest of the women, then walked heavily up the winding road toward her house.

When Allie turned back to the clinic, she sighed. For some nagging reason—probably the fact that she didn't know much about Sophia's medical history—her condition bothered her.

As she watched the women pack their cleaning supplies and paraphernalia, sending her shy glances and hesitant smiles as they walked out the door, Allie was certain of one thing: There were more nice women like Sophia in the village.

A whole lot more.

That gave Allie hope.

Because of her late morning nap, Allie didn't sleep during the heat of the day. She finished unpacking her suitcases, then spent the afternoon in the shade of her vine-covered veranda reading a traveler's handbook on the history of Greece.

She had just finished reading about Minoan Crete and the Mycenaean civilization on the mainland and their famous Trojan War and was about to start on archaic Greece and the rise of the city-states, when the spicy scent of roasting chicken wafted in the wind that ruffled her pages.

Her stomach growled.

Oregano and pepper scented the air, and she lifted her head and sniffed as Jeannie's adorable little Siamese cat might. She hadn't realized how hungry she was.

Weighing her book down with a ceramic pot to keep it from taking flight, she went into the kitchen to see what she had to eat.

A can of sardines and a box of breakfast cereal were in the cupboard, while eggs, yogurt, and milk graced the shelves of the refrigerator. Nice food, but definitely not ideal for lunch and supper every day. She closed the fridge with a small kick. The time had finally come for her to learn how to cook. Her father and brother had done all the cooking while she was growing up, and her aunt when she'd been in medical school. After that, Allie had eaten most of her meals at the hospital or had called out. As she padded back out to the veranda, it suddenly occurred to her she wouldn't be able to call out for food in Kastro. She had to learn to cook now. There was no choice.

She wanted to. It was something basic, something real, and as the aroma drifted on the wind to her nose once again, she wondered if maybe she should follow the scent and see if that housewife might be convinced to teach her.

Sighing, she picked up her history book again and read how the country of Hellas came to be known as Greece. That had always intrigued her. When asked his nationality, a person from the country would not say he was Greek, but rather, that he was *Ellanas* if a man, or *Elannitha* if a woman.

Allie couldn't help but laugh when she read that the words Greece and *Greek* were actually derived from misunderstandings. When Hellenic colonists met the people in what is now known as southern Italy and were asked where they came from, they gave the name of their small city, Graia, rather than the overall area of Hellas.

It stuck.

From then on, the Hellenes became known in Latin as Graeci—the people of Graia—rather than the correct Hellenes. Thus came into being the adjective and noun *Greek*, or *Grecian*, while the name of the country became known as Greece, instead of the correct Hellas.

But as she started reading about ancient Sparta, the most military-oriented society of ancient Hellas, Allie's stomach again interrupted her as her nose registered the scent of frying zucchini.

Zucchini was her favorite vegetable in the world, a culinary feast, and Allie hadn't eaten any in a very long time. Her mouth salivated.

That would be the first thing she'd learn to cook, she decided, as she ignored her tummy and continued to read. She was into chapter five, having read about the glory of Ancient Athens, *Athena*; the Persian Wars; and the original marathon, when there was a knock on her door.

Padding on bare feet across the wooden floor, she glanced at her watch and was startled to see it was nearly six. But when she opened the door, she was given a much greater surprise.

Alone and smiling stood Stavros.

"Hi," he said, and there was a shy tone to his voice that almost confounded her.

"Hi," she returned softly, his shyness contagious.

"I've come bringing a peace offering."

"As long as it isn't a wooden horse," Allie quickly quipped. But at his questioning look, she dipped her head and explained, "I've been reading Greek history all afternoon."

"Ah," he said, "the famous wooden horse of the Trojan War from which we get the expression 'Beware of Greeks bearing gifts.'" He chuckled. "A true military feat of genius," he commented and smiled. "But no. Unlike the Trojan horse, the gift this Greek American offers is genuine. A picnic dinner."

"A picnic?" Allie repeated and blinked. But when her tummy chose that moment to voice its desire, they both laughed, sharing in friendship.

Waving his hand down toward the rumble, he said, "I think I've just been given my answer."

"You most definitely have," she admitted. "When is this picnic to take place?" It touched her deeply that he had asked her out.

"In about fifteen minutes?"

She nodded again and moved to step back into her home when he motioned down to her bare feet. "Oh, and wear tennis shoes or hiking boots."

"Boots?"

He nodded. "I thought we'd go up to the castle."

"The castle?" She glanced up with trepidation at the low vegetation along the path leading up to the gaping entrance of the citadel. Most of it was dried a beautiful gold in the heat of the August earth, with only cactus to add bits of green. "But aren't there snakes up there?"

He chuckled, a sound that was more like a verbal caress than a laugh. "I think, darling Allie, that you've found more snakes down here than you will ever see up there," he replied, and she knew he had heard about her latest problem. Her spine stiffened as she readied herself for a fight. She didn't want to hear his opinion on her living in, or rather leaving, Kastro again. But when she saw the definite flicker of admiration in the shining darkness of his eyes, the armor within her slowly dismantled.

"But if we do run into snakes, darling Allie," he continued with admiration in his tone, "fearful or not, I feel sure you will know how to handle them." Chuckling lightly, a low sound Allie definitely liked, he turned and went around the veranda toward the door of his house.

Allie stood for a moment at her door even after he had disappeared around the corner. She couldn't believe he had complimented her. Nor that he had invited her out for a picnic dinner.

Her clinic was all cleaned and ready to be set up in the morning, and now this.

Kastro, she thought as she looked up at the castle that was glowing pink in the evening sun, was getting to be friendlier and friendlier.

And hadn't Stavros called her "darling Allie"?

Not once, but twice?

Maybe the prince of the bus was finally replacing the toad of the house. But she slowly shook her head as she closed the door.

Stavros had never been a toad.

Not ever.

Chapter 15

The path up to the castle was steep.

But it was also fragrant and thought provoking, and Allie soon forgot all about snakes, both the variety that slither on the ground and the two-legged kind, as she followed Stavros up the zigzagging path.

The quiet of the medieval surroundings settled on and around her with a sense of timelessness and peace unlike anything she had ever experienced. Something elemental, it made her feel at one with the people of history during the last three millennia of which she had just been reading.

After the last zigzag, Allie saw the arched gate in the west curtain wall ahead of her. Two ancient cypress trees guarded the entrance—two soldiers on the alert—while large supporting buttresses jutted off to each side.

Looking at the walls of the castle up close, Allie noticed that it was well preserved. Even though its ramparts were crumbling in places, they were still serviceable. She could easily imagine knights and their ladies riding through the gate with their men-at-arms marching behind them, the prince's standard fluttering in the wind from the tallest towers.

"What do you think?" Stavros asked.

"It's beautiful," she said but didn't tell him her true thoughts. Knowing his distrust of fairy tales, she suspected that he wouldn't appreciate them.

"I thought you'd like it." He lightly touched her shoulder to guide her around to face what the castle had guarded for centuries. "But the view is the best part."

As she turned and her eyes registered the beauty of the 180-degree scene stretched out below and beyond, she gasped. She had expected to see the patchwork valley and the mountains surrounding it like a protective hoop, but what she hadn't anticipated was the Ionian Sea, shining like a crystal world of enchantment, to the glimmering west.

"I didn't know the sea was visible from here or that Kastro was so close to it." She reached out her hand, feeling as though she were a titan who, with just three or four steps, could cross the golden valley and wade into the waters that, even from this distance, were the famous blue of Greece.

"As a crow flies, Kastro is only about forty kilometers from the sea," Stavros explained. "It was for this"—he stretched out his arm to encompass the land and seascape before them—"that this fort was built here. Even invaders by ship could be detected early."

"Amazing," she whispered in awe, while absently lifting her braid off her neck to let the wind touch her skin.

"Are you hot?"

With a rueful smile, she let the braid swing back into place. "Surely you jest? With all this arctic coolness?" she replied facetiously, holding out her hand to the hot wind. "You?" she questioned.

His eyes opened wide in an "of course" gesture as he motioned toward the castle. "That's why I've ordered air-conditioning for dinner." Walking toward the steps leading up to the huge portal, he waited for her to follow.

"Air-conditioning?" Allie moved toward him. "What's that?" She hadn't felt air-conditioning since leaving the States, and she certainly hadn't expected to find it in a deserted castle high above the village. But after trailing Stavros just three paces into the interior of the vaulted passageway, she understood. Within its deep walls, the temperature was at least ten degrees cooler, if not more. "It's wonderful!"

"Ancient and medieval man's answer to scorching days was to hide behind his thick castle walls."

"And we of the modern world think that we are the only ones with the advantage of air-conditioning."

"No," he returned, and Allie thought she detected an ironic note in his voice. "We've just forgotten how to build houses of thick stones with deep foundations on solid rock that protect us from more than just the elements of the earth," he declared, and his jaw muscles became as tight as a bowstring.

Allie suspected that he was speaking figuratively and was referring to much more than just the physical home. The verses from the sixth chapter of the Gospel of Luke came to her mind. She spoke them without hesitancy.

"It has been well recorded that a very wise man once said, 'I will show you what he is like who comes to me and hears my words and puts them into practice. He is like a man building a house, who dug down deep and laid the foundation on rock. When a flood came, the torrent struck that house but could not shake it, because it was well built.'" She paused.

"Jesus' words," Stavros murmured.

She nodded, somewhat surprised that he recognized them. But it was a pleasant surprise.

"Please continue."

Feeling as if something very important was happening, she did. "'But the one who hears my words and does not put them into practice is like a man who built a house on the ground without a foundation. The moment the torrent struck that house, it collapsed and its destruction was complete.' "

Only the sounds of the natural world around them—the swallows playing in the evening sky, the trees, bushes, and dust of the earth being moved by the wind, bees buzzing—could be heard for a few moments as the words of the Lord settled between them.

"I am not an infidel, Allie." His voice was deep, but with a quality Allie could only describe as resigned sadness. "I believe that Jesus Christ is God's Son and that He came from heaven to earth to set all people free from sin so that we might have everlasting life."

Her soul sang to hear his declaration, even as she asked, "But even still, you don't trust Him to care for you here and now, do you?"

He rubbed his hand over his face and sighed, the deep, troubled sound of a man who had walked too long along life's rough paths alone. She wasn't surprised when he changed the subject. "How about if we eat?" he asked.

Allie smiled her agreement as she watched him pull the backpack from his shoulder. Knowing that he did believe in the redemptive work of Jesus was like learning that the vital signs of life were still present in a person who suffered from a serious illness. She was beginning to have an idea of what she was dealing with in him. She only hoped that before this night was over, she would learn more.

For Stavros Andreas was becoming very special to her.

Feed her he did.

But much, much more.

Stavros asked her to wait outside the castle entrance, beyond the supporting buttresses, while he set up the meal. When he called her in, he had transformed the entrance area into a hall fit for a king. Medieval tapestries hung upon the old walls, flickering sconces cast friendly shadows, and Allie thought that Emperor Alexius Comnenus himself might come riding in to join them.

Awed, she took in the lace tablecloth, the sterling silverware, and the hand-dipped candle of softest violet, lit beneath an antique crystal globe. She looked up at him. "Stavros, this is unbelievable." *And he claims not to believe in fairy tales!*

He smiled and pulled out one of the two chairs for her to be seated. "Since there aren't any fine restaurants in the vicinity of Kastro, I've had to learn how to improvise."

She laughed, but only to hide the unexpected stab of jealousy. "Oh? Do you bring many women up here?" she asked, slanting her eyes over at him as he took the other chair.

"You're the first."

She was confused. "Then. . . ?"

"Jeannie. I bring Jeannie up here at least once a month," he explained, and

Allie's lips turned up at the corners, both in unexpected relief and in happiness for the girl who had such a caring and doting father. "She loves it." He indicated the table. "The lace, the crystal, all of it. I keep a lot of stuff—table, chairs, lamp, plates, glasses—here permanently."

Allie looked at the items in alarm. He was talking about crystal and sterling, not glass and steel. "People don't steal them?"

"Crime in Greece is very low—probably the lowest in Europe. Here in Kastro it's practically nonexistent."

"Except if there is a feud?" she suggested wryly.

He lifted his brows in sad agreement. Then, leaving that subject behind—something she was happy to do, too—he raised his glass. "To friendship," he said and smiled, a slow and giving smile.

Lifting her long-stem glass of bubbly mineral water, she knew that it was a pledge more than a toast—one she wouldn't argue with. She lightly touched the rim of her glass to his and accepted what he was offering with a joyful heart. "To friendship," she agreed before sipping the sweet, refreshing water.

"Tell me," she asked after a quiet moment of harmonious reflection. "Martha mentioned that you moved here from Washington, D.C., three years ago. What were you doing when you lived there? Teaching?"

He reached over to the stone bench beside the table for a food container. "Yes. Medieval literature."

"What?" That was the last thing she had expected him to say.

"I'm a professor of medieval literature."

"A professor?" She had always known that there was more to this man than what he presented.

He nodded, and she asked, "Where did you teach?"

"Georgetown University."

She took a sip of water, then said, "I'm impressed."

"What I do here in Kastro is of far more lasting importance. Nothing is more wonderful than having the privilege of helping form young minds."

"Oh, I agree," she was hasty to assure him. "But having university qualifications makes you of greater worth to those budding brains simply because you know more. Tell me, what do you most enjoy about teaching kids?"

"That they are so honest. They tell it like it really is, like they see it. The world and everything to do with it."

She rubbed the stem of her champagne glass between her forefinger and thumb. "I've found that to be true when dealing with children in medicine, too. They want to know what I'm doing when I examine them. Why? Will it hurt? Everything. Even the diagnosis."

"And do you tell them?"

"If I can."

"Meaning?"

"You've probably discovered in teaching the same thing that I have in practicing family medicine—that often dealing with the parents is the most difficult part of the job."

He smiled in agreement. "How true."

The remainder of the meal passed with the same sort of companionable conversation.

A little later they sat on the steps of the castle, enjoying both a bowl of grapes and the view. The sun-ripened fruit tasted so fresh that Allie felt as though she could taste the sun in them, while the view was panoramic and alive with activity. She could almost envision Thumbelina riding on the back of a swallow that dipped in the breeze close to them. Without thinking, she spoke her thoughts. "All this—the meal, the view, the castle—it's truly like a fairy tale."

"This castle was anything but part of a fairy tale, Allie," he immediately cast back.

She didn't want to have another disagreement with him—especially during this very special evening. Holding up her hands in a conciliatory fashion, she said, "I didn't mean to imply—"

"Do you know the amount of blood that has been spilled right here where you now sit munching on your grapes so charmed by the view? Hundreds, thousands, of people have lost their lives," he said. "No, Allie, this land was too wealthy, too strategically located to be left to the fairy tales."

She regarded him steadily for a moment, angered that he had intentionally misunderstood her. "Oh yes, I forgot," she said sarcastically. "You don't like fairy tales, do you? Not even for children."

"Particularly not for children."

"Why, Stavros? Why are you such a pessimist that you can't let a little whimsy into your life? Into your daughter's life?"

"I'm not a pessimist, Allie. As I told you last night, I'm a realist. And my daughter is fine without idealistic stories to create unrealistic expectations within her little head."

"So you think you are being a realist by ignoring the lovely, the enchanting, the fanciful things in life? You think by ignoring them you can prevent hurt and pain in your life, in your daughter's life?"

"No," he ground out, "but I do believe that unrealistic expectations can be avoided that way. I don't believe in happily ever afters."

Allie sucked in her breath. "That's sad, very sad. Happily ever afters, those which have God in the equation," she qualified, "do exist, Stavros."

He regarded her for a moment. "Tell me, Allie Alexander, what's your idea of happily ever after?" he asked but immediately held up his hand to stop her answer. "No, wait. I know. It's to marry the handsome, modern-day prince"—he opened his palms outward in a gesture that said he found it unbelievable—"and to live happily ever after, of course."

That was a bit too simple, but also, too close to reality. She lifted her chin. "And why not?"

"First and foremost, because you're a career woman."

She blinked. Had she missed something, a non sequitur, along the line? "What?"

"You're a professional," he repeated, as if that clarified everything.

"So?"

"You're married to your work."

She blinked again. "I am not!"

"Oh, come on, Allie. You just told me you don't even know how to cook," he said, referring to part of their mealtime conversation.

"So what you're saying is, one has to know how to cook in order to live happily ever after?"

He made a disgusted sound. "What I'm saying is I don't believe that professional women can have it all. They can't have a family and their profession. It doesn't work. Somebody always pays. The children, the woman, or the man." He paused. "Somebody."

Allie looked at him as a physician studying a patient. What she saw was pain deep in his eyes, pain that must often plague him. She had seen the same look in desperately ill people many times before. Consequently, she didn't get angry. What she did was get personal. "Tell me, Stavros. What exactly did your wife do to you to make you hurt so badly?"

As if someone had struck him, he flinched, and tears sprang into her eyes at the raw pain that filled his face. She moved her hand up between them and spoke softly, her bubble of self-righteous directness now popped. "I'm sorry. I had no right—"

"No," he waved her apology aside. The question had changed his demeanor, too. He spoke softly, no longer antagonistically. "No. Actually"—he paused and gave her a wry smile—"I want to tell you." He paused again. "I've never told anyone but my mother and Papouli what I am about to tell you but—"

"Stavros—"

"I want to tell you," he repeated, and nodding, she waited. "My wife—" He rubbed his hand over his eyes and took a deep breath. "She didn't want Jeannie. Not ever."

Allie couldn't help the gasp that came from her. She didn't know what she had expected him to say. Just—not that. Never that. But so much about the man she was coming to care a great deal about was explained by those words.

"When my wife," he continued, "found out she was pregnant, she wanted—" He stopped speaking and grimaced wryly. "Let's just say that until my wife was past a certain week in her pregnancy, I didn't let her out of my sight for fear of what harm she might do to our unborn child—my little baby—to Jeannie." He looked out over the valley, and Allie knew he wasn't seeing the view but that very difficult time instead.

Allie reached out and touched his upper arm. His biceps bulged beneath her hand. Such a strong man, and yet the strength that he had had to exert to protect his unborn child had been so much greater, a might, Allie was sure, from which he was still recovering. Allie didn't have to be told in any plainer words that his wife had wanted to abort Jeannie.

"Jeannie told me," she ventured softly after a moment, "that it was as if her mother was dead, even"—she paused—"when she was alive."

Like eagle eyes zooming in on the prey, his gaze swiveled back to hers, startling her. "Jeannie said that?" he asked in a strangled tone.

Perplexed by his piercing look, Allie shook her head in confused question. "What does she normally say about her mother?"

"Nothing."

Her eyes widened in shock. "Nothing?"

"Absolutely nothing. To no one," he confirmed. "The topic of her mother is the only thing she never talks to me about. No matter what I do to try to get her to speak." He opened his hands before him, a parent's helpless gesture.

That Jeannie felt something very special toward Allie to have so honored her in speaking about her mother was obvious to both of them. She shrugged. "I don't know what to say."

"I do." He turned to face her, and reaching out, he softly ran the back of his fingers against her jaw. His eyes darkened, and as she read only nice and wonderful things in their depths, things so different from what she had seen there just moments before, she breathed out a prayer of relief within her. "You are a godsend," he said, surprising her, but Allie could tell from the catch in his voice that he felt the same amazement over his own words.

He continued, "I believe, Allie Alexander, that you were actually sent by God—directed to come to Kastro even—to help my little girl and me. Her not talking about her mother has been a heavy burden for me to bear. Because I knew it was so unhealthy, I think it was the last thing that kept me from allowing my heart to trust God again. In spite of my wife, God has been good to us," he admitted. "I have known this intellectually for quite some time." He breathed out deeply. "My heart was just too hard and heavy to admit that which my mind's eye could see. "

His lips slowly turned up at their corners, and Allie watched as the most remarkable smile spread across his face. It matched the smile in his eyes. "You are quite some physician, Dr. Alexander. Not only does my little girl open up to you in a way she hasn't to anyone else, but"—he placed the palm of his hand over his chest—"I feel as though my heart, which has felt more like a heavy block of ice than a beating pump, is finally beginning to melt."

"Oh, Stavros." She covered his hand with hers. Then, twining their fingers together, she scooted closer and rested her head against his chest, against the beating of his heart. She closed her eyes as its steady sound filled her ear. "I hear it, Stavros. I feel it. It's warm, my darling. It's warm and strong."

He squeezed her closer to him and spoke into her hair. "Maybe in God sending you to Kastro and to me, I can finally start to believe that He really does care about me, about Jeannie."

"Oh, Stavros," Allie whispered and, sitting back a little, looked up at him. "He does. He really, really does."

"My life was just so perfect until"—he paused—"my wife became pregnant." A faraway look came into his eyes. "I never knew that she didn't want children."

"You never talked about having a family someday?" That seemed inconceivable to Allie. Her family had always talked—and prayed—about everything.

He took a deep breath and shook his head. "No. I just assumed that someday we would start a family. It wasn't an assumption my wife shared."

"Did your wife. . .I mean, did she believe in God?"

"That's the funny thing." He clicked his tongue against his cheek. "She did." He shrugged his shoulders. "I guess she got lost somewhere along the way." He looked at her as if he were trying to measure her. "You told me last night you would never have made it to Kastro if you hadn't lived your life God's way rather than your own. What did you mean?"

As if she had been doing it forever, she turned and leaned her back against him. She breathed in deeply of the pure air, while her eyes took in the surrounding beauty. The sun was riding low in the sky, highlighting the blue of the sea, while the earth was rejoicing in the rest a star-filled night would soon bring to it. Looking out over the world bathed in the setting sun and holding his arms close around her, she prayed for wisdom in answering.

"When I sit at a place like this, I feel so thankful to be alive and to know who it is that keeps me safely in His grip." She squeezed Stavros's hand. Then, turning her head to look up into his waiting eyes, she answered him directly. "My mother died when I was just a little girl, and even though I had the most wonderful father in the world and a brother who would have given me the moon itself had I asked him for it, I would not have been a happy girl if I hadn't been assured of my heavenly Father's love. There is only so much people can and should expect of their fellow humans. I learned at a very young age that people leave us—people we love and who love us. The only constant in life is God, as revealed by Jesus Christ. He is here with me now, just as he was in New York City and Athens, too. If I had tried to live my life without that constant, I know that I never would have left what seemed like my secure world. I would have lived life my way rather than God's way. He directed me to go to Athens to continue my studies." She gave a shaky laugh as she remembered that time. "And believe me, that was no small decision. Just as He then directed me to Kastro."

Stavros shook his head. There was an amazed yet a respectful quality to his voice as he said, "I think what you have is a very mature working faith in God."

She smiled self-consciously. "That's what my brother, Alex, has always said. What about you, Stavros?"

He took a deep breath and confessed, "I've always believed in God. I never stopped believing, even when I felt He didn't care about Jeannie or me or all the rest of the hurting people in the world." He grimaced. "But I think that the measure of my faith went along with how well everything was working out in my life. When things went wrong—particularly when my wife didn't want our baby—I think I decided that God really didn't care. My faith became as weak as my life, when just the opposite should have happened." He shook his head. "I don't know. Maybe I was an idealist, one who felt as though my happily-ever-after life was ripped wrongly away from me when my wife didn't want the baby I thought our love had conceived. Perhaps I was even one, as you said, whose principles were shattered—shattered into a million pieces."

"To be an idealist is not something bad, Stavros. It's only when you believe in your ideals more than you do God, or when you rely on your belief of how everything should be rather than on your faith in God to work all things out for your good, that it's not advantageous."

He nodded. "I'll concede that. It's very shocking, though, when things don't work out as one plans."

"So be a hopeful realist, like me."

"Hopeful realist." He seemed to taste the expression. "I like that." Then, standing, he pulled her up with him, effectively but nicely ending their discussion as he had on so many other occasions. Allie didn't mind. She had learned so much about him during the last few minutes, really important things that had brought them very close.

"Come. It's getting dark. I'd better direct you down the path before it's too dark to see."

"Path," Allie murmured the word she found key to his sentence—to their conversation—and recited a favorite verse from Psalm 119. " 'Your word is a lamp to my feet and a light for my path.' "

He paused, and the smile he gave her in the waning light of the day made her wonder if he might just be the knight—the Christian knight—she had been dreaming about her whole life. "You're quite a physician, Allie Alexander," he said, repeating the praise he had given her earlier.

"Oh, but it is the Great Physician who is working in your heart, Stavros Andreas. Not I."

He clicked his tongue against his cheek as they walked together down the path to the village, and she heard him whisper, "I think, maybe, both of you are."

Chapter 16

The days that followed were, on a personal level, some of the most wonderful Allie had ever experienced. That she and Stavros had been brought together by God, and that their growing feelings had been ordained by Him, was something of which they were both becoming certain. When Allie wasn't at her clinic, she was with Stavros and Jeannie at their apartment, or they were with her at her apartment, or the three of them were visiting with Papouli and Martha, or they were walking the countryside around Kastro, hand in hand. It was as Jeannie had proclaimed when the three of them had returned home from Papouli's together on Allie's first night in Kastro—it was as if they were a family.

But the clinic was still a problem.

It wasn't that things weren't going well; rather, things weren't going. Period.

She had no patients. Not even the elderly came to have their blood pressure taken, something Allie had been told was a favorite pastime for the senior citizens of the village. That Drakopoulos had instigated a boycott on the clinic was obvious.

Allie thought about threatening the Men's Club with going to the Department of Health again, as she had after the office had been vandalized. But after much prayer, she knew God wanted her to trust Him and to leave the situation in His capable hands. Casting all her anxieties on Him, she put on the virtue of patience and waited.

Allie didn't mind for herself. She used the free time to acquaint herself with the people she was to serve through the numerous and meticulous medical ledgers her predecessor had left behind. But she did mind for Sophia.

Because of Sophia's tenuous position—her husband being Tasos Drakopoulos's brother—the woman didn't come to the office as Allie had asked her, nor did she feel comfortable enough to allow Allie to examine her at her home. This disturbed Allie. Her professional intuition warned her that Sophia and her baby might just become real victims of this feud.

On the fourth day the clinic was open, Allie decided that if the people of the area wouldn't come to her, she would go to them. She read in the medical records about a family of four children who lived up on the mountain with their father and had not received their current inoculations. She decided to pay the family a visit. When she leaned from Stavros why the family lived all alone up on the mountain, her heart went out to them.

The man's wife had died in childbirth three years earlier. Angry at the so-called civilized world, which had not been able to save his wife and baby, Petros Petropoulos had taken his four children and returned to his ancestral home to live an extremely basic life. When Stavros went on to tell her that Petropoulos was in fact the man who had disembarked from the bus with the chickens on the day she arrived, Allie was further intrigued. She couldn't help but think of Johanna Spyri's beloved heroine, Heidi, who had lived high on a mountain with her grandfather.

When Stavros offered to take her to the family on his horse, her house call turned into a very romantic trip up the mountain. Especially when Papouli, ever the matchmaker, prompted Jeannie to stay behind with Martha. They were going to make *hilopitas*—or "thousand pastas"—homemade pasta cut into a thousand little squares.

"Well, Dr. Alexander," Stavros said, as he came to stand before Allie when his daughter and the priest left the clinic. "It seems as though we can spend some quality time alone this morning." He motioned in the direction where the old priest's laughter and the little girl's chatter could still be heard as they made their way up the village road toward Papouli's home. "I love my daughter." He rubbed the back of his hand against Allie's cheek, and she watched as his dimples, a sure sign that he was happy and content, deepened around his mouth. "But I am glad to be alone with the woman I am coming to love, too."

"Love?" Allie whispered hesitantly. She was glad he had been the first to mention what was obviously in the air between them, but at the same time, she just wasn't sure she could make such a declaration with her job in Kastro still so tenuous.

He nodded, then placing his finger against her lips and seeming to read her mind, he said, "Let's get your situation here settled." Leaning toward her, he placed a feather soft kiss upon her lips. "Then we have to talk."

"Talk?" she repeated, her heart giving a little flutter.

"Hmm. . .but first your position here has to be set." He smiled sheepishly, as they both remembered how difficult he had made her stay in the beginning. "I understand now how important it is to you—and to the health of the people in this rural location—and I will not do anything—anything else, that is—to make it any harder for you than it already is."

"Thank you, Stavros," she said. "You know, with your support and God's constant care, I feel as though I can do almost anything."

She had always thought that she really needed only God in her life. Now, after having come to have such strong feelings for Stavros, she understood that to have both God and the love of a man of faith—and Stavros was now, indeed, just that—was ideal. But then again, hadn't God Himself ordained that man and woman should pass through life together? No wonder the joy she felt in having Stavros by her side was so perfect.

He wrapped his arms around her and pulled her near him. She reveled in the feel of having him so close, both physically and emotionally. "You can do anything, my love," he whispered in her ear. "You can."

⁓⊱◦⊰⁓

"There. Now that didn't hurt much, did it?" Allie asked two hours later of the wobbly lipped little boy named Vassili as she rubbed the spot on his hip where she had just inoculated him.

"That nail I stepped on yesterday hurt a whole lot more," the boy assured her, trying his best not to let tears slip from his eyes.

Concerned, Allie asked, "What nail, *agori mou*—my boy?"

The boy lifted his bare foot and showed her the makeshift bandage that covered the puncture.

"I washed it and put iodine on it, *Yatrinna,*" sixteen-year-old Maria explained, holding her youngest sibling's hand. Allie smiled at the sweet girl. She felt sorry for Maria. It was as if childhood had totally passed the girl by. Allie wished she could somehow convince the children's father to move back down to the village where they might have some help.

When she turned back to the boy's foot and removed the bandage, though, Allie had to use all her bedside manners not to flinch at the angry cut she found there. It was red and infected in spite of Maria's ministrations. "You did a good job, Maria." Allie knew the girl had done all that could be done under such primitive conditions, but to the boy she asked, "Do you still have the nail?"

"Sure do! I saved it!" The boy answered as Allie suspected he would. From both her brother and Dale, Allie knew that boys liked saving things like nails. Especially nails they had stepped on. "It's in my jar."

"I'll get it," Stephanos, the oldest boy, who was a year younger than Maria, offered, and walking over to the bed on the other side of the large, one-room house, he pulled a ceramic jar out from under it and brought it to his younger brother.

The boy rummaged through his treasures before presenting the nail to Allie as if it were a trophy.

She couldn't help widening her eyes. It was the rustiest, most jagged piece of metal she had ever seen. Although it had probably been a nail at one time, it hardly looked like one anymore. She thought it was probably left over from some Byzantine building. "Hmm, I guess that hurt a bit."

"A lot," the boy corrected her.

"Well, I'm afraid that you are going to have to have another shot."

"But why?" His lip wobbled again.

Talking on his level, she answered, "To make sure that rusty ol' nail doesn't make you sick."

"Oh." That seemed to calm him down. "I don't wanna be sick."

Allie ruffled his nearly blond hair, which, she had noticed with some surprise, was very clean. All the Petropoulos children were clean, as was their rustic but very quaint home. "You won't be."

But as she prepared the injection, she glanced up at Stavros. They both knew that if she hadn't come today the little boy might have become very ill with tetanus. She glanced over at Kyrios Petropoulos. She was surprised to realize he seemed to know it, as well.

He nodded at her, but in an enigmatic way, as if he had just made a big decision. "When you're finished here, Yatrinna, please come out and we'll talk." Motioning for Stavros to precede him, the two men walked out the door.

Allie watched them go before turning back to her job. She liked Petros Petropoulos. When he wasn't holding squiggling, squawking chickens, as he had been that day on the bus, he was a very calm, articulate man. He remembered her and had been amazed when she rode up with Stavros. He was more amazed still when he found out she was Kastro's new doctor. Not because she was a woman, but because she cared enough about his children to ride all the way up the mountain to check on them.

After the children were all taken care of, she left them with one of the many puzzles she had brought for the children of the village and went out to join the men. They were sitting at a table made from the trunk of a big oak tree with matching stools from the same tree's branches. Expertly shellacked, it was a natural and beautiful patio set, and Allie knew that people in New York would have gladly paid top dollar for it.

"How's the boy?" Petropoulos asked quickly, exhibiting all the concern a doctor could want in a patient's parent.

"He'll be fine. I've left an ointment and some tablets for him to take." She paused. "That nail was very rusty. Didn't you think he might need a tetanus shot?"

"I only got back this morning. I was up in the pine forest checking on my trees. The children told me about it. I hadn't seen the nail. I was as shocked as you."

Allie wondered how he would have felt had his child suddenly and needlessly developed tetanus. "Kyrios Petropoulos, you're a long way from civilization and help if you ever needed it. Why don't you move the children back down to the village? I'm sure someone could be found to help with the housework, and your children could go to school." Allie had already discovered that all of the children were extremely bright.

"I think you're right," Petropoulos answered without even pausing.

Stavros turned his head toward him as quick as a whiplash. "What?"

Petros smiled. "I said, I think the doctor is right."

"But I've been trying for the last two years to get you to move off this mountain and back down to the village."

"Yatrinna!" Vassili called out. "We finished the puzzle. Do you want to see it?"

Allie flashed Stavros an amused smile before she stretched out her legs and rose from her seat. She could tell he was not only amazed by Petropoulos's answer but flabbergasted. She bit her lip to keep from laughing at his expression and, turning to Petros, said, "I'm glad you're going to move to the village. I'm looking forward to seeing a lot more of your children—and I don't mean only for medical reasons," she qualified before excusing herself and returning to the well-behaved siblings.

"Einai koukla," Petros said of Allie just as he had that day at the bus stop.

Stavros stiffened. "Is that the reason you're moving back down? You're interested in the doctor?"

"Don't be ridiculous, friend. You and she are meant to be together just as my Emily and I were."

Stavros was surprised that Petros had not only so quickly noticed but said something about it. The woodsman was a man of few words, giving each one he spoke more weight. "Then why are you suddenly coming down off this mountain?"

"Because I have a good enough reason to move now." Petros nodded toward the door Allie had just walked though. "That doctor will do everything humanly possible to make sure no more of my babies die."

"But Kastro has had other doctors. Don't you think they would have, too?"

Petros made a disgusted noise. "They never even cared enough to come looking for us," he spat out, and Stavros knew that he spoke the truth. Both of the other two physicians were eager to leave Kastro. They had only wanted to serve their required year and get out, definitely not anything above and beyond the call of duty. Allie Alexander, they weren't.

Stavros frowned. He wondered why he hadn't thought of that before. Allie was the only doctor who had come to Kastro because she wanted to and not because of requirements. And everyone, including him, had made life difficult for her.

~~~

A little while later, clip-clopping down the mountain on their return trip to Kastro with Allie seated before him on Charger, Stavros kissed the sensitive part of her neck where her elegant braid fell. "Thank you, darling Allie."

The saddle creaked as she squirmed around and looked up at him in question. "For what?"

"For coming to Kastro and being instrumental in saving two recluses—Petros and me."

She put her hand up to his face. "Oh, my darling, don't you know you have done the same for me?"

Stavros was glad that Charger knew the way back to Kastro. He only had eyes for the beautiful woman he held tightly in his arms.

At Allie's request, Stavros—and Charger—left her at the clinic. She wanted to complete some paperwork plus be available during the evening hours in case someone decided they needed a doctor more than they needed to be a part of a silly feud. After two hours, when still no one came, she closed up and headed for home, deciding to stop at Sophia's shop on the pretense of needing something.

Pushing through the beads, Allie expected to see Sophia in her usual place behind the carved counter. She wasn't there; rather, she was sitting on a hardback café chair with her head resting against the wall and her eyes closed. Allie walked quietly up to her and placed her hand against her forehead. She became alarmed when she felt how clammy the woman was.

Sophia's eyes fluttered opened. When she saw Allie, she smiled.

"Yatrinna." Her voice was even softer than normal, and slowly, wearily, like a very old woman, her hand reached up to take Allie's. Allie took the chance to feel for her pulse. She was relieved to find it normal.

"Sophia, you're exhausted. What are you doing here?"

"Yiannie, my husband, had to check on something in the fields—the vines—I didn't want to shut the shop."

"Let me put you to bed and examine you. Please, Sophia. I'm worried about you—"

"There's no need." A harsh voice spoke from behind, and Allie didn't need to turn around to know to whom it belonged. Allie would have known the Wicked Witch of the West, the evil Elani Drakopoulos, anywhere. "My relative doesn't need a stranger looking after her," she continued and grabbed Sophia's hand away from Allie.

"Kyria Drakopoulos, your relative is a very pregnant woman who is utterly exhausted. She should be in bed, preferably a hospital bed, where she can have tests performed."

The beads from the back of the house rustled, and they all looked up as a man whom Allie assumed to be Sophia's husband entered. He was of medium to short height, and Allie thought him a man of medium to short personality, as well, for allowing his wife's health, and that of his unborn child's, to be put in danger because of some archaic feud.

"Elani? Sophia?" He glanced at Allie in question, and she extended her hand. He took it. Allie held it for a moment. She wasn't surprised to find his grasp extremely weak.

"Kyrios Drakopoulos, I'm Dr. Alexander. I strongly suggest that your wife be taken down to the hospital and given complete rest, as well as tests."

"Don't be ridiculous," Elani cackled. "She's fine. Just a little tired from a day of making hilopitas."

Allie turned to Sophia aghast. "Hilopitas!" she exclaimed. Ordinarily, making the pasta wasn't a very difficult task for village women. But a full day of mixing dough, rolling it out into paper thin sheets, cutting it into a thousand tiny pieces, then putting it in the sun to dry was definitely something Sophia shouldn't have been doing. "Sophia, that's too much for you in your condition."

"It's okay," Sophia whispered, and Allie noticed that speaking seemed too much for her now.

Allie turned to her husband. "I strongly suggest your wife be taken down to the hospital—"

"No," Elani forcefully interrupted. "She doesn't need a hospital. Just her bed."

Ignoring the other woman's outburst, Allie continued to speak to Sophia's husband. "Kyrios Drakopoulos, I think that your wife is suffering from a mild case of heat exhaustion. She needs care."

Indecision weighed heavily on the man's shoulders. He was definitely a weak man who had probably been in his brother's shadow all his life. But for a moment, Allie thought she saw something like agreement flicker through his eyes. But his sister-in-law moved, making her position clear.

"I'll put Sophia to bed now," she said, expertly taking charge, and Allie watched in amazement as Sophia's husband shrugged his shoulders in compliance—something he had probably done a thousand times before.

Allie felt defeated. "Sophia?" She appealed to the exhausted woman.

"I'll—be—fine, Yatrinna," she whispered as she allowed her sister-in-law to guide her toward the back area.

With those words Allie knew there was nothing more she could do. Feeling as though she had been slapped in the face, she returned in her most professional tone, "Drink plenty of cool drinks and don't hesitate to call me if you need anything." Turning, she walked out the shop door.

But all the way up the cobbled streets toward home, Allie was mad, so mad she was sure steam could be seen coming from her ears. She didn't understand how people could be so careless with their health, with the health of their unborn children. What these people needed wasn't a doctor but a good swift kick in the rear end.

She only hoped that dear Sophia wouldn't be the one to get kicked.

But at the moment Allie couldn't even understand how the shopkeeper could be so silly as to make hilopitas. True, it hadn't been over 110 degrees as on the previous days, but it had still reached well up into the nineties. Hot. Too hot for a woman who was at least forty years old and about to have a baby for the first time to be making her winter supply of pasta.

As Allie stomped her way into the garden of her house, she decided that dealing with the mentality of these villagers was much more difficult than tackling their diseases. She walked toward the fountain in the garden. Not having running water in her house to have a bath made it almost unbearable. Allie knew she was behaving unreasonably, but when the broad leaf of the banana tree reached out and slapped her arm as she stormed passed it, she balled up her fist and swung into the leaf. Not once, not twice, not three times, but more, and she probably wouldn't have stopped swinging if an iron grip hadn't taken hold of her arm from behind and halted her.

"Allie!" Stavros called out. "Have you gone mad?"

"No!" She whirled around to face him, forcing him to let go of her. "I haven't gone mad, but I am mad. Mad, mad, mad!" she yelled out. "Sophia could die, or the baby, or they both could, and nobody cares because of this stupid feud—one whose origin nobody can even remember. Not even Papouli. It's getting to be a tedious excuse."

With extreme gentleness he pulled her close to him, and the fight left her like air from a balloon. She leaned against him, and relief settled around her like a cloud.

She needed him.

She needed his arms.

She needed just to be held.

After so long, so many years of standing like a tall cypress tree at guard, Allie needed to lean like a weeping willow. And she needed this man to bend toward, to depend upon.

Stavros ran his hand across her back, a caring gesture.

She squeezed her arms tighter around his neck, a needing gesture.

He responded by holding her closer and by raining little kisses of tenderness on the top of her head, down her cheek, on her throat.

Turning her head, she sought out his lips.

They were like the wonderful heat of the hot sand after staying in the cold sea too long. They warmed her soul, her spirit, and she knew that with this man she wanted the happily ever after to be theirs.

"Stavros. . . ," she whispered against his mouth.

Gingerly, with infinite care, while keeping her in the circle of his arms, he stepped back. "Tell me what happened."

She told him. "Sophia isn't taking care of herself, and whenever I start to make headway with her, Elani Drakopoulos always seems to appear and tells her how she doesn't need me." She leaned her head wearily against his shoulder. "I'm just so worried about her."

Stavros reached beneath her fancy braid and started kneading the tension that was as thick as a gnarled olive tree branch out of her neck. "I know. . . darling. . .I know."

Her eyes closed as she luxuriated in the magic his fingers were working on her neck. "Mmm. . .that feels so good."

"Close your eyes—"

"Well, well," Tasos Drakopoulos's nasally voice droned out from his place next to the open garden gate. "What have we here?"

Allie's muscles bunched as she almost reflexively stepped apart from Stavros. But with a slight pressure, he held her fast. They hadn't been doing anything wrong.

"Drakopoulos." Stavros greeted the other man.

"Thaskalos." Drakopoulos called Stavros by the title of teacher, just as the children and most of the parents in the village did.

"Why don't you let the doctor examine Sophia?" Stavros asked directly.

"That's not up to me." Drakopoulos spoke as if he were totally innocent. "That's up to Sophia."

"We both know that's not so."

"Do we?" the nasally voice returned.

Allie addressed him, the fire of injustice in her voice. "If she dies, or her baby does, I'll hold you and your wife responsible," she warned and was sure she didn't miss the flash of concern that went through his narrow eyes. But it passed, leaving only the latent anger of before.

"Sophia and her baby will be fine," he declared and returned to his favorite pastime, making her life miserable. "What I'm certain about, though, is that everyone is going to be very interested in learning how you two spend your days—and your nights," he snickered, and Allie and Stavros stood together as they watched him walk away.

"What an awful man," Allie said between gritted teeth.

"Be prepared for some bad days."

"Worse than the ones I've had?"

He slanted his gaze down to hers. "He just found us in one another's arms."

"But we haven't done anything," she protested.

"I know." A muscle jumped in his jaw. He motioned toward the house. "But we live here together. People will believe what they want to believe."

Allie sighed and leaned her head against his shoulder. She knew he was right. Hadn't she gone through this once before with the soccer player? But this time Stavros and Jeannie were involved, two of the dearest people in the world to her.

She wouldn't let them get hurt.

She closed her eyes and knew that not for anything would she allow that.

Chapter 17

It wasn't quite as hot in the morning as it was the previous day, but it was windless, and Allie soon learned that a scorcher in Kastro without the hot wind was worse than one with it.

She wanted—no, needed—a bath. She had opted for sponge baths since her second evening in the village, not wanting the chore of carrying bucket after bucket of water up the stairs. This morning, however, nothing would do except for full immersion in the elegant tub.

Donning a pair of shorts and T-shirt, she pushed the IN USE sign under Stavros's door, then walked down to the faucet in the garden and proceeded to fill the four metal buckets that sat ready by its side. Papouli walked into the garden, and Allie happily greeted him, but from the somber look on his face she knew that something was wrong.

"Is it Sophia?" she asked, shutting off the spigot in anticipation of having to run quickly down to Sophia's house.

Papouli held up his hand. "No, it's not a medical emergency."

"Then what—?"

Stavros opened his door and looked down on them from the veranda. "Papouli?"

"I need to speak with both of you," the older man said, looking up at him.

Leaving his door open, Stavros immediately came down and stood beside Allie. "What is it?"

Papouli got right to the point. "Some ugly things are being said"—he paused and looked over the rim of his glasses from one to the other—"about the two of you."

"Drakopoulos." Stavros spoke the man's name almost as if it were an epithet, and Papouli nodded.

"He's sitting in the kafenion telling everyone that you two"—the wise old man's eyes went questioningly from one to the other—"have been behaving improperly."

"That's not true, Papouli." Stavros answered the question in the priest's eyes without hesitation.

"I didn't think so," the old priest said, but Allie could tell from the way his shoulders relaxed that he was relieved. He might be a priest, but he was also a man and understood about temptation.

She gently laid her hand upon his arm. "Papouli, we aren't going to lie to you. As you might have suspected, Stavros and I are very attracted to one another. But we haven't done anything that would compromise our working in this village. Nothing which you—or God—would disapprove of."

That's all Papouli needed to hear. He was satisfied. "Thank you, Yatrinna. You didn't have to tell me this."

"You didn't have to warn us."

"Exactly what's being said?" Stavros asked, and Allie could tell that the priest didn't want to answer.

"Please, Papouli," Allie prompted, and the older man nodded.

"They're calling for Stavros's immediate resignation as teacher because he's 'carrying on' with you, the village doctor."

"What?"

"You've got to be kidding!"

"I'm afraid not," Papouli said, answering their disbelief.

"But this is my home. I love these kids, and they're all doing so well. Last year all the high school students who took the test for the university were admitted." Allie could hear the pain beneath Stavros's words, and she was amazed he really thought that made a difference to people like Drakopoulos. Unless Drakopoulos had a drastic change of heart, she doubted he would ever think of anyone over his own selfish desires.

But Allie also recognized that it was because of her and her insistence on living in Stavros's house that she had not only shaken, but was about to topple, the secure world Stavros had painstakingly built for his daughter and himself. She wasn't sure his newly reestablished faith would be able to withstand it.

"I'll take care of it," she said, and forgetting all about her bath, she left the pails of water where they were and pushed passed Stavros toward the stairs.

He reached out for her hand. Hesitantly, she turned to him. The pain in his eyes over the priest's revelation was countered by something good, something strong. She was amazed when she realized that it was a sense of togetherness. "We'll take care of it," he corrected her.

She appreciated his offer—loved it—but shook her head. "No, Stavros. It's not your problem."

"Not my problem?" he shot out questioningly. "How do you figure that?"

She gently squeezed his hand to stop further protest. "Don't you see, my love, they are just trying to get to me through you." *And they have*, a little voice whispered within her. They finally attacked her where she was vulnerable. Stavros and Jeannie. She could withstand attacks against herself, but not against those she loved. And she loved the Andreas family very much. "I'll handle it," she repeated with conviction.

"And just how do you plan on 'handling' it?" he asked through a jaw that had suddenly gone tight.

She smiled down at her shorts and T-shirt. "I'm going to go dress—extremely professionally," she qualified and lifted her brows at the amused look that jumped into his eyes. It felt so nice to be able to say something like that to him now and not to receive a negative response. After much talk he understood that his wife's professionalism had been to the extreme and that there were many woman who could successfully juggle a career and a happy home life. The key was wanting to and knowing who to rely on to make it work. "Then, I'm going to pay the men at the Men's Club a little visit." Giving his hand another little squeeze, an encouraging one this time, she let go and, swiveling around, started running up the stairs.

Stavros followed close on her heels. "Allie. I want to come with you."

She spun around. With her eyes shining with how cherished his words made her feel, she explained why having him by her side at this time wouldn't work. "Thank you, my love, for wanting to, but don't you see? It's my profession that is being attacked, and because of this, it's something I must handle on my own and in my own way." She gave a light chuckle, then looked between the two men. "Which will actually be—"

"Not alone, but with God and. . .in God's way," Stavros finished and returned her smile with one of admiration.

"Ah. . . ," the wise old priest said, "if only more people knew that secret."

Allie's gaze moved to his. "But I will most gladly accept any prayers you both might like to put forth on my behalf."

"Done," Papouli said.

Nodding, Stavros copied the older man. "Done," he whispered.

As Allie turned away, the admiration and love coming from Stavros's whole being gave her courage. Knowing she had the love and prayers of such a man not only on her side but by her side was a blessing straight from God, one she accepted with a thankful heart.

~≈≋⟐≋≈~

Dressed in a pale green suit of linen, Allie walked into the kafenion.

It was full of men, smirking little men that made Allie ashamed for the rest of the masculine gender. Sour-faced Ireni—as usual the only woman in the room—gave a defiant tilt of her face before disappearing into the curtained-off back room.

Allie didn't care. She turned to the table where she knew Drakopoulos would be holding court.

He immediately spoke. "I told you the people would all be very interested in learning about what I saw last night," his nasally voice gloatingly informed her.

Allie wasn't even going to justify his statement with one of her own. Instead, she asked, "What is it that you want?"

"I want you to leave."

"Why? Do you think your son will come if I go?" she asked directly and knew that she had hit a sensitive cord when there was a general movement around the room. Even though everyone knew the reason for Drakopoulos's behavior, no one had spoken it.

Blood vessels popped in the man's red forehead, and Allie was sure that his blood pressure was up. "He should have been given this job. Not you," he sneered.

Allie shrugged her shoulders. "That had nothing to do with me. I applied for the position, and it was awarded to me. Maybe your son applied too late. Or maybe," she paused dramatically, "he didn't apply at all because he didn't want to live around you."

Drakopoulos jumped up. He towered over Allie. But she didn't let so much as a muscle move. "How dare you?"

"Dare I? It's you who is causing all the problems. I only want to do my job."

"And sleep with the schoolteacher," the man spat out. "Something easy to do with that central hall. How do we know what really goes on there night after night?"

"You don't. You can only think what your wicked little minds allow you to think." She wasn't going to defend herself to this mindless group. Papouli knew the truth. She did. And Stavros. That's all that mattered.

"Well, we've decided." He gestured at all the men in the room. "If you're not on the afternoon bus, the teacher will not be allowed to teach at our school this year."

"Yes, I've heard that."

"So."

"So that's how you got me here. Now tell me what it is that you want."

"I told you. I want you on the afternoon bus."

"Mr. Drakopoulos," Allie began quietly but firmly, "currently, everything is fine in your world—your wife is well, your friends." She waved her hand around the room. "But I wonder. How would you feel if I got on that bus and tomorrow or the next day your wife should fall ill, or a friend of yours should suffer a heart attack, or one of the children in the village should fall and need a doctor, and you know that you are responsible for my leaving and thus for the people you care about not having the help they need?"

"Another doctor will come—hopefully, my son."

Allie laughed, a sound that was like a lawyer's laugh of contempt. "Do you honestly think I would leave this village and not tell the Department of Health how I was threatened into leaving? And knowing the reason, do you honestly believe they will allow Kastro to retain control of the Rural Physician's Station for this area?"

"We'll tell them you were behaving improperly," he threatened, and although Allie felt that old tightening in her stomach over the false accusation, she didn't even let so much as her voice waver or her hand shake as she continued.

"I like Mr. Andreas. I like him very much," she admitted. "But we have never behaved in an improper manner."

That old evil smile, that smile that showed his gold teeth in the back of his mouth, stretched across his face. "But you don't have proof."

She had proof, the ultimate proof. But that was only her business and that of the man she eventually married—hopefully Stavros. "I tell you what we are going to do." She tapped her nails against the tabletop. "I'm going to pretend this episode never happened—write it off to the heat doing things to your brain—and I'm going to go to my office right now, and if anyone has a need, they can find me there during office hours or at my home after hours. I hope no one needs my skills," her eyes touched on individual ones in the room, "because that will mean that all in this village—your wives, your children, your mothers, your fathers—are well. But I will be available if I am needed, and I will help everyone to the best of my—"

"Ireni! Ireni!" A woman ran into the café, and everyone turned to her.

Ireni appeared instantly from behind the curtain where she had obviously been listening to what was going on. "What is it?" she rasped out.

"It's Sophia. She's collapsed!"

"Oh, dear Lord!" Allie breathed out and went over to the other woman, one whom Allie recognized as having helped clean the clinic after it had been vandalized. "Where is she?"

The woman glanced over Allie's shoulder at Tasos. He was scowling, but Allie was relieved to see that the woman didn't seem to care. This was an emergency, and in emergencies nothing mattered except the person in need—definitely not the opinion of Tasos Drakopoulos. "In front of her store. She'd been hanging clothes out, walked into the street, and fainted."

But Allie heard the tail end as she ran out the door. Moments later, she tore into the clinic, thankful that it was located so close to Sophia's home. Grabbing her medical bag and miniature ICU case, she ran up to Sophia's house. A crowd of people had gathered around the spot where Sophia was lying in the road.

"Let me through!" Allie shouted. The crowd parted, and Allie was further appalled when she saw that hardly anything was being done for the unconscious woman. Elani Drakopoulos was uselessly fanning Sophia's face. When she saw

Allie, she looked up and snarled like a dog. "We don't need you."

Ignoring her, Allie set her bags down, reached for Sophia's pulse, and grimaced. It was disturbed, her skin was hot, and she wasn't sweating. "Heatstroke," she murmured and took precious seconds to speak to Sophia's husband, who was hovering over his wife impotently. "If you don't let me treat your wife now, she is going to die and your baby, too."

Before Allie's very eyes, she watched a weak man turn into a strong one.

"She's just trying to scare you!" Elani Drakopoulos shouted, but Sophia's husband pushed her back and, like a lead dog protecting his territory, snapped at the people. "We will do exactly as the doctor says."

That was all Allie needed to hear. She got to work. "Let's get her inside where it's cool," she instructed, and several men immediately lifted Sophia and carried her to the room behind the store, where a bed was located. "I need ice, lots of ice, and electric fans," Allie told them, and they quickly scurried away to comply. While she was setting up an IV, she instructed the women, "Get her clothes off her and get wet towels onto her. She's burning up, and we've got to get her fever down," she informed them while inserting the needle into Sophia's hand.

"Here's a fan." One of the men returned, and Allie instructed him to get it blowing directly onto Sophia. Within moments, two more fans were in place, and cool towels covered Sophia's body. Allie took her temperature and shook her head.

"What is it?" she heard a deep, gravelly voice ask, and she looked up into Papouli's concerned eyes.

"One hundred and six degrees."

"Is there anything I can do?"

"Pray."

Papouli smiled. "I'm good at that."

"Yatrinna," Mr. Drakopoulos hesitantly asked, "is she going to be okay?"

"I'm going to do everything I can to make sure that she is."

"But she's still unconscious."

Allie nodded as she placed her fetal stethoscope up against Sophia's bulging tummy. "But she's breathing well."

"And the baby?" he whispered, hardly daring to voice his fear.

Allie smiled. "So far the baby is undisturbed. The little one's heartbeat is normal. But as soon as we get Sophia stabilized, we'll transfer her to the hospital for both their sakes." Since the baby wasn't distressed, Allie opted not to tell him that was one of her main fears. If the time came, she would tell him. But for now, his worrying wouldn't do any of them any good. And maybe the baby wouldn't even reach that point. She prayed not.

"More ice is coming," a man said as he placed two bags of ice next to Allie.

"Get it around her." Allie instructed the women in how to place it.

"Stavros has gone to the next village for more."

"Good," Allie said as she took Sophia's temperature and shook her head. "I'm afraid we may need it. I won't be happy until it's down to 102 degrees. And when it's there, we'll transfer her. Call for an ambulance," she instructed no one in particular. It would take the ambulance at least an hour to get up to Kastro, but Allie knew it wouldn't be safe to transfer Sophia before then, anyway.

"I called," a woman said with fear lacing her voice. "But there are none available. A fire has broken out near Olympia, and all the ambulances are there."

"Okay, we'll transfer her ourselves. Does anyone have a car with air-conditioning?" Allie prayed that someone did. Sophia would never make it without that modern convenience. Not in this heat.

"The schoolteacher does."

Allie nodded. She didn't even know Stavros had a car. She thought he only had his horse. "Is it big enough to transport Sophia?"

"Plenty big."

"Good," Allie responded.

Later, when Sophia had regained consciousness and her temperature had dropped to 102 degrees, Allie was glad for the comfort of Stavros's Jeep. She didn't know that one could be so luxurious. Stavros was able to turn the rear seat into a bed, so Sophia was as comfortable as she would be if she were in an ambulance. The cool air that blew through the vents was exactly what the woman needed.

Sophia's husband rode with them. He was solicitous in a way Allie wished he had been before, sponging his wife and talking to her, effectively helping to keep the frightened woman calm.

Allie continually monitored the baby. After driving forty-five minutes down the mountain, Allie registered a lowering in the baby's heartbeat. She knew they had just about run out of time. The baby was distressed, and the little one had to be taken from Sophia before it developed problems or even died.

Not wanting Sophia to know how dangerous the situation was for her little baby, she spoke to Stavros in English. "If you can add wings to this truck, I would appreciate it. The baby is suffering, and we've got to get to the hospital—stat."

"You've got it," he answered and applied his foot to the accelerator. With lights flashing and horn blasting, he took the curves and turns as fast as any race car driver ever could.

Yiannie looked at Allie in questioning concern.

Allie slightly shook her head and motioned for him to continue to care for his wife. Sophia seemed amazed by the concern her husband was showing and was reveling in it. Allie was glad for the distraction. It was imperative that the woman not become distressed.

As routinely as she had done before, Allie again put the fetal stethoscope against Sophia's tummy. She had to use every ounce of bedside manner not to let her concern show when she registered yet another drop in the baby's heartbeat.

She turned toward the front of the Jeep and spoke in English again. "Stavros, we're going to lose this baby. . . ."

"Five minutes, Allie."

"That's about all the time this baby has. Under normal circumstances, I would perform a C-section myself, but with the heatstroke, I'm afraid for Sophia's life."

"Hold on, Allie. We're almost there." Judging the speed they were traveling, Allie thought Papouli must have been praying for angels to indeed guide their truck. It took less than five minutes for the hospital to come into view. Medical personnel were waiting for them. The doors flew open, and Allie quickly filled in the obstetrician and internist on Sophia's condition while they sped her down the corridor. She watched as Sophia was whisked through double doors and was gone.

Allie knew her job was done.

She had administered medical care that had kept both the baby and Sophia alive, and now she could wait for the men and women at the hospital to do their jobs.

She felt Stavros's arm go around her shoulder and was glad to lean her head against his. "Well done," he murmured.

She looked up at him and smiled. "You, too."

He shrugged his shoulders. "All I did was drive. You saved her life and the baby's."

"That's still not a sure bet," Allie whispered to him, not wanting Yiannie to hear.

"Yatrinna—" Yiannie softly spoke from her side, and Allie reached out her hand for his. "I know my Sophia has only made it this far because of you. Thank you, and forgive me for not supporting you earlier."

Allie smiled a weary but happy smile and squeezed the man's hand. "Kyrios Drakopoulos, all we need to do now is pray that your little baby will be okay. I. . ." She didn't want to tell him, but she believed that all rational adults had a right to know what she, as their physician, knew. "I'm afraid the baby was distressed during the last part of the drive."

"I know." He looked up at Stavros. "That's why you were speaking in English. But I know you did everything possible. No matter what the outcome, I will always be grateful." Tears formed in his eyes, tears of self-recrimination. "I should have let Sophia come to see you during these last few days. None of this would have happened if I had listened to her and you, rather than to my brother and his wife."

There was no denying that what the man said was true, so Allie didn't insult him by offering empty words. "Because of Stavros's skillful and quick driving"— she looked at him—"I think your baby has a good chance of making it."

Yiannie nodded and walked over to the window. Allie and Stavros left him to his own thoughts and prayers and went over to the chairs that were placed up against the wall. They sat and held hands, a man and a woman in love, giving one another strength. Together they offered prayers for the woman and baby behind the closed double doors.

They didn't have long to wait until they received an answer to their prayers. When the obstetrician walked through the doors, Yiannie turned to him with the look of a man who was waiting to hear whether his world was to be whole again or broken beyond repair.

"You are the father of a healthy little girl." The doctor reached out and shook hands with Yiannie, whose face looked ready to split with joy.

"And my wife?"

"She's doing fine, although the heatstroke is still affecting her. But the internist thinks that by later tonight, she will be nearly back to normal. Holding her little baby was the best medicine in the world for her."

"May I see her?" Yiannie asked.

The doctor nodded. "You may see both of your ladies."

Yiannie started to follow the doctor through the door then stopped. "Yatrinna? Are you coming?"

Allie shook her head. "No. This is your moment. Give her my love and tell her that I'll come back tomorrow to visit."

"Thank you, Yatrinna. For everything," he whispered and went through the door.

"More than just a baby was born this afternoon," Stavros said and nodded after the new father. "I think a man was born, as well."

"Mmm," Allie agreed, and resting her head on Stavros's shoulder, she let him guide her toward the car. She didn't think she had ever been more content.

Chapter 18

On their return trip to Kastro, Allie watched the silvery countryside slide by her window, with a mature appreciation that had been lacking on her first trip up. They rounded a bend in the road, and Kastro sat gleaming in the sun—like a necklace of rubies and pearls—exactly as it had when she'd first arrived.

She sighed. "It's so lovely."

Stavros turned his eyes momentarily from the road to her. "A land of enchantment?"

She laughed, delighted that he could even suggest it. "As well as a land filled with real people who have very real emotions," she admitted.

"A good place, perhaps, for a hopeful realist to live permanently?" he suggested, and the question slanted her green eyes toward his.

"A perfect place for a hopeful realist to live permanently," she agreed softly. When a quick smile lit his features, one that held secrets but no verbal answers, she offered up a prayer that his question meant what she hoped. To walk the same path through life that Stavros walked would be the perfect happily ever after to Allie.

They pulled up into the village square. As had happened when she first arrived, people came out from everywhere to greet the vehicle. Only this time there were more people. And this time they were all smiling.

When Allie alighted from the car, all congratulated her. They welcomed her back and made her feel like the much-wanted member of the community she had yearned to be. She glanced up at Stavros. At that moment, she knew that happiness could have been her middle name.

Understanding, he leaned down and whispered, "Enjoy, my love. I'll be back for you later. I'm going to put the Jeep away." She nodded as the children swept her on a wave of good cheer into the kafenion.

Papouli was there, as were all the usual members of the Men's Club. But this time their wives and children were with them, as well as numerous other villagers who had smiled shyly at her during the previous week. There was a festive feeling to the air as everyone cheered Yiannie and Sophia's baby a good long life and Sophia a speedy recovery. Even Tasos Drakopoulos and his wife, Elani, who were sitting together at Tasos's normal table—with a handsome young man

123

whom Allie didn't recognize sitting between them—were raising their glasses in good cheer. In such a small community, the birth of a new citizen was always welcomed grandly. The extenuating circumstances surrounding this birth made it extra special.

To Allie's surprise, the normally sour-looking Ireni served her a cola and *galaktobouiko*—custard pie—along with a smile.

"Sophia's husband, Yiannie, called and told us everything. We're so proud of you and thankful for you, Yatrinna." The priest's kind old eyes twinkled their joy in not having underestimated her.

She smiled back at him, her heart warming with love for him as it had for her own father. "I just did my job, Papouli."

As her words pierced the guilt most of the villagers felt over their lack of welcome and support toward her, silence reigned in the room.

Finally, Tasos Drakopoulos cleared his throat. "I," he said, glancing at the young man who sat beside him before continuing. "I apologize. . .Yatrinna." Allie's brows rose at both his words and his use of her title. "My son"—he motioned to the young man—"as well as the events of the day, have made me realize just how wrongly I mistreated you and the position you represent. I hope you will accept my apology."

"And mine." His wife, Elani, quickly spoke from his side.

Allie looked at the woman. Her Wicked Witch of the West persona had melted away, and all Allie could see now was a woman of remorse who wished only for a second chance.

The young man shifted in his chair, and turning, Allie couldn't help but notice that he had the bluest and gentlest eyes she had ever seen. He was also one of the most handsome men. He would definitely be some woman's idea of a prince. "My parents—" he began, then broke off what he was going to say in order to introduce himself. "I'm sorry, Yatrinna. I'm Dimitri Drakopoulos."

"It's good to meet you." Allie smiled as Dimitri continued, but she had a hard time believing that this very courteous, articulate man was Tasos's son.

"I must take some of the blame for my parents' behavior toward you. I should have been honest with them and told them from the start that I had no desire to practice rural medicine." He shrugged his broad, but unlike his father's, straight shoulders before looking around the café to make sure that he had everyone's attention. "The Angelopoulos family member who has connections with the Department of Health did exert his influence to save this position for me. That's why Kastro was without a doctor for so long. I declined it without informing my parents that I was the one to do so. I'm very sorry. When Papouli called and told me what was going on—that the ancient and ridiculous feud had been rekindled because of this position—I came directly to set the record straight." He looked back at Allie. "I'm very sorry you suffered because of it."

Allie walked to the Drakopoulos's table. She held out her hand first to the father, then to the mother, then to the son. "Thank you. I appreciate what you have all done here, apologizing in front of your friends and family. Since Sophia and her baby are going to be fine, I more than accept your apologies, and I just ask that this situation—as well as the ridiculous feud—be forgotten. I like Kastro." She looked at Tasos, who now looked nothing like an ogre but, rather, a penitent old man. "Unlike your son, Kyrios Drakopoulos, I want to practice rural medicine. And I want to do it as everyone's friend." Her gaze went between that of the mayor and his wife. "Including both of you."

"Thank you, Yatrinna," Tasos rasped out. "I will do whatever I can to ensure that no one ever again reenacts the feud."

Even with the apology, an uncomfortable and tense silence hovered over the room for a few long moments until the light, lilting voice of a woman—one Allie vaguely recognized—spoke from behind her. "Goodness." Allie turned and gasped in pleasure when she saw Natalia walk from the direction of the door. "As my father has pointed out many times—who even knows how the feud began?"

"Hear, hear," said the villagers, and a sigh of relief seemed to ripple throughout the room.

Allie held out her hand to the young woman. "What a nice surprise. What are you doing here?"

Ignoring Allie's outstretched hand, Natalia hugged her instead and explained. "When Dimitri told me that he was driving up here for just one night, I decided to come with him. I missed Baba and Martha," she said simply and truthfully. "I just had to see them and talk to them about some things."

"Eh. . .Yatrinna, what daughters I have," Papouli exclaimed. His eyes twinkled with a father's love at his youngest child. Natalia smiled fondly back at him before excusing herself when Dimitri motioned that he needed to speak to her.

"That you have, Papouli," Allie said as she watched the exchange between the young doctor and the art student. Allie couldn't help watching them. No one in the café could. They were two of the world's really beautiful people with facial features of perfect proportions and bodies that only fictitious characters should be allowed to have. But as Allie watched, she knew that there was something more between them, or, at least from the expression Dimitri wore, something the man obviously wished was between them.

"Dimitri's going to have to wait a few years if he wants a life with my daughter," Papouli commented sagely. "She's got a very long path to follow before she settles down to family life."

"She's smart. She knows who to turn to in order to make the correct decisions."

Papouli nodded as they watched Natalia quickly leave the kafenion. "Yes, I've been very blessed in my children. They all know Jesus as their personal Savior and have the same faith as their ancestors, who received the gospel from the very disciples of Christ."

"Such an amazing lineage," Allie agreed, gazing around the crowd of people searchingly. "But where is Martha? And little Jeannie Andreas, too?"

"Ahh. . ." was all Papouli said. But behind his glasses, his eyes danced. "They had something to do. They'll be here soon."

Allie would have asked what they were doing, but a little old lady, who had to have been Papouli's senior by at least ten years, waddled up to her. "Yatrinna, how about doing your job and taking my blood pressure?" she asked, and as all of the people in the kafenion seemed to hear her, there were chuckles all around.

In the name of professionalism, Allie refrained from giving a little laugh of her own and only allowed her lips to crack into a smile. "Definitely. I open the clinic at 8:00 a.m. So do come."

"Why can't you take it now?" the old lady demanded, and everyone laughed again.

"You didn't know how good you had it, Yatrinna," said one middle-aged man—a former member of the Men's Club.

"Yeah," another agreed. "You're going to see so much of us, you'll think there are nine thousand of us in this village rather than just nine hundred."

"Oh dear," Allie played along as if the idea made her nervous. "Are so many of you sick?"

"Bah!" the old lady said. "Most of us just want our blood pressure taken."

"But some of us," a man in the rear spoke up, "just want our children looked after."

Allie's smile widened when she saw Petros Petropoulos walk up to her. "Mr. Petropoulos, have you moved back to the village already?"

He nodded his head. "We spent all of last night packing. Just arrived this morning."

There was a gasp of amazement before happy pandemonium erupted as all the people welcomed Petros back. When they learned Allie's part in his finally moving back, they looked at her with, if possible, even more kindness. Petros and his wife had been stalwart members of the community, and the villagers had not only mourned the passing of his wife and baby, but the loss of Petros and his four other children, as well.

After a moment when the attention was off her, Allie turned to Papouli. They shared a smile. "God really does answer prayers, doesn't He?"

Papouli glanced down at his watch and stood. "Ah. . . Yatrinna. That He does. But I think the time has come for some more prayers to be answered. Some that have had my special interest for the last several years."

She drew her brows together in question.

"Come." He directed her toward the door of the café. As everybody else seemed to take that as their cue and followed, Allie looked around, perplexed. They all walked out to the plane tree in the village square. It seemed to Allie as if all were waiting expectantly for something to happen.

"Papouli—" Allie started to question what was going on but stopped when the sound of clip-clopping against the cobbled stones of the road could be heard.

She looked in the direction of the sound just in time to see Charger's gorgeous white head round the corner of a stone house. But when she saw Stavros and Jeannie sitting on his back, she gasped. Her eyes widened even more as she took in how the two were dressed.

Jeannie was arrayed like a medieval princess, with a green gown of soft velvet and flowers woven masterfully into her hair, flowers that matched the bouquet in her hands. Stavros was dressed similarly to how he had been the first time Allie had set eyes on him, with a flowing silk shirt and proper riding britches—the prince of her dreams. The castle, highlighted pink in the evening sun behind them, couldn't have made a more perfect background for the fairy-tale scene Allie was sure Stavros had created for her benefit.

The horse halted beside her, and she saw a clarity to Stavros's gaze that had never been there before. It made the hopeful realist in her dare to believe that what she had prayed for—a happily ever after with Stavros—might just come to pass.

She didn't say a word.

This was his show.

She watched as he gently lowered Jeannie to the ground. Jeannie turned and walked with all the grace of a medieval princess toward her. Allie wished she hadn't been wearing a tailored suit. She yearned for something flowing and romantic, something to fit in with the mood Stavros had so expertly created.

Just then, Martha, Maria, and Natalia walked up behind her and placed a robe of the softest chiffon over her shoulders. Allie gasped her pleasure as the gossamer fabric wrapped around her like a cloud. She looked up again at Stavros.

He smiled, and just as teachers at school performances were experts at doing, he motioned for Jeannie to commence her part in this lovely, romantic show.

"Yatrinna—"

Stavros cleared his throat.

Jeannie smiled. "I mean, Princess Allie." She indicated the bouquet in her hands. "These flowers are for you from my father, who awaits your permission to take you on his white stallion, Charger, up to the castle."

Allie reached for the flowers, and while bringing the arrangement close to her nose and inhaling the fresh, sweet fragrance, she lifted her gaze toward the prince and spoke. "I would be honored to ride up to the castle with your father—Princess Jeannie."

Jeannie's face split with a smile. "That's what you're supposed to feel like, Yatrinna. A princess! Isn't it wonderful?" A good-natured laugh went around the crowd at the girl's exuberance.

Leaning down, Allie kissed the little girl's cheek and said in agreement, "It is wonderful, Jeannie." She turned her gaze up to the girl's father again. "Wonderful," she said to him and continued with, "it makes me feel as if I am part of a fairy tale."

His eyes crinkled at their corners, and as he reached down and pulled her up behind him, he whispered, "Darling Allie, it is a fairy tale. But the best kind. One that has God in the story. He is the One who leads this hero and heroine."

"Oh, Stavros," she whispered into his ear. "Not even I could have imagined that such joy was possible to feel."

He chuckled softly. "That, from my fairy tale–loving lady, is a great compliment." Then, more softly, for her ears only, he spoke words that he had needed to say for a long time. "I'm so sorry, Allie, for all that I ever said to you. You can have it all. Your profession—which saves lives—and the happily ever after." The first cool breeze anybody had felt since the heat wave started nearly a month ago blew across the cobbled streets just as he finished. All murmured at how wonderful it felt against their skin. Stavros laughed and held up his hand to the wonder of it. "You can even have cool air, my love."

"I'll gladly take it all, Stavros," she said, and as she wrapped her arms around him, she marveled at how so much had changed in her life in such a short period of time. Her gaze met that of Papouli's, her fairy godfather. The older man shrugged and motioned toward the cross that sat atop the blue-domed church. His gaze very clearly said, "With God all things are possible."

Nodding and smiling in agreement, Allie mouthed the words *thank you.* She knew then what the dear man's prayers of the last several years had been—that Stavros would not only find his faith once again but the love of a woman, too. The fact that a man she hadn't known had been praying for her to come into the life of the one she now hugged close was nothing less than one of those amazing things of God. *Thank You, God!*

After Maria, Natalia, and Jeannie fixed her robe so that it draped perfectly over the horse's flank, Stavros clicked his cheek and directed Charger to walk at a slow pace out of the village. The village children—young and old alike—ran alongside and cheered.

Allie leaned forward and asked in his ear, "Why are they cheering?"

He chuckled, a laugh that she felt rather than heard. "Maybe because there are a whole lot more people around who like fairy tales—nice ones—than I ever realized." And feeling her questioning gaze, he turned his head halfway to her and said, "In a moment, darling Allie, I'll answer—and ask—everything. For now, just enjoy the ride."

She did. A ride of enchantment, a ride of wonder, but mostly it was a ride of love. The path the stallion took up to the castle was different from the one they had walked together. It meandered along the backside through silvery olive groves filled with cicadas and the cool breeze that serenaded their upward journey. The green-and-golden valley shimmered below them, and the sky above was the ethereal Greek blue that poets and bards had written about since the beginning of the written word. As they followed the path farther and farther up, Allie knew that she and the man whose back she hugged close to her were exactly where God wanted them to be. She squeezed her eyes shut and silently gave thanks for the miracle of knowing.

When they came to the entrance of the castle, Stavros swung himself off the horse, then reaching up for her, his hands lightly grasped her waist as he lowered her to the earth. He didn't let go of her but gently pulled her into his arms. "Darling Allie," he spoke against the top of her head. "I have one very important question to ask you"—he took a deep breath and, stepping back half a pace so he could look directly into her eyes, he sighed out—"but I'm going to do it right this time and ask a few other ones first."

She nodded. She was quite certain of the one important question. She wondered about the others.

His shirt sleeves billowed out in the breeze as he continued. "I know your feelings about God, but do you feel confident we believe in a way that would be compatible to joining our lives?" he asked with a solemn quality to his voice that she respected and appreciated.

Her eyes searched his. What she saw there—a man with a deep faith in Christ—made her confident of her answer. "Since you have reaffirmed your belief, dear Stavros, yes, I do believe that our walk with God is compatible."

He lightly ran his fingers down her cheek and smiled, a smile of love and friendship before he softly continued. "Darling Allie, how would you feel. . . about becoming Jeannie's mother?"

Tears—liquid joy—touched Allie's eyes at the question. She knew how much he loved his daughter. For him to ask this of her was the highest compliment he could pay her. She reached up and touched his forehead. "Dear, dear Stavros, I would be honored to be Jeannie's mother. Her legal mother," she qualified. "I would want to adopt her so that should we be blessed and able to have children together, she would be certain that it would never make her any less my daughter."

Tears now washed his eyes, and they fluttered closed. "Thank you, Allie." He sighed before opening his gaze—his very vulnerable gaze—to hers again.

"For what?"

"For wanting children with me. For wanting to be Jeannie's mother. Her natural mother didn't even—"

She placed one finger against his lips, stilling his words. Shaking her head, she said, "Don't judge her, Stavros. We don't know what went on in her mind, but I'm sure it couldn't have been anything pleasant. Just be thankful she left you with that wonderful little girl." Allie smiled. "I know that I am."

"Oh, Allie—" He rubbed his hands over her back. "What did I do to deserve you?" he questioned into the wind. "You are so wise, so beautiful, so—"

She stilled him with a mighty laugh. "What I am is impatient. Are you going to ask me *the* question, darling Stavros, or shall I ask you?"

He let loose with a generous laugh of his own. "Wouldn't that ruin the fairy tale if the princess asked the prince for his hand in marriage?"

She slowly shook her head from side to side. "Darling Stavros, I don't think anything can ruin this fairy tale. . . ."

As her words were swept out over the land on the cool, north wind, he lowered himself to one knee. "Allie—Princess Allie—I love you. Would you do me the honor of becoming my wife and of giving to me all your ever afters?"

With her robe fluttering out and around her, Allie reached down and pulled him to stand tall and straight before her. Looking up at him, she replied, "Dear Stavros, I would be honored to become your wife, the mother of your daughter, Jeannie, and the mother of any other children whom God might grant us. My ever afters are your ever afters, and because we have been redeemed by Jesus, we can even look forward to sharing an eternity of ever afters in the true land of enchantment, wonder, peace, and joy—God's heaven."

He shook his head at the import of her words. "I love you, Allie," he murmured, just before his lips captured hers, and Allie's words of love remained unspoken, but not unsaid, as her lips told him what was in her heart. She loved him, loved him more than she had ever imagined she could love someone.

And someday soon they would marry, and she knew that because their union was ordained by the God of Jesus Christ, they would live. . .happily ever after. . . .

Fairy-Tale Romance

For my daughter, Sara—the fashion designer, arrAs (www.arrasboutique.com).
Your love of New York City inspired this story.
Many thanks for your help with fashion questions
and as a guide to New York City at Christmas.
You are the best!

Prologue

He asked you to go to New York to become a model, Natalia? I don't know about this," said Martha Pappas, Natalia's much older sister.

Hopping up from the chair, Martha grabbed a sponge and began wiping the already immaculate kitchen table. She stopped, though, when their baba put out his hand to still her.

"Martha, sit down," he directed, his voice raspy but kind. He looked over the rim of his glasses at Natalia, his youngest child, and the only one of his six children who was adopted. "Tell us everything that happened. From the beginning."

Natalia nodded. Never had she been happier for the equilibrium of her father than at this moment. He was the clergy in the village of Kastro, so everyone referred to him as Papouli. But to his six children he was their beloved baba, and Natalia felt honored to be his daughter.

She reached for her glass of lemonade, took a sip, then started recounting the events that had brought her back unexpectedly to Kastro for the night. "Yesterday, feeling dissatisfied with the courses I'm following at school—" She paused and grimaced. "That's something else I have to talk to you about, Baba."

"Tell me about the modeling first," he instructed her gently.

She pushed her shoulder-length hair behind her ears. She was glad for his leading. "I decided to go up to the Areopagus, your favorite place in Athens." She referred to the hilltop location where the apostle Paul was purported to have preached to the Athenians in Acts, chapter seventeen. Her father went there whenever he visited the capital. "I was questioning whether I was indeed following the path God had laid out for me when a man came up to me and in a very nice way—and in English—asked if he might speak to me."

"English?" Martha asked, her brown eyes as round as basketballs.

Natalia nodded. "His name is Jasper Howard, and he is the president of Smile Modeling Agency in New York City."

"How can you be sure of this?" Martha asked. Natalia wasn't surprised. Martha had always been protective of her.

"Not only did he give me his business card"—she pointed to it on the table before her father—"but he removed from his wallet his passport, driver's license, and social security card so I could see for myself that his identification proclaimed him to be Jasper Howard."

"And he wanted to talk to you about becoming a model for his agency?" her father prompted.

Natalia shrugged her shoulders. "That's right."

"What sort of modeling?" her father asked.

"Tasteful, fashionable clothing, nothing I might consider at all compromising."

"I don't know," Martha said again, and Natalia could hear the anxiety in her tone. "I've seen fashion shows on TV. I usually have to change the channel. They are"—she searched for the correct words—"well, you know."

"I know." Natalia reached out to comfort her. Martha was thirty-two years her senior; since their mother had died when Natalia was only ten, Martha was in many ways more a mother to Natalia than a sister. "That's why I told him the only way I could consider such a thing would be for him to come here and meet both of you, along with Allie and Stavros, who are Americans and know how things are done there." She referred to the village doctor and schoolteacher; doing so brought smiles to all three of their faces.

For at that moment they knew Stavros had taken Allie, who loved fairy tales as much as they did, up to the castle that sat above the village to ask her to marry him. Allie had come to the village about a month ago and had changed the lives of Stavros and his daughter, Jeannie. Natalia, Martha, Papouli, and, in fact, the entire village knew that, if it was God's will, a romance was about to come to that deserving couple, and they would live happily ever after.

"But tell us," Martha asked in her quick way, "what did this Jasper Howard say when you asked him to come here to meet us?"

"He agreed to do so," Natalia replied.

"He did?" Her father's eyebrows shot upward. That seemed both to surprise and impress him.

"Yes."

"When?" Martha asked, jumping up from her chair.

Natalia pulled her back down. "Tomorrow. So calm down, Martha."

"Tell me." Her father leaned forward as he always did when he was about to ask something very important. "How would you feel about moving to New York?"

"That's the part about this whole thing that surprises me the most, Baba. Not only do I want to go, but somehow I almost feel pulled to the city. It's as if it's the path God wants me to take—the path He has laid out for me."

"You said you aren't happy with your courses at the fine arts school you are attending in Athens?" her father asked.

Natalia held her hands out in front of her, then let them drop onto her lap. Her father had given so much to send her to school in Athens, and she hated to disappoint him, but she knew she had to be honest. "It's not at all what I was expecting, Baba. It's too general and too abstract. It's wonderful for people who like that kind of art," she qualified, "but I don't. None of my classes has anything to do with fashion design." Ever since her mother had showed her how to hold a pencil and sew a straight seam, Natalia's hobby had been to draw and design dresses and make them into garments she could wear.

Her father was quiet for a moment, as if he were thinking over the matter. Suddenly he said, "Then perhaps you are meant to go to America at this time. I have always known God would somehow lead you back there."

Natalia had no idea about this. "Baba?"

"As you know," he began, "I feel certain that your birth mother was from the United States. That is why I have insisted upon your learning to speak English so well." She knew that at a great expense he had made sure her English was as perfect as it could be. Even Jasper Howard had commented on how fluently she spoke.

"But why do you feel this way, Baba? Not even the American embassy would recognize that I might be from America."

"The letter that was pinned to you from your birth mother said you were American. Plus you were dressed in that American flag suit when Baba and Mamma found you at the bus station," Martha said. Natalia knew her sister still had the infant sleeper she had worn then; it was carefully wrapped in tissue paper and tucked away in her dresser drawer. "And the blanket you were wrapped in was emblazoned with the American flag."

"But that still doesn't prove my nationality is American. Anyone of any nationality could have written that letter or dressed me that way so I would be taken to America."

"True. That was the reasoning at the American embassy," her father admitted. "Plus, not a single American citizen had reported a missing baby." He sat back and settled his palms upon his skinny knees. "I don't know how to tell you why I feel as I do, Natalia. It's just something God has put into my heart." He looked at his daughter over the rim of his glasses. "And in the same way I have always known God would lead you back there someday, somehow, too." He lifted his hands, then dropped them upon his knees again. "Maybe it is God's will that you search for your real parents."

"Baba!" She was aghast. "You and Mamma are my real parents!"

He smiled and patted her hand. "Yes, we are, and you have been such a blessing to us. I know your mother fought her illness and lived as long as she did only because she wanted to raise you—her sweet-natured, fair-haired child—for as much time as she could."

"I loved her so much," Natalia whispered as she thought about the loving smiles and gentle voice of her mother. The aroma of jasmine drifted through the open window. That was her mother's scent. Natalia savored it and could almost feel her mother's presence.

"We all loved her," Martha said. "Still do."

"She was a very special woman," their baba agreed, and his eyes sparkled brightly with remembered happiness. It was a joyous look, but also the only time Natalia thought her father looked close to eighty years old. Even after eight years he missed his wife dearly.

He took a deep, settling breath. "Your mother was never angry at the woman who left you in the bus station. She always felt, as did I, that there must have been a reason, a good reason. Women do not give up their children without one. Maybe someday you will be led to her."

"That is not the reason why I want to go to America, Baba." Natalia wanted to make that clear. "I don't feel one way or the other about her, neither angry nor sad." She shrugged her shoulders. "I'm just glad I'm a part of *this* family."

"A very big part," Martha added quickly.

Natalia smiled over at her. "I don't know why I feel drawn to America—why something jumps in my soul at the idea of going—"

"God's leading, *agapi mou*—my love. God's leading." Her baba spoke with the authority of his calling. "Not only do you feel pulled to go, but also the way has been opened for you. I never would be able to afford the plane ticket for you, much less the other expenses involved with your living in New York City. If this *Jasper Howard*"—he spoke the unfamiliar name in a heavily accented tone that made Natalia smile—"is indeed the man he says he is, and if he can assure me you will be well taken care of, then I say go."

Chapter 1

Six Years Later, New York City

Noel Sheffield glanced at his watch as he dashed from Seventh Avenue up Thirty-fourth Street on his way over to Fifth Avenue. It was an overcast day, and one might consider it gloomy with dusk falling earlier than usual. But the excitement of Christmas left no room for dreariness in the air. People were smiling and chatting like high school students at pep rallies do.

Noel glanced up at the pine that adorned the windows of Macy's Department Store and took a deep breath. Not only was it beginning to *look* a lot like Christmas, but it was beginning to *smell* like it, too. Who would have imagined that midtown Manhattan could smell like a pine forest?

This was Noel's favorite time of the year. Judging from the smiles as big as the state of Alaska on the faces of people wrapped in brightly colored scarves, he felt certain he wasn't alone in liking the season.

Christmastime in New York. He took a deep breath of satisfaction as the city he loved danced and pulsated to its own special holiday melody all around him. *What could be better?* he wondered as he stood at the traffic light at Herald Square where Broadway and Sixth intersected Thirty-fourth Street.

He glanced at his watch, and a sobering sigh of annoyance whistled through his teeth.

Of all days to be running late.

He had planned to leave the high school, where he worked as a guidance counselor, earlier today to ensure that he didn't miss his yearly rendezvous. Then a problem with one of his students had arisen. He sighed. Sixteen-year-old Rachel was running in the fast lane and was going to find herself in big trouble if she didn't listen to reason. But Noel knew it would have been easier for him—for anyone—to reason with a mouse than to try to persuade the girl of that fact.

The light changed. As Noel dodged holiday-garbed people coming toward him, he wondered again how he could make the girl understand that her lifestyle would lead only to heartache.

He took his position as counselor to the students at Westwood High School seriously. He felt that if he could catch a problem in a person and solve it at the high school level, it would be one less individual who would need the other profession for which he had trained: criminal lawyer.

But Noel didn't know if he had succeeded this time with Rachel or if he ever would. The girl was in trouble from a lack of good judgment. *Humph*, he thought. *A lack of judgment, period.* She had gotten herself into circumstances that needed much more wisdom than Noel could offer.

He drew in a deep breath.

But he was the girl's only chance. Her parents had paid thousands of dollars to private clinics and therapists in order to help her.

Nothing had worked.

As Noel had seen too often in the fast-paced world of today, busy lives precluded parents from having sufficient time and energy to solve their children's problems themselves. That was the challenge of the whole situation. Most kids longed for their parents—at least one of them—to be around. After two years of counseling problem kids, Noel had decided they wanted quantity time with some of the overlauded quality time.

But it was what so few received.

To know that their mother or father was in another part of the house with them, to know that at least one parent was at hand whenever they—the child—wanted to ask a question or sit and talk, meant everything to young people.

Noel had to give Rachel his best shot. Since she seemed to listen to him more than to anyone else, her parents had begged him to do whatever he could. He didn't want to let them down.

As he neared the famous shopping street, Fifth Avenue, the throngs of people were growing thicker and thicker. Even though Noel normally didn't mind rush-hour crowds—he found it exhilarating to be among so many people all in one spot at one moment and somewhere entirely different the next—it annoyed him today. He might miss the young woman with the dog.

The Rockefeller Center tree had been delivered during the previous night. Noel had seen it leave on the first part of its journey from his parents' home in New Jersey. He now had a tryst to keep with the tree *and* the woman.

For the past three years she had come to the center with her dog—a gorgeous German shepherd—at dusk on the day the tree was delivered. She always sat on the same bench in the Channel Garden and gazed up at the tree with a look of both yearning and joy. She had captured Noel's attention the first time he'd seen her. Noel knew she came to visit the tree on this day because he had done so ever since he was a little boy. His father used to bring him and tell him how *their* tree would one day stand at that "blessed spot."

Noel didn't know the woman and had never talked to her. He hoped to change that today. As he picked up his pace, his trench coat flapped out behind him like a flag.

He would speak to her this time in honor of *his* tree—the one he had grown up with—finally being the one to stand at the center, to grace the city of New York.

New York.

He glanced up at the decorated lamppost and flashed a smile at the red bow and Christmas flowers suspended from it. This city was the greatest place on earth, to Noel's way of thinking.

Especially at Christmas.

⟡

"City sidewalks, busy sidewalks, dressed in holiday style. In the air there's a feeling of Christmas!" Natalia sang softly the refrain from one of her favorite holiday melodies as she walked briskly down Fifth Avenue. Her four-and-a-half-year-old German shepherd, Prince, clipped by her side in perfect canine posture. With a plaid ribbon and bow of green and red tied around his neck, he was as well tailored in the Christmas way as the city of New York itself.

This was Natalia's favorite time of the year in the city. The hustle and bustle, the songs filling the atmosphere, the decorations, but mostly the way people seemed to smile at one another a little more as they passed by brought warmth to her heart.

But as an arctic wind whipped around the corner of Central Park South and Fifth and caught her under her jaw, she gave a slight shiver and snuggled deeper into her down-filled ski parka.

"It's cold, Prince," she said.

He hunched his shoulders forward, looked up at her, and sent her his friendly, if lopsided, doggie grin.

Natalia laughed and wondered how anybody could be frightened of him. But people were, and she realized they had a right to be.

Prince would do anything for her, and most definitely anything to protect her. He was as docile as a lamb—unless someone looked at her the wrong way. Then he was all guard dog. She smiled. She knew that fact made her baba and her sister Martha happy. Her baba might be a man of faith and trust God to look out for his youngest child in far-off New York, but he certainly didn't mind letting one of God's creatures help with the job.

She and Prince had returned the previous day from visiting her family in Kastro, Greece. As was her custom whenever she flew home, she had spent two glorious weeks there. She had moved away from the village six years ago, but not too much had changed, which of course was one of its main charms. Allie and Stavros, the village doctor and schoolteacher, had just added another child to their brood, making little Jeannie Andreas, who wasn't so little anymore, a very happy big sister. Jeannie loved her two brothers and her new baby sister to distraction. A smile curved Natalia's lips as she thought about Jeannie. The girl loved her stepmother, Allie, as dearly as any child could ever love a natural parent.

But that thought stole the rosiness the cold city day had put into Natalia's fair cheeks. Her baba had surprised her—shocked her even—on this trip home by almost insisting she search for her *own* natural mother. He hadn't said too much about it in the six years since she had left Kastro. But this time he had told her all that was in his heart; he felt that God wanted her to look for her biological mother or at least be open to finding her or to the possibility of her mother discovering her. The time was right, he said.

Natalia wasn't so sure.

She had done some research about people looking for biological parents; contrary to the stance of sentimentalists, it wasn't always so wonderful. Sometimes people didn't want to be found. Plus Natalia now had the added disadvantage of being what she called herself—a "genetic" celebrity. Because of the genes she had inherited from her unknown biological parents and the career she had chosen, her face was quite well known, at least in magazine layouts and on billboards.

Most models looked different in person than they did in magazines. Natalia was glad she was one of them. Further, she rarely wore makeup while going about the city, thus adding to her disguise. And one of the reasons she loved walking with Prince was because he was a good distraction. Most people looked at him more than they did her.

She smiled down at the dog.

Prince kept the tabloid photographers at bay, too. They preferred to snap pictures of famous people who didn't have a large dog with a mouth full of sharp teeth walking by their side rather than bother with her.

Jasper Howard had done more than make Natalia into a model. He had turned her into a modeling star. Not only was she famous in certain circles, but she had also made more money than she ever knew existed for individual people. She gave large percentages of it away—something that gave her a sense of contentment that amassing it in banks could never hope to achieve. Her father had often preached that God required good stewardship of those He'd blessed materially. And just as Jesus had taught in the parable of the talents, the more she gave, that much more she seemed to receive—a never-ending cycle of receiving and giving.

She wouldn't mind giving to her biological family should they be in need—she would be happy to do so. But she thought that she had to be careful because of the mystique behind being a model. Had her natural mother put her up for adoption, it would have been different. But the woman had deserted her: She had left her in a bus station in a foreign land, if indeed she had been American as her father suspected. If the woman had left her in an orphanage, at least Natalia would not have felt as uneasy about looking for her. But to be left in a bus station? What sort of woman did that?

"The desperate kind," a voice seemed to answer her. *"A woman desperate in a way you have never had to experience—because of her actions."*

Natalia sighed.

She didn't know what to do. The truth was, her birth mother might have deserted her, but no one could have asked for a better set of parents than the ones who had loved her for much longer than she could remember. Her adoptive mother died when Natalia was only ten, but that didn't take away the joy she had in being that lovely woman's daughter.

The sound of a Volunteer of America Santa ringing his Christmas bell drew her attention. He was a joyous figure in red splashed against the backdrop of the city. Natalia reached into her pocket for some bills.

"Merry Christmas!" she said as she dropped them into the bucket.

"Ho, ho, ho," he sang out and rang his bell loudly. "Merry Christmas to you, too, young lady. And many thanks."

Nodding to him, she walked on, a warm feeling of hope and good cheer washing over her. She looked up at the green lamppost above her. Its artful arrangement of bows and poinsettias made her smile widen.

She loved New York.

Loved it passionately.

She wouldn't want to live anywhere else.

But she knew that having the means to live in a nice area meant she had a responsibility to give back in full measure.

That thought inevitably returned her to her father's views on searching for her biological mother. His opinion was too wise to ignore. She breathed a prayer into her plaid, cashmere scarf, adding to the many she had said while flying the previous day across the Atlantic. "Dear Lord, Your will be done in this matter, please. If You want my natural mother and me to find one another, so be it." She paused and smiled as a professional dog walker handling seven dogs passed her. "But if my natural mother could now be a woman who loves You, that would really help." With that, she let go of the thoughts that had been plaguing her about her biological parentage. She wanted only to enjoy this very special moment of being back in New York City.

Natalia was heading for the tree at Rockefeller Center. She'd heard from her doorman, Roswell Lincoln, that it had been delivered during the night. It had become her personal tradition to see it each year before it was decorated. She loved the trees when five miles' worth of lights graced their branches, but there was something special about seeing them in their almost-natural state.

The WALK sign flashed on in yellow letters. She tightened her grip on Prince's lead, then motioned the dog forward and crossed the intersection. Glancing to her right, past the horse-drawn carriages and the Pulitzer Fountain ringed with twinkle lights, she saw the towers of the Plaza Hotel.

Natalia smiled as she remembered the first time she had walked into that building, which was styled after a French château. It hadn't been dressed and waiting for the arrival of Christmas as it was now, sparkling in holiday adornment, with lights aglow along its towers and bunting festively arrayed across its entrance awning. But it had still seemed like something out of a storybook to her. Jasper Howard had rented a suite of rooms for her there upon her arrival from Kastro.

She'd felt like a little girl who had just entered a fairyland castle. But it wasn't a fortress-type castle like the one of thick stones and buttressed walls she had played upon in Kastro; rather, it was like a palace where kings and queens might live in splendor. With all that velvet and mahogany, crystal and gold, it was opulent and exquisite with rich detailing and an elegance that Natalia had never experienced before. She was thankful Jasper's wife, Janet, had come to meet her there. Taking one look at Natalia's tired and flabbergasted face, she had understood that the Plaza was not the place to ensconce a young woman fresh from a Greek mountain village.

Janet had immediately invited Natalia into their spacious apartment, where she had resided like a beloved daughter for nearly a year. Natalia now had her own apartment in the same building on the Upper East Side and was still very close to Janet and Jasper. They were her mentors, her friends, but, most of all, her sister and brother in the Lord. They had wanted her to live with them longer, but when the three-bedroom apartment came up for sale, she knew it was time for her to move.

She loved her apartment. Although it was bigger than what she needed, it was the one area in her life where she had splurged and felt no guilt in doing so. Because of it, her numerous brothers and sisters—but mostly Martha, the sister she was closest to—and her father had often come to visit. It never failed to amaze her father that he could look out the window and see a good portion of the trees that filled Central Park. He took daily walks in the park whenever he came. On her most recent trip home, Natalia was pleased to see that, at eighty-five years of age, he hadn't changed at all in the six months since she had last seen him. She felt certain the final verse in Psalm 91, "With long life will I satisfy him and show him my salvation," applied to her dear baba. Even though he was semiretired, he was still the village priest, still as strong as he had been ten years earlier, and still helping others, both physically and spiritually.

Prince looked up at her as he came to a stop at the corner of Fifth and Fifty-eighth. She reached down, adjusted his collar, and rubbed his neck beneath it.

"Good boy," she whispered to him and smiled. Prince was trained never to cross a street without first stopping to check for traffic. She gave the command for them to continue and looked up at the sophisticated decorations at Bergdorf Goodman. Holiday wreaths adorned every window of the building.

But it was the giant snowflake suspended high over Fifth and Fifty-seventh she was searching for now. She gave a light laugh when she saw it lit resplendently above the avenue, then spoke to her dog.

"I love snow, but I'm sure glad snowflakes aren't really that big." She patted the dog's thick, woolly fur. "Even you would have a problem walking through the amount of snow such flakes would produce, dear Prince."

Crossing over Fifty-seventh Street, she pushed up her sleeve and glanced at her watch. It read 4:25. She increased her pace. If she didn't hurry, she wouldn't make it to Rockefeller Center until too late. It had been her tradition the last few years to see the newly arrived tree as day faded into night.

But even more important, she wanted to get there in time to see the handsome man who had filled so many of her romantic thoughts during the last three years.

Because of her work and studies, but mainly because she hadn't met anyone she wanted to know better, Natalia had shied away from dating during the years she had been in New York. But something about that unknown stranger tugged at her.

She had first seen him three years ago.

He was tall and dark, with a ruggedly handsome appearance, and she had noticed him standing by the corner of the South Promenade that first year, gazing at the tree with a sort of longing and thoughtfulness, which had touched her. The strangest thing, though she would never admit it to another living soul, was that he looked like the man she had dreamed about ever since she was a little girl, the man she knew God would someday bring into her life and with whom she would spend the rest of her life. It wasn't that he was so handsome—those kind of men could be found anywhere—rather, it was an elusive *something* that drew her to him.

She had found herself thinking about who he might be, what he did, and what he believed at strange times throughout the years. She supposed it was because she didn't want to date, and thoughts about him were safe.

But when she saw him again last year, not only on this day but also at the Macy's Thanksgiving Day parade and again at the Lincoln Center's annual performance of the *Nutcracker* ballet, she had thought she'd conjured him up. New York was a large city, and it was rare to meet the same people at various locations that weren't connected with daily activities repeated at the same time each day—such as catching the subway or walking an identical route to work or school.

But with all the longing of a woman who loved fairy tales, she hoped she might see him again today. He could easily be her "Prince Charming."

She shook her head at the silly notion and, reaching down, rubbed her fingers across the velvety softness of her dog's ears. "You're my only Prince, aren't you, boy?"

The dog looked up at her with that look in his eyes he sometimes got that made her think he understood her perfectly. Giving a little laugh, she said, "Never mind," and turned back to the avenue upon which they walked.

Even though it was barely mid-November, the sounds of Christmas filled the air—bells, music, laughter. Some people said it was too early, too commercial. Natalia didn't agree.

Maybe it was commercial, and perhaps many people didn't allot enough time to think about the true meaning of Christmas. But Natalia saw it all as being in honor of the Babe who had been born so long ago. *Well, maybe not all,* she conceded as a street vendor called out to everyone to buy his "cheap, barking, 'dog' toy." But the Babe born in Bethlehem was the original idea behind the celebration of Christmas. Natalia felt that the so-called Christmas feeling or spirit so many people loved at this time drew many to look again at the birth of Jesus.

Maybe some of the people she passed on the busy street with their holiday bags and Christmas colors adorning them didn't have any insight into the "mystery that had been kept hidden for ages and generations," until Christ's arrival. But perhaps the celebration of Christmas appealed to so many because something stirred within them at this time, something that made each person somehow know a mystery had been made known to mankind upon Christ's birth. She wasn't sure, of course. But that's what she thought.

She looked around her as her steps carried her farther down the world-famous shopping avenue. It was festooned with red and green and lit in a Christmassy way. As she crossed one street after another, she remembered how her father had taught her that Christmas, from the beginning of its formal observance in A.D. 354, was more for nonbelievers to draw near to Christ than for believers who were close to God all year long. With so many Christmas scenes all around her, she believed it was probably still the same.

The Gothic spires of the cathedral on the next block down and across the street caught Natalia's gaze. As a structure built to honor the Prince of Peace, it was superb. When its construction was first considered back in the mid-1800s, no one could imagine how the city of New York would grow up around it. Until skyscrapers appeared in the 1930s, she had read that the 330-foot spires of St. Patrick's Cathedral had towered above the city and had been part of its skyline even then.

It was counted as one of the largest cathedrals in the world, and, throughout the last six years, Natalia had often found solace and peace within its welcoming walls. It didn't matter that it wasn't a church building of her persuasion. What counted was who was honored and loved there: Jesus, God's Son. People representing the entire world might be passing by its huge bronze doors, but the peace and tranquility she found in that Gothic structure made it one of her favorite places in the city.

She glanced up at the sky.

It was dusk now. *Perfect for seeing the tree,* she thought.

She turned onto the North Promenade and gasped.

It was like a fairy world.

In the dusky mistiness of the late autumn evening, the horn-blowing ensemble of wire-sculpted angels was aglow, reminiscent of those actual angels that had heralded the birth of Christ so long ago. The stars that twinkled around them made them seem as if they were part of the heavenly host.

And the tree. . .

Natalia stood in awe of the Norway spruce. It was bigger and fuller than any she had seen before. Framed by the seventy stories of the General Electric Building behind it, the ice rink and Channel Garden before it, the tree stood, majestic and beautiful, a monument to the wonder of God's work on the third day of Creation.

She repeated softly the words in Genesis as she gazed at the tree's regal beauty: "Then God said, 'Let the land produce vegetation: seed-bearing plants and trees on the land that bear fruit with seed in it, according to their various kinds.'"

In this city of concrete and steel, the tree was like an oasis, a small part of nature that God, the bestower of everything good and wonderful, gives life to and shares with His creation. The workmen who had built Rockefeller Center during the Depression back in the early 1930s had brought the first Christmas tree, starting a yearly tradition. Meant to gladden their spirits, as well as those who passed by and saw it, similar trees had been placed yearly at the center—a tradition that had been practiced for more than seven decades.

Natalia inhaled a deep breath of air. The tree's limbs still held their natural clean fragrance. This was another reason she looked forward to seeing the evergreen upon its arrival. Soon it would no longer have the freshness of countryside scent upon it. Having grown up in the mountains of Greece, Natalia craved that natural aroma.

She walked over to one of the benches situated beneath an angel and sat down.

She knew that once the tree was lit, she wouldn't find a place at this time of day. That, and because she wanted to watch the faces of the people as they rushed along Fifth Avenue and see the childlike brightening that filled them when they spied the tree, was yet another reason she always came now. Their expressions were as unspoiled as the tree.

A lovely representative of the Tree of Life and the redemptive work of Jesus Christ, the Christmas tree in its celebrated place would catch most by surprise. Young and old, rich and poor, people from all over the world would pause for a moment on their journey through life and look up at the pine. Without fail, a dreamy sort of smile would soften the lines around their eyes, their mouths; the sight of this year's Christmas Tree—for just a moment—making them forget their worries and cares.

The conifer proclaimed the arrival of the Christmas season in New York City. Christ's incarnate birth was soon to be celebrated once more.

And that made Christmas-loving Natalia very happy.

She scanned the Channel Garden. But seeing the prince of her romantic daydreams would make her woman's heart beat even brighter.

Chapter 2

Noel turned the corner of the South Promenade next to the French Building. Before he even looked up at the tree, he searched for the woman he had hoped to see again this year.

He spied her immediately. She was sitting on a bench opposite the fountains, like an angel in a forest of celestial beings. He skidded to a halt.

Her head was uncovered, and her hair, as golden as the radiant beings that surrounded her, glowed luminously in the cozy duskiness. She was gazing upward toward the ninety-foot tree, but to Noel it was as if she were looking at much more than the tree he had played upon and beneath as a child. The tilt of her profile made her seem as though she were trying to see into her future, contemplating what it might hold. He wished it to be one full of sunshine and beauty—and him.

Usually he would pause for a few minutes, wondering if the next year his tree would finally stand in this special place, and send covert glances in the girl's direction.

But today everything was different.

His tree—one of the most beautiful, most symmetrical, and most cherished trees in the world—was in the place it had been marked to grace since Noel's grandfather had witnessed the first tree placed in Rockefeller Center in 1931. When six of the ten Norway spruces planted at the same time as this one had succumbed to last winter's severity, his parents decided to let this Christmas be its turn at the center. The official gardener of the center, who had kept his professional eye on the spruce during the last two decades, agreed it was the right decision. It was very old and might not make it through another hard Mid-Atlantic winter.

And because of his tree, Noel wasn't going to wonder about the girl any longer; he was going to go over and talk to her.

With long strides, he let his feet carry him the short distance to the North Promenade.

The dog was the first to notice him. He turned his noble head with his finely chiseled jaw in Noel's direction. Noel casually looked into the dog's eyes. From growing up with German shepherds, he sensed this one had to have been well treated and was probably one of the gentler ones—unless his mistress had a need. Noel knew he didn't need to fear him. Seeming to come to the same decision about him, the dog's long, feathery tail started to brush softly against the ground, and Noel was glad to be recognized as a friend. Feeling the dog's movement, the girl turned.

She looked up at Noel.

Their gazes met.

Her blue eyes blinked.

His blue eyes blinked back.

Vitality and excitement seemed to flow through every line of her. He had thought she was beautiful when glancing at her from a distance. But from only about eight feet away and looking directly at her, with her soul seeming to shine through her eyes, she carried Noel's breath away on a cloud of enchanting white.

Golden and light, blue and bright, she fit in perfectly with the twelve sculpted Clarebout angels that surrounded her. If he didn't know better, he would say she was one, too, of the highest order. He hoped she wasn't, though. He didn't want to fall in love with an angel.

He wanted to fall in love with a woman.

With this woman.

And as superficial as it might sound, even to him, he knew he was already in love with her, or at least he was the closest he had ever been to that elusive emotion. Something about her, something almost familiar in her eyes—a certain light—made him love her when their gazes came together in an embrace of mutual interest. At that moment their souls seemed to merge and sing like a celestial host proclaiming something wonderful and right. Noel felt an explosion within his head as bright with lights as his tree would soon be, and even more he felt as if he were the happy prince in a wonderful fairy tale.

As strange as it might sound for a healthy, red-blooded American male to admit, Noel loved fairy tales now as much as he did when he was a little boy, especially those in which the guy and the girl lived happily ever after. He only hoped he might soon be living one with this remarkably beautiful girl who caught his interest and wouldn't let go. Her beauty encompassed much more than the fine placement of her features upon the planes of her face; rather, it reached out and touched the core of him.

～～◦◎◦～～

When Natalia looked up and saw the man she had wondered about during the last few years standing before her, she blinked, thinking her recent thoughts about him had conjured him up.

His eyes were blue, something that surprised her. With such dark hair she had expected brown. But she wasn't disappointed. Who could be? They were the warm and restful blue of the Grecian sky in summertime. Besides, she didn't think that anything about him could disappoint her at this moment. His appearance was everything she could ever want in a man. A part of her almost didn't want to know him any further; he was perfect now.

As he nodded his head toward Prince, she knew he was going to speak. She braced herself for what he might say, for what might come out and shatter the illusion she'd built. She hoped he wouldn't say anything that might turn her prince into a toad.

⁓◦⦿◦⁓

Noel, not indifferent to the impression he created—and finding courage in it—pointed to the dog and said, "He's a magnificent beast."

Her head dipped slightly in response. Scratching behind her dog's ears, she said, "I'm glad you like him."

"What's his name?"

She tilted her head and smiled at him with an almost self-conscious turning up of her lips. "Promise not to laugh."

His mouth quirked. She sounded like one of his students admitting to an embarrassing occurrence. "I promise."

"Prince Charming."

In light of his thoughts a moment earlier, Noel wouldn't have laughed even if she hadn't asked him not to. "I like it."

"Really?"

"I guess you must like fairy tales then."

"I grew up on them. Love them," she admitted quickly. "Romantic movies, too."

"Is that why you come here to see the tree year after year on the day it arrives? Because it brings a little fairy-tale wonder to New York?" He could tell from the way her eyes widened that his observation had startled her.

He knew he was being blunt. But now that he had finally talked to her, he wasn't going to play games. She didn't know him, and she might think it strange if, even after a few minutes of talking, he told her he'd seen her before. He didn't want her to think he'd been stalking her.

After a short moment her pale brows lifted. Nodding in the direction of where he usually stood leaning against the French Building, she returned, "Is it why you come, too?"

Now it was his turn to be taken aback. His mouth narrowed. He hadn't expected that. But the fact she admitted to it told him something about her character. She was honest. Not a game player.

He liked that—a lot.

Most of the women he had met during the last few years played the male-female game. That was the reason he hadn't formed a lasting relationship, even though it was something he desired.

"I love the holiday season," he answered. He was glad for his training that enabled him to think about several things while answering something entirely different. "Perhaps because the city does take on a fairy-tale type appearance during the Christmas season."

"I agree. Except I like to think of it as a God tale," she said.

Her description of the Christmas season stunned Noel. His parents often compared the season to being a God tale rather than a fairy tale. He had never heard anybody else describe it like that. It unnerved him.

"Christ's birth is proclaimed around the city, around the world," she continued, oblivious to the sensation her words brought to him, "in its decorations, lights, and pageantry. It's really nice and—"

Not even Noel's training kept his thoughts on her words then as the realization that the reason she had seemed so familiar to him was because she was. . . similar to his parents. The bright, open look in her eyes, one of wholesomeness, forthrightness, and an otherworldly sort of wisdom, was analogous to what he often read in his parents' eyes and general way of being. She had to be like them, a person who made her relationship with Christ the center of her life; one whose life found worth in that God-human relationship. It had always disturbed Noel a bit concerning his parents. He had a thing about fanatics of any kind and not understanding their relationship with God, he was afraid it bordered on extremism. But incredibly, he discovered that he didn't mind the trait in this young woman at all.

In fact, somehow, it made her seem even better to him.

Because of his parents, he had a good idea what sort of character she would have and, as important, wouldn't have.

It was as if he held a secret knowledge about her.

He liked that.

He had rejected his parents' all-encompassing religious lifestyle, but he found he could accept it in her.

This was quite an ironic revelation for Noel.

~~∞◇∞~~

Natalia stopped speaking.

At some point in their conversation, she realized she had lost him. She wondered if it was her description of the Christmas season being a God tale rather than a fairy tale. It made her feel sad, really sad, that this might prove a stumbling block to their getting to know each other—because she really did want to know him— but she didn't regret saying it. It broke her heart to see the beauty of the true story behind Christmas turned into a multitude of fairy tales. Loving fairy tales as she did, she believed they definitely had their place. Didn't she hope for her own Prince Charming someday? But he would have to love God and would have to believe that Truth came into the world the day God came to earth as a human baby.

"I'm sorry," he spoke after a moment. He waved his hand as if he were trying to clear his thoughts while his strong, square-cut chin lifted a fraction of an inch in a way Natalia would call considering. "Your words caught me by surprise. You see, my parents have always described this season that way."

She felt her pulse pick up its rhythm. Did this man whom she had thought about often during the last few years believe as she did? Whether a person was a Christian or not had not been something she had given thought to when growing up—everyone in the village had been, albeit of varying degrees—but coming to New York City, she had learned just how unusual that situation actually was. Motioning to the bench, she did something she had never done before. "Would you like to sit down?" Her sister's teaching on safety in the big city had been deeply ingrained in her, and she had always been careful about strangers.

"Thanks," he said, lowering his tall frame with an easy grace onto the bench. She wasn't surprised when Prince stood, instinctively putting himself between her and the man.

"Hey, Prince Charming." The man slowly extended the back of his hand for the dog to sniff. "You're a handsome fellow."

The dog stood in perfect German-shepherd pose, with his hind legs stretched back, his chest out, and his head held high. Natalia laughed. "Careful—he's already too vain."

The man turned his head to get a good look at the dog's lines. "He must come from championship stock."

"Sit, Prince," she commanded the dog, who promptly obeyed. "Yes, his grandfather was the world champion a few years ago." She leaned down and nuzzled her nose against the velvety smoothness of her dog's ears. "But I don't show him. He was a gift and is champion enough for me without the ribbons. You know about German shepherds?"

"I grew up with them," he returned. "My parents still have two. Ten-year-old Laddie and his son, Harry."

Well, we definitely have a love of dogs in common, she thought. That was good, especially if. . .they should get to know one another better as she really hoped they would. "I hope you don't mind my asking, but are your parents Christians?"

A smile tugged at the corners of his mouth. "I don't think anybody could be any more so."

She returned his smile. Did that mean he was, too? "I doubt they feel that way. Being a Christian is a work in progress. I don't think any Christian feels he or she is living the Christian life perfectly."

"I think they would agree with you."

"And you?" Her gaze narrowed. She wanted to—no—had to know.

He took another deep breath. "I'm not sure. I guess I haven't wanted to give my parents' beliefs a chance because"—he flashed that endearing grin again, but with a touch of remorse to it—"it's what *they* believe."

She'd heard of that before. Janet and Jasper had had a similar experience with their oldest son—a man now in his forties—until he met a special woman of faith. Natalia decided it was better not to comment.

His response wasn't what she had hoped it would be, nor was it entirely negative. He might be open to learning *if*, like Janet and Jasper's oldest son, he had someone other than his parents to show him the way.

"So, tell me, do you believe in fairy tales?" he asked, obviously redirecting the conversation back to their original discussion.

"Of course. I've seen them come true often enough."

Noel turned his head to the side. "You mean with real princes and princesses?"

She shook her head and smiled. She had met real ones—European and Asian—while being in New York, but that wasn't what she meant. "No. Between a doctor and a schoolteacher. Between the president of a modeling agency and a museum director. And, well, between my own father and mother." She shrugged her shoulders. "Simple people like that."

He chuckled. "I don't think there's anything simple about being a doctor or a schoolteacher or any of those things. And for a child to think of her parents' marriage as a fairy-tale romance must mean you have remarkable parents."

"Very."

"I do, too," he quickly returned and smiled at her. She smiled back. It was as if he knew what a gift his parents had given him, as her parents had given her: a family unit in which a child could find that special place of peace and security and love.

In this age of divorce and light romantic flings, his words made Natalia's heart sing. They had something basic and important in common: parents who loved one another and who loved God. She nodded her head, but as the star on the top of the tree flicked on—the tree's only light—and caught the corner of her eye, she exclaimed, "Oh, look! Isn't it beautiful?"

Noel turned his gaze toward the tree.

Seeing his tree at this famous plaza and finally meeting this young woman made him feel glad—as if the whole world was a bright and beautiful place. It was a way he hadn't felt since he was a child on Christmas morning and he first beheld all the presents waiting for him under the tree. Lowering his gaze to her profile which was silhouetted against the Rockefeller tree, he whispered, "Beautiful."

Both the girl and the conifer were.

And no matter what the future might hold for them, this moment would be one of his most cherished memories.

"This night is almost more thrilling than the tree-lighting ceremony. We are mostly alone"—she waved her arm toward the heralding angels and laughed—"except for our heavenly host, of course, and we have the expectation of the coming holiday season before us."

"I like this time of the year more than any other," Noel admitted. He didn't know why, but the lights and happy music, the ringing bells and merry decorations seemed to make something within him jump to life.

"I think hearts are more open to God's truth at this time than at any other. Maybe"—she looked shyly toward him—"that's what you feel." She motioned toward the people rushing along the avenue in buses, taxis, and cars; on Rollerblades, scooters, and feet. "Perhaps everyone does."

"The spirit of Christmas," Noel whispered, thinking that explained what she described.

She looked at him in a contemplative way, as if she wasn't sure she should speak. He'd seen the expression often enough in his students to recognize it. As with them—no, much more and in a different way than with the teenagers he counseled—he wanted to know what she was thinking. Every word she spoke was important to him.

"Tell me," he prompted.

Her eyes smiled up at him in question. "Are you sure? I have quite strong opinions about things, and once I get started—"

"I'd like to hear them," he interrupted. He wanted to know everything she thought, everything she believed. If he had his way about it, he'd like to spend a lifetime learning.

Amusement now glinted in her eyes. "If you're sure," she said, and after he nodded in encouragement, she twisted a strand of golden hair behind her ear and spoke. He wasn't disappointed. "Well, the expression 'spirit of Christmas' is actually from the Middle Ages and describes a jovial medieval figure."

"Really? I had no idea. If I had thought about it, I would have said it came from the pen of Charles Dickens."

"Most think that. But it was around long before that great writer's time. And there is a big difference between the 'spirit of Christmas' and that of God's Spirit touching people's hearts in a personal and holy way. God is real. Not an invention of man."

His parents might have said the same thing to him in the past, but he hadn't paid attention. He found himself wanting to pay attention to this golden-haired woman with perfect features. "Go on." He motioned for her to continue. He liked watching her lips curve as she spoke.

"Are you sure? As I said, I have a lot of thoughts about these things." She laughed, a light tinkling sound that reminded Noel of fine crystal touched by the wind.

"I want to hear what you believe." He really did. She was a thinker. He was glad she was so much more than a pretty face. It didn't surprise him.

"Well, I think God's Holy Spirit can more easily touch the hearts of people now. Christmas makes people wonder a little more than they normally do about God coming to earth as a little baby." She pointed behind them to the statues of the heralding angels.

Could that be the reason I love Christmas so much? Noel wondered. It was an interesting thought, but he doubted that was it. To believe in the message of Christmas, a person had to believe God did, in fact, come to earth as a baby. He wasn't so sure about that. It seemed like a nice fairy tale. But that was all. He believed in God and thought Jesus had been a remarkable man.

But God born as a human baby?

He wasn't going to tell this young woman that now, though. It wasn't the time or the place. And more than anything he wanted to meet her again, and he doubted—

His thoughts ground to a halt as she reached for her dog's lead and stood. "You're going?" he asked.

Nodding, she motioned for Prince to take his correct place beside her left heel. She glanced at her watch. "I have to."

He quickly stood up. "Wait—I mean—" He looked down. The dog watched him carefully, without his tail wagging. Noel knew German shepherds well enough to know he'd stood too suddenly for the dog's liking. "I'd like to see you again."

The girl reached down and patted the dog between his ears, assuring him all was well. She flashed her bright and lovely smile. "I have a feeling we'll meet again next year right here."

"I'd like to see you before then." *And learn what you think about and believe,* he wanted to say. Instead, he watched as her gaze roamed over his face; something in the way she looked at him told him she wanted to see him sooner, too.

"I'll be at the Macy's Thanksgiving Day parade," she offered.

He grimaced. "You and several million others."

She smiled at the truth of that statement and went a step further and offered him the area she would be in. "Well, I'll be at Herald Square." She looked up at the tree one more time. "It was special to talk to you finally."

He wondered if she could hear his heart pound louder at her admission. "Kind of like a fairy tale," he said.

She flashed him a high-wattage smile of agreement and, giving a command to Prince, turned and walked through the Channel Garden, around the corner, and out of sight. It was only as he watched the dog's feathery tale disappear around the edge of the building that Noel realized he hadn't asked her for her name.

He banged the heel of his hand against his forehead and laughed. There had to be poetic irony in that. The study of names was one of his favorite hobbies, and he'd even written a book titled *What's in a Name?* It had recently made the *New York Times* best-seller list. He turned and walked in the direction of his tree. For a few days more she would have to be the girl with the dog who visited the tree on the day of its arrival.

But that didn't matter. He had something more important than her name; he had a glimpse of the soul her beautiful exterior housed. And he was beginning to think it was more attractive than her appearance—he glanced in the direction she had walked—if that were possible.

He doubted that Cinderella or Sleeping Beauty could have had souls any nicer than his very own fairy-tale princess.

Princess, he mused, gazing at his tree. He wondered if her name might be Sara. It meant "princess."

"Could very well be," he muttered to himself. He felt better than he had in a long time. He could almost break into Gene Kelly's rendition of "Singin' in the Rain" and click his heels at any moment. He bowed to a family of tourists who looked at him as if he were the perfect specimen of one of those "crazy" New Yorkers they had heard about, one who walked along the streets talking to himself.

But Noel knew he *was* crazy.

Crazy in love with a woman he had only talked to once, a woman he would meet at Herald Square in a little over a week.

Noel did click his heels.

And the tourists practically ran away from him.

Chapter 3

Less than a week later he turned from a side street onto Fifth Avenue and saw her. She was standing in line with Prince to see the Christmas windows unveiled at a famous department store. Noel felt as if he were living a fairy tale.

What were the chances of their running into one another like this in New York City? Slim to none, he knew. Noel didn't believe in chance or destiny or that New Age mumbo jumbo. Enough of what his parents believed had rubbed off on him to trust that God had a hand in directing the steps of people. Noel liked the way his steps had been pointed this day.

The woman who had occupied much of his thoughts was standing not far from the end of the line. He walked up to her. As at the Rockefeller Center, the dog noticed him first. Noel was glad to see her canine friend did his job so well.

"Hi, Prince," he greeted the dog, putting his hand out for him to sniff it. The woman turned to him. Pleasure covered the smooth lines of her face. He knew his own face had to be wearing the same emotion.

"Hi!" she exclaimed, and Noel felt as if the joy of the season were expressed in the brightness of her gaze. "This is a nice surprise!"

"Nice surprise." Something jumped inside Noel at her words. "I couldn't agree more."

"What are you doing here?" she asked as if he were an old friend and not a person whose name she didn't know.

He motioned to his camera, then toward the decorated windows before them. "I understand each one resembles a Victorian dollhouse set this year. My mother loves dollhouses and collects and makes them, so I wanted to take some shots for her."

Her mouth dropped open as she touched her chest. "I collect dollhouses, too! That's why I've come today, even though"—she hiked up the sleeve of her coat to check her watch—"I don't have much time."

He wondered what she did to make her so pressed, but he only said, "I'll have to get you together with my mother. She has several scattered around her home. She's built Victorian homes herself—one from a kit and the other from scratch, plus another modeled after her own home, also from scratch."

"Really!" Her eyes widened in appreciation of the work that went into making three houses. "That's impressive. I've only just finished building my first Victorian. And that from a kit," she said. "I would love to see them. Does she live here in Manhattan?"

"She used to, but now my parents live in a big old home with lots of land around them in New Jersey." It was actually a mansion, one that had been in Noel's family for several generations. But he didn't tell her that.

"Hey, buster," a man with a heavy Queens accent who had a little girl by his side called out to Noel from about three places behind them. "If you're goin' to see the windows, you have to move to the back of the line. No line breakin' allowed."

Grimacing, Noel turned to the man. "Sorry. I just ran into—"

"Yeah, yeah. I've heard that story before," the man said without giving Noel the chance to explain.

Noel stiffened at the uncalled-for accusation, but sensing the woman's soft touch on his arm, he swallowed the retort he'd been about to make.

"Let's move to the end of the line," she urged him and, not waiting for his reply, motioned for Prince to turn around.

"But you said you were in a hurry—"

She shook her head. "It doesn't matter. We're only about"—she glanced toward the end—"thirty places from the rear anyway. If it makes that man happy, then why not? Maybe he's had a hard day. It's an easy way to show him people care about him, even people he doesn't know."

If Noel hadn't already thought she was a remarkable woman, he would now. She seemed to be wise in a way that was far beyond her years.

And—her appearance aside—he understood why he was already in love with her.

As they walked back, the belligerent man's gaze followed them in surprise. Noel noticed that his anger seemed to evaporate off his broad shoulders like snow under the shining sun. "Hey—thanks. If only more people were so fair."

The woman smiled over at him with a look that could have melted the largest iceberg in the Arctic. It definitely warmed the man's disposition. He stared at her with his mouth hanging open and his eyes as round as saucers, and Noel guessed he was probably falling in love with her, as well.

"I wonder," Noel said as they took their place at the end of the line, "how much better that stranger's day will be because you agreed to move back." Her action wasn't too unusual for Noel. He had seen his parents do things like that many times. But never someone near his own age. "You didn't have to come to the back with me."

"I wanted to," she replied quickly, and Noel wondered if he dared suppose she wanted to know him as much as he wanted to know her?

She smiled. "I know we weren't in the wrong. I could have come early and saved a place in line for both of us." Noel liked the way that sounded. That would mean they were a couple, or at least friends. "But," she said, shrugging her slender shoulders, "my father always told me if I could do something to calm another person, especially something that cost so little, a place in a line"—she shrugged her shoulders again, a cute habit Noel was beginning to associate with her—"then why not? Who knows what's going on in that man's life?"

"Sounds as if you have a wise father."

"I do," she agreed as they took short steps forward toward the display. "So tell me," she said, changing the subject, "where in New Jersey do your parents live?"

"Madison."

Her brows came together thoughtfully. "I'm not sure where that is. I haven't seen much of New Jersey, but I hear it's beautiful." She flashed her smile and gave her tinkling little laugh. "Much more than the New Jersey Turnpike, that is."

He chuckled in agreement. Most people thought New Jersey looked like the industrial area that followed the turnpike across its length, not realizing the state was one of the prettiest on the East Coast. "That it is. But, shh," he said, leaning toward her. At her scent—clean and fresh like powder on a baby's skin—his senses reeled, and he took a hasty step back to clear his head. "It's one of the best-kept secrets."

"Then I won't tell," she said in a conspiratorial way. Craning her neck toward the first window whose brightly lit display was becoming visible, she said, "Now you know one of my favorite hobbies is collecting and building dollhouses." She turned to him. "How about you? Do you have a hobby?" In the chill of the evening, her frosted breath mingled with his, a cloud that connected them together. Holiday songs piped out onto the street from the department store turned the moment into one of total Christmas enchantment. *"It's that time of year, when the world seems to say. . .Merry Christmas!"* And Noel wanted to lean toward the woman who, because of the crowds, was standing as close to him as a girlfriend might and kiss her.

But, of course, he didn't. At even the slightest start, Prince might grab his leg, but, even more important, Noel knew it wouldn't be right.

He stood up straight and fought to remember her question. His hobby? "Names," he managed to reply. He was pleased he could get the word past his throat. He felt as tense as the tightest setting on a windup toy.

She blinked back at him in confusion. "Names?"

He nodded his head. "I enjoy onomastics."

"Onoma—" She paused. Then, as if a light had suddenly switched on, she exclaimed, "You mean you like the study of names?"

Now he was the one to be surprised. "I'm impressed." He was. Most thought onomastics had something to do with gymnastics.

"Don't be." She laughed, a sound that to Noel sounded like the bells of Christmas ringing out over the wintry world. She shook her head and explained. "*Onoma* is the Greek word for 'name.' If you know elementary Greek, it's easy. *Onoma* is, of course, one of the first words a person learns. *Ti enia to onoma sou?*—What is your name?"

To say he was astonished would be to put it mildly. He was flabbergasted. He was normally the one explaining the history of a word to another. "How do you know Greek?"

She touched her gloved hand to her heart and, in a way he could only describe as proud, replied, "I am from Hellas. . .from Greece."

"*You're* Greek?" That was the last thing he expected. He had met many Greek people or Americans of Greek ancestry. Most had fair, olive skin and straight, thick hair that was either light or dark brown. This woman was as blond as a towheaded toddler. And it was obvious from her pale lashes and skin that the color was natural.

A smile touched the corners of her mouth. "Yep."

"Do you have any more secrets to tell?"

"Oh, I have a few," she assured him with a mocking glance.

He was sure she must. He would enjoy getting to know each of them. If she would let him. "Well, how do you speak English so well?"

"Most people in Greece speak English—actually, several foreign languages. But, for personal reasons, it was important to my father that I learn to speak English well with as little accent as possible." He listened to her carefully now and could detect a slight difference to the way she pronounced words. She softened the English language. Not an accent exactly, but more a treat for his ears, a caress he rejoiced in hearing. "I had lessons from a very young age."

"Greece. . .that's neat. I went there once," he said, "when I was a little boy." It was shortly after his parents had married. The thought always brought a smile to Noel's lips. How many couples include a young boy on their honeymoon? But that's how it had always been for Noel and Jennifer, the woman his father had married. He considered Jennifer his mother in every sense of the word; she had included Noel in everything. He doubted a woman could love a child of her own body as much as Jennifer loved him, and he loved her. The three of them—Noel, his father, and his stepmother—had a very special relationship. Probably his parents' faith in God had a lot to do with it, he admitted to himself. "I don't remember too much about Greece," he continued. "Just that I liked it. How long have you lived here?"

"More than six years."

"Alone?"

⁓⁓⁕⁓⁓

Natalia wasn't sure she liked that question. She didn't know much about this man, and she had made it her way never to be too open with anyone. People had preconceived notions about models—some of them arrived at correctly. But not where she was concerned. He didn't know she was a model—at least she didn't think he knew—but that possibility existed. So this was getting too personal for her. In case he did know—had, in fact, seen her picture and was using their "chance" meetings as an excuse to talk to her, though she didn't believe it—she wasn't going to give too much information away.

"Of course not." It wasn't a lie. She lived with Prince.

"Oh." She could tell from the way his face clouded over that he assumed she meant with a man. His disappointment was palpable. "You're married?"

"No."

"Oh," he said.

She groaned inside. That "oh" meant he thought she lived with a man without being married. She couldn't let him think that, especially since he knew she was a Christian.

"So you're in a relationship right now?"

She prayed that her thoughts about his being a decent person were true. "No. I don't live with a man. I would never live with a man who wasn't my husband. But I wasn't lying," she assured. "I live with Prince." She ruffled the dog's fur. "And I live in the same apartment building with my surrogate family here in New York."

The relief that crossed his face almost made her laugh and definitely made her thankful she'd been totally honest with him. "I'm glad," he admitted on a frosted breath that made his words seem to dance in delight around his head. She wasn't sure if he was glad because she didn't live with a man or because she hadn't altered his idea of how a Christian should behave. "It might sound funny in this day and age," he continued, "but it's nice to find a woman with old-fashioned values."

He was glad because of my second thought! That made her feel tingly down to her toes. "My principles aren't really old-fashioned as much as God-fashioned," she clarified.

He nodded thoughtfully, something in itself that astounded her. Often such declarations on her part had been scoffed at. "Like my parents," he said.

She let out the breath she hadn't realized she'd been holding. "I think I'd like your parents," she admitted.

He chuckled. "I *know* they would like you."

The music, the sounds of happy shoppers on the street, taxis and buses and trucks passing them, faded as they looked deeply into one another's eyes, into one another's souls. What Natalia saw in the blueness of the man's eyes made her heart rejoice. That something very special was happening between them, an emotion deeper than time, was obvious. Natalia only prayed it was something God ordained. Somehow she felt that it was.

Tearing her gaze away from his, wanting to lighten a moment that was becoming too heavy, she turned toward the front of the line. She was relieved to see they were almost at the first window. She pointed to his camera. "You'd better get it ready." She glanced behind them. About a hundred people were there now. "With so many people wanting to see the windows, we can't stop for long."

She was relieved when, taking her cue to lighten the mood, he reached for his camera. She liked him and wanted to get to know him, but the emotions swirling around her needed a break. She had always been open about her beliefs, just had never told so many of them so quickly after meeting a person. But he seemed to pull her thoughts out of her. It was as if he really wanted to know what she believed. As if he really cared.

After a half hour of gazing together at the artistically re-created rooms in the store windows, all from the Victorian age and decorated for Christmas with garlands and tinsel, wreaths and ribbons, and greenery of every kind, Natalia glanced at her watch. "I really must go."

"Too bad. I was going to ask you to go to a little café and get a hot chocolate or something."

She gave a slight shiver, and for the first time since he had walked up to her side, she felt the cold. She fixed her scarf closer around her neck. "Perfect evening for it. I would have loved to. Maybe another time," she suggested.

"Definitely. But"—amusement glinted in his dark eyes—"if we're going to meet each other again, maybe we should exchange names."

She laughed. "Since you love onomastics, I'm surprised that wasn't your first question."

"It normally is," he answered, his lips turning downward. "But with us nothing seems normal." The way he looked at her—with the gleam of a man who considers a woman special—made her forget about the cold again. "I like that."

"Me, too," she heard herself whisper back.

He stood back, held out his hand, and softly introduced himself, "I'm Noel Sheffield."

She extended her gloved hand to his waiting one. "Nice to meet you, Noel." She paused, then decided quickly to give him her real name, something she rarely did. "Natalia Pappas."

He nodded in appreciation of it. "Now that's some name. To be called

Natalia, meaning 'of or relating to Christmas,' you must have been born around Christmas. And Pappas—well, you could most definitely be nothing other than Greek." His brows came together in a thoughtful question. "Isn't *pappas* what priests are called in Greek? I suppose there must be a long line of priests in your family."

"Very good." She was impressed. "And yes on both accounts. As a matter of fact, my father is a Greek Orthodox priest, as was his father, and his father before, and, well, I guess all the way back to the beginning of Christianity."

He whistled. "That's some lineage."

"It is kind of neat to know I was raised in a tradition that goes back almost two thousand years, practically to the twelve apostles and Christ Himself. But—" She dipped her head and clamped her mouth shut. There she went again, speaking too much.

"Please continue," he encouraged her as he had at the tree the other day.

"Are you sure?" She grimaced slightly. "Once I start talking with you, I don't seem able to stop, and I have very strong beliefs, and—"

"I want to hear them, Natalia," he whispered. "All of them."

All? She saw in his eyes an interest that went beyond the superficial. It was a heady feeling. Her father had always wanted to know everything her mother was thinking; anything important to her was important to him. Could this man feel the same way? And if he did, what did that say? That he cherished her? Cherished her thoughts? She still hesitated.

"Please go on." His eyebrows rose slightly, and he gave a quick, reassuring nod.

What else could I ask for? she thought. Taking a deep breath, she plunged in. "Well, the most important thing is that my father—my mother too when she was alive—has always made God the center of his life. Consequently, God has always been the heart of our family's lives."

"I think that's as important to you as it is to my parents," he commented.

"It's the most important thing," she admitted and hoped he understood what she was trying to say. For them to have a future together, something she wished might be theirs, it would have to be the same for him. She hoped he understood that.

His right hand reached out toward her. When it settled on her left shoulder, heat enveloped her, and the noise, the bustle of the evening, seemed to slip away. It was as if they were the only two people on the avenue again as he smiled a crooked little smile down at her and said, "Well, we must meet for that cocoa sometime." He spoke softly with a husky, romantic sound to his voice that made her feel like the most valued woman alive. "Because I find I want to hear all about your beliefs, Natalia Pappas."

He looked away and squinted toward the bright lights. From the way his jaw clenched and unclenched, it seemed to Natalia as if he were considering something of importance.

"You might find it strange, but where I have never wanted to sit down and listen to my parents talk about their beliefs"—he looked back at her—"I want to with you. Very much."

She reached up and wrapped her gloved fingers around his. "It's not at all odd, Noel. How many children honestly ever want to pay attention to their parents?"

As a counselor Noel knew that was true, but also as a counselor he felt convicted by her words. Was he ignoring the best advice his parents had to give? Since meeting this woman, he was beginning to think he was being as ornery as some of his high school students, even Rachel, whom he was so concerned about these days.

"Well, Noel." She let go of his hand and lowered hers to the dog's lead. The emptiness he felt over not holding it any longer was keen until she spoke her next words. "How about if we meet at the grandstand of the Thanksgiving Day parade? At seven in the morning. Perhaps we can go for cocoa afterward." She shivered slightly. "I heard the weather report last night, and it's supposed to keep getting colder and colder until Christmas. I think we'll have to thaw out after sitting outside for so long. I have tickets for the stands outside of Macy's, so we can enjoy the show up close."

"How do you have tickets?" he blurted out, then smiled sheepishly. "Sorry," he apologized. He knew grandstand tickets were hard to come by and much coveted. If he hadn't already realized there was something special about this woman, having grandstand tickets was one more indication.

"My surrogate parents, whom I mentioned earlier, receive them each year. But they won't be using them this year, so they've offered them to me." She patted Prince's head. "I was going to bring Prince as my date, but if you'd like to come. . . ?"

"As your date?"

If his tree at Rockefeller Center sparkled half as much as her eyes did right now—like soft blue diamonds reflecting the many-colored lights on the avenue—then he knew it would be the most beautiful tree ever. "As a friend," she said with a smile that made her lips crinkle at their corners in such a cute way he wished he could touch them.

To be a friend was good. He would take that. For now. "I'd like that."

She nodded. "Me, too."

Chapter 4

It was fantastic to see the Macy's Thanksgiving Day parade arrive at Herald Square with its world-renowned performers, the huge balloons fashioned in whimsical characters, the marching bands, the clowns, the magical floats. But to Noel the best part of the morning was being with the girl and her dog and going for hot chocolate afterward to a little café off Broadway. The arctic bite in the air had combined with the wind to give them both rosy cheeks. The warmth of the café was a welcome change from the outdoor elements.

Soft Christmas music filled the café, continuing the sounds heard on the city streets. Ginger and cinnamon and sugary delights mixed with the scent of pine to please their sense of smell, as much as the parade had that of their hearing and sight. Evergreen and wood, windowpanes frosted naturally by the elements outside, and a stone fireplace running the full length of an inside wall with a tall Christmas tree to its side helped make the café cozy and festive. Each little marble-topped table came complete with its own miniature tree decorated with lights that softly winked and blinked, too.

Noel and Natalia found a table near the fireplace. They laughed over some of the antics of the people trying to keep the huge helium balloons from taking off in the high winds.

"I thought one of the young girls holding the tin soldier was going to lift off just as Santa's sled was mounted to do!" Noel exclaimed. He mimicked the shock on the girl's face as her feet rose an inch off the ground, and they laughed until tears glistened in their eyes.

"Ah, Santa!" Natalia sighed as she wiped the corners of her eyes with her red holiday napkin. "Of course, the Santa Claus float is the best of all. His arrival in Herald Square officially opens the Christmas season in New York City and America."

That statement brought a quizzical frown to Noel's face. "You don't mind children believing in Santa Claus?" he asked, not waiting for a reply. He wanted to explain his question. "As Christians, my parents seem to be in a quandary about that. I was allowed to believe in him, though, when I was a young child." At the time his father hadn't seen any harm in letting Noel. But his father's views had changed through the years.

"That's a tough question," she replied. He watched her take a sip of her cocoa. "The Santa myth is such a delightful one for children to experience, especially here in America. It's become an American tradition, and I think Christians have to bear that in mind. But like many things surrounding the celebration of Christmas"—she pointed to the lights, the trees, the tinsel all around the room—"if we remember the reason behind it, then I think it's fine."

"Meaning?"

She shrugged. "Well, first of all, I think parents have to teach their children that Santa Claus was actually a man. He was a bishop in the church, and his name was Nicholas. He lived in Myra in Asia Minor and did much good, all in the name of the One he believed in and served his entire life—Jesus Christ. Even after Nicholas died, people remembered his life as an example of a wonderful Christian."

"You're talking about the man referred to as *Saint* Nicholas, right?"

She nodded. "Saint Nicholas of Myra."

"Okay, but what about children believing he lives forever?"

"Well. . ." She let the word roll off her lips in a hesitant way. "The truth is, as a Christian he *does* live forever. Bishop Nicholas was purported to have died on December 6, around the year A.D. 330. That day is celebrated as the first day of his life with Christ in paradise. In that manner, through his faith in Jesus, Nicholas of Myra, like all Christians, does indeed live on."

Noel knew his mouth dropped open at her words, but he couldn't have kept it from happening. She was saying things he had never heard before. "How do you know all this?"

She seemed to understand finally how much he enjoyed hearing her share her views, for excitement shone on her face, enchanting Noel with her eagerness. "Well, remember that my father is a priest—in the same tradition in which Nicholas of Myra was first a priest, then a bishop. Back in those days, Myra, the city in Asia Minor where Nicholas served as bishop, was a major part of the Greek world." She glanced toward the tree's lights and squinted in a way that almost seemed sad to him. "Until a few decades ago, the city of Myra was Hellenic with mostly Greek Christians living there, even though the Turks from Asia had taken over the land politically during the Middle Ages."

Once again he realized there was more to her than outer beauty. Behind that golden hair, the blue eyes, and the features that looked like a master craftsman had sculpted them were brains. And she was knowledgeable about different things, things he had no idea about. As one who studied the etymology of names, he liked that. "I had no idea about any of this."

She sipped her cocoa, then said, "That's one of the nice things about cultures mixing with one another." She looked at him above the rim of her cup before replacing it on the table. "I'd never heard of some of the more current men and women of faith from this area of the world until coming to live here." She held up her hand and counted off a few people on her fingers. "D. L. Moody, Peter Marshall, and Billy Graham, for example. Those men and their walks through life should be remembered as much as the early Christians."

"I agree that history is very important. Does Myra still exist? I mean, are there still ruins from the time of Nicholas?"

"Oh, sure," she said, nodding. "Ancient Greek, Christian, and medieval Greek ruins are all over what is now modern Turkey. In Myra, the actual church where Nicholas taught, which was built during his lifetime, is still there. My father visited it when he was a young man. In fact, the church in our village is very similar in appearance."

"Wait a minute." Noel leaned forward. "He visited the exact church where Saint Nicholas preached?"

She nodded.

He whistled. "I never knew there was so much to the man who inspired the legend of Santa Claus."

"Not too many people in this part of the world seem to know much about the early Christians, Saint Nicholas included. I've noticed since moving here that everyone knows about the apostles, and then there seems to be a break until about the time of Martin Luther. But we grew up learning about early Christians in Kastro, the village I come from. Rather than having our rock stars or football stars, we have those men and women who gave their lives so today we could have the same knowledge they had about Christ. Saint Nicholas, the real man, has always been one of the more important Christians to remember. Even today."

Noel shook his head. "So Santa actually was real?"

"Definitely," she said without hesitation. "And because he was a Christian, he still lives. So that's true, too. A Christian's body might die, but not the spirit. So to say Santa still lives is true in the same way that all Christians live even when our bodies die." She returned to her original thought. "When a person knows Santa Claus was actually a wealthy young man who became a priest in the church and gave in Jesus' name so generously his deeds were talked about for generations, then it's fine to enjoy that tradition. But a person should not believe in him, rather in the One whom Saint Nicholas believed in and followed—Jesus Christ. Otherwise I think a child is in for a great disappointment on learning Santa doesn't live at the North Pole or fly through the sky on a sled pulled by reindeer. The myth shouldn't be confused with the reality, the truth."

Noel heaved a deep sigh. "To be honest, that realization was one of the hardest for me to accept." He had learned it at about the same time his mother died, when he was six. The two losses coming together were— Another thought, an aggressive, almost angry one, intruded upon the first. For the first time, Noel understood he was angry at God about both events: His mother had died, and as crazy as it sounded for a man nearly twenty-eight, Santa had died, too.

Worse—Santa, as such, had never really lived.

It was a startling thing for Noel to realize.

Maybe it was one of the reasons he never wanted to believe a baby born in a stable could be the God of the universe. If Santa was just a myth, then wasn't the idea of a baby born as fully God and fully man also a myth?

But he knew enough to know there was a fallacy in his thinking.

There was a big difference between the two examples.

But not to a six-year-old child who had just lost his mother. To a grieving child it would be the same thing.

Worse even—for the baby who was God should have been able to save his mother for him. Noel remembered asking both Santa and Jesus to save her that year.

Neither had.

But he didn't want to get into this with Natalia now, so he kept the conversation on Santa Claus. "And I guess his name must have been derived somehow from the actual Nicholas."

"That's right. With your knowledge of names, can you figure it out?" she asked just before taking another sip of hot chocolate.

"Well, Nicholas is an ancient Greek name that means 'victory of the people.'"

She nodded. "Even today we say *nikisa* for victory. But more important we are certain Nicholas was Greek, of Hellenic heritage, by his name."

Now she was speaking on a subject with which he was familiar. "Absolutely. Back then names were never given lightly. They always told something about the person. Particularly from where they hailed. So let's see." He felt that thrill he always got when considering the history of names. It was like a tasty morsel to his mind. "How did his name go from being Nicholas, Greek bishop of Myra, to Santa Claus? There has to be an interesting etymology here."

"Want me to tell you?" She leaned forward and asked with all the eagerness of a child wanting to tell a secret.

He smiled and, sitting back, indicated with his hands to go ahead. He loved watching her talk, the way her mouth curved around each word as if it were a treasure and the way her eyes opened wide with an excitement similar to reading a good book.

"Well, the Dutch settlers of New Amsterdam"—she pointed out the window to the city, using the name by which it was first known to colonists—"brought with them their beloved *San Nicolaas*. Americans said it fast with a stress on the broad double *a* of the last syllable. A *t* slipped in after the first *n,* and we got *Santy Claus*. From there it was just a short step to Santa Claus. That's how American kids started calling the early Christian cleric from the Greek world Santa Claus!"

Noel shook his head in appreciation. "That's one of the more remarkable etymologies I've heard. But," he conceded, "it sounds correct."

"You're the expert in names, of course, but I think it is," she said with a bright smile. "Now enough about Santa." She glanced at her watch. "I have to get going soon or I'll miss Thanksgiving dinner. But how about telling me what you do?" She laughed. "We still seem to talk about everything but the normal things."

They hadn't had even one moment of boring "small talk" between them. "It's nice," he said. It was one of the things he liked about her.

She nodded and glanced at her watch again. "I agree, but if I'm going to tell my surrogate family about you at Thanksgiving dinner in about an hour, I should at least be able to tell them what you do."

He was pleased she was going to tell the people she was close to about him. It meant she must be beginning to care for him. Maybe even in more than just a friendly way.

He liked that. A lot.

"Okay." He sat up straight and wondered what he should tell her. He had told her about onomastics as a hobby. What he hadn't told her was that he was a writer and his current book was a huge success on the *New York Times* best-seller list.

He decided against enlightening her about it, though. People always seemed to change toward him once they learned he was an author—particularly a successful one. He doubted she would, but he didn't want to take that chance. He didn't want her to act any differently than she had been. "I come from a very long line of lawyers, one that stretches back to revolutionary days."

"That's quite a lineage," she said, repeating his earlier words about her and her priestly ancestry.

"By American standards, it is. But I guess it kind of pales when compared to Greek ones."

She shook her head. "No. Don't say that. Everything is relative. The United States is a new country. That has to be respected in the same way that an ancient one is."

"Tell me something." He leaned forward. "How old is the church in your village?"

Her gaze searched the ceiling, as though she might discover the answer there. "I don't know. It's from Byzantine times, so it must be at least five or six hundred years old, maybe older."

He held up his hands and smiled. "I rest my case."

She laughed. "You spoke just like a lawyer. Are you one, too?"

"Only by degree."

Her brows came together. "What do you mean?"

"I studied criminal law, even graduated from Harvard Law School, but I'm a high school counselor." He shrugged his shoulders. This was what most women couldn't understand. Why he would be a high school counselor when he could be a high-powered, highly paid criminal lawyer with one of the oldest firms in the city. But she didn't know about his wealth—that he never had to work a day in his life if he didn't want to—and, for the moment, he would keep it that way.

He was surprised when he saw a look of wonder in her eyes. Just the opposite of what he normally saw in a woman's face when he told of his career choice. "Really. Well, a counselor is a counselor whether it is to direct people in the ways of the law or children in the way of life. I think, of the two, you chose the better."

He was taken aback. "You do?"

"Of course. You have the chance to shape young minds so that maybe they won't need the help of your other profession when they grow older."

She couldn't have shocked him more had she said she was going to walk across the Brooklyn Bridge. "That is exactly my reasoning. Precisely why I decided to counsel high school–age people."

"I know someone else who did something similar. Stavros Andreas is my village's schoolteacher. Because the village doesn't have too many children, he teaches all ages. But he left a career as a university professor here in the States—at Georgetown University, I think—and went to live in his ancestral village. That is my village of Kastro, and he did it so he could raise his daughter himself and, as he has often said, 'to help form young minds.' He has never regretted his decision. Especially since Allie Alexander, the village doctor, left New York and came to the village, and they fell in love—"

Noel held up his hand. "Wait a minute. Is this the fairy-tale romance between the teacher and the doctor you mentioned the other day?"

Her face brightened even more as she nodded. "They are living out a 'happily-ever-after' life if ever anybody did."

"They sound like interesting people."

Her smile deepened. "They are. Stavros's faith had been, well—let's just say he had been really hurt by his first wife—"

"He's divorced?"

"No. His wife died. But they had been separated. She had hurt him terribly. His wife hadn't wanted their little daughter, Jeannie." Natalia shrugged her shoulders. "From what I understand, the woman never wanted to be a mother. She was a lawyer who wanted a career, and she deserted both her little girl and her husband."

"That's tough."

"But it's another case of God taking something terrible and making something wonderful. Allie, Stavros, and their four children couldn't be happier. Stavros regained his faith and was given the family he had always yearned for, as well." She looked down at Prince who was sleeping by their feet under the table. "Prince is from their dog's litter of puppies."

"Really?" He glanced down at the dog. Who would have thought such a handsome German shepherd would come from a Greek village? Leaning forward, he reached for Natalia's hand. It was warm and soft, so soft he felt as if he were holding a cotton puff. "Now. I've told you about me, and you've told me about Allie and Stavros, and even Prince." He smiled down at the dog. "How about telling me about what you do so I can tell my parents when they ask me about any special people in my life?"

When the pupils of her eyes seemed to expand and swallow up some of the crystal blue of her irises, he was afraid he had gone a bit too far in describing how he felt about her. But as her lips softly curved up at their corners, he knew she didn't mind. Maybe she even liked it.

"Well, I—" She paused, and he thought she was trying to decide what exactly she should tell him. He understood. She had to be careful. They had met several times now, but they didn't know anyone in common. And this was New York City. "I'm a fashion-design student at Fashion Institute of Technology."

"No kidding?" That meant she was an artist. "You mean you're one of those people who can sketch clothes superquick?"

She laughed. "Believe me, Noel—sometimes I don't think quickly enough."

"I can't seem to draw a straight line, so people who can draw anything at all really impress me."

"I've always liked it a lot."

"How much longer do you have until you graduate?" Now that she was talking about herself, he was going to ask as much as he could.

"Next term."

"Fantastic. And then?"

She took a deep breath. "Then I hope to start my own line of clothes."

"And you have been going to school for six years?" That's how long she'd told him she'd been in New York. But he knew she must have been doing something more than just going to school. She had to support herself. New York was an expensive place to live. And he already knew what her father did.

"Yes, but part-time. I've been working, too."

"Doing what?"

"A bit of modeling," she murmured.

That surprised him. Not that she was a model. She certainly could be. Just that he didn't expect a strong Christian to be in that industry. "What type of modeling do you do, if you don't mind my asking?"

"No, of course not." She tucked a long strand of hair behind her ear, and he had the impression this line of questioning had made her uncomfortable. Giving her the benefit of his own experience, he suspected it was for the same reason he didn't like telling people he was a writer. People treated him differently.

She flashed a self-conscious smile before continuing. "For some reason I'm often asked to model nurses' uniforms."

"Nurses' uniforms?" He had the feeling she had modeled more than nurses' uniforms, but he didn't push her.

Her mouth turned up in an amused way. "Tell me—do you think I look like a nurse?"

She was giving him the chance to look at her, really look at her, and it wasn't an opportunity he was going to pass up.

From her soft forehead to her full lips, he let his gaze roam over her face. Did she look like a nurse? He wasn't so sure about a nurse, but he thought the look of gentleness and wisdom in her eyes, plus her height, which must be close to five feet ten inches, probably got her jobs modeling the white nurses' uniforms. An aura of purity seemed to surround her like perfume. Other than being gorgeous to see, she had a look of capability about her. Yes, he could imagine her dressed as a nurse.

"Hey!" she exclaimed after a moment, reaching for Prince's lead. He knew he'd taken too much time and had made her feel uncomfortable.

He quickly leaned forward. "No, wait." He touched her hand. "Yes. I can see where you might make the perfect nurse. You give a feeling of competency."

She loosened her grip on the lead. "Thanks. That's a nice thing to say." She glanced at her watch. "But I have to go—"

"Me, too." He had to catch the train out to New Jersey in fifteen minutes; otherwise, he would be late for Thanksgiving dinner at his parents'. And he didn't want to do that. "But look. Since we both love Christmas activities, how about if you and Prince, if you like, come with me to the tree-lighting ceremony at Rockefeller Center in three days? I have passes for the guest section."

Her pale brows rose. "The guest section? How?"

"I have a connection with the tree."

"With—the—tree?" she questioned in staccato.

"Don't worry. I'm not into any mysticism connected with trees. I have the passes because my parents donated the tree this year. It comes from their property in New Jersey."

He had the satisfaction of seeing her eyes widen. "It did?" But immediately they narrowed. "Oh, how could they part with it? That is the only thing about the trees at Rockefeller Center that has bothered me. They are cut down."

"No, it's okay," he assured her. "This tree has been marked for Rockefeller Plaza since, well, ever since my father was a little boy. Norway spruces have a life span of only 80 to 110 years. My great-grandfather planted this tree over 100 years ago. It wouldn't have been able to survive many more hard winters. Either that or it would have soon died of old age."

"I didn't realize their lives were that short. So your family wanted it to have a chance to show its beauty to the world?"

"That's right," Noel agreed and was glad she understood. "Please come with me to see it lit, Natalia. It would mean a great deal to me to have the woman by my side who loves and appreciates Rockefeller Center's trees so much she comes to welcome them upon their arrival every year." It would mean that and so much more. He wanted her to attend the special ceremony with him more than he could ever remember wanting anything in recent years.

Her lips curved up into that giving smile he was coming to expect from her. As her fingers squeezed his gently, Noel wondered at the way she made him feel, as if he wanted to hold her, protect her, never let her out of his sight. She was the mate of his soul, the woman his eyes yearned to see every day, forever. "I would be honored, Noel."

His heart seemed to bang louder inside his chest. A date. A real date. One that might end with his placing his lips on hers. "May I pick you up at your home?" he pushed out past his throat, which had suddenly gone dry.

"No. Not at my home, but at my surrogate parents' home." She reached into her purse for a pen and, leaning over, wrote something on a napkin. "This is their address. I would like for you to meet them before we go out."

"On our *date*?" he asked, placing special emphasis on the word as he slipped the napkin into his pocket. He had to make sure she saw it that way, too. It would change their relationship. He wanted it. But did she?

She flashed that million-dollar smile of hers, one that made her whole face shine like the sun. "Yes, on our date," she agreed, and Noel felt sure his smile had to be a reflection of hers.

Finally, he would have a date with Natalia, a real one. Not just an outing as friends. As he paid and they walked out of the café together, it took every ounce of his self-control not to skip down the sidewalk.

Chapter 5

It took a lot to impress Noel. But the apartment building did just that when a uniformed doorman let him inside on the afternoon of the day his tree was to be lit. He knew the prewar building was one of the great luxury apartment buildings in Manhattan. He rode the gilt elevator to the top floor.

"Welcome and come in," a woman greeted him, smiling warmly. She ushered him into the entrance hall. It had stone detailing on the walls and marble on the floors, reminding him of châteaus he had visited while in France. "You must be Noel. I'm Janet Howard, Natalia's, well—" She gave a light laugh that was full of good cheer. "I call myself her surrogate mother."

Noel shook Janet Howard's hand. "I've heard her refer to you in that way."

"My husband and I have been blessed with three sons." She guided him into the living room where the soothing strains of Christmas carols played softly in the background. "We are happy to count Natalia as a daughter. But please come in and sit down. Both my husband and Natalia will be out shortly," she said and motioned to a spacious room that made Noel feel more like he was in a Parisian apartment than one in Manhattan. Then he looked out the many windows at the panoramic view it had of Central Park and knew he could be nowhere but in his beloved New York City. The apartment sat just above tree level. The park was laid out below in its leafless, wintertime splendor.

"That's beautiful," he said, motioning to the view before he sat on the velvet sofa behind him.

Janet stood for a moment more and looked out the window at the view. Noel thought she must have gazed upon it a thousand times before. To him, she seemed to be breathing it in as if for the very first time.

"My husband and I have lived here for the last forty years, and yet"—she shook her head at the wonder of it—"I never tire of looking out these windows. It's one of God's greater blessings in our lives." She sat in a chair adjacent to his. "I grew up on a farm in Connecticut," she explained. "To have trees within my view is almost a must for me." She turned and smiled at the older woman who brought in a silver tray laden with tea and coffee, cakes and sandwiches. "May I offer you something?" she asked with a gracious wave of her hand over the tray. "Juanita makes the best coffee in the world."

Noel leaned forward. That was of interest to him. He was a connoisseur of great coffee. He smiled at the older woman in the maid's uniform. "In that case I'd like a cup. And a piece of that chocolate confection, too."

Though employer and employee, the two women were obviously friends, and they shared a laugh of mutual delight. "Just what we like, right, Juanita? A man who both appreciates and admits to wanting delicious food." Janet Howard waved the other woman aside as she started to serve. "I'll take care of it, dear. Thank you."

Noel nodded at the maid as she smiled and left the room.

Janet glanced up at the Charles X clock on the mantel. "Her favorite show is coming on TV," she whispered to him. "I hate for her to miss it," she said, pouring the coffee. "Cream? Sugar?"

"No. Black is fine."

Janet nodded and handed it to him, then sliced the silver knife through the luscious-looking cake. "Are you planning to go out anywhere after the tree-lighting ceremony?"

Noel looked at her in surprise. It had been years since a date's parents, or even parent-type figures, had asked him what his plans were for the evening.

Janet returned his gaze with a steady one, and he realized she was serious. She passed him a plate with a slice of cake. Where Natalia was concerned, he could understand the older woman's care and appreciate it. "I've made reservations at the Tavern on the Green for afterward." He referred to the famous restaurant located in Central Park.

"Oh! That's one of Natalia's favorite places, especially at this time of the year. It's decorated for Christmas. It has become our tradition to take her there for her birthday each year." She looked up, startled. "Oh, that's next week! I must remember to make reservations."

Noel paused in putting a forkful of cake in his mouth. "Her birthday is next week?" His own birthday was, too. He wondered if it might fall on the same date.

"The first day of December. That's why she's named—"

"Natalia," Noel finished for her, and his eyes widened. They shared the same birthday.

Janet looked at him in surprise. "Why, yes."

"That's why I'm called Noel," he explained. "My birthday is December the first, too."

"Oh!" Janet clapped her hands together at the coincidence of it. When Natalia and an older, distinguished-looking gentleman walked into the room arm in arm, she turned to them. "Natalia, you and Noel share the same birthday!"

Natalia's blue gaze met his. To Noel, as he stood up, it was as if the other two people weren't there. She had been beautiful the other times he had seen her, but now, dressed specifically for him and for their first real date, she looked like a modern-day, fairy princess should. She wore a burgundy cowl-neck sweater with a matching knee-length velvet skirt and high black boots that had ankle straps with antique brass buckles on them. But it was the look in her eyes that made all the finery fade almost beyond consequence. Her eyes shone like diamonds reflecting the light, and Noel had to remind himself to breathe.

"*Your* birthday is December the first?" There was that quality in her voice of a young girl pleased by the discovery.

He could only nod.

She moved forward. Actually she seemed to float toward him.

She extended her slim hands to him, her expression softening.

"Oh, Noel." She paused as the thought occurred to her. "*That's* why you're called Noel?"

He nodded. "It means 'Christmas.'" The meaning behind his own name was one of the reasons he had started studying onomastics.

"And yours means the same," Janet Howard said. "How remarkable."

"Something else we have in common," he whispered to Natalia, and she nodded her golden head slightly before turning to the man who was standing behind her. "Jasper Howard, I'd like for you to meet Noel Sheffield." Extending the same honor to Noel, she said, "Noel, Jasper Howard."

"It's good to meet you, sir," Noel replied and shook hands.

"Sheffield?" The older man looked at him with the narrowed gaze of a man trying to place another. "Is your father Quincy Sheffield of Sheffield, Brokaw, and Thomas?"

Noel saw in the man's eyes that light of interest he was used to seeing when someone recognized his prestigious family. He stiffened but nodded. He didn't like having to be associated with his family's law firm in order to see that look in another's eye. He was actually disappointed to see it in this man whom Natalia thought of so highly. But since it had happened all his life, he was used to it and answered truthfully. "Yes, sir."

"But Natalia told us you don't work in your father's firm?"

"No, sir, I don't. If I did, though, I would work with my father, who does mostly pro bono cases."

"Yes, I've heard that. Your father is a Christian, isn't he?"

That surprised Noel more than anything else the man could have asked. No one, with the exception of Natalia, had asked him that before. Noel stood a bit straighter as he answered, taking sudden pleasure from doing so. "Yes, he is."

Jasper shook his head and smiled. "I've heard many good things about your father. The world would be a much better place if there were more men like him in positions of responsibility. You must be very proud to be the son of a man of such well-placed principles."

Noel hadn't realized how highly he esteemed his father until that moment. "Yes, I'm proud of both my father and my mother."

Noel saw Natalia flash a see-I-told-you-so smile at her surrogate parents before saying, "We must be going." While she gathered her coat and scarf, Noel realized he didn't feel the need to make a hasty retreat from these people as he had when he was a young adult wanting to get away from a girl's relatives. It was a strange but good feeling.

"It was nice to meet you both," Noel said and shook hands again with Jasper. To Janet he said, "Please tell Juanita her cake and coffee were delicious."

"Juanita must take credit for the coffee, but the cake was my creation."

Noel's brows lifted in surprise. Most women he knew who had full-time help didn't do much in the kitchen. "It was fantastic."

Jasper Howard put his arm around his wife's waist. "Everything my wife does is fantastic," he said in a loving, yet not boastful, way. Noel could feel the air around them radiating with the love they felt for one another, exactly as it did around his own parents. It was something wonderful and perfect and special. He only wished, as he helped Natalia on with her coat—a gray, double-faced, cashmere design that was soft to the touch—that he and this woman whose birthday he shared might find such a love someday.

The older couple walked with them to the door. "It must be very special to see *your* tree being lit," Janet Howard commented.

Noel looked over at Natalia. The boots she wore almost made her his height. "It's even more so by having Natalia with me," he admitted and looked back in time to catch Janet and Jasper Howard exchanging amused glances.

"Have a wonderful evening, you two," Jasper said while Natalia reached over and planted a quick kiss on first his cheek, then Janet's.

"We will."

As they stepped out the door, Noel stopped suddenly. "Hey! Haven't you forgotten someone?"

The three looked at him in confusion.

"Where's Prince?"

Their faces settled into smiles, and Natalia slipped her left arm through his right one. Noel couldn't remember the last time anything had felt better. "I thought I would hold onto you tonight."

Noel looked over at her surrogate family and gave them a small wink. "I like the way that sounds."

~~~

The tree-lighting ceremony was everything and more than Noel had thought it would be. The only thing that would have made it better would have been to have had his parents with them. They had planned on coming into the city for the occasion, but his mother had developed a cold. Having suffered from pneumonia the previous winter, they deemed it prudent to stay at home and watch the ceremony on TV.

Noel missed them but was glad he had Natalia with whom to enjoy it. When the giant TV screen at the center showed his tree being trussed, then cut down on his parents' property, Noel thought it had to be the most novel way to introduce a girl to his parents' affluent home.

When the Tudor-style mansion was shown, Natalia leaned toward him and whispered, "Your mother has made a model of *that* house?"

He nodded but braced himself for what would most likely follow—her understanding of his parents' wealth.

"Must be a beautiful dollhouse."

Noel turned to her. She was actually thinking about the difficulty in recreating the mansion as a dollhouse rather than about what the historic home represented—generations of wealth.

That was a first for him.

By this time he would usually see dollar signs in the eyes of women. He saw none in Natalia's. They still sparkled like diamonds, but for the occasion and not for his wallet.

He quickly realized the fallacy of his jaded thinking. Her beliefs wouldn't allow her to be impressed by wealth except, like his parents, in the context of how it might help others. After seeing the Howards' luxury apartment, he should have known the stateliness of his parents' home wouldn't faze her. Her own apartment was located in the same building.

The show included famous singers performing Christmas songs, Olympic champion skaters, the Radio City Rockettes, and even someone dressed as Santa waving and dancing to a merry tune across the stage. Then the time for the lighting of the tree finally arrived.

"Noel." Natalia leaned over and spoke directly into his ear. With all the happy noises going on around them, that was the only way to be heard. Noel was glad; he liked the closeness, savored the way her perfume scented the air around them. "Do you know who is going to turn the switch that lights the tree this year?"

"I think the mayor will."

It was the mayor, and soon the countdown began. "Ten. Nine. Eight. Seven. Six. Five. Four. Three. Two. One!"

A gigantic shout erupted.

The switch was flipped.

Thousands of lights lit the tree. And everyone looked on it with childlike wonder, the multicolored glow illuminating each person.

"It's a fairyland of delight!" Natalia said among all the "oohs" and "aahs" and clapping around them.

Noel had to agree. It *was* like a fairyland—a beautiful place of wonder and enchantment, goodness and light. And *his* tree was at the center of it all.

"How do you feel?" Natalia asked into his ear.

He turned his head so their gazes met.

How *did* he feel? The word that came to him he had never used. But it was the only one that described what this moment meant to him. He leaned toward her and spoke it.

"Blessed," he said. Her eyes narrowed as if to ascertain she had heard correctly. He nodded and mouthed the word again. "Blessed."

She reached for his hand and patted it gently, and a feeling of blessedness that even he could recognize as coming from God increased within him. As everyone started singing "Joy to the World" and praising the One whom the tree was meant to glorify, Noel wondered how he had ever lived without the feeling singing through his soul. And how he had ever lived without this remarkable girl.

~~~~~

"That was one of the most wonderful things I've ever experienced," Natalia said after the host at the Tavern on the Green seated them at their table. "The tree couldn't have looked better. And what a surprise this is." She looked around the restaurant. "I usually come here only for my birthday."

"So Janet told me. That's how we found out you and I share the same one."

"Why don't you come with us this year?"

"That would be great, but I always spend it with my parents—"

"Of course you do." She felt the heat of embarrassment fill her face.

"But that's in the evening," he was quick to point out, apparently trying to relieve her discomfiture. She appreciated it. "How about if we make a *date*?" He paused as he accentuated the word.

Understanding he meant it in its true form, as a romantic appointment, she smiled.

"Let's make a date," he repeated, "to come to the park first thing in the morning of December 1. To be here"—he waved his hand over a small section of the huge park—"before anybody else. That would be a fun way to celebrate our birthdays. And with this freezing weather, we might even have snow that day."

She felt laughter bubble up inside her. This was one of the things she liked about Noel. He did different things. No movie and a dinner date for him. "I'd like that. I've never come out very early because of safety reasons."

"Well, I'll come to your apartment and get you. Between Prince, me, and"—he pointed upward—"your faith in God, you'll have nothing to fear."

She liked the fact that he had included God in the list, although she wasn't quite sure whether it was in a mocking way or not. When his next words came out, they not only settled the question in her mind, but thrilled her.

"I must admit, I'm beginning to envy you, my parents, and the Howards for your faith in God."

She reached for his hand and gave it a gentle squeeze. "It's not something you have to envy, Noel. It's something that can be yours so easily. It's about your volition, your choice, as a human being to believe or not to believe Jesus is who the Bible and the church say He is."

"I believe He was a great man, Natalia, a great politician, a great moral teacher. Probably even the most important person in history to have ever lived," he conceded. "But God's Son?" He sighed, and she heard the regret in his tone. "That I don't get."

Natalia felt her heart beat fast with the desire to hand this special man her faith. But she knew it didn't work that way. It went back to volition, that gift of choice from God that made humans—well—human. To decide whether Jesus was who He said He was, was something people had to choose for themselves.

But Noel was questioning now, probably things his parents had been praying he would for many years. Saying a quick prayer of her own, she reached for the crystal goblet of water and took a sip before speaking. She knew she could speak her mind because Noel had encouraged her often enough to do so. "Noel, do you know that on many occasions Jesus declared Himself to be God?"

"God's Son," he corrected her.

"Yes, He said He was God's Son—one Person of the Trinity—but also that He's God."

His brows came together in a frown. "Where did He say that?"

She breathed out deeply and said a prayer that her father's teachings might come back to her. "Well, in the book of John it's recorded that He said, 'I and the Father are one.'"

"So what does that mean? To my way of thinking, it means He's God's Son—'I *and* the Father'—not God."

"Actually it means both. With those few words He's telling us He is both God's Son and God. Listen: 'I and the Father are one.' My own father"—she touched her chest as she referred to her baba—"once gave a lesson on the fact that the term *one* in Greek is neuter, meaning 'one thing,' not 'one person.' In other words, the two—Jesus the Son of God and God the Father—are one in essence or nature, but they are not identical persons."

He frowned. "So how many Gods are there?"

"One."

"But you just said"—he paused as he seemed to listen in his mind to exactly what she had said—"'one thing,' not 'one person.'"

"That's right. The verb 'are' used here indicates the Father and the Son are two persons. Distinct, but united in essence, will, and action. God is one entity but made up of three persons—the Father, the Son, and the Holy Spirit."

"The Trinity?" he asked.

She nodded, relieved he knew the concept and she didn't have to explain where the three persons suddenly seemed to come from.

"Okay, so Jesus is saying He is God here in this one place—"

"And He says it elsewhere."

"Where?"

Natalia drew in a deep breath and was grateful the waiter chose that moment to take their order. She was glad she'd told Noel to order for her—anything but liver—so she could get her thoughts together. She had relied so long on her father to guide people that it was a bit strange for her to be the one to do it now. Even with her years in New York, no one had ever asked her point-blank so many questions of such deep import. *Dear Lord,* she prayed silently, *please give me the words, the words my baba might use.*

And it was as if a voice answered her. "Just think about what your baba has taught people—you included—throughout the years. You have heard it often enough. Just think. And My Holy Spirit will guide you. Only trust."

The waiter left, and Noel sat back and looked at her. "You look pale. I'm sorry. I probably shouldn't have asked so many questions—"

"No." She held up her hand. She wouldn't let this opportunity pass. "Your asking me makes me very happy, Noel." She cupped her hands together on the edge of the table. "Believe me—it's like a gift. What would hurt is if you didn't want to know."

"I really do want to learn. It's strange. My parents have been trying to teach me things for years, but until now, until meeting you"—he held his hands out in a shrugging way—"I had little real interest. But you intrigue me. And the fact that you believe so strongly makes me want to know why. Does that make sense?"

Her heart seemed to pick up its tempo. "It makes perfect sense. I would want to know if the situation were reversed."

"You would?"

Emotion threatened to clog her throat. "You are becoming very special to me, Noel. But the fact that you don't know Jesus. . .would prove"—she had to swallow—"to be a stumbling block to our forming any lasting relationship. So your asking is hope—for me, for us—that we might"—she paused and, holding her hands together against her chin as if she were praying, ventured to finish with—"have a future together."

"Natalia," he whispered. Rather than her words scaring him away, as she feared they might, they seemed to have done just the opposite—draw them together. "I so badly want that with you. I have from—"

"Shh." She touched her finger to her lips. "Let's not say anything else yet. It's too soon."

He nodded, but she didn't think it was in agreement to its being too soon. "So you said there are other places where Jesus declared He's God, not just God's Son?" he asked.

She took a deep breath and let it out slowly. "If I had my Bible with me, I could show you."

"That's okay. Whatever you remember." He surprised her with his encouragement. But she shouldn't have been. Wasn't he always encouraging her to speak her thoughts, her beliefs? How could she do otherwise?

"Okay. Well, in the Gospel of John, the fourteenth chapter, Jesus said some of His most forceful words about His deity. In the sixth verse He said, 'I am the way and the truth and the life. No one comes to the Father except through me.'"

"I've heard that before. How does that prove His divinity?"

"Well, 'the way and the truth and the life' is a person. It's another name for Jesus."

"You mean those are all His names?"

She had forgotten about Noel's love of onomastics. "That's right. Well, some of His names anyway," she clarified. "He has a lot of them." *Ask him to study My names.* The thought popped into her head. *Yes, Lord,* she answered. *Yes!* "Noel, you love to learn about names, right?"

"Yes," he answered slowly.

"Why?"

"Why what?"

"Why do you like to study names?"

"Because they're important. In older times a name identified a person. Among other things, like telling where a person came from—as we said the other day concerning Saint Nicholas—they were used to reflect personal experience or express or influence one's character."

"Exactly!" she exclaimed, but then she lowered her voice when she saw people from a nearby table glance in her direction. "And nowhere is that truer than in Bible times, both the Old and New Testaments." She opened her hands before her. "So why don't you study the Lord's names? Maybe you'll come to know who He is through learning about His names."

Noel sat back, and she could tell from the way his dark brows nearly touched that the thought intrigued him. "Hmm, might not be a bad idea." He leaned forward. "As a matter of fact, it's a good one."

"You know, I've heard of people—lawyers even—who started out to prove to the world that Jesus was a fraud only to fall at His feet in worship of His divinity. And all because of their studying about Him."

"Natalia," he said, his voice husky, "I would be very happy if the same thing happened to me."

"Me, too, Noel." She blinked at the tears that had gathered in the corners of her eyes. *Dear God, please,* she implored. *Please give him Your understanding.*

"Do you remember any other places where Jesus says He's God?" he asked after a moment. Ducking her head down, she smiled. God seemed to be answering her prayer by Noel's persistence. He wanted to understand.

"Well, in the same chapter of John, He said, 'I am in the Father and the Father is in me.' That means—"

"That He and the Father are one in essence and undivided."

She was impressed. She thought it must be almost impossible for a person without a softened heart to grasp the concept even if that was precisely what it meant. "That's right."

He whistled softly. "That's quite a statement. Someone would either have to be a lunatic or, in truth, God to say such a thing."

"Precisely! That's why for you to say, as you did earlier, that you believe Jesus was a great man, a great politician, a great moral teacher, is an absurd declaration. On many occasions Jesus also declared Himself to be God."

A frown slashed across his face. "I see what you mean. The one crosses out the other, doesn't it?"

"How can a person be a great moral teacher if people don't believe all He said about Himself? Jesus said He was God. He said it so often the leaders and people of His day wanted to kill Him."

"And didn't they? Kill Him, I mean?"

"They didn't do anything to Him that He didn't allow, Noel." She lowered her voice. "When the time was right for Him, He allowed them to kill Him, after He had completed His ministry on earth. And with His resurrection He established His church, the rock upon which believers in Christ's redemptive work would flourish."

Noel repeated the words she had spoken a few minutes earlier: " 'I am the way and the truth and the life. No one comes to the Father except through me.' "

Natalia felt adrenaline flow through her body. To see Noel try to understand the Christian message was the most thrilling thing she had ever experienced. It was almost like watching a baby try to walk for the first time.

"That's right," she said. "And because of what Jesus did, if we choose to believe what He said about Himself—all His words, not just a select few—we will be resurrected as He was. We will be given brand-new bodies that will never perish, never get sick. And we will see loved ones who have gone on before us."

From the way his gaze intensified and his blue eyes darkened to look like a midnight sky, she felt that was something very important to him. For the first time she wondered if perhaps he had lost someone close to him to death's sting. "Best of all, though," she continued, "we will be in complete fellowship with God for eternity."

She looked at the happy people around them and smiled. No one could say there wasn't something special about how people acted at this time of the year in America. In Greece it happened both at Christmas and at Easter time. "I like to think of this season, when goodwill seems to abound more than at any other time, as a glimpse of what heaven will be like, though it will be far more wonderful." Reaching over to the tree to her right, she detached a beautiful, handcrafted Christmas-tree ball from it. Moving the golden globe around in her hand so that all the colored lights from the room were reflected in its shiny glass, she said, "I think heaven will be so much more superior, though, like the sun in the sky is to this Christmas-tree ball."

"I wonder if that's why I've always liked this season most of all. Because it is a bit like everyone's idea of heaven."

She replaced the ornament and, taking his hand, lightly squeezed it. "It could be, Noel."

"Natalia, I *want* to believe. I really wish I could say, 'Okay, I believe you.' It's just that—"

"Shh," she said. "I understand."

"You do?"

She sat back and took a sip of water before answering. "People come to know the Lord in different ways, Noel. It's possible your way will be through the study of His names. Even then I can't be sure." She replaced her glass and, resting her palms on the linen tablecloth, said, "But I feel it will happen."

"I *want* it to happen, Natalia. It's the only thing that has stood between my parents and me. I feel somehow it's true. I just have to know it is in here." He touched his heart.

She couldn't agree with his reasoning more. "That's the only way God wants a person, Noel. Many have the wrong idea about God. But, you know, I think one of the reasons God gave us the ability to read and study is to learn about Him. Perhaps it's laziness and the traditions of ancestry that keep people from opening the Bible, going to church, and learning."

"Funny, but that's something I often tell my students."

She could understand laziness but not the other. "Tradition has to do with their not learning?"

"You'd be surprised how many kids think an education should come to them by osmosis. Or because their parents learned or didn't learn and they did okay, so the kids think they shouldn't have to study, either. So many waste the marvelous education they have available to them at the school where I work."

Growing up in the village of Kastro, Natalia had never seen that. And the competition for entrance into her university had been so tough that most felt privileged to be there. "I suppose you're right." Then another thought came to her. "Noel, do you have a Bible?"

"Sure. I even have a study Bible with a concordance. My parents gave it to me a few Christmases ago." He shrugged his broad shoulders. "I haven't read more than the Christmas story." He twisted his head to the side. "Guess I should study it, huh?"

The waiter came then and placed their artistically designed plates of scrumptious-looking food before them.

"It's your choice, Noel," Natalia said. "Either it can stay dusty, or you can brush it off and use it, and"—she smiled brightly, trying to give him hope—"you can learn."

Chapter 6

Later that night in his brownstone town house on the Upper West Side—ironically directly across the park from Natalia's apartment on the Upper East Side—Noel wondered about the things they had discussed. After searching his bookshelf, he found his Bible in a back corner. It was in such a forgotten location that not even his competent housekeeper's vacuuming had managed to keep the dust off its upper edge. Noel blew on it and coughed as the particles swirled around his head.

He opened the book. It seemed so foreign to him. Something his parents should be reading. Not him.

Walking over to his four-poster bed, he sat on the thick burgundy quilt. He was careful to move the ecru afghan his mother had made for him to the side. He'd told Natalia he would try to learn about Christ by studying His names. But how could he study Jesus' names when he didn't even know more than a couple?

He sighed. That was a cop-out. But he was too tired to reason it out. He put the Bible on his night table.

He would start tomorrow. Maybe.

⌒⌒⊙⌒⌒

"I don't know, Prince," Natalia said to her dog about a half hour after Noel brought her back to her apartment. She sat on the thick white *flocate*, a rug from Greece made of sheep's wool, in front of the fireplace.

She glanced up at her dollhouse on the table to her side. Its windows were ablaze with the little electrical lights she had installed herself, and in honor of the season, wreaths hung on each door and a lighted tree stood in the bay window.

A gas fire burned in the apartment fireplace while Handel's *Messiah* played softly in the background. She was brushing the dog's shiny fur. It was a nightly winter ritual they both enjoyed. "I think Noel wants to learn, but the tradition of his not knowing and believing in his own brand of Christianity will be tough for him to break. And even though I suggested he start learning about Christ by studying His names, I doubt that's enough. I don't think he knows how to begin, Prince. I want to do more. But what?"

The dog turned his large head to her and nudged his nose against her hand. It was a comforting gesture he often gave her. Natalia put the brush down and, wrapping her arms around his back and chest, leaned her head against his clean fur and listened to the rhythmic *beat, beat, beat* of her beloved companion's heart. Steady and clear, it never failed to ease the worries of Natalia's own heart. "Dear Lord," Natalia prayed to her heavenly Father, "please show me what to do, how to help Noel."

The rest of their evening at the Tavern on the Green had progressed much the same, with him asking questions and her answering to the best of her ability. By the time dessert came, they had moved on in conversation to talk about his work, and he had told her about the student, Rachel, with whom he was particularly concerned.

Natalia's heart reached out to the confused teenager. It amazed her how people went from being little kids to acting as grown-ups and dating so quickly in modern American culture. Teenagers here seemed in a big rush to become adults; it was not that way in Kastro. Natalia might be nearly ten years older than Noel's student, but she knew she was far younger in terms of the dating game, for which Natalia was very grateful.

Until Noel, no other man had truly interested Natalia as a possible life mate.

Growing up in Kastro, her friend Dimitri had hoped for more with her than the brotherly love she had always felt toward him, but even he had finally admitted to their not having that "special something" that should exist between a man and a woman. She was thankful he had finally turned to Maria, who had loved him all her life. From Martha's reports on the romance, Natalia was almost certain she would soon hear wedding bells pealing for Dimitri and Maria.

But Natalia knew everything was different with Noel. For the first time, she felt that "special something" for a man, and she knew Noel felt it for her, too. If his beliefs could get into line with the precepts of Christianity Jesus had laid out, she would be very happy to spend her life with him.

As it was, she could hardly wait for their mutual birthday in three days' time. Their early morning date at Central Park sounded like something out of a dream to Natalia. She wished she could see him sooner, but both her work and school precluded it. Not only did she have an intense modeling shoot in Harlem, but she had her demanding portfolio class to prepare for over the next three days, too.

As her favorite part of *Messiah*—the choir singing Isaiah 9:6—started to play on the stereo, Natalia reached over for her remote control and turned it up. She could never hear those beautiful, prophetic words the prophet Isaiah penned several hundred years before Christ's birth without chills running up and down her spine.

"For unto us a child is born, unto us a son is given," she sang along with the choir and wished her voice could do it justice.

"And his name shall be called Wonderful, Counsellor, The mighty God, The everlasting Father, The Prince of Peace!"

Natalia stopped singing as the words moved over and around her, and the Spirit within seemed to guide her in how to help Noel start his study of Jesus' names.

Isaiah 9:6. Handel's wonderful oratorio *Messiah*.

Scrambling to her feet, she ran over and picked up the newspaper. She flipped to the entertainment section. She was certain she'd seen it listed there. A special performance with opera stars was to be given one night soon at Carnegie Hall. But it was sold-out. That didn't deter Natalia. Picking up her phone, she dialed her agent's number. If anybody had spare tickets, it would be David. She glanced at her watch. It was late, but then he hardly ever slept.

When his cheery voice answered, she knew she was correct in calling him, even at such a late hour. "David, it's Natalia. I need a favor. . . ."

After talking with him for scarcely thirty seconds, she hung up the phone, then picked up a pillow and hugged it to her chest. It was done. As she'd expected, David had tickets, which he'd happily offered to her. He usually bought extra tickets for special events for his clients. Also, as she had expected, they were the best seats in the house.

Natalia knew now how she could help Noel in his search. She would let the wonder of the Christmas season and the wondrous truths heralded so perfectly in Handel's monumental work speak to Noel's heart. With God's Holy Spirit going about His holy business and the music filling Noel's being, it had to be a combination that would work.

It just had to!

⁓⁓⁓⊱✦⊰⁓⁓

Three days later, while the earth still slept in predawn slumber, and Natalia did, too, the phone by her bed rang out shrilly.

Reaching over to her table, she fumbled around for the noisy contraption. "Happy birthday, sleepyhead!" Noel's voice sounded as cheery as a robin singing in the spring.

"Noel! Happy birthday to you, too!" she croaked and, pushing her hair away from her eyes, tried to focus on the numbers displayed on her clock. When she saw what time it was, she gasped. "Noel!"

"I know—I know. I said I'd come and get you at six. But something has changed."

Alarm filled her. "You won't be able to make it?" She had been looking forward to this morning with the same anticipation she normally reserved for Christmas and Easter.

"Not at all—just the opposite. We need to leave earlier than planned if we're going to get the full benefit of the wonderful gift to us today, the anniversary of the day of our births."

She shook her head, trying to wake up. "What are you talking about?"

"Put your feet on the floor, walk over to your window, and look out."

Carrying the phone with her, she did as he instructed. She pulled back the curtains and was instantly wide-awake because of what she saw. "Noel!"

" 'The moon on the breast of the new-fallen snow gave a luster of midday to objects below. . . ,' " he quoted. She recognized part of the poem *The Night before Christmas*.

"Oh, Noel," she whispered into the phone. Her eyes took in the beauty of the park covered in a glistening blanket of the purest white. "The first snow of the season. . ."

"And in time for our birthdays."

"Thank You, God." She whispered her thanks to the One she credited with this minor miracle.

"It is rather amazing, isn't it? Especially after our conversation the other night at the restaurant." But before she could reply, he quickly said, "Tell me how it looks from your window."

She didn't hesitate. "Like a pristine world that's at once familiar and yet so utterly unfamiliar. I can see the tops of the buildings across the park, but they look as if they are floating above the trees, not connected to the ground at all." She squinted. "Almost as if they aren't really there." She gazed at the trees directly across from her window and placed her fingertips against the windowpane, not minding that it was freezing. "And the branches that seemed so bare yesterday are now covered by garments made to fit each of them perfectly. Like haute couture."

Her voice lowered to a whisper. "And it's so quiet, Noel. Even the light from the park lamps glowing among the branches seems to be hushed." She gave a little laugh. "As if light can be described as hushed. But it is." She paused. "There is no noise, Noel. No noise from the city at all. Everything is hushed with a serenity, a beauty, a solitude that is at once so humbling I feel as if I'm in the most beautiful cathedral in the world, and it makes me want to fall to my knees and pray. And yet"—she took a deep breath—"it is so thrilling, too, that I want to shout for joy. Oh, Noel! I've never seen the city look so perfect!"

"Few have, Natalia," he responded softly, and she could hear the smile in his voice. "Can you and Prince be ready in twenty minutes, birthday girl?"

She glanced down at Prince. He lifted his head from his mat and cocked it to the side in question. "Prince already has his coat on. We'll be ready and waiting for you, birthday boy!"

Chapter 7

Exactly twenty minutes later, looking every inch the abominable snowman, Noel stood at the entrance to her building. He was covered from the top of his head to the toes of his boots in snow.

Natalia giggled at the sight of him.

When Roswell, the doorman, allowed him inside, an icy blast of air shot into the relative warmth of the hall. Without pausing, Noel reached out for her, picked her up, and twirled her around. She couldn't keep from squealing in delight.

"Happy birthday, birthday girl!" he said.

"Happy birthday, Noel," she returned softly in his ear. The smell of the snow on his shoulders was clean and fresh and cold.

She could have stayed in his arms forever, but Prince wasn't so certain about the situation. Noel as a "snowman" was not a familiar sight to him. When a soft growl emanated from the four-footed friend, Noel stopped twirling her and put her down.

"It's okay, Prince," she assured the dog. "He's a *friend*." He listened to her words, and she knew he understood the term *friend* from the way his head tilted to the side; but still it was obvious from his stance that he wasn't convinced. Only when Noel removed his glove and held out his hand so Prince could identify his scent did he relax. His tail started brushing back and forth in happiness over seeing Noel again, too.

Natalia praised him. "Good boy, Prince. Good boy."

"That beast takes his job seriously," Roswell said from behind them.

"That he does," Natalia agreed, then turned to Noel to introduce the two men. "Noel, I'd like for you to meet the best doorman in New York City, as well as a dear friend." Then to Roswell she said, "Noel is not only a very special person in my life—one you may let in whenever he comes calling—but it is his birthday today as well as my own."

"Oh!" the older man exclaimed. "That it is. The first day of December." He looked at Noel. "And it's your birthday, too?"

"For the last twenty-eight years," Noel replied.

"Isn't that fine? You share the same day. Very special. And Advent season, too." He pointed to the snow that was swirling around the streetlights like a dancing troupe of white moths. "And you have the first snow of the season as a gift sent straight from God. A happy birthday to you both!"

"Thank you, Roswell." Then pointing to the key the older man held with uncertainty within his large hand, Natalia said, "You'd better do as I say and go up to my apartment and rest. Your wife doesn't need a sick husband for Christmas this year, too."

Before Noel arrived, Natalia learned that Roswell had been unable to return home the previous night because of the snow, but his replacement had made it in. So she offered him the use of her apartment while she was gone. She could tell that reminding him of his illness the previous Christmas was all the encouragement the older man, who should have retired years ago, needed. He loved his wife dearly and never wanted to cause her distress.

"You are so right. Mary deserves me well this year," he said. "Thank you. I will take you up on your offer, Miss Natalia. But if I fall asleep, you must promise to wake me the minute you step through the door."

"I promise," she replied. She knew the older man had a code of ethics that would be disturbed at the thought of her being in the apartment while he slept. She understood it perfectly; it was how men in Kastro, her baba included, would feel.

"Now at least I know why it had to snow so hard last night," the older man continued as if a mystery had been solved. "The good Lord has blessed this, the anniversary of your birthdays. You two young people are about to enjoy New York as few do. My Mary and I once went to the park early in the morning on the first snowfall of the season. But that was when we were as young and strong as you," he said. A special gleam came into his eyes as he recalled that time. Then he continued. "Central Park will be more marvelous right now than you have ever seen it before." With a flourish, he opened the door so the three of them could go on their way. "Have a wonderful time! And a very, very happy birthday to both of you!"

Roswell's words about the park being "marvelous" were correct, Natalia thought. It was that and so much more.

They shuffled through half a foot of the fluffy crystals that had settled on the avenue's sidewalk and stuck out their tongues like children to catch the new flakes as they fell from the sky. Soon they walked through one of the park's many gates and found themselves in a winter wonderland of delight that took their breath away on puffs of joy.

Were they in the park she knew so well? Natalia wondered. They walked with hushed steps across terrain she at once recognized yet didn't. It was as if Someone were sprinkling a deep layer of powdered sugar over the park, reminding her of the Greek Christmas cookies *Kourabiedes.*

She'd gone out at the first snowfall in Kastro many times and trekked up to the castle with her father, Martha, and older brothers several mornings to watch the sun rise over the white world of rural wonder.

But this was different.

This was New York City.

They were standing in the middle of one of the biggest cities in the world, and yet it was as if no one else existed.

Noel, Prince, and she were alone in a landscape as unfamiliar with its white pearly covering as it was familiar in its layout. She looked around as if she'd never seen these surroundings before. *Perhaps I haven't,* she thought. *Not in this light.* The character of the land had been transformed, made more perfect somehow—cleaner, smoother, crisper. She could hardly believe she had been living above these same trees for six winters but had never seen them looking quite like this before.

"Oh, Noel," she whispered and watched her words float to him on a wisp of icy breath. "Have you ever seen anything more excellent?" she asked as her boots crunched through the snow. It felt like a crime to mar the smooth path with her footsteps, as if she were trampling on something holy.

They were standing so close they were almost touching. "It's as if the snow has created the perfect landscape," he said, pointing out different things to her. "Look at the branches of the trees, the earth, the little creek with its stones that look like powder puffs with the snow piled upon them." He swept his arm up to the tall, ghostlike buildings that rose above this "rural" scene. "Even those structures look as if they're an illusion and not places where thousands of people are sleeping." He paused. Natalia took her gaze off Central Park in the predawn, snow-painted day and turned to him. "But most of all," he said, glancing at her curiously, "it's as if the great Artist Himself has reached down from heaven and with a palette of pure white re-created the world exactly as He might wish it to be. Pure, without anything to mar it, nothing to blemish it."

Searching his eyes, she saw sincerity in their depths as well as a clear vibrancy that she thought must come to a person when he recognized Truth. She was almost certain God's creation was speaking to Noel's soul.

She spoke softly. " 'For since the creation of the world God's invisible qualities—his eternal power and divine nature—have been clearly seen, being understood from what has been made, so that men are without excuse.' "

"That's in the Bible?" Noel asked. She heard awe in his voice.

Slowly, reverently, she nodded. "The New Testament. The Book of Romans."

He took a deep breath, one that made his chest expand, before turning back to the vista of trees and fields and hills that stretched out before them like a silk painting. "Something about this moment, Natalia," he whispered, "makes me feel as if that and everything you said at the restaurant about Jesus being God couldn't be anything but real." He sighed. "It's as if all this were created for our eyes alone." He shrugged his shoulders. "But I know it wasn't. It's for any of the millions of people in this great city who make the choice to get up early and come out and see it. Come out and see how God, during the restful night, has painted this special spot of His earth."

He turned to her again, and his gaze searched her own, as if he were trying to pull knowledge, her knowledge, from her. Like at the restaurant, it was something she wished to give freely.

"Isn't that like what you said the other night about human beings' choice? This"—he waved his hand out but didn't remove his eyes from hers—"is here for all the people in this city. Not just us. It's perfect right now, the best I've ever seen it; and yet I've never bothered, never made the choice, to get up early enough to come and experience it."

"It's exactly like that, Noel." She paused and smiled. "Except God doesn't require us to lose sleep when we make the decision to believe Him."

"Natalia," he breathed out her name. Wrapping his gloved hand gently around the back of her head, he slowly, respectfully, leaned down and brushed his lips against hers.

She closed her eyes.

She didn't think anything she'd ever felt, not even the warmth of the Grecian sun upon her skin in the summertime, was better than that of Noel's lips on hers. It was right and good and brilliant in the way she had always thought the kiss from her "Prince Charming" should be. And she knew she would never want to join her lips with another man's again.

Seemingly of its own volition, her mouth moved against his, and the motion deepened into a dance like a ballet of warmth and love.

"Natalia," Noel whispered against her lips, "I love you. With all my heart I do."

"And I love you," she heard herself respond and knew, even as the declaration sent her pulse spinning, that it was true. She couldn't have kept the truth of it from him any more than she could have kept the snow from swirling like a perfect dream around their heads.

They stood with their foreheads and noses resting together, making a silhouette of a heart with their profiles—that complete heart that could only be made by a couple in love. It was a romantic picture often represented on greeting cards with a sunset behind the couple. Natalia liked the fact that they had a sunrise.

After a moment Noel took a half step back and smiled, that all-encompassing smile of a man content with his world. She knew her smile had to match his. Her pulse was beating so fast she was certain he could see it move in her temple. She was just beginning to wonder where they would go from here in their relationship when he suddenly grabbed hold of her hand and started running.

"Come on!"

"Where are we going?" she squealed out as their boots crunched over snow.

"Somewhere special," he said and laughed. "You'll see!"

Prince pranced all around them, first kicking up the snow, then plowing through it like a burrowing animal building a tunnel. Letting go of one another's hands, they reached down, scooped it up, and tossed it at one another as they frolicked down the cozy, lamplit path. But when they reached a certain point and were ready to drop from their merry-making, they sat for a moment. They were panting as hard as Prince.

When Noel removed his scarf from around his neck, she looked at him in question. "Are you hot?" Playing had warmed her but not enough to be without her scarf. Central Park this morning was as freezing as it was beautiful.

"I want you to see the place I'm taking you from a certain vantage point. And I don't want you to look at it until then. So I want to tie this around your eyes and guide you there."

She looked out over the park. Except for the tall buildings surrounding it in the distance, it looked like a wilderness. But she trusted Noel. This would make it more of an adventure and more fun. "Okay," she agreed and, turning slightly, let him fix it. "Umm, the scarf is warm from your neck." It felt good. Her skin was tingling from the cold bite of morning air. "But I want to hold Prince close to me. Prince!" she called to the dog, who immediately stopped his snowplowing and came to her side. She attached his lead and wrapped her arm around him. "What a good boy you are," she cooed into his ear.

"And me?" she heard Noel ask from behind her as he secured the knot that held the scarf. "Am I a good boy?"

She reached out her arms and brought his face close to hers. "No. You aren't a good boy. You're a good man."

"Hmm." She could hear the pleasure in his voice and was sure his head had tilted to the side, as Prince's often did. "I like that. Come on." He reached for her right hand. "Let me show you the most perfect spot in all of Central Park."

They walked quietly down the path.

Seeing the white world was one thing, but feeling it and hearing it now that her eyes were blindfolded was another thing altogether. The snow crunched beneath their feet while her nose lifted and sniffed. She loved the way snow smelled. It was a clean, fresh scent, the same whether it fell in the wilds of Kastro or in the middle of this city of concrete and steel. But never had it smelled or felt better than it did now. She had never walked through the snow with the man she loved. She hugged Noel's arm closer to her.

He chuckled, and she knew he was looking at her when he asked, "Are you scared?"

"No, I just like the excuse to hold you close."

He paused. And she knew a moment before it happened that his lips were going to touch hers. She sensed them coming close. "I like it, too." His voice was deep and husky. "But you don't ever need an excuse. That, dear Natalia, is something you are welcome to do for no reason at all."

Natalia placed her head on his shoulder. She hadn't known that to be so close to a man would feel so good. She was aware of the muscles beneath his coat as he moved, the way his breathing sounded, the soft scent of his aftershave, and even his height as he crunched along beside her. It made her feel warm and toasty and feminine.

"We're here," Noel said after a few minutes and situated her in a certain direction. "Stay like that," he said as he undid the scarf. "And keep your eyes closed until I tell you to open them."

"You're certainly full of orders," she teased.

"Not usually." She could hear the smile in his voice. "There—got it." As the scarf fell away, a sharp, sudden chill stung her skin, but she hardly noticed it as she concentrated on Noel and his surprise. "Not yet, not yet," he spoke slowly. She felt as if he were a cameraman telling her to hold a pose until the lighting was perfect.

"Now!"

She blinked her eyes.

"Oh!" She couldn't help the gasp that came from her at the vista before her. The little Gothic castle, Belvedere, which sat on a rocky outcropping to the west had always been one of her favorite places to visit—probably because of the castle in Kastro. But she had never seen it looking like this.

To the east and behind them, the dawning sun had found an opening in the clouds. It highlighted the castle with golden light even as snow still swirled around it like laughter falling from the sky. Natalia half expected to see a rainbow appear at any moment.

And one did!

Shafts of sunlight lit up the blanket of snow in the glen before the castle, and the snow sparkled like that of a rainbow in the sky.

"Oh, Noel," she breathed out. "It's enchanting."

"Perfect for our fairy-tale romance?" he asked.

Turning from the castle to him and with her heart thudding heavily in her chest, she wrapped her arms around his neck. "Absolutely perfect."

He reached out and tucked a strand of her hair that had come loose from her hat back under the fabric. "Happy birthday, Natalia."

"Happy birthday, Noel," she whispered back.

"It's been perfect."

"And it's not even seven thirty in the morning yet!"

He nodded toward a man walking from the opposite direction. "I'm glad we came out so early and got to see the castle like this. Now that the sun is coming up, the park will soon be filled with joggers, dog walkers, and even cross-country skiers out to practice their technique." Noel squinted toward the man who was cutting a wide arc so as not to disturb the pristine snowscape. "But I think that man is here to try to capture this moment forever for a book or a calendar."

Natalia looked at the man. The camera equipment he had strung across his shoulders told its own tale. "He might capture the scene," she agreed. "But one can only experience the moment, the enchantment, by coming here into God's world and feeling it. It is so special, so ethereal, so—"

"A part of God?"

That was exactly what it was. "Do you feel it, Noel?" she whispered. "Do you feel God speaking to your soul through this encounter with His creation?"

"I do, Natalia. It's something I feel here." He tapped his chest. "I know God exists. I just don't know Him as I'm realizing I should." He sighed. "I wanted to tell you today that I started my study of Jesus' names. But I didn't know where to begin, even though I've found my Bible and have it on my bedside table now."

"I thought that might happen," she said softly.

"You did?" His chin lifted a fraction of an inch in reaction to the news. "How?"

How can I explain it to him? she wondered. *"The way it actually is,"* a voice replied within her. So she did. "It's just something God put into my heart."

"Really?"

She nodded. "I think you'll soon see how He does that."

"Do you think so? I want that. I want what you have and my parents have. . . ."

"That want is God knocking on the door of your heart, Noel. 'Here I am!' Jesus says in His revelation to John. 'I stand at the door and knock. If anyone hears my voice and opens the door, I will come in and eat with him, and he with me.'" She gazed out over the beautiful park. "It's the way you hear His 'voice' here today."

"That's beautiful," Noel murmured. "I'm beginning to see the Bible is a very poetic book. Every line seems to contain music."

Her heart beat faster. "Do you like music, Noel?"

"Love it. Especially classical composers."

Of course he does, she thought, and smiling, she reached into her pocket and pulled out an envelope she had decorated with a length of candy-cane-colored yarn and gave it to him.

"Here," she said. "This is my birthday present to both of us."

"To *both* of us?" he countered, with an amused lift of his dark brow.

"They go together like the celebration of our birthdays does."

As the world slowly started filling with people—the joggers, dog walkers, and cross-country skiers Noel had anticipated—he removed the yarn from the envelope and pulled out two tickets. He turned them over, read them, then looked back at her. "Natalia. . .Handel's *Messiah*. . .I don't know what to say." So he didn't say anything else with words; rather, his face bent toward hers and touched his lips lightly to hers. She wrapped her arms around his neck and rested her head against his shoulder.

"I think you just 'said' everything perfectly, Noel," Natalia whispered.

Chapter 8

With the first sounds of the orchestra, Noel knew he was in for an experience he'd never had before.

Normally he was a visual person. But this performance of Handel's *Messiah* was already making him use his sense of hearing unlike any time before. And that sense seemed to demand that another one was to be employed, different from the five physical senses he was so accustomed to relying upon.

As the notes filled the air around them, Noel glanced over at Natalia.

Her eyes were closed. Her lips were moving as if in prayer.

It was something Noel almost felt like doing.

When the tenor sang the first word, "Comfort," Noel smiled to himself. What a poignant way to start a work titled *Messiah*. Nearly everyone needed comfort in some form or another.

Noel sat back in his seat. But as the music combined with the wonderful words, he found himself leaning forward. The Word of God, which he hadn't known how to start reading a few nights earlier, was proclaimed beautifully by some of the world's most highly trained voices. What struck Noel, too, was that they sung only the words written in the Bible.

Nothing else.

And those words did things to Noel.

They stirred him in a way he had never been moved before.

When the choir sang, "And the glory of the LORD shall be revealed," it made Noel want to stand up and sing with them. A thrill went through him. It was as if a chorus of angels were on stage glorifying the Lord.

He didn't understand what they meant by "all flesh shall see together." But he wanted to find out.

The bass singer came in with the words, "He will shake the heavens and the earth," like thunder giving an exclamation to what had been sung. "The Lord, whom ye seek, shall suddenly come to his temple" was like a wake-up call to Noel. Something like tears formed at the back of Noel's eyes when the bass singer asked, "But who may abide the day of his coming? and who shall stand when he appeareth?" Noel wondered if he would be able to. He suspected that, as he was now, he would neither abide nor stand when the "He" they referred to, Jesus the Christ, the Messiah, should appear.

197

"He is like a refiner's fire" sounded ominous to Noel.

"But who may abide the day of his coming?" the singer repeated the question, and Noel, like a child, wanted to shout out that he would. He would stand! But to do so he thought he had to learn how first, like a child learning to stand on his feet for the first time.

The choir came in singing, so sweet and calming, like a rest after the bass's ominous question. But what was this angelic-type choir saying? Noel leaned forward to catch the words. "He shall purify."

Whom shall he purify?

"The sons of Levi," the choir seemed to answer him, "offer unto the Lord an offering in righteousness." Noel wondered who the sons of Levi were and what they had to do with him. It sounded like a glorious hope to him, though.

But wait! What was the alto proclaiming now?

"Shall call his name"—His *name*—"Emmanuel: God with us."

Emmanuel. God with us! She sang it only once, and for a moment Noel wondered if he had heard correctly.

He glanced over at Natalia. Her face was glowing with a light that had nothing to do with that found in the dimly lit auditorium. It was a light shining from her face.

"Behold your God!" the alto sang. "The glory of the Lord is risen upon thee." And Noel knew that was exactly what was upon Natalia. The glory of the Lord had risen upon her face. Noel looked around him. On so many faces—Caucasian faces, African faces, Oriental faces, Indian faces. And yet they all looked the same, almost as if light was upon them, and it in turn was shining out from their souls!

The choir sang the same words, "The glory of the Lord is risen upon thee!" It was joyously sung, and Noel's heart thumped to its glorious beat.

Then the bass sang again. A soulful sound of sadness. Noel listened to his words and realized he sounded so sad because the words he recited were sad. "For, behold, darkness shall cover the earth, and gross darkness the people."

Gross darkness? Was that how he was? Was he living in gross darkness by not getting to know God the way his parents knew Him? He glanced over at the woman he loved. The way Natalia knew Him? He looked at others seated around him. The way so many people in this auditorium apparently knew Him?

The music changed again, and Noel felt expectation in the melody, though still sad, that now diffused throughout the room. "The Lord shall arise upon thee. Upon thee, and his glory shall be seen upon thee! The people that walked in darkness have seen a great light! Have seen a great light!"

Yes! Noel sang within himself.

Light!

That was it!

The people around me—Natalia, my parents—they have seen a great light, a light Noel was beginning to realize he wanted to see.

"And they that dwell in the land of the shadow of death"—Noel had heard his parents refer to that phrase often—"upon them hath the light shined."

With shock Noel realized the Light referred to must be Christ, the Messiah, the Son of God, the Light of the World! He knew that was one of Jesus' names. People didn't have to be an expert on the names of Jesus to know that one.

The choir lifted up their many voices in song again with a part of this work Noel had heard many times but had never listened to before. It permeated every corner of the hall.

"For unto us a child is born, unto us a son is given: and the government shall be upon his shoulder, and his name shall be called Wonderful! Counsellor! The mighty God! The everlasting Father! The Prince of Peace!"

Noel felt goose bumps break out over him.

Names!

Christ's glorious names filled the hall.

Names of the Man—the God—Natalia and his parents wanted him to understand. Amazing names. Descriptive names. Significant names. Names for him to study and help him know the character of the Man, the God, who meant so much to so many people he loved.

He glanced over at Natalia.

She turned her gold-crowned head to him and reached for his hand. "His names," she mouthed. He knew then why she had bought these tickets for them.

Nodding, he smiled. And chills of wonder, of hope, flowed through him because he knew the only barrier between this woman and him having the life together they both so desired was his faith. He was beginning to think that along with his lack of faith—though he had always believed in God—was a lack of knowledge about the nature of God, about who God is. He could read and study, and he had ignored probably the most important book ever given to the world. The Bible. The Word of God. The Word these beautiful voices were proclaiming a small portion of so magnificently and mightily.

The choir sang in allegro. As before, Noel wished he could sing with them. His soul yearned to sing the declaration, the praise, the acknowledgment.

"Wonderful!"

"Counsellor!"

"The mighty God!"

"The everlasting Father!"

"The Prince of Peace!"

Something inside Noel jumped to the fullness of the resounding sound. He wanted to hear it over and over again.

And yet, even when it ended, which seemed too soon, he found he couldn't be sad. For the pastoral symphony that followed the chorus was like a gentle caress on the excitement of his soul. One that gave him the chance to rest and listen to the remainder of the story.

Noel now had several names to study: Emmanuel, Light, Wonderful, Counsellor, the Mighty God, the Everlasting Father, and the Prince of Peace. All names that described the person of Christ.

He glanced over at Natalia, who was dressed in a sequined gown of soft, royal blue that winked and blinked with her movement. She turned and looked at him. He knew he didn't have to tell her how he felt. She could see it.

And he was certain it pleased her.

When the soprano started singing again, they turned their gazes toward the front, but their hands remained intertwined as the words flowed around them and through them.

"There were shepherds abiding in the field, keeping watch over their flock by night." Noel knew this. It was the Christmas story. "And the angel said unto them: Fear not: for, behold, I bring you good tidings of great joy, which shall be to all people. For unto you is born this day in the city of David a Saviour, which is Christ the Lord."

Savior! Christ the Lord! More names! Noel's mind reverberated with the belief that was supplanting the disbelief within him.

"Glory to God in the highest!" the female members of the choir sang. "And peace on earth!" the men returned. When they started singing in a round, exhilaration filled Noel. "Good will to men!" The many voices, both male and female in turn, overflowed into the room with a joyful noise that seemed to seep into every pore of Noel's body. He felt himself break out into a light sweat, an amazing thing considering the snow that covered the ground outside.

"Rejoice greatly," the soprano sang, sounding like bells chiming, like Natalia's laughter. "Behold, thy King cometh unto thee. . .speak peace unto the heathen."

Heathen. The word stuck in Noel's brain. For the first time he realized belief in God was not enough. Belief in a Supreme Being made him little more than a heathen. There was much, much more to belief than believing in God.

The words *"Yes, belief in God's redemptive work through His Son"* marched through his brain. He wasn't sure when he had heard them, but he thought they were probably some of the many bits of knowledge he'd picked up from his parents through the years. Before this evening they were just words; now they were so much more. Now they were truth. A truth Noel was coming to accept.

"Then shall the eyes of the blind be opened, and the ears of the deaf unstopped; then shall the lame man leap as an hart, and the tongue of the dumb sing." That was what Noel was feeling at this moment, as if he were seeing and hearing and his heart was jumping in knowledge of God's greatness for the first time. And like a man who had never had the use of his tongue, he wanted to speak it out and sing it out, too! The thought went through his mind that he had been dumb for years because he hadn't bothered to proclaim truth, the truth of God.

But what was the alto saying now? What truth was coming forth from the notes of her mouth? "He shall feed his flock like a shepherd: he shall gather the lambs with his arm." The imagery was beautiful.

And now the soprano sang, "He will give you rest!" Noel wanted that. The choir was singing the best sermon he'd ever heard. The music was moving his heart in a direction he'd long yearned to travel but, at the same time, had long fought to go.

"And ye shall find rest unto your souls." Noel recognized that rest for his soul was something he'd never had. Oh, he didn't have any major problems—he wasn't an unhappy person at all—but there had always been an unease, as if he were missing out on something in his life, something great.

The choir came in now, singing words that sounded like a springtime dance, reminding Noel of butterflies flittering around daisies. "His yoke is easy; his burden is light!" And he smiled. Almost laughed.

"Behold the Lamb of God," the choir now sang in largo. Noel knew he was hearing another name of Christ's, one he'd heard as a child in Sunday school. *Jesus, the Lamb of God.* He recalled the lambs in his Sunday school coloring books, lambs with Jesus in the picture.

The next words filled Noel with sadness. "He is despised and rejected of men: a man of sorrows, and acquainted with grief." But when Noel realized he was one of those men who had rejected Him by simply ignoring Him, by not believing all His words, only a select few, the grief and sorrow and conviction that filled him were nearly overwhelming. The section was so long and slow he thought Handel had probably written it like that for a reason: to give each man and woman time to let the full import of the words sink into their souls.

They sunk deeply into Noel's soul. Very deeply.

Sadness filled him as he realized by his lack of interest in God's Son he had, in fact, rejected Him. He hadn't taken the time to get acquainted with Him or, as Natalia had pointed out that night at the restaurant, to learn all about what Jesus said while He was on earth as a man.

Here he was, a counselor, always advising parents and children to get to know one another. God had given everything for people to do that, but Noel had spent the first twenty-eight years of his life practically ignoring Him.

As the sad, convicting words filled the glamorous hall, Noel remembered his father telling him once, "God has given us everything we need to know Him. He has given His Son, His Holy Spirit, His Church, His Word to hold in our hands and read, and the testimonies of men and women from the earliest days of Christianity to the present as witnesses and examples of true belief. All that plus the gift of volition. God, the Builder and Designer of the infinite universe and the smallest leaf on a tree, has left it up to us whether we puny, sinful humans want to know Him or not."

Noel felt a keen sense of conviction upon remembering his father's words and hearing the current ones sung in the auditorium.

He suspected that George Frideric Handel must have loved God very much to write such inspirational combinations of sounds to go to the arrangement of biblical words.

That was Noel's thought when the music stopped and the lights in the auditorium flicked on for intermission.

As people all around them rose from their seats, Noel and Natalia continued to sit in silence.

Finally, when he could speak, he admitted to her, "I am speechless." He squeezed her hand gently and whispered, "It is so wonderful, so convicting." He touched his free hand to his heart. "I have so much learning to do, so many decisions to make."

"Only one decision, dear Noel," she corrected him quietly.

He nodded slowly. "Yes," he agreed. "Only one."

After the intermission the music continued to wash over Noel. When the choir in magnificent allegro broke into singing, "Hallelujah, for the Lord God omnipotent reigneth," Noel felt something sacred was happening.

He thought he'd been moved earlier when the choir had sung, "For unto us a son is given." But it was nothing compared to the emotions that filled him on hearing the voices of the men and women when they praised God in this refrain. He was not even surprised when everyone—like a giant wave—stood up for the words filling the airwaves of the room. The question would have been, how could anyone not stand in the face of such a magnificent sound of praise? It was the most heavenly sound Noel had ever heard, and he imagined angels taking part in the singing. It was too beautiful to belong only in the human realm.

As the glorious combination of words and music rose higher and higher, a majestic crescendo proclaiming glory to the one and only God of heaven and earth and to the Messiah, the Christ, who is One and the same God, Noel's unlearned heart cried out to believe in Jesus as God's one and only Son.

To the "King of Kings, and Lord of Lords!"

For these were not words composed by men but glorious truths God had given men of things to come. At that moment as the choir sang, "The kingdoms of this world are become the kingdoms of our Lord, and of his Christ," Noel knew it was the truth. "He shall reign for ever and ever! He shall reign for ever and ever! King of Kings, and Lord of Lords!" Noel knew this to be true, too, and he wanted to live under that rule. He didn't want to be left behind or not allowed to be present when the King of the universe reigned, simply because he hadn't taken the time to know God's Son now—while he had the chance.

The choir ended, again too soon for Noel, and the people sat down to experience the rest of the prophetic and inspired words Handel had set to music. Noel resolved not to tell Natalia about his decision yet. It was something personal between him and God and too new for him to share even with the woman he loved. He still wanted to learn about the names of Christ. Then he'd tell her he finally understood that Jesus is the Christ, the Messiah.

He looked over at her as the chorus of amens was sung, and he smiled.

It was enough to know that because of his decision, his new and as yet unrevealed one, he and this most wonderful of women now had the prospect of a future together. Because second only to his new relationship with the Lord Jesus Christ—which he somehow knew must always hold first place in his heart, in the hearts of all humans—was his relationship with this woman. Next to God and his parents, she was becoming the most important person in his life.

And he prayed, yes, prayed, as she turned her sparkling blue eyes upon him, that they would be granted a long and lovely life together.

Chapter 9

It was snowing again—bright, fanciful flakes that flittered and danced around their heads—when they walked out the doors of the concert hall.

"It's wonderful!" Natalia laughed and held out her ungloved hand to the crystals. Surprisingly, for something so cold, they only seemed to add warmth to the ambience of the night. She felt Noel's arm go around her shoulder, and she gladly snuggled against his side.

"This has been one of the most wonderful nights of my life, if not the very best," he said.

Natalia didn't think she'd ever been happier. "Me, too, Noel. I'm so glad you enjoyed the oratorio."

"*Enjoyed* is not the word to describe what I was feeling in there," he admitted, and she said a silent prayer of thanks for his declaration. She thought it had moved him. She only wondered to what extent.

He guided her over to the line of people waiting for a taxi. He paused and looked up at the swirling snow falling from the nighttime sky. She waited without comment, allowing him the time to speak his thoughts, as he had so often allowed her. "It was almost as if. . .the door to my heart were somehow opened, as if those wonderful words somehow drew me near to God. I don't know. Here's yet another metaphor for you." He looked at her. "I felt almost as if God were embracing my soul as my father used to hug me when I was a little boy. Does that make any sense to you?"

"Perfect sense," she replied, watching their frosted breaths mingle together and wrap around their heads like a happy cloud. "Jesus said, 'But I, when I am lifted up from the earth, will draw all men to myself.' "

"That's it!" Noel exclaimed softly. "I feel as if I want to learn all about Him and that I can believe everything Jesus told us when He was here on earth, even that He is God."

She didn't say a word but wrapped her arms around him and squeezed the man she loved close to her. Their heavy wool coats were between them, but it didn't matter.

Wool was just material.

What had been between them before—Noel's lack of belief in Jesus as God's Son and as God—was something she could not have taken away herself. Only the anointing and urging of the Holy Spirit could do that. And faith.

The change she sensed in Noel was as pure and wonderful and refreshing as the snow that danced around them and settled upon their heads, their shoulders, the ground upon which they stood, as well as the lighted building tops that soared into the sky above the city of New York.

To say it was a magical moment would be to take something away from God. There was no magic involved. This was a God-sent moment, one of those special instances when eternity and time seem to make everything still and sweet and as similar to heaven as people on earth can imagine. It was a passionate moment but one that had nothing to do with the passions of the body, rather, everything to do with the passions of the spirits, the souls, of two of God's children. For although Noel didn't say it, Natalia was almost certain he had made the most important decision a person could ever make, the one about Jesus, during the soaring sounds proclaiming His prophecies, life, work, death, resurrection, and future reign. Natalia was certain Noel was God's child by conscious choice now.

The verse "No one who denies the Son has the Father; whoever acknowledges the Son has the Father also" went through Natalia's head. Somehow she could sense the change in Noel; his spirit was no longer denying the Son His glorious place in the Godhead.

As much as she might want to, Natalia wouldn't press Noel for any more information right now. Neither God, her heavenly Father, nor her earthly father, her baba—the wisest person she knew in the ways of God—ever pressed a person; rather, they both waited until the person was ready on his or her own to speak.

Natalia would wait. It was enough to feel this change, this heaven-sent change in the man she loved.

He turned and, with his nose almost touching her nose, said, "This feeling of belonging, of being drawn to something so right and good as what those words in there"—he pointed to the concert hall—"proclaimed, is like coming home after a very long absence. Almost as if I'd been lost but now am found."

"Dear Noel," she said, reaching up and touching the snowflakes that made his dark hair shine as if with stardust, "do you know you repeated some famous words in the Bible almost verbatim?"

He tilted his head to the side, and she knew he was waiting for her to continue.

"In the story about the prodigal son—"

"Wait," he interrupted her. "I know this story. From Sunday school when I was a little guy. It's about a man who takes his half of his father's inheritance and squanders it on immoral living. When he runs out and sees the pigs where he's working are eating better than he is, he realizes he must go home and apologize to his father."

She nodded. "And when he returned, his father said, 'Let's have a feast and celebrate. For this son of mine was dead and is alive again; he was lost and is found.'"

Noel clicked his cheek thoughtfully. "That's another good metaphor to describe how I felt while listening to that music—how I still feel. I feel as though I was dead before, as if the life I led before this evening was almost totally different from the one I want to lead now."

If their turn for a taxi hadn't arrived then, Natalia wasn't so sure she could have kept from asking Noel what had happened to him during the concert, about the decision he'd made. But as she bent down and scooted into the warm cab, taking care not to muss her gown—an arrAs original—she knew it had to be God's timing. Noel would tell her everything at the right moment.

But for now he had told her enough.

The man she loved was coming to know God. That's all she needed to see.

Noel instructed the driver to take them to the General Electric Building where he'd made reservations for them at the Rainbow Room. Reaching into his breast pocket he asked, "Do you mind if I turn on my phone? I'm concerned about Rachel, that student I told you about."

"Of course. Switch it on."

"I think she's at an intersection in her life now. She can either go the right way or— " He let out a deep sigh and smiled. "She should hear the *Messiah*."

"Do you know how many people's lives have been touched by it during the last 250 years?" she asked.

Noel looked at her in surprise. "That long? I didn't realize Handel lived 250 years ago."

Enjoying history as much as she did, Natalia studied things she particularly liked, so she knew a little about the composer. "Handel was born in Germany in the late 1600s and moved to England in the early 1700s. Ludwig van Beethoven said he was the greatest composer to have ever lived."

Noel's brows rose. "Beethoven said that?"

She nodded. "And most people considered Beethoven the greatest."

"I think if anybody should know, he would."

She smiled. "When Handel composed *Messiah*, he was fifty-seven years old. But just before its success, he was depressed, plagued by rheumatism that didn't allow him to sleep, and afraid to answer his door for fear he'd be hauled off to debtors' prison."

He looked at her curiously. "Are you serious?"

"It's sad, but so many people who have given the world such mighty works or used their talents in one way or another have had very difficult lives. But I've always thought it might be something like the apostle Paul and his thorn. It made these very gifted people realize His 'grace *is* sufficient' for them, and it was the thorns that made people strive for new heights. Heights in writing, like people living under persecution, and in music like Handel's *Messiah*. God's grace was sufficient for them."

"I've never thought about it like that."

"I read that while composing *Messiah* Handel was said to have seen visions about the subjects he was writing, especially during the 'Hallelujah Chorus.'"

Noel whistled. "Now that's something I can believe."

"You can?"

"It was"—he held his hands out before him—"as if angels were singing."

She nodded thoughtfully. "The amazing thing, though, is that it portrays not angels, but humans who have come out of the Great Tribulation and are proclaiming the 'Lord God Almighty reigns' and He is the 'King of Kings and Lord of Lords.' It's a prophecy for us today, who wait for Christ's second coming, as much as what was written hundreds of years before the birth of Christ in Isaiah, 'For to us a child is born, to us a son is given,' was for those at the time of Christ's first coming."

He looked at her with the same admiration in his eyes she remembered seeing in her father's eyes for her mother. It made Natalia feel warm and cherished and adored. "You amaze me. How do you know all this?"

She shrugged. "My parents and family have tried to live by the teachings of the Church, by the Word of God—"

"I have had that, too, though," he interrupted her. She knew it was true. His parents were believers.

"Yes, but I didn't fight what my parents taught me by their wise counsel as you have fought yours, Noel." When his gaze seemed to glaze over, she felt heat rise to her face as embarrassment flooded her. She took his hand in hers. "I'm so sorry, Noel. That sounded so pompous, so self-righteous. . . ."

"No." He reached up and touched her cheek. "It sounded only like honesty to me. I don't mind that."

"I don't want to hurt you."

"Don't you think I know that?"

"I just want you—"

"To 'get it'?" he asked.

"Do you?" she whispered. They were in a taxi zipping through midtown Manhattan, but the world seemed to stand still as she waited for his answer. "Has everything changed tonight?" she asked in spite of her best intentions not to press him. She was almost certain of it, though. Her spirit could sense it.

In less than a heartbeat he covered the few inches that separated them. And just before his lips touched hers, he whispered, "My darling, I think you might count on it. . . ."

The kisses they had shared in Central Park had been special because they had been the first ones and given with a declaration of love. But this kiss was like a merging of souls going in the same direction. Natalia wished the moment to last forever.

But the trill of Noel's phone in his pocket would not allow it.

He pulled away and reached for the phone. "I sure hope that's a wrong number."

Glancing at the name on the screen, Noel frowned. "It's Rachel—that girl I told you about." He put the phone to his ear. "Rachel—" Natalia watched him raise his hand. "Wait a minute. Start from the beginning." It was clear the girl had a problem. More than the usual. Natalia leaned forward and sent up a prayer on the girl's behalf—and on Noel's that he would know what to do. "Yes, of course I can come." He gave Natalia a questioning look, as if to ask for permission.

"Of course," she whispered. Their plans to go to the Rainbow Room could wait for another night.

"Okay, where are you?" He glanced at his watch. "Sit tight. I'll be there in ten minutes." Ending the call, he turned to Natalia.

"I'm so sorry—"

Natalia stopped him. "Don't be. Is there anything I can do?"

A sheepish grin crossed his face. "I was counting on your asking. Would you mind coming with me? I make it a practice never to meet students away from the school alone. In this situation I would normally ask another counselor to accompany me, but I don't want to waste time. The girl sounded very frightened, and I'm afraid—"

"You don't need to explain," Natalia said, smiling. "I would be very happy to come."

"You're amazing, you know that?"

It thrilled her that he thought so. Reaching up, she placed her hand against his cheek. "Since you're the one who's going to the rescue of a disturbed teenager, I think *you're* the amazing one."

⁂

Not ten minutes later they walked into the diner where Rachel sat slouched in the last booth in the corner. And Noel learned that Natalia was even more remarkable than he had thought.

Rachel looked up then and saw them approaching the table. The look of astonishment and pleasure that crossed her face on seeing Natalia was so out of character for the normally ill-tempered teenager that Noel thought she was a different girl. She seemed to change before him. She went from having eyes that resembled mud on a stormy day to ones that looked as bright as a travel brochure of Bali might.

"Oh! Oh! Oh!" The girl scrambled to her feet and stood before Natalia with barely constrained glee. "Mr. Sheffield, how did you know? How did you know?"

"Hello, Rachel," he heard Natalia say and was further surprised by the way she was unflustered by the girl's reaction to her, almost as if she were used to it.

"Audrey Shepherd!" the girl exclaimed. "You're my favorite! My absolutely favorite model! I want to be just like you. Oh, I know I don't look like you. I've got dark hair, and you're very blond. But, oh, I would love to be a model like you someday!"

"*A model like you someday?*" Noel heard the girl gush and knew she couldn't be referring to someone who modeled nurses' uniforms. That wasn't Rachel's style. The girl wore only the latest, trendiest, and most expensive fashions on the market. For Rachel to react this way, Natalia had to do much more than "a bit of modeling." And much more than nurses' uniforms.

The way she carried herself, her expensive address, taking six years to complete the program at the university, her clothes. Yes, now that he thought about it, he should have known. There were other things, too. The way people often looked at her, almost as if they knew her. It hadn't registered that they were looking at her that way because she was famous rather than because of her lovely appearance.

But he couldn't be angry about her omission.

He understood it.

Hadn't he done the same thing by not telling her about his book that was now six weeks on the *New York Times* best-seller list?

Rachel stopped speaking and pressed her hand against her stomach. "I don't think that will ever happen now." She turned to Noel. "Mr. Sheffield, I think I might be pregnant."

Noel's eyes widened. He couldn't help it. He'd never had to deal with this area of counseling before. The female counselors at school took these cases. He'd known he might eventually confront it, but did it have to happen now, with Natalia present?

"Now calm down, Rachel," he said and motioned for the girl to be seated. "Are you sure you are? Have you seen a doctor?" He and Natalia sat down also. He was glad Natalia chose to sit next to the girl. In her gown of sequined jewels, which even the fluorescent lights in the diner caught flashing from between the folds of her cashmere coat, she might have looked out of place in the diner. But she didn't. She looked as wonderful as she had at the concert.

"No," Rachel mumbled, sounding like a six-year-old. He brought his attention back to the girl, rather than where he would prefer it to be, on Natalia.

"Then how can you be sure?" he heard himself ask.

"I'm not," she shot back sullenly. "But I'm late. And I'm never late." Her voice was hard, until she seemed to remember who was sitting next to her. She looked at Natalia and asked with a sugary sweet voice, "What have you done when you've found yourself in this situation, Audrey?"

Audrey? Noel frowned, then remembered. The girl had said Natalia's professional name. Audrey something—Audrey Shepherd. She must have chosen *Shepherd* for *German shepherd.*

He watched as Natalia took a breath. He wanted to hear the answer as much as the girl. Even though he knew Natalia, in light of her profession, he wondered how she *had* coped.

"Well, first of all, my real name is Natalia, and you may call me that," she said to the girl.

"Thanks." The girl looked down but not fast enough for Noel to miss seeing she was pleased by the honor.

"Second," Natalia continued, "I have *never* found myself in that situation, Rachel, because I have never been married."

"You've *never*—I mean—I didn't think models thought they had to be married before. . ."

Natalia smiled wryly. "Some, no, but as with all groups of people and professions, not all. Many are wise about their relationships. A few are not, and they are the ones by whom people judge all others."

"Wow! So you're—I mean—since you haven't been married before—that means you're a. . . ?" She let the last word trail off, but it was obvious what she was asking. Natalia smiled at the girl before she turned back to Noel.

"That's right," she responded. Noel was glad she answered, even if he hadn't asked—and would never have asked—such a thing.

He had known all along she was pure; he had sensed it the first time they spoke at the tree. But the way he felt upon hearing her words was as if she were handing him a gift.

"Wow!" Rachel repeated her earlier declaration. "That's amazing."

Natalia looked back at her. "Not really. What is, though, is that young men and women would do things that could forever alter their lives, either through illness or"—she paused and spoke more softly—"through bringing a child into the world."

Rachel moaned. "What am I going to do?"

"Have you talked to your parents about this?" Natalia asked.

"No way!" the girl exclaimed. "They'd tell me it was my fault, and they'd probably want me to get rid of it." Natalia cringed at her words. Noel could tell that Rachel saw her cringe, too, because she was quick to assure Natalia. "But I couldn't. That's one thing I couldn't do. Even if being pregnant disfigured my body so I could never be a model, I would never do that."

"I'm glad." Natalia took the girl's hand in her own. "If you are pregnant, God already knows your child and wouldn't want you to hurt him or her."

Rachel looked up at her with what Noel could only describe as awe. "Do you believe in God, too?"

Natalia smiled and nodded her head. "Absolutely."

"If you believe in Him, He must be real. Would you teach me about Him? I think I need Him," the girl admitted.

Noel couldn't believe what he was hearing, but he knew it was true.

And he understood it.

It was simple really—Natalia's life was a witness to this young and impressionable girl.

He heard Natalia respond with an offer of friendship. "I would love to teach you about God." When a big smile spread across Rachel's face, Noel felt that, for the first time since meeting the troubled young student, she would be okay.

Where his counseling and talking had failed, Natalia and God would not. The witness of God in Natalia's life would turn the girl around.

Of that Noel was almost certain.

And it made him glad.

Chapter 10

Two evenings later Noel stood gazing into the miniature house—a perfect, doll-sized recreation of the home in which he had been raised. Even the tree—the one that now graced Rockefeller Center—was included in the model. The Sheffield family would never forget it, especially Noel, because it had brought him and Natalia together.

All the miniature lights were lit in the dollhouse, giving it the warm, cozy feeling of Christmas. His mother had made tiny wreaths for every window as identical wreaths hung in the windows of the actual house.

Noel leaned down and peered into the replica of the comfortable den in which his parents and he now sat. A tree—similar to the one that stood in the corner beside the hearth—was there. Even dolls that represented his parents, him, and the two German shepherds that were lounging by the side of the fireplace were in their proper place. A miniature woman with soft platinum hair was sitting on her sofa. A man with wings of distinguished silver around his temples was ensconced on his recliner watching television. And a young man in slacks and a polo shirt stood looking at the replica of the dollhouse, which was even represented in the dollhouse itself.

Noel breathed out a sigh and turned to his mother. "I don't know how you did this. It's fantastic."

She laughed, a light tinkling sound that reminded him of Natalia. It wasn't identical, just flavored with the same pitch of happy humor. He suspected it probably had to do with his mother's and Natalia's faith. "To be truthful, I'm rather amazed I did it, too."

"It was a labor of love," his father declared and gazed over at his wife. His face had that special look he reserved for the woman he loved.

His mother glanced around the room. "This home has given me much joy since the day I came to live here. I guess the model is a small way of returning some of the love I've felt within these walls since you two welcomed me and made me a part of it and a part of your lives." She placed the afghan she was crocheting to the side and reached out for the older Sheffield's hand, which was never too far away. "As your wife." She looked at Noel and sent him that wonderful look of a mother's love he had so craved when she and his father had first married and one he still treasured seeing. "And as your mother."

"It's Noel and I who have been blessed by your being here with us," the elder Sheffield was quick to respond, and Noel nodded. "I don't know what we men would have done without you, Jennifer. We would have rattled around this big, old house and driven one another nuts." His eyes twinkled in humor.

All three smiled.

They all knew they'd gotten along much better than most fathers and sons could ever hope to.

After a moment Jennifer Sheffield turned to Noel. "What I'd like to know is why the special interest in my dollhouses? You've made the rounds of all three of them this evening."

Noel grinned. He should have known she'd notice. "Because, Mother, I've met a young woman who shares your love of the same hobby." He'd told Natalia at the café on Thanksgiving that he was going to tell his parents about her, but he hadn't. His feelings for her had been too new for him to share with someone else then.

Jennifer clapped her hands together, then reached for the remote control. She turned the volume down on the Christmas special until only the faint sounds of carols filled the room. "Is she the reason for that special gleam I've seen shining in your eyes lately?"

"What gleam?" Noel was prepared to tell his parents about Natalia now. But he was going to enjoy watching their curiosity run rampant first.

"As if you have a secret, but one that is too wonderful for you to believe might be true," she replied without pause.

Noel laughed. "You know me too well, Mother. But it gets even better, especially from your standpoint."

"What do you mean?"

"She's a Christian. I mean a Christian like you and Dad are Christians."

"Hallelujah!" his mother sang out. Noel wasn't surprised when he saw tears fill her eyes. She was an emotional woman. "That's an answer to our prayers for you, son."

Noel's father reached out and placed his hand on his wife's arm. "Now wait a minute, dear," he said with the steadiness of his legal profession. "Noel didn't say he was marrying her."

"But I'd like to." Noel didn't want to leave any doubt in their minds concerning his intentions toward Natalia. He had the pleasure of seeing shock, unlike any other time before, cover his distinguished father's face. He chuckled. "Dad, I think I've finally gotten the last word." That was a joke between them. Quincy Sheffield was a brilliant man, and it was a rare moment when someone said anything that could close his mouth.

The older man, whose appearance was a good indication of how Noel would look in thirty years, chuckled back. "Most definitely," he conceded before his face turned serious. "But if she is, as you say, a Christian, who holds Christ as the center of her life, then I'm sorry, son, but—" He paused and looked at his wife.

Her joy seemed to wilt like a flower left without water on a hot summer day, though with a nod she encouraged him to continue.

"What, Dad?"

His father turned back to him. "I'm sorry, son, but I doubt she'll marry you without your being one, as well."

Noel walked over to the dogs and, kneeling down, patted the head of the older German shepherd. Laddie responded with his happy-go-lucky doggie grin and his tail tapping happily against the floor. Noel smiled at the dog, then stood and faced his parents.

"She took me to see the oratorio *Messiah*, by George Handel, the other night. To say I was emotionally moved would be a gross understatement." He paused and looked up toward the star that twinkled on top of the tree. It made him remember the star it signified. The star that heralded the birth of God's Son on earth, the star that told the world that a whole new volume in the world's story was starting.

He looked back at his parents and smiled. "What I experienced," he said, "was something almost life changing. No." He corrected himself. "It *was* life changing. During that performance, I realized I wanted all the promises of those amazing, prophetic words. I wanted to believe everything. And you know what, Mom?" He looked at his mother, then turned to his father. "Dad? I do. I might not know much, but I believe. I believe with all my heart that it's true—that Jesus is God's Son, that He is God."

"Hallelujah!" his father's voice sang out.

Noel saw tears come into his father's eyes, but he wasn't concerned. They weren't the sad ones of the only other time he had seen them in his strong father's eyes—the day they had buried the wonderful woman who had given Noel life. These tears were happy ones. And with his limited understanding, Noel could grasp why his father felt so moved that tears would fill his eyes now.

"Tell us about her," his mother whispered, dabbing at the corners of her own eyes. "Tell us about this woman who we've been praying for many years would enter your life."

"You've been praying for her?"

She nodded. "We suspected that only a woman you loved would be able to lead you to Christ."

"That's why we've been, well, leaving you alone," his father added.

"We always hoped that such a woman would come into your life and share her faith with you," his mother explained.

"That's the truth," his father agreed.

"Natalia is wonderful and—" He stopped speaking when he saw his parents' faces turn ashen. "What?"

"*Natalia* is the girl's name?" His father reached over and took his wife's hand.

The atmosphere in the room changed from joy to apprehension. Noel felt the muscles along his shoulders tense and forced himself to relax.

"Natalia Pappas—"

His mother gasped, and Noel stopped speaking. She seemed to wilt against his father while her slender white hands covered her face. His father cradled her against him.

Noel was at a loss. Then his mother lowered her hands from her face, and he saw a rapturous expression coloring her features.

"Has she. . .by any chance. . .mentioned to you whether she was adopted?" she asked.

Noel frowned. "Adopted?" An uneasy feeling ran through him. "No. She's never said anything to me about being adopted. The only thing I know is that she loves her family very much. Her father is a priest—"

His mother's gaze searched his face. "A Greek Orthodox priest? From Greece?"

"How—?" He held out his hands in question.

For a moment it was almost as if he weren't there. His mother turned to his father, and Noel heard the older man say, "All in God's timing, my dear. It's all in His hands."

She nodded, and her soft, platinum blond curls bobbed silkily against her shoulders. "That's what you've always told me, my dear, wise husband. And it seems you have been correct."

Ordinarily Noel wouldn't interrupt such a moment between his parents, but he had to know what they were talking about. It concerned Natalia. "What's 'all in God's timing'? What's 'in His hands'?"

The older Sheffield narrowed his eyes, silently asking his wife for permission to tell. She nodded slightly, and his father turned to him. "You recall we told you that before your adoptive mother and I met, she gave birth to a little girl. What we haven't told you is that she deserted the little girl in a bus station in a small city in Greece on Christmas Eve nearly twenty-five years ago. We've been praying for the little girl every day since we met. A Greek Orthodox priest and his wife adopted her. She was born on December 1, the same day as you, my son, three years later. That little girl, Natalia Pappas, grew into a young woman who models under the name Audrey Shepherd."

Except for the clock striking the hour of ten and the soft breathing of the dogs, silence reigned after his father stopped speaking.

Noel knew he was staring at his parents.

His mouth hung open.

But he couldn't help it.

Never in his wildest imaginings would he have considered such an amazing story as his father had just described. The fact that his adoptive mother had given up a baby, when she herself had been little more than a child, wasn't news to him. His parents had never made a secret of the life she had led before she met his father and, more important, before she met the Lord Jesus Christ. Both occurred at about the same time.

No.

What astonished Noel was that the little girl his father referred to, and the woman he had thought about since the first time he had seen her looking at the Rockefeller Center Christmas tree three years earlier, were one and the same. Natalia!

He smiled at his parents to ease their minds in case they were wondering how he felt. And a thought kept playing through his head: The Supreme Being had been orchestrating the events of their lives as much as the conductor had orchestrated the *Messiah*.

"Hallelujah!" Noel finally managed to whoop out. He reached for his parents and engulfed them in a gigantic hug.

The three stood together and laughed with relief, joy, and thanksgiving. Then, in the twinkling lights of the Christmas tree, with the soft strains of carols playing inside and the snow falling gently to the earth outside, they cried happy tears.

~~~~~~

Natalia looked away from the slow-burning fire to the Charles X clock on the mantel in the Howards' living room as it struck ten o'clock. She sighed. The sound of Christmas carols from the special the Howards were watching on TV and the softly falling snow lit by streetlights outside the huge window gave a cozy feeling to the night. It was a moment of family comfort, one Natalia treasured to have found in New York City. Kneeling down, she rubbed her fingers absently across Prince's velvety ears. The dog lifted his head, seemed to smile, yawned, then lowered his head to the carpet. Prince liked a warm place to lie down and a thick carpet beneath him.

Only one thing would make this moment more perfect, Natalia thought. And that would be to have Noel by her side. She sighed as she looked out the window again. That wouldn't happen for a few days. She had to go to Maine on a modeling shoot early the next morning and wouldn't return until the following week.

"You really like him, don't you?" Janet Howard asked from her place on the sofa.

Natalia looked over at her. "Who? Prince? Of course I do."

"Oh, darling girl! Don't you think I know you well enough to know when you sigh over your dog and when you sigh over the man you—love?" she asked.

Her husband chuckled softly. "She has a point," Jasper Howard agreed with his wife, tilting his recliner forward.

Natalia knew what that meant. He was ready for a serious discussion.

Her gaze went back and forth between the two people she loved as much as she did her own family. She knew they wouldn't be put off. She was glad. She wanted to tell them. "I do. . .love. . .him," she admitted. She let the smile in her soul shine out and laughed. "I do!"

Janet clapped her hands together. "It's like a fairy-tale romance."

"It is!" How many times had she herself used that expression? "Made even more wonderful because the prince of my dreams wants to welcome the Prince of Peace into his life."

"Oh, darling girl!" Janet exclaimed.

"That's wonderful," Jasper said.

"I was going to ask about that," Janet admitted. "But I trusted your judgment."

"Just pray for him," Natalia implored. "We haven't really had a chance to discuss it, but I'm certain he made a decision the other night at the *Messiah*." His answer, after she had asked him if everything had changed, *"My darling, I think you might count on it,"* had been going through her head like a glorious refrain for the last two days. "He hasn't said anything specifically," she continued, "but I don't think he will until his decision to believe can be justified by his knowledge of who Jesus is."

"Many people need to let their intellect catch up with their belief, especially when it's new and profound," Jasper pointed out. "Don't worry."

"Oh, I'm not," Natalia said, smiling. "I just can't wait for these next few days to pass so we can see each other again. He loves onomastics, the study of names, so I challenged him to discover who Jesus is by studying His names and—"

"That's it!" Janet exclaimed and jumped up, startling both Natalia and Prince. Prince jumped up suddenly, too, and stood at canine attention while Natalia gathered the pillows that Janet's sudden movement had scattered all over the floor.

"What's 'it'?" Natalia asked, looking at Jasper. His eyes crinkled at their corners. He was used to his wife's sudden movements.

"That's where I've seen him before!" Janet clicked her fingers together. "I *knew* he looked familiar."

Natalia frowned as she instructed Prince to lie back down. "What are you talking about?"

But Janet only waved at her as she dashed over to the bookshelf. "Here it is!"

She pulled a book off the shelf. *"What's in a Name?* by Noel Sheffield."

"What?" She reached for the book Janet passed to her. She turned to the back jacket and gasped when Noel's smiling face stared up at her. Rubbing her fingertips over the beloved features, she whispered, "Noel."

" 'Loves onomastics, the study of names,' " Janet repeated. "Darling girl, he's one of the foremost authorities on the meanings of names. Not only that, but this book has been on the *New York Times* best-seller list for weeks. And I think he's had other successful books, as well."

"He never said a word."

"Does that bother you?"

Does it? Natalia wondered. She shook her head. "No, it really doesn't. I didn't tell him much about my modeling career. Probably for the same reason he didn't tell me about this. He didn't want me to judge him by it any more than I wanted him to judge me by my modeling." She held up the book. "Is it good?"

"Wonderful," Janet answered. "I bought it in case one of our sons ever decides to make us grandparents. I'll have it ready for them to search out names."

"Umm." Natalia wasn't thinking about Janet's words nor the Howards' married-but-childless sons. She had turned to the beginning of the book Noel had written. It was his thoughts, his words. That made it important to her.

"Why don't you read it?" Janet suggested.

"I think I've already started," she admitted wryly.

Janet and Jasper exchanged amused and knowing glances, then settled back and watched the Christmas special.

"Happy reading," Janet said.

Natalia gladly lowered her gaze to the book.

But out of the corner of her eye, she saw Jasper wiggle his left ring finger with his wedding band glistening around it, then motion to her. Janet nodded and smiled. Natalia knew they thought wedding bells might soon be pealing for her.

Natalia hoped they were right.

~≈⊙⊙⊙≈~

"I still don't see how you could have kept from going to her and telling her every-thing once you found out she was living here in New York," Noel said for about the tenth time to his parents.

The Christmas special had ended long ago, although, after his parents' rev-elations, no one had paid any attention to it. The three were sitting around the fireplace talking. They had a lot to talk about.

"I wanted to," his mother admitted. "Oh, how I yearned to. But after much prayer, I didn't think it was right. Maybe if I'd put her in an orphanage, I would have gone to her. But, Noel, I had deserted her in a bus station and in a foreign country. It would be difficult for anyone to forgive another person for that, especially the person who had given you life." She shrugged her shoulders, a gesture not unlike one Natalia often made. "It goes against even the most primitive laws of how a mother is to act toward her child."

"Mom." Noel squeezed his mother's hand. "I know Natalia. She will forgive you. In fact, I'm sure she already has without knowing you."

"But, from what you've said, she hasn't even mentioned she was adopted."

"That's true. But I don't think it's a reflection on you as much as a reflection on how much she loves the family that raised her. She loves them dearly."

"I am so glad for that, so thankful," his mother said. Noel could feel the truth of that declaration. It radiated from her.

"Please let me handle introducing the two of you," he said.

His mother beamed at him. "Would you do that for me?"

"Of course, Mom. What do you think? I have no choice really. I love both of you. I now know something that concerns Natalia in a very personal way." He paused. "Other than that, would you understand me if I said it's something I feel led to do?"

His parents nodded.

"God's leading," his father said, his voice filled with emotion. "It's a wonderful gift God gives a believer in His Son, Jesus, by the Holy Spirit."

Noel nodded. "I have a lot to consider while Natalia is away on her photo shoot." He had already told them she would be in Maine for the next several days. "Not only do I have to consider how I will tell her what you've told me about her parentage, but I have an assignment from Natalia, too. She's charged me with learning about Jesus through studying His names."

His mother gasped. "Oh!" She hopped up from her chair like a surprised cat and dashed over to the tree. Kneeling down, she rummaged through the gaily wrapped presents until she found one. Coming back to Noel, she held it against her chest for a moment. "I ordered this several weeks ago. It arrived today." She handed it to him. "Please open it now."

Noel glanced over at his father, who shrugged his shoulders.

He gave his attention to the Christmas gift paper that covered the book. The Christ child was depicted on it. He rubbed his fingers over the golden image. *"For he shall reign for ever and ever!"* He didn't think he would ever look at manger scenes again without the music from the *Messiah* going through his head and thrilling his soul. He removed the paper carefully. It was his turn to gasp when the title of the book was revealed to him.

The Names of Jesus.

He looked up at his mother and didn't try to hide the tears that had gathered in his eyes. "You. . .and your. . .daughter—" He paused. "You and Natalia are so much alike, Mother." He looked down at the book again. "What a coincidence."

"Son." His father rested his large hand upon Noel's shoulder. "You will soon find that with God"—the older man cleared his throat—"there are no coincidences."

Noel nodded. That was something he was fast learning.

Chapter 11

Natalia arrived at her apartment at 10:00 p.m. the following Tuesday night. The phone rang one minute later.

She answered it, and Noel's voice greeted her. "I'm glad you're back in town," he said.

She took off her coat, flipped on the tree-lights switch with her toe, and plopped down on the sofa to gaze out at the flurries of snow that danced among the trees in the park across the avenue.

"Me, too," she responded. "I missed you."

"Not nearly as much as I missed you."

She pushed her hair behind her ear and smiled into the phone. "That's debatable."

"Well, how about we debate it tomorrow?"

"When and where?"

"Central Park. Noon. By the statue of Balto."

She laughed. "I think you've set me up."

"That's only the start. I have a very special Christmas surprise for you."

"But it's not Christmas yet." They still had a week to go before that most wonderful day.

"Ah, dear Natalia, I'm beginning to think that Christmas, for those who believe, is an event to be celebrated every day."

"Noel—" she whispered then hesitated. "Does this mean—?"

"Tomorrow," he interrupted her. "You told me the first day we spoke that you believe in something similar to fairy tales, what you called 'God tales.'"

The delight she felt at his words made her weak. She was glad she was sitting.

"Well, let me organize tomorrow. Trust me and"—he paused and his voice lowered—"trust God. It will be a day you won't ever forget. I promise you. A day that will change your life, mine, and probably several others' forever."

She squeezed her eyes shut. She was sure he was going to tell her he believed—in that personal, life-changing way all people on earth are called to do—and then he was going to ask her to marry him. She knew what her answer would be. It was a fairy-tale romance, made perfect because her prince had finally discovered why he liked the Christmas season so much and let the Spirit of

God—not just the Christmas spirit—work in his heart.

"Okay. Tomorrow. Noon. By the statue of Balto."

"Good night, my love," he whispered.

After they hung up she looked down at her dog. Why did Noel want to meet by the statue of Balto? It had been built to commemorate the brave dog that had led the last relay team of sled dogs over treacherous terrain in 1925 to bring antitoxin to the stricken people of Nome, Alaska.

She shrugged her shoulders. It might be a strange place for a man to propose marriage, but she didn't care.

Kneeling, she rubbed her hand through the soft fur of her tired dog. Prince loved traveling. But after being transported first by helicopter, then plane, then car, he was ready to rest. "Sleep well, Prince Charming, my boy!" Natalia sang out. "For tomorrow we're going to see Prince Charming, the man of my dreams!"

After being away from each other the last four days, seeing Noel waiting for her by the statue made her feel warm and special all over. That such a man was waiting for her was indeed a fairy tale come true. Snow from the previous night still spotted the ground and clung to Balto's curly tail. She detached Prince's lead from his collar and watched her beloved canine friend dart over to Noel.

Jealous, Natalia ran, too. Noel lifted her off her feet and twirled her around in his arms. Crystal flakes of snow flittered around them as Noel's lips touched hers. Even though the day was cold, Noel's lips were warm and welcoming.

The kiss ended much too soon for Natalia. But sensing he would soon speak words that would enable them to have a life together, she stood back and looked up at him, leaving her hands locked around his neck.

"I've missed you, and I have so much to tell you," he said, his blue eyes vibrant with a clear light that seemed to originate in his soul.

"Tell! Tell!" She could hardly wait.

"You aren't curious, are you?" he asked and laughed, a deep, rich sound that reverberated around the bare trees, filling the air with joy and her with even more warmth.

"I am!" she admitted and laughed, too. She felt as free and happy as she had when she was a child. "I want to know what happened to you the night of the performance of the *Messiah*. What did you mean when you told me I might count on everything having changed for you? And I want to know why you believe Christmas should be celebrated every day." She let go of him and climbed onto the rocky outcropping on which Balto's statue stood. She wrapped her arms around the statue as she had her own dog so many times. "And I want to know why you wanted to meet here." She stood up straight. "I love this spot and what this statue represents, canines who have given so much in service to humans."

She looked at Prince, who was playing in the snow in the clearing to their right. He had served her on a daily basis by offering her unconditional protection, companionship, and love. "But I'm intrigued as to why you chose it. I know you have a good reason."

He stepped up beside her and laid his hand on the ears of the stone dog, worn smooth by children rubbing them for more than seventy-five years. Natalia had often thought people were trying to resurrect the dog, rubbing it like Aladdin's magic lamp, yearning for the same goodness. But if they had only known much more remarkable goodness and truth could be theirs simply by believing in the redemptive work of Jesus, the Man who was resurrected.

That thought brought all others to a stop.

She guessed, even before Noel spoke, that that was the reason he'd wanted to meet here.

He must have seen the resemblance between Balto and his teammates' heroic drive in the dead of an Alaskan winter to save the people of Nome and that of the much greater redemptive work of the Lord Jesus Christ who came to earth to save humanity with the medicine He brought for sin: His own death and resurrection.

"Did you know it took twenty mushers and that many teams of dogs to carry antitoxin to the people of Nome, Alaska, who were dying from diphtheria?" Noel began speaking without preamble. He patted the dog, who had been about the same size as Prince. "And that Balto was the lead dog who got them through, using his God-instilled instincts in the blizzard during those last crucial miles into town?"

She nodded. She knew but didn't want to interrupt what Noel was saying.

"I've known it, too, since I was a little boy." He indicated the shiny ears. "I helped polish them by touching them so much when I was a boy. Whenever I could I came here." He sighed. "Like who Santa Claus represented, I loved this dog and what he symbolized." He jumped down and pointed to the plaque in front of the dog.

" 'Dedicated to the indomitable spirit of the sled dogs that relayed antitoxin six hundred miles over rough ice across treacherous waters through arctic blizzards from Nenana to the relief of stricken Nome in the winter of 1925.' "

He was silent for a moment; it seemed to Natalia as if the angels in God's heaven waited with her for Noel's next words.

"The night of the performance I finally started to realize that a rescue mission was exactly what Jesus did for the town of earth by coming to us as a baby. It was something much grander than what God's creatures and the men who drove them did for the town of Nome all those years ago."

"Hallelujah," she whispered.

In the space between the snowflakes falling around them, she was certain she heard angels sing out the same word of praise.

"I used to think that if Jesus had been anything more than a good man or a prophet, He would have taken the misery and pain out of the world. But I finally realized that His coming to earth as fully man and fully God, more than two thousand years ago, was just part of the story. A climax in the story of God's redemption of mankind, to be sure," he added, "but only part of the story."

He gazed into her eyes deeply, and Natalia saw the love of a man for a woman—for her—shining out of his eyes. It was a love she readily recognized because she had seen it often between people she cared a great deal about: her parents, Stavros and Allie, her married brothers and sister, and Janet and Jasper. But to see it directed toward her, a true love—not one of infatuation or for the beauty of her outward self—was an experience that nearly took her breath away. His next words did that, however, for what he said had maturity to it, an unusual understanding for a new believer.

"I finally realized we are only partway through the Book—that the patriarchs, judges, kings, and prophets of the Old Testament, the birth of Christ, even the church, are part of the story. They are climaxes in the novel, but not *the* climax. That climax will be when Christ returns. That will be the 'happily ever after' of the story. Sickness and pain will be no more, and the heavenly choir of angels as well as believers will sing, 'He will reign for ever and ever!' " His eyes widened in joy. "And you know what, Natalia? Both of our voices will now be part of that choir."

"Oh, Noel!" She pulled him to her. "I am so glad. So glad."

"Wait. There's more."

"What else could there be?"

"You'd be surprised," he replied in a way that perplexed her. "First, did you know there are more than a hundred names for Jesus? That's because not one name, or even three, can contain all of who He is."

"Noel! How did you start studying them? Using the *Messiah* as a guide?"

He moved over to the rock outcropping, sat down, and pulled her onto his lap. She felt cozy and wonderful and cherished, everything a woman sitting on a man's lap on a cold December day could want to feel. "Well, now, here's something amazing."

"Something else, you mean?"

He rubbed his nose against hers. "So many great things have happened the last few days."

"Tell me," she prompted. "I promise not to interrupt."

He laughed. "Is that possible?"

She laughed, too.

"Well, when I told my mother about your having advised me to learn about Jesus by studying His names, she gave me a gift she had oddly bought for me this Christmas—a book called *The Names of Jesus*. I thought at first it was a coincidence."

Natalia was about to tell him she didn't believe in coincidences when he seemed to pull the words right out of her mouth.

"Of course, I now understand that nothing is happenstance. God had your advice and my mother's gift coordinated."

"Coordinated. Hmm. I like that." She had never heard it put that way, but she thought it perfect. She could see that Noel would add fantastic thoughts to a believer's efforts to understand God. Life with him would be an adventure.

She paused. If he ever offered to share his life with her.

But when would she hear the words from his mouth?

He leaned toward her until his forehead came down to touch hers, then moved his head back a fraction of an inch. "I still have more to tell you, things I've—recently—learned." He hesitated over the words, and she felt fingers of apprehension move up her spine.

"What things?" She thought he was referring to his career as a writer. But he said things he'd recently learned.

He glanced at his watch. "I'll tell you on our way."

"On our way?" She looked at him, even more puzzled now. "On our way where?"

"To meet my parents."

Chapter 12

Arm in arm, talking and laughing the entire way, Noel and Natalia walked across the park to the garage close to Noel's brownstone town house where he kept his cars: a Jeep and a red sports car. Since the weather was inclement and Prince was with them, he pulled out his Jeep. After a while of Noel maneuvering the Jeep across Manhattan's busy streets, Natalia turned to him with a grin. "So when were you going to tell me about your publishing success?"

He grimaced. "How did you—?" he started to ask, then stopped. "Actually I was going to tell you about it today." He glanced over at her as they drove onto the George Washington Bridge. "Are you upset?"

She offered him her hand, and he took it. "I hardly have the right, Noel, since I didn't tell you the extent of my modeling career, did I?"

"Being a writer isn't who I am—"

"Any more than being a model is who I am."

"Exactly."

She was glad they agreed.

"It's a wonderful book," she said as they crossed over the state line and into New Jersey.

The corners of his mouth turned up in surprise. "You've read it?"

"Uh-huh, a few nights ago. Janet Howard had a copy. That's how I found out."

"I think the next one will deal with the names of Jesus found in the *Messiah*."

"Noel!" she exclaimed. "That's wonderful."

"No," he corrected her. "*He's* wonderful."

She certainly wouldn't deny that. "But on a human level you are, too, my love. You are a wonderful counselor. Look at what you've done for Rachel."

"Me?" His glance left the road for a second to meet her steady and open gaze. "Don't you mean *you*?" he corrected.

"I haven't done much," she demurred. "Just talked to her by phone a couple of times."

"'Haven't done—'? Natalia, giving the girl your personal number and allowing her to call you is—"

"Just trying to be a good steward with what God has given me, Noel," she finished for him. "If the profession in which I make my livelihood can help

226

somebody simply by its nature and by the way I live my life within it"—she shrugged—"then that gives my work real worth."

"Well, the example of your life has turned Rachel's around. She doesn't wear skimpy clothes to school anymore, she's cleaned up her speech, and I don't think she'll lead a wild life any longer. Her parents don't think so, either, and they couldn't be happier." He drew in a deep and satisfied breath. "They were so concerned about her and didn't know what else to do. That was why they asked me to help her as much as I could in my capacity as her high school counselor. It's so rewarding to see that family drawing together."

"I'm glad for them. And of course you must know she's not pregnant. It was a false alarm."

"But one that God used in His plan for her."

Natalia let her gaze roam over his profile. He had chiseled male features that appeared to be cast in bronze as he concentrated on both the road and his thoughts. But she knew what warmth was there, that of a man who cared about a young high school student, about his own family, about her, and now about the things of God. The degree of his understanding amazed her. Seldom did a person come to believe and learn so quickly. But he had been around parents who believed all his life. That had to have made a difference. "You're absolutely correct," she agreed after a moment and turned her gaze forward as the Jeep ate up the miles. She felt such contentment. Her world seemed to be falling into shape perfectly.

"If only *my* mother had had a role model like you to talk to when she was young," he continued after several minutes of companionable silence. "She might not have become wild."

Her glance slid to his face again. "Your mother was wild?" She knew from earlier conversations that his mother was a strong Christian.

"Well," he replied, "my biological mother was a very strong Christian. My father has laughingly told me in the past that she probably never did anything wrong in her entire life."

"Your '*biological*—'?" Her eyes widened. "You mean the woman you refer to as your mother is your *stepmother*?"

"No, she's actually my mother, too," he stated. "She adopted me legally when I was nine."

"I had no idea." But as with his being a writer and her, a high-fashion model, she wondered what else they might have neglected to share with one another. She had never told him she had been adopted, either, but only because the subject had never come up. And even though her father had encouraged her to be open to finding her biological mother, she had given the situation to God on her first day back in New York from Kastro, and she really didn't think about it. At some point she knew she must tell Noel. But right now he was telling her about himself. And there was no way she was going to interrupt that.

"It isn't something that's in my mind. I remember my biological mother with much fondness and love, but Jennifer *is* my mother."

"I can understand that." *Could she ever!*

"I imagine you can," he said evenly.

She looked at him sharply. Did he know about her having been adopted? Or was he simply referring to her being able to empathize with him? But as the car covered the miles across New Jersey on the way to his parents' home, he continued to talk about his family, so she decided to let it go. She had plenty of time to tell her story.

"My natural mother died when I was six. Remember the conversation we had about Santa Claus at the café the day of the parade?"

Surprise flickered across her face. Santa Claus? What did Santa have to do with this? "Yes."

"Well, I finally figured out a few days ago that one reason I was so negative about letting my parents teach me about God was because I was angry about the death of both my mother and, as strange as it might sound, Santa. Finding out Santa wasn't real, he didn't live at the North Pole, and he didn't fly through the sky with a sleigh full of toys every Christmas Eve was very traumatic for me. It was almost as if he had died, too."

Her heart went out to the hurting little boy Noel had been. In Kastro, little Jeannie Andreas had been wounded in a similar way by her mother's desertion of her. But at least Natalia had been able to hug the little girl close to her and do fun things with her to try to ease her pain. Then Jeannie's new mother, Allie, had come into her life and filled it with the mother's love the little girl had so craved. But Natalia couldn't do anything for the boy Noel had been. She could only be thankful for the new mother who had adopted him—the boy who had grown into the man she loved—when he was nine.

"That's one of the dangers associated with the secular myth about Santa." Her answer was soft but firm in its psychological affirmation of what had happened to him. "What concerns many is that kids are taught to believe in Santa and his powers, rather than being taught that the true Santa Claus was a Christian, who believed in Christ with his whole heart. Children are given a tarnished and untrue image of Christ to believe in, as a sort of Christmas spirit, rather than the real God. All these things would, I think, make that dear old clergyman Nicholas from the Greek world long ago very sad."

"You know, Natalia, I can remember crying out to both Jesus and Santa to save my mother." There was a steely quality to his voice as he thought back. She reached over and placed her hand over his. Instinctively his hand grasped hers.

"When neither did, I decided they were both fake."

"But, Noel, just because Jesus didn't save your mother—"

His hand tightened on hers before he let go of it to take the exit ramp off the interstate. "I know that now. But try getting that into the head of an angry six-year-old who just lost the most important person in his life, as well as the Santa he thought could give him his wish for Christmas—his mother's health." He turned into a gated roadway and pulled the car to the side. He cut the engine, and peace enveloped the car. Only the sound of Prince's breathing could be heard in the hushed world that surrounded them.

Natalia gazed out on one of the most beautiful wintertime vistas she'd ever seen. A Currier and Ives print couldn't have painted the snow-covered world any better. Rolling hills, distant barns, stately homes, the bare branches of trees silhouetted against the horizon, and a few brave conifers holding out their needle-clothed arms, filled the white world of earth and sky. It was still and wearing its snow mantle, perfect and pure.

Noel turned to her and took her hand in his again. His fingers were warm, firm, sure. "I know I'll see my mother again because of what God, born as a baby, did for us all. And in Jennifer I was given a wonderful second mother."

"From how you've talked about her, it's obvious you love her very much."

"I do. She's a very special woman."

Natalia thought that now was the time to tell him about her own background. It wasn't important to her because she had always considered *Mamma* and Baba her very own parents, but she knew she had to tell Noel. Whether she wanted it or not, her biological parentage was part of who she was. She leaned toward him and placed her hand on his cheek.

"That's something I can understand, Noel." She was silent for a moment. "You see, I was adopted, too, by both of my parents. I never knew my natural mother or father."

When he didn't respond, by word or even by a flicker of emotion in his face, she felt apprehension slicing through her again.

Finally, he admitted in a low and husky tone, "I know you were adopted, Natalia."

Then fear ran in to keep her apprehension company.

That was the last thing she'd expected. Her hand fell from his face, and she sat back. *How did he know?* "You know? Did the Howards tell you?" That would be the only way he could have known. Not even the tabloids had that information.

"No. My father told me a few days ago."

"Your father?" Now panic ran through her system like a fire alarm might a building.

"Until then I had no idea of what I'm about to tell you."

"Noel." She hugged herself, rubbing her hands against her arms. She could feel the goose bumps rising beneath her cashmere sweater. "You're scaring me. How could your father have known?" Then suspicion filled her. "Have you had me investigated?" She nearly choked on the word and reached for Prince who, picking up on her fear, had stuck his head into the front of the Jeep. His great head, with its mouth full of teeth, was between her and Noel. She was unexpectedly glad she had her trusted canine companion with her.

Dear Lord! Have I been wrong to trust Noel? To love him? She cried out to God, the One who would always be with her and could always be counted upon.

"No," a voice spoke calmingly within her. *"Everything is in My control. Just trust."*

"I know this seems strange to you—"

"Strange!" Her voice shook. "Noel, how do you know—?"

"I know because Jennifer, the woman my father married when I was nine, was a very wild teenager. More so than Rachel. And, unlike Rachel, when my adoptive mother was sixteen, she did become pregnant. Then, when she was seventeen, she was backpacking around Greece with her boyfriend—"

"Greece!" Natalia gasped. *I know! I know what Noel is about to say.*

She saw him reach for her, but she barely felt his arms as they wrapped around her. She went numb and had to force herself to hear his words through the pounding in her brain.

"—when she gave birth to a baby girl."

Gave birth to a baby girl!

As if a gigantic vacuum had pushed its way into her chest, Natalia's breath was sucked out of her. It would have been easier for her to understand if Noel had announced he was going to take a trip to the moon rather than grasp the words he'd just uttered.

"I—was—that—baby?" She finally managed to gulp enough air to ask against his shoulder. Tears flooded her eyes at the unexpected wave of euphoria that washed over her upon discovering her mother's whereabouts. She had always been so blasé about meeting her biological mother. Suddenly she realized her cool indifference had been a facade. Now it was melting like an ice sculpture under the warm rays of the sun. And she knew her baba had been right to encourage her to meet her natural mother someday.

She heard answering tears in Noel's voice. "Yes, you, my darling. My adoptive mother—is your biological mother. She gave birth to you in Greece—on December first—three years to the day—after I was born." Emotions clogged his throat, halting his speech.

For a moment they held one another, and Natalia knew the arms holding her were the ones she wanted around her—"for better or for worse, for richer or for poorer, in sickness and in health"—forever.

His clean masculine scent filled her senses. She was so glad Noel was the man she had thought he was. "My baba always encouraged me to find my biological mother, or at least be receptive to her finding me," she whispered.

He moved just far enough back from her on the leather seat so he could look into her eyes. "Really?"

She nodded.

"And are you, my darling? Receptive to her finding you?" She thought from the way the blue of his eyes became as deep and intense as a mountain lake in winter that it was something for which he fervently hoped.

She wiped the tears from her eyes as the miracle of God's timing swept through her. "It's something I prayed about and gave to God the afternoon we met, Noel. The only other thing I asked of Him—" She stopped speaking as the wonder of it filled her, and she turned her gaze to the pristine world of white that surrounded them.

"What, my darling?"

She turned back to him and, remembering her plea to God, repeated it. "I asked Him, if possible, that my biological mother might be a Christian now," she said softly.

Making a sound of joy, he pulled her close to him and, like leaves rustling on the ground, said, "She is, Natalia. Not only that but"—he spoke with more force—"she's been keeping an eye on you through your doorman Roswell for the last five years—ever since she realized the modeling superstar Audrey Shepherd was her daughter."

She blinked. "Roswell?"

He nodded. "She came to your apartment building, and after understanding what sort of man Roswell was, she confided in him. That's why the dear man hasn't retired. He's been staying on for my mother." He gave a small laugh and touched the tip of her nose. "Your mother."

"My mother. . ." *To have a mother again.* It was a gift, especially since she knew what sort of woman she was from hearing Noel talk about her so much.

"But now Roswell will retire and live in the beautiful carriage house on this estate with his wife and family for as long as they wish—now that he no longer needs to give her weekly reports about you. When he met me the morning of our birthdays, he didn't know I was Jennifer Sheffield's son. He just found out yesterday when I told him."

"And your mother—my natural mother—wants to meet me now?"

"With all her heart. And—to ask your forgiveness."

Natalia shook her head. That thought seemed almost absurd to her.

"I've had a wonderful life, Noel. I grew up in a land that seems like something out of a fairy tale with the most wonderful family imaginable. Then God brought me to America, and I've lived like a princess in a storybook. And now the man I love, the prince of my dreams"—she ran her hand over the fine contours of his face—"has not only discovered the Prince of Peace but has welcomed Him into his life." She shook her head. "No, Noel, I don't have to forgive my natural mother for anything. I only have to thank her. I would not ask for a different life."

"Natalia," he whispered and pulled her close to him. "Dear Natalia. That mind of yours keeps up with your heart in a way I wouldn't have believed possible"—he leaned back and held her face between his hands—"if I hadn't lived with Jennifer for nearly twenty years. She has filled my world with the same mature wisdom. You and she walked different paths—something unusual for mothers and daughters to do—and yet God has brought you both to the same blessed one. You are so much alike. It is—" He stopped what he was going to say. "Well, it *would* be unbelievable if I didn't understand how the Great Conductor works."

Natalia nodded. "Amazing, isn't it?"

"More like miraculous."

She laughed lightly, thrilled to hear Noel speak in such a godly way. "I'll agree with that."

His eyes narrowed. "Are you ready to meet your mother, my darling?"

She nodded slowly. "That is something for which my earthly baba and my heavenly Father have been preparing me for several years. Yes, Noel. I'm ready."

Chapter 13

To say that Natalia was delighted with the woman who had given her life would be putting it mildly. God had ordained their reunion so there were only tears of joy and much laughter. Natalia felt more like a beloved child coming home after a long absence than a daughter who had been deserted so many years before. If she had been given a choice of any woman in the world to be her biological mother, it would have been Jennifer Sheffield. She loved her mother upon sight, and she knew her mother loved her, too, as Jennifer held her and kissed her and explored her face, looking for the infant of so long ago. All the days of their lives they would cherish finding one another after so many years.

The tree lights twinkled, a new snowfall drifted down past the windows, and the three German shepherds lay happily near the fireplace, for Prince had become fast friends with Laddie and his son, Harry. And Noel and his father sat quietly while Natalia and Jennifer held hands and talked about everything—the far distant past and the more recent one.

"You must remember, Natalia, that I was a very foolish young woman," Jennifer said. "To put it succinctly, I was a spoiled brat. I had been given everything money could buy, and I spurned it and the lifestyle it bought for me. But, worst of all, I left you, my precious baby, in a bus station in a foreign land. The only right thing I did was to wait and make sure good people found you. When that wonderful man—that Greek Orthodox priest—and his wife held you, I knew they would love you and never let you go." She glanced at the older Sheffield and sent him a look of thankfulness. "Until I met Noel's father, I was a very lost, very nasty young woman. Quincy's faith and his love of God got through to me as nothing else could—not the doctors my parents took me to see or the rehab clinics from which I repeatedly escaped."

Natalia squeezed the long and slender hand that so resembled her own. "That's an amazing testimony. . .Mother." The title rolled easily off her lips. She had always called her adoptive mother Mamma, so calling her natural mother "Mother" did not conflict with the special relationship she'd had with her mamma at all. Natalia knew too that her mamma would have been glad.

"Mother?" The older woman squeezed her eyes together. "What have I done that you'd call me that wonderful name?"

"You gave me life," Natalia responded, "and it's a life I've liked very much. Thank you."

"But can you forgive me, dear daughter? Can you ever forgive me for being so immature, so wrong, to leave you behind?"

Natalia was slow to answer. She wanted to do so with care. "By giving me away, I think you gave me the best life you could at that time. To grow up in the loving family you found for me was a rare treasure. Not only is my family very special, but the village where I was raised is, too."

"We went to Kastro once," Jennifer confessed and motioned to both Noel and her husband. "The three of us did."

"What?" Natalia and Noel asked in unison and looked at one another in disbelief.

Jennifer nodded and answered Noel. "That's where we went on our honeymoon."

"*Kastro* was where we went?" Noel turned to his father for confirmation. The older man's smile widened. "That's it."

"I remember the village." Noel squinted, as he seemed to search through his memories. "It was a beautiful place. There was a castle on the top of the mountain and donkeys and chickens and kids. Lots of kids."

"Certainly sounds like Kastro," Natalia said, chuckling. She turned back to Jennifer. "But Noel went with you on your *honeymoon*?"

"I had already left one child behind," Jennifer said quickly. "I wasn't going to leave another I was blessed to have come into my life."

"They took me with them everywhere," Noel interjected. "That's why I didn't remember Kastro at first. We went to so many places."

"Plus, you were just a little boy of nine," his father pointed out, sounding like a lawyer with a mind for details.

"Did you see me?" Natalia had to know.

A dreamy look came into Jennifer's eyes, and Natalia suspected she was recalling memories she often liked to contemplate. It made Natalia feel very special. "Yes, we saw you. We went to church service Sunday morning. You were there dressed in a little yellow sundress with white flowers and matching yellow ribbons that held your nearly translucent hair back in a ponytail."

"I remember that dress." She did, even though it was long ago. "My sister Martha made it for me. It was one of my favorites."

"You were so happy. So carefree. So loved. Your whole family was there." She laughed. "So many people."

"I have five brothers and sisters, and I think several of them were already married then."

"And your father was such a man of God. I knew that day as I watched you with your family that God had taken my bad actions and brought good out of them."

"Did you talk to my baba?"

"No. I couldn't do that to the dear man. I learned that his wife, your mother, was quite sick. You were the apple of his eye. I didn't want to chance scaring him. Plus, how would we have communicated without any misunderstandings? I didn't speak a word of Greek then."

Natalia caught the word *then*. "'Then'? You do now?"

"Malista," Jennifer replied, surprising Natalia with a yes. Greek was not a language many people spoke. She listened as her mother continued to speak in perfect Greek. "I thought if I should ever be blessed to be reconciled to you, I wanted to be able to communicate with you. So I've been studying Greek for years. I didn't know, until you became Audrey Shepherd, that you had learned English so well."

A million words never could never have conveyed to Natalia the depth of her biological mother's love for her as that act of learning Greek in the hope of their meeting did. It told its own tale and touched Natalia deeply.

"Fharisto poli, Mother," she said, thanking her mother.

"Parakalo." The older woman responded with "You're welcome." "Your English is superb, Natalia. And with only the barest trace of an accent. Very lovely. How did you learn to speak so well?"

"My parents were certain I was American, even if the American authorities wouldn't acknowledge it."

"The little sleeper I dressed you in and the blanket I wrapped you in were emblazoned with the American flag. I wasn't thinking too clearly back then, but I remember I thought everyone would know from those things that you were American. I also wrote a letter saying you were. But I'm not sure exactly what I wrote. I'd started taking drugs by then."

"Drugs?" To see her, Natalia didn't think it was possible.

An almost haunted look entered Jennifer's eyes. "I was very confused, Natalia, and I did a stupid thing. A woman does not desert her child in a bus station without having major problems. I didn't know what else to do. I was desperate."

Natalia remembered the day she'd met Noel. On her walk to the Rockefeller Center Christmas tree she had been praying about her birth mother. She had wondered what kind of woman would leave her newborn baby in a bus station. And God had told her, *"The desperate kind."* Exactly what her mother was admitting to having been—desperate.

She looked deeply into Jennifer's eyes and, seeing how sad recalling her past made her, decided now wasn't the time to question her further. She would sometime but not today. Those questions could be asked and answered in the days and weeks and years to come. They had time.

She went back to Jennifer's question about her learning to speak English. "In the event I ever searched for my roots, my parents wanted me to be able to speak English well."

"And did you?" Jennifer asked with a degree of yearning in her tone that almost made Natalia feel sad. Particularly since she knew her answer. "Ever want to find your roots, I mean?"

Natalia didn't want to hurt this woman who had been such a wonderful mother to Noel, but she had to be truthful. She spoke softly, tenderly. "Not really. I mean I always wanted to come to America, but—oh, please don't feel bad—I never really felt the need to find my biological parents. Even though it was something my baba always encouraged me to do."

"He is a very special man. A man of faith, who, I think, has a great understanding about human nature and need."

Natalia thought about her dear baba and all the good he had done for the people in Kastro throughout her life and more. "Yes, he does," she agreed. "I always knew I was adopted." She touched her blond hair. "I looked so different from my brothers and sisters, and my mother was too old to have had children when I came along. I assumed you had given me up for a good reason. That's what my parents told me, too. Either you couldn't care for me, or I was an embarrassment to you because you were unmarried, or you were sick. Something." She quickly continued, "I've had a wonderful family. One I thank you for finding for me."

"It was God." Jennifer held her hand upward.

Natalia smiled her agreement. "But when Noel told me you were my natural mother, at that very moment I realized how important it was to have you in my life, how right my baba was to encourage me to find you or be open to your finding me. And even though it wasn't something I thought I needed, having you in my life is one of the most important things to me now. I'm so thankful to have met you after twenty-six years."

"Thank you, Natalia," she whispered. "I don't deserve your forgiveness, but I thank you from the very bottom of my heart." She dabbed at the corners of her eyes, then blinked and sent Natalia a bright smile. "I thank God He gave you wisdom not to question my motive in giving you up, as if it had been a reflection upon you. Never that! And I thank God for the wonderful people who raised you to be such a lovely young woman. But mostly, right now, I thank God He has brought us together again."

Leaning toward one another, they fell into a natural embrace. Natalia took a deep breath of the essence of the woman who had given her the gift of life. She smelled of peaches and freshly washed clothing, wholesome and clean. Natalia whispered a prayer of thanksgiving to God for protecting her mother through her wild years. "What about my biological father?" Natalia felt compelled to ask after a moment.

Her mother sat back but still held her hand. Natalia was glad. She didn't want to let go, either. "He was as bad as I."

"Did he know about me?"

Jennifer nodded sadly. "He told me to get rid of you."

"So you did." Natalia didn't mean for the words to sound so harsh. She offered a thin smile to soften them.

"Yes, but after you were born. Thank God—and only Him—I at least gave you life. On the first day of December. I always loved Christmas." She looked at the tree sparkling from its place near the decorated hearth, and a pensive quality came into her tone. "Even when I was a terrible, disrespectful, immoral young woman, I loved the Christmas season, and I thought it was very special you were born then. That's why I left a note saying exactly when your birthday was." She looked over at Noel. "I couldn't know it then, but it was the exact day, though a different year, as the young boy I was to someday call my son."

"The day my parents found me," Natalia explained, "was Christmas Eve, my mamma's birthday. Her name was Natalia, but she was always called Talia. So I was named for both Christmas and my mamma."

Jennifer's mouth formed an *O*. "Your mother's name was Natalia?" She laughed. "What an amazing humor our God has to have orchestrated everything so perfectly. For your mother to find you on her birthday, for her name to be Natalia, for the Christmas season to be something that spoke to my hardened heart even then." She shook her head at the miracle of it all. "From reading Noel's book, I know Natalia means 'of or relating to Christmas.' "

Noel nodded. " 'She who is born at Christmas.' Just like my name means 'born at Christmas.' "

"It is the name I would have chosen for you, Natalia, had I been a responsible mother then."

There was a moment of silence in which Natalia lifted up her thoughts and prayers to God, and the other three people seemed to do the same.

Then Natalia, wanting to know one more thing, asked, "Where is my biological father now?"

A look of sadness crossed Jennifer's face.

"He never changed. He died of a drug overdose a couple of years after you were born. But his parents are still alive. I think meeting you, their granddaughter, would be one of the most wonderful gifts they could ever receive." She turned her head in a searching way. "You inherited your exceptional outward beauty from him." She let her fingertips slide across Natalia's face. "Your fine, high cheekbones, your sparkling blue eyes"—she touched the ends of Natalia's hair—"your true blond coloring. He was a handsome man."

"I always wondered who I looked like." Natalia thought most adopted children wondered that, whether they admitted it or not. It wasn't important, just nice to know.

"Your father. Totally." She sighed. "I don't have any pictures of him, but his parents do. It would do his parents good to meet you. After they saw how my life changed, they've been leaning toward Christianity." She shrugged. "But they haven't been able to let go of the bitterness even after all these years. He was their only child. Someday, when you feel ready, maybe we can invite them over."

"I would be honored."

She nodded. "Tell me about your baba. Is he well? And your brothers and sisters?"

That Jennifer should ask about her family cemented the love Natalia already felt for the woman who had given her life. Maybe she hadn't done much more than that in the beginning. But it was more than many received in these modern times. And that was something.

Natalia happily told her about her baba and Martha and her brothers and sisters. Jennifer asked if they might call and talk to her baba, and even though it was very early in the morning in Greece, Natalia didn't hesitate to call him. This was one phone call her baba had been waiting for, for a very long time.

As it was, he had just returned from church, where he had felt the desire to go and pray. Natalia told him what had just transpired, and the dear man understood.

"Ah." His deep gravelly voice spoke through the wire and satellite to his daughter so far away and yet so very close spiritually. "That's why *O Theos*—God—directed me to get on my knees this morning and pray extra hard for you, *Kali mou Kori,* my dear daughter. He knew."

"Malista, Baba, He knew," Natalia agreed. And when she told him that Jennifer had learned Greek and the reason why, the man was overjoyed to be able to speak to her. Smiling, Natalia handed the phone to Jennifer.

Her mother's first words, with tears of joy and thanksgiving, were, 'Papouli, thank you so very much for raising Natalia in such a God-centered and wonderful way." Natalia took Noel's hand then and walked with him over to the picture window.

For a few moments they stood and looked out at the pristine world. Snow still fell softly, a blanket of righteousness and protection for the winter's night.

"King of Kings and Lord of Lords," Natalia heard Noel whisper by her side. She turned to him.

He turned to her.

They nodded their heads with a degree of oneness that could come only from an understanding of the words Noel had spoken.

Those words said it all.

Everything.

And using only two of the Lord's names.

But for the couple who believed, those two names were enough.

More than enough for them to build a lifetime of happiness and commitment in a continuing fairy-tale romance that would forever have God at its center.

~~∞⊙∞~~

And, beside his tree at Rockefeller Center on Christmas Eve, on bended knee Noel asked Natalia to be his wife. All were present—Jennifer and Quincy Sheffield, Janet and Jasper Howard, Mary and Roswell Lincoln, and Rachel; and, through the amazing technology of cell phones and computers, Natalia's baba and sister Martha and a multitude of friends in Kastro; as well as Prince who, as was his job, watched everything carefully. And they clapped their hands in joy when Natalia, to the sound of church bells ringing and the singing of Christmas carols in New York City, said, "Yes!"

Well, not Prince. He thumped his tail against the pavement and smiled his big doggie grin.

Prince seemed to understand he was soon to see his canine family in Kastro again. By Natalia saying yes, a wedding would be planned. Probably for March. And since Papouli would officiate, they would all be flying to Kastro.

Prince thumped his tail harder against the pavement.

That was something that appeared to please him very much.

A Land Far, Far Away

With love to my cousins, Dr. Stephanie Dellis,
and her brother and my best childhood friend, the late George Dellis.
For the magical summers the three of us spent together in that land far,
far away on the Upper Peninsula of Michigan:
To our "Lady of the Forest," children-size castles made of driftwood and sand,
chipmunk studies, freezing but wonderful picnics on the beach,
and parsley eaten fresh from your grandparents' garden.
Although physically far away from me,
you have both always been near to my heart. . .and always will be.

Chapter 1

Martha clapped her hands together. "Now it's my turn to have news for all of you," she said to her family and friends who were gathered in the kitchen of what had been her home for all of her fifty-six years. But her news was soon to change that.

"News?" Natalia, Martha's much younger sister, asked with a tilt of her famous blond head. "What news?" she persisted, and Martha took the moment to regard her sister.

She knew that the fondness she felt for Natalia had to be evident in her face. Natalia was Martha's adoptive sister, but because Martha was thirty-two years her senior, Martha thought of her more as a daughter than as a sister. And just as a mother might feel upon the return of her child for a holiday, Martha had loved having Natalia and her husband, Noel, home for these few days.

The Pappas family had adopted Natalia when she had only been a few weeks old. Although their mamma had been beyond her childbearing years and their father—Baba—had been quite old to be the father of an infant, Martha doubted that any girl could have been showered with more love than Natalia while being raised in the village of Kastro in Greece.

"*Ella, koukla mou*—come, my doll. What is it?" Baba encouraged when Martha didn't immediately speak. Martha turned to her father. Her smile deepened. Although the calendar declared him to be eighty-five years old, he was as thin and spry as a man half his age might be. Only the gray of his beard, the deep crinkles around his eyes, and the rasp of his voice indicated his advanced age.

As did his wisdom.

He was the wisest man Martha knew, and when people compared her to him—as they often did—they extended to her the ultimate compliment. But right now she liked the way her baba still referred to her as "koukla mou." How many fifty-six-year-old women had fathers who called them "my doll"?

Hurriedly rising from her seat next to the recently whitewashed and now flower-bedecked tzaki, she went over to the sink and to the curtains that fluttered in the soft May breeze above it. She tied back the light floral fabric.

"What news, Martha?" Allie, the village physician, asked from her place beside her husband. But when Martha only turned back to her friends and family and smiled, Allie flicked her long French braid behind her shoulder and gave a slight laugh before continuing. "Honestly, Martha. I've never known you to take so long to say or do something."

That brought chuckles of concurrence from all, and Martha couldn't keep one from escaping her own lips, either. She knew that Allie hadn't meant it in any way unkindly.

Besides, Martha knew that she was taking a long time. Especially for her. She was normally as quick as a buzzing bee in both speech and action.

"Well, this decision took quite awhile to arrive at, so it deserves to be stated slowly." She took a deep breath and swallowed down the unfamiliar butterflies that were flittering around in her stomach. But somehow the proverbial butterflies were pleasant, too, because they meant that there was soon to be an exciting and new adventure in her life. And that thrilled Martha as much as if she were a child going off to school for the first time. "And even more, I want you all to know that I have said many prayers concerning it, and I'm certain that I'm moving in God's will for my life by following through on it."

"Martha. . ." Natalia groaned and clasped her long, slender hands together. "I promise that I won't ever tease you about being too quick again. Tell us!"

But Martha still didn't, immediately. She took her time and regarded the two couples. Except for her father, who was a longtime widower, she was the only single person in the group. But that was not something that had ever bothered her. Her unmarried state had never given her cause for alarm because she had lived a very fulfilling and free life without the "bonds" of matrimony. First, she had been the youngest of five siblings, then, when all of her older brothers and sisters had married and moved to various towns and cities, Natalia had joined the family. Because of Mamma's long illness and subsequent death, the primary care of both the baby girl and her mamma had fallen upon her, something Martha had never minded.

Natalia was now a world-renowned fashion model living in New York with her husband, Noel. Her father had found joy in spending his time between Natalia in America, her brothers and sisters in Athens, and her in Kastro. But Martha knew that because of the research he was doing for a book about the fathers of the church—a dream of his forever—that he only spent time in Kastro because she was there. And that was silly, especially since Martha had been led to follow a dream of her own.

"I'm going to be opening a shop in Ancient Olympia," she blurted out and had the satisfaction of seeing every mouth in the kitchen drop open in shock.

She laughed.

Then happy pandemonium broke out as everyone started laughing and talking and congratulating her all at once.

Natalia squealed and pulled her into a hug. "So that's the reason you've been going to Olympia nearly every week to visit our relatives there."

Martha squeezed her tall and slender sister back tightly. Even with Natalia living an ocean and a continent away, they were so intuitively connected. She should have known that Natalia would figure that out quickly. "Exactly. And I have grown to love the town. It's where our mamma's ancestors hail from, after all." Martha knew that along with its history and the peaceful, thoughtful quality of the green and fertile valley in which the ancient site was situated, that was one of the things that made Olympia so appealing to her. Her mother had grown up there. She had only left the town of Ancient Olympia when she had married.

"How absolutely wonderful! And exciting," Allie exclaimed. "So similar to my own adventure when I first came to Kastro."

Martha grimaced, remembering back to Allie's reception to the village. "Well, I hope the people of Olympia are a bit friendlier to me than Kastro's population was to you!"

Stavros groaned, and his dark eyes narrowed in guilt. "Don't remind me." The village schoolteacher, he had been one of those who had tried to get Allie to leave those first days after her arrival.

His wife nudged him and, slanting her eyes at him, said, "But you soon came to your senses, darling."

His mouth twisted downward in remorse for his behavior before he leaned toward her and gave her a quick kiss. "That I did," he agreed. Then to Martha he said, "With you moving to Ancient Olympia, at least I know where to bring the kids for a field trip next year."

"You'd better." That idea pleased Martha. It would be a connection with her home that she would treasure.

The only thing Martha had left to do to make her move official was to sign the papers for the property on Ancient Olympia's main street. She had fallen in love with the meticulously restored traditional Greek town house. The ground floor was meant to be a shop, while a two-bedroom apartment with polished plank floors, recessed, shuttered windows, as well as vine-covered verandas for living was above it. Compared to most of the town's buildings, which were post–World War II, nondescript, flat-roofed structures of concrete and glass, it was a real find.

But without her father's blessing, she wouldn't follow through with her plans. Martha turned. "Baba?"

His lips moved a moment in the sweet way of older men filled with emotion before words came out. "I am so proud of you, *kali mou Kori*—my dear daughter," he rasped. "You were a wonderful girl, and you have grown into one of the most thoughtful and elegant of women. You have done nothing but bring joy into all of our lives every single day with your sunny smile and your quick and sure ways."

Behind the lenses of his glasses tears touched upon his fine old lashes. But Martha wasn't concerned. She knew her baba well enough to know that this moisture came from joy, not sorrow.

"I feel that God has many more wonderful things in store for you, kali mou." He reached out for her hand with his right one and, looking over at Natalia, motioned for his youngest child to take his other. Leaving her place beside Noel, Natalia quickly did so. Squeezing his two youngest children's hands close against his heart, he spoke to Martha. "I am only thankful that you have the faith to make this change in your life. Since I spend so much time in Athens and New York, leaving you behind in Kastro has weighed heavily on my mind."

"But your following your dream of writing a book and having to spend time away from here to research it is the reason I feel free to pursue my own dream, Baba. Moving to Ancient Olympia and opening a shop there is something I have wanted to do for a very long time."

She turned to Natalia, who had been extremely generous with the money she'd earned from high-fashion modeling. "I've saved practically all the money that you've given to me though the years." She glanced down at her linen suit and grimaced. "With the exception of having spent quite a nice amount on clothes."

Chuckles were shared around the room, and Martha knew that it was because she had become touted, quite unexpectedly, as one of the most stylish and fashionably in-tune women in Kastro—and the surrounding area, as well.

It had all started when, having more than enough of her own, Natalia had asked designers in New York to send clothing to her sister in Kastro. After several boxes of designer clothes arrived in Kastro, Martha soon discovered that she liked the way fine fabric felt against her skin and how well-designed clothes fit her figure. The garments made her feel womanly and feminine in ways she liked. It was one of the few frivolous things she had allowed into her life and one for which she felt no compunction.

"So." She flashed them all a bright smile, refusing to feel self-conscious. "Other than buying clothes, I have saved everything. I have more than enough to buy and open my own gift shop and keep it running for the next two years, even should I not make a profit." Her gaze returned to her father's. "Your travels between your children's homes and your work is the catalyst directing me on this adventure. For the first time ever, I feel free to pursue something different. Not that I have been unhappy in the life I have led until now, Baba. I haven't," she qualified quickly. She had no regrets about the years spent caring for her father's home. She had always thought it a privilege.

"Don't worry, Martha. I understand what you're saying. The truth is"—he looked at her above his glasses—"you are free now. And I am proud of you for following the path God has laid out for you. Natalia did that, and look where it led her."

"Straight to Noel's arms!" Allie sang out, and with a great big smile of concurrence, Natalia left her father's side and went back to those very arms.

Noel smiled as he held his wife tightly against his side. "Unfortunately, it took a few years, plus"—he glanced down at the German shepherd that reclined by their feet—"having Prince here as a chaperone." They all knew the story. Natalia and Noel had seen each other for several consecutive years at the same place—Rockefeller Center in New York City at Christmastime—before they even got up the nerve to talk to each other. And that was using Prince as the excuse.

But this line of thought concerned Martha, and a frown pulled her brows together as she returned to her chair. She leaned over and picked up her Siamese cat, Needlepoint. The cat had done her favorite trick of jumping up on Martha's seat as soon as Martha had vacated it. They had all been amazed at how the cat and the dog could be in the same house together, even more, in the same room. But the two animals had been tolerant of one another from the first, even friendly.

Martha placed her cat on her lap and rubbed her feline friend's silky fur while Needlepoint went in a circle to settle herself. "I don't want you all to think that I'm moving to Olympia in order to search for a—" Martha had to swallow, and even then she stumbled over the final word of the sentence, "hus–band."

"Why not?" Allie, always the hopeful realist, asked with a twinkle in her soft eyes. "Do you feel as if you are too old for romance?"

"And if you do, then that's just silly," Natalia interjected.

"No, of course not. Age has nothing to do with it." Martha defended her position. "But Jesus' response to his disciples' question about marriage as recorded in the nineteenth chapter of the Gospel of Matthew does. I think it fits perfectly for my life. Among other things He said, 'others have renounced marriage because of the kingdom of heaven. The one who can accept this should accept it.' "

"Bah," her father softly intoned, and Martha turned back to him in surprise. "I disagree, Martha-Mary." She didn't expect that response from him. And the use of her two names was a sure indication as to how serious he was, even if his voice remained as calm and sweet as always. He only used both her names when he wanted her full attention.

"I don't think that verse refers to you at all." He spoke to her more as Papouli—the village priest—than that of father to his child. "To renounce something means that you have given up all rights to it. I don't think you have done that; rather, I think that the man you are to marry has not yet come into your life. You have been needed in this home for so long—God only knows how much we all needed you"—he qualified—"that you are confusing service to your family with that of having renounced marriage."

Shock reverberated through Martha. She had had no idea that her father thought that the man she was to marry hadn't yet—*yet*—come into her life and that was the reason she hadn't married. Placing Needlepoint on the floor, Martha hurriedly moved to her father's side again and, taking his thin hands in her own, said, "Baba, I have never been unhappy in being single. I've led a very fulfilling life, and I'm not moving to Olympia to look for a husband. I'm not unhappy in who I am."

He looked at her above his glasses. "I know that."

"Then?" She was confused.

Between his beard and his mustache, his lips curved into a kind smile. "I'm only taking issue with your using that verse in Matthew in respect to your life," he said with that playful twinkle in his intelligent eyes that she so loved in him. "I feel you are misapplying it."

"Oh." She had lived with her father long enough to know better than to discount anything he might say. So clamping down on her ready protest, she listened. His words astounded.

"As Solomon wrote, 'There is a time for everything, and a season for every activity under heaven.' " He reached out and, as he had done a million times before, ran his hand in a father's loving way across her cheek. "If you want to use a verse from the nineteenth chapter of Matthew in reference to your life, Martha-Mary, then I think the correct one might be, 'with God all things are possible.' Even the fulfilling of my longtime prayer for you—that a wonderful man might come into your life so that you, the most deserving of women and the most self-less, might know the joys of married life, just as I was privileged to know with your dear mother. God rest her soul."

Martha was speechless. Literally. A very unusual occurrence for her. She had had no idea that her father had been praying for a partner for her. Her tongue, which normally worked as quickly as her hands, remained still as her father continued.

"None of us would have had the wonderful life we have enjoyed without your ministrations and care. You embody all the good characteristics of Jesus' friends Martha and Mary. Your mother and I named you well when we gave you the double name of Martha-Mary. Even though we call you only by the first part of your name, you are both Martha and Mary. You are Martha, the tireless worker and hostess, and you are Mary, the one who sits at the feet of Jesus and learns from Him. More than anything, moving to Ancient Olympia will give you more time to be a Mary, and for that I am glad."

Martha felt tears—those coming from being profoundly touched and edified by her father—form in her eyes. She knew that her father had always appreciated her running his home since the day her mother had taken ill almost three decades earlier, but she had never realized just how much until this moment. She blinked the moisture away. "Baba, I don't know what to say."

He chuckled, a deep, throaty sound, and patted her hand. "Just say that you will take care of you—of Martha—just as you have always taken care of us. And. . .that you will let God lead you in this wonderful new path He is taking you down. . .every step of the way. Even if the steps seem uneven to you at times."

She blinked, and leaning over, she put her arms around his skinny, but very strong, shoulders and whispered into his ear, "I will, Baba. I promise."

Chapter 2

Two Months Later

H ello." Martha's heart seemed to do a double beat at the sound of the voice, the rounded and full, masculine one with which she was becoming familiar. She knew before looking who was standing above her—the man she had often said hello to as they passed one another in and around Ancient Olympia.

As she raised her eyes from the verses in the Bible she had been reading into the deep-set eyes of the tall and slender man, she willed her pulse to slow down. She normally saw him while in motion, either while walking in opposite directions or as he whirled past her on his fancy bicycle. His features were every bit as fine and classical as she had thought, even with lines—made from both smiling often and time—permanently etched into the skin around his mouth. Probably a little bit younger than she, he had the look of a man who had always been in top physical form. His hair was dark and thick with silvery feathers of gray at his temples and behind his ears. It lent him that distinguished look men past the age of fifty who were still in good physical shape were blessed to wear.

And as always, when in his presence, she felt her heart pound against her chest in a very unusual but exciting way. She was beginning to think it was anything but abnormal to feel this way around this man. It happened every time she saw him, which had been nearly every day of the two months she had lived in Ancient Olympia. Seeing him had become a highlight of her day.

She returned his smile, but she sincerely hoped that it didn't appear as wobbly as she felt on the inside. "Hello."

He motioned toward the ancient piece of stone masonry that she had made into her bench. "Mind if I join you?"

Martha scanned the tree-filled grounds of the archaeological site of Olympia. Brightly clothed tourists, dressed for summer fun in Greece, formed splashes of bold coloring against the pastoral setting as they inspected the jutting columns and low foundations that, with just a little bit of imagination, told of how magnificent the ancient precinct had been once upon a time. Since she was hardly alone, Martha scooted over and offered him the place beside her. "I'd like that."

"I'd like that?" Had she—cautious Martha—actually said that? She was only glad Natalia wasn't around to hear her. How often had she warned her sister when she had first moved away from Kastro against talking to strangers? But Martha wryly remembered that it hadn't done any good. Natalia and Noel had first talked to one another at Rockefeller Center in New York City the previous November: two strangers who ventured to converse. And now look. Not even a year later they had been married for several months.

The man lowered his tall frame to the bench, and turning to face her, he smiled, a smile full of white teeth that matched the gleaming of the columns of the site, with eyes that flashed silver green like the olive trees in the grove. And Martha forgot all about Natalia.

"Since we both seem to live in Ancient Olympia, and we see one another every day"—he had noticed that, too—"I thought that it was time that I stopped and introduced myself. I'm Leo Jones," he said and extended his hand.

Martha looked at it for a moment before placing her much smaller one within it. But when she did, her mouth almost couldn't form her own name. If she thought seeing him and greeting him did things to her, it was nothing compared to the way his hand enfolding her own made her feel. For the first time ever, she was cognizant of the calluses that a lifetime of cleaning, mending, and activity had added to her hands. At that moment she wished for Natalia's soft, pearly smooth, picture-perfect hands.

She was just noticing that he had even larger calluses on his palms, though, when he prompted, "And you are?"

Martha felt as if all the blood in her body had decided to convene for a convention in her face. She was reacting like a silly schoolgirl. She hadn't even behaved like that when she had been a schoolgirl. But then there had never been a boy in Kastro who had made her feel the way this man did, as if her very being was somehow tied to his. All the boys she had grown up with had felt like brothers or cousins. This man most definitely did not.

"I'm Martha Pappas."

"Martha," he repeated and seemed to taste the individual sonances and nuances belonging to its two syllables. "A name of substance. As well as being pretty, it belonged to one of my favorite Bible characters, too."

Her brows shot up to almost meet the brim of her straw sun hat. If she had been wearing sunglasses, they would have risen above the rim. "Martha is one of your favorites? Martha? Mary and Lazarus's sister?" she returned quickly, wanting to make sure that they referred to the same person, even though she didn't think there was another Martha mentioned in the Bible.

"That's the one."

"Martha normally gets bad press in the story about her in the tenth chapter of Luke." She patted her white, leather-bound Bible. "It's her sister, the contemplative Mary, whom most admire."

"I respect her, too," he was quick to qualify.

"Then?" She pushed her chin-length hair behind her ears. The stiff breeze was blowing from behind the bench and pushing it into her eyes.

He spoke quickly and with a degree of knowledge that intrigued her. "I don't think of them as being on opposing teams," he began. "We need both Marthas and Marys in the world, but even more, Martha had to learn from Mary, and Mary had to learn from Martha. I think that was the most important lesson taught by that story: one of balancing life."

"Balancing life," she repeated. "That's an interesting thought." And a very good one.

He smiled and continued, "It might seem that by Jesus' saying, 'Martha, Martha. . .you are worried and upset about many things, but only one thing is needed. Mary has chosen what is better. . .' that He was reprimanding her for complaining that her sister wasn't helping in the preparation of the food. But I don't think His words were intended just for Martha of Bethany, but rather for all the wonderful Marthas—ladies—throughout time who have served their families and made home a wonderful and safe haven of harmony." He squinted out over the site before continuing. "I think the Lord was telling all homemakers who might read about Martha and Mary to calm down and not to be distracted in their walk with Him by the day-to-day activities and stresses that can so easily overwhelm. In other words"—he flashed a quick grin her way—"one pot roast instead of three entrees is better so that they can then have the time to sit at His feet and eat spiritual food. That was something Martha obviously learned, as we can see from her declaration a few months later, as recorded in the twenty-seventh verse of John, chapter eleven, when she answered Jesus, 'I believe that you are the Christ, the Son of God, who was to come into the world.' "

Martha was impressed. This was a man who clearly knew the Bible. And one who was quick to get his thoughts across. She really liked that. "That sounds like something my father might say." She thought. "Hmm. . .has said, even. But he's a very wise, old man." She turned so that she could look directly at the man named Leo Jones. "How did you come to be so smart?" She couldn't believe she had asked that. It was the closest to flirting she had ever come.

"My wife."

Wife. Wife. Wife. The cicadas in the Aleppo pine above them seemed to scream out the refrain as fingers of mortification crawled up Martha's spine. That's what she got for being so bold with a stranger. She should have listened to her own advice to Natalia. She shouldn't have talked to someone in this way with whom she hadn't been properly introduced. What had come over her? She shouldn't have talked to him in this flirtatious way. Period.

But of course this man had to have a wife.

The women of the world would have had to be blind to leave him alone. Even she, of all people, was attracted to him. But she wouldn't, nor couldn't, allow herself to covet another woman's husband. That was something she had never done, and at fifty-six years of age, nearly fifty-seven, it was not something she would start now.

But why, why did she have to be so attracted to him? For the first time she really understood her young friend Maria and her dilemma with Dimitri Drakopoulos. Maria had been crazy about Dimitri all her life. But Dimitri had only had eyes for Natalia. . . .

Martha had never really understood that attraction bug, that thing some called chemistry.

Until this moment.

And she found herself bitten by it. That she was highly attracted to, drawn to, fascinated by this man, by this stranger who was sitting beside her, was not something she could deny.

But he was a married man.

Off-limits.

Totally.

She would remove herself from his company before the seed of temptation could be planted even a centimeter deep into the matter of her mind. Gathering her purse and Bible close to her in preparation to leave, she replied, "Your wife sounds like a very smart lady."

"She was."

Martha stopped in the motion of arising and looked closely at his face. Was? Was?

Yes, was.

Definitely past tense.

She could see the truth of it in the reflective, steely color in his deep eyes. It was the same opaque sorrow that she had often seen in her father's over the loss of her mother.

The world seemed to stand still as sadness moved in to replace the guilt of thinking she was attracted to another woman's husband. Martha sat back and hesitated over the question. "Your wife. She has. . .passed on?"

He nodded, took a deep breath, and turning his head to the right, looked out over what had been the Altis—the sacred precinct of Olympia. But Martha was certain that he wasn't seeing the home of the original Olympic Games as he murmured, "Six years ago."

Her eyes shut briefly. The pain of losing his wife was in the pronunciation of each vowel, each syllable. She recognized it as the same sound that had come from her father and friends in Kastro who had lost their mates.

"I know it's inadequate, but I'm so sorry."

He breathed out deeply and narrowed his eyes. "Thanks." He sat back. "And thanks, too, for not immediately assuming that my referring to my wife in the past tense meant that we were divorced." His head moved up and down softly in a contemplative way. "I know people don't mean to, but it hurts when they immediately assume that my Susan and I ever could have stopped loving one another." He stretched his long legs out in front of him and heaved a heavy sigh. "I know it's just a sign of the times in which we live, with people so lightly sharing wedding vows. But it can really hurt."

"It never even crossed my mind," she murmured. It hadn't.

A sudden smile filled the lines around his mouth. "Where do you come from? Must be somewhere the rest of the world hasn't touched."

She laughed softly. If Kastro was anything, it was that. Not one couple had ever divorced there. "Actually it is. I was born and raised and, until two months ago, lived all my life in a village called Kastro. It's about two hours by car from here." She pointed toward the north. "As a crow flies, just over that broad range of mountains."

He did a double take. "You're not American?"

She tilted her head to the side. The question surprised her. "Why would you think that?"

"Your English is superb." He gave a little laugh. "Probably better than most native speakers'."

"Thanks." Several Americans, Brits, and Australians who had visited her shop had told her that. "I like the study of languages. And especially"—she grimaced guiltily—"grammar."

"Ouch." He tapped the heel of his hand against his brow as if he had just been hit. "That's my nightmare."

She had heard that from many people. But it seemed inconceivable to her. "Grammar is like a puzzle to me. I really enjoy it."

"So you've been studying English all your life?"

"No. Actually, on a formal basis, just for the last six years."

He stared at her, and his eyes narrowed as if he had a hard time believing it. "Are you serious? But you speak it so well."

His praise made all the years of hard study worth it in a way nothing else ever had. And that was saying something, since she had had many compliments about her ability to learn foreign languages, and even more, to get the accents down perfectly. Needing to do something with her hands, she let her fingers play with the leather of her purse strap. "When my younger sister moved to America, I started studying English," she explained. "I didn't want her to fall in love someday and marry an American, leaving me unable to communicate with her husband."

"And did she? Fall in love and marry?"

Martha smiled as the image of Natalia and Noel on their wedding day went through her mind. Wearing a wedding gown that she herself had designed, Natalia had not only looked like the famous cover girl she was but like the heroine in the most perfect fairy tale, too. She had had a fairy-tale romance with Noel, so Martha hadn't expected anything less. "Noel and Natalia married last March. And now a baby is on the way." They had told her the blessed news just the previous evening during their weekly phone conversation. That new little human was whom she had been praying about—while using the words of the Bible—when Leo had walked up to her.

"A baby. . .how wonderful," he responded, and she thought that she detected a wistful quality, almost one of sadness, before he looked at her in a speculative way, almost with apprehension framing his eyes. A mix of diverse emotions, it confused her. "And how about you?" He asked with an edge to his voice. "Are you married?"

Then she understood.

And she could hardly believe it.

What she now saw in his face was the same anxiety she had felt when she had thought he had a wife. He was afraid that she had a husband! In the same way that the wind touched the leaves on the poplar trees that shaded them, she could feel his trepidation. It was a heady experience. Slowly she shook her head. "No, Leo," she spoke his given name, feeling that the moment deserved it. "I've never been married."

His eyes softened, and he regarded her as if. . .if. . .she was the most beautiful woman on earth! She couldn't believe that he might actually be as attracted to her as she was to him. "Where have all the men in Kastro been?" His voice was husky, almost a caress.

Excitement, thrilling and grand, coursed through her veins. But pushing right behind it, like one of the floods that had covered the land where they now sat for centuries, came unease. A deep, chilling discomfort that she might be falling for a "line" that was older even than the civilization that had flourished almost three millennia earlier where they now sat assailed her. Goose bumps pricked her skin.

She was acting like an ingénue. She might not be very experienced in the ways of men on a personal level, but she was a mature woman who had seen enough of life to know very well the consequences of trusting unwisely.

In her haste to stand, she dropped her Bible. He reached down and dusted it off on his jeans before standing and giving it back to her. He was looking down at her curiously, undoubtedly trying to understand her sudden change of attitude.

But it wasn't something she was prepared to explain. He was, after all, still a stranger.

"I must go," she said quickly and motioned in the direction of the modern town that was about a half mile in the distance. "My cousins are expecting me for dinner this evening." She felt safer letting him know that she had family close by. But even as she did, she knew that she was being ridiculous. Deep down she was certain that she didn't ever have to fear this handsome, courteous gentleman. Because he was just that—a gentle man.

He didn't challenge her abrupt change in attitude or manner, but instead, with a tilt of his head, indicated the long broad path that led to what was both the entrance and the exit of the ancient site. "May I walk with you? To the exit," he qualified, and she liked the way he didn't ask to see her home. He seemed to understand that she needed time to become acquainted with him.

As she looked up at him and watched the hopeful expression on his face, she knew that to get to know him was something she really wanted, too.

Coming on top of her momentary apprehension, it was one of the most incredible feelings she had ever experienced.

Chapter 3

After a long moment, she nodded. She didn't trust the emotion he might hear in her voice if she spoke.

Seeming to understand her unease and wanting to calm her, he glanced around at their location and motioned to what remained of the early Christian basilica to their left. "It's beautiful here. So peaceful. I find it poignant, too, that Olympia, which was built in honor of mythological gods, should have a Christian basilica upon the very spot where Zeus's seated statue—one of the seven wonders of the ancient world—had been sculpted by the master craftsman Phidias."

He had touched on a subject near and dear to her heart, Olympia's history and that of the Olympic Games in relation to Christianity. She ambled over to what had been the three-aisled basilica, which had been built of sandstone with later brickwork placed above it. She put her hand on one of the columns that had supported its wooden roof. It was warm and rough to her touch, but nice, real, something solid from a time long ago that connected the early Christians of the land with the Christians of today. "I think it was the early Greeks' way of dedicating this land, and all that was good about the Olympic Games, to the God who had been made known to them by the apostles of Christ in the first days of Christianity."

He stood beside her, and his gaze traveled around what had obviously once been a beautiful church. It was the earliest and simplest type of church building. A rectangular central hall or nave was separated from side aisles by rows of columns. The building type had originated in antiquity as an assembly hall—a basilica.

"The Greeks certainly made sure to do that with the first modern Olympics held in Athens in 1896," he said. "There can be no doubt in anybody's mind who both the athletes and the organizers were honoring during those historic games."

She smiled, impressed by his knowledge. "Opening day was on Easter Monday—Bright Monday—the day after Easter. Easter is the holiest day in Greece, even more so than Christmas, so that was as loud a proclamation as any that the Hellenic planners could give as to whom the games were intended to honor."

"The day after Easter," he murmured, and even though she didn't know him well, she could tell that that day held a special significance for him. She suspected from the way the corners of his eyes seemed to turn downward, a sad one, too. He shrugged, visibly trying to rid himself of some memory. "I'm sorry. My wife miscarried our child—a little boy—on that day many years ago. I can never think about it without melancholy seeming to grab ahold of me."

Her heart went out to him, and she understood then that she'd been right when she thought she'd detected a wistful sadness when she mentioned Natalia and Noel's baby a few minutes earlier. "You have nothing for which to apologize. That is one of the hardest things a couple can go through." Mamma had miscarried a child. Every year on the anniversary of the babe's birth—and death—they had all gone to the cemetery. Her parents had always told her how much they regretted never having had the opportunity to get to know that child and that that was something they were looking forward to doing in heaven. The fact that they had six other children made no difference to the loss of that one. Except in terms of having been blessed to have had other children, a family.

He nodded. "It was the closest my wife and I ever came to having marital problems. It had nothing to do with our love for one another, but everything to do with pain over the loss of our child. Really hard, especially since we were never blessed to have other children."

She could tell from the way his shoulders hunched that that was a grief that he still felt keenly. For him to mention it to her, a virtual stranger, proved how much it was still on his mind. She doubted that the loss of a child, even with the grace of God, ever totally left a person.

"It's something couples have a very hard time ever recovering from. Often marriages suffer because of it." That was the only time couples had almost broken up in Kastro. She had often been asked to be present when her father had counseled them, comforted them.

"And we went through that tragedy alone, without our Lord to lean on. He was there of course; we just didn't know it, didn't know Him. Not in the full meaning of His being. Not with Him being the Lord of our lives."

She had thought he was a Christian. She'd seen him in church every Sunday since she'd moved to Ancient Olympia; it was something that seemed to be imprinted on the very fabric of his being—just as it should be with all Christians. She couldn't help how happy it made her to hear him declare it with words, though. She didn't pause to wonder why that should be.

"Did you ever consider adopting a child?" She had thanked God practically daily that her parents adopted Natalia. She knew that single women often adopted children today, but that wasn't something she had even thought about doing twenty-odd years earlier.

He breathed out deeply. "We were completing the paperwork on a young girl from Eastern Europe when my wife became ill." He shrugged and looked out around the site. "I would have liked to have brought her here. She's eighteen now. I've often wondered about where she's living and about the couple that became her parents. I hope she's happy."

"So." Martha paused and licked her lips, not really sure she should continue. This was a highly personal subject. But the way he looked at her, as if he needed to talk to someone about the children he'd loved and lost, compelled her to continue. "In truth, you've lost two children. Not just one."

When a poignant smile lifted the corners of his lips, she knew that she had been correct to speak. "You're a very perceptive woman, Martha. Most people don't realize how deeply I feel the loss of that little girl, too."

"She was almost your child every bit as much as the baby your wife miscarried. Of course you miss her."

"How is it that you seem to understand? You said that you'd never married, so I assume you don't have any children." It was a statement, but a questioning one.

"Ah. . ." She smiled and bantered back. "But you don't know that for sure. As it happens, I do have a child."

A frown sliced across his forehead as a myriad of questioning emotions covered his face. Disappointment. Amazement. Gladness. It was as if he didn't know which one to settle on. She decided to enlighten him.

"When I was thirty-two, my parents found a newborn baby in the bus station of the city close to our village."

"Found?"

She nodded. "Yes, they actually found an infant in a bus station. She had been abandoned there. To make a very long story short, since there wasn't a trace of the baby's biological parents, and no one claimed to have lost one, my parents adopted her, adopted our Natalia. But because my mother had just been diagnosed with a severe illness, the care of Natalia became mine. So in every way important, and even though we refer to one another as sisters, we're actually more like mother and daughter. I couldn't love a child of my own body more than I love Natalia. And even though I have never been blessed to share in the marriage relationship, as you were with your wife, God has blessed me in giving me a child to raise and love."

He whistled out through his teeth. "That is most definitely a testament to God's provision. He not only gave your sister a loving home, but you, a child."

She thought about Natalia and the way she'd brightened all of their lives, especially Mamma's, during those ten years of her illness. It was because of Natalia that their mother had lived so long, because her mother had wanted to be with her youngest child for as long as humanly possible. "God is gracious. As the saying goes, 'When God closes a door, He always opens a window.' "

He nodded, and she watched as he scanned his gaze out over the thoughtful valley and breathed in deeply of the sweet summer air. "Olympia is that window for me," he said after a moment. "I love living here. It makes me feel as if I can do anything. It's almost as if I am a young man again, free to dream and grow and do so much with my life."

"Umm, I know what you mean." She nodded and let her own gaze wander the tree-covered site full of historic stones, memories, and curious people from the world over.

Moving here had been good for that reason, too, and even though Kastro was beautiful at this time of year, there was something extra special about this valley she now called home. Although it was July and most of Greece was baking brown in the summer sun, the valley of Olympia was still green and fragrant.

"This outdoor church"—she motioned to the roofless one in which they still stood—"is one of my favorite thinking spots in the world."

"Thinking spots?" A smile brightened his features. "I like that." Then he motioned down to the white Bible that she held in her hand. "You must have a lot of Martha's sister, Mary, in you. Not only do you seem to know about human nature, but also when I walked up, you were deeply engrossed in reading. And it's not the first time I've seen you sitting here doing so."

"You've seen me here before?" The question came out before reason could keep her from voicing it. She'd seen him around town, but never at the ancient site, a place she made a point to visit at least once a week.

He shrugged his broad shoulders. "You've always looked so thoughtful that I haven't wanted to bother you." A quick grin sliced across his face. "I couldn't help myself today."

"I'm glad," she admitted and thought that she would have stayed with her gaze fastened to his all evening long if the strong gusting wind hadn't chosen that moment to pick up the brim of her hat and nearly blow her straw bonnet off her head. "Oh no!" she exclaimed and laughed. Her hat would have left her head completely and traveled through the ruins of Olympia on its own if Leo hadn't placed his hand on top of her head and held it in place while she adjusted the silky scarf straps beneath her chin. "Thanks."

He smiled, and standing back so that she could precede him from what remained of the church building, he motioned toward the path that led to the exit. Except for the crunching sounds of their feet upon the earth, they walked in companionable silence. They passed the foundation of the huge temple of Zeus, then the Philippeion—a circular building offered by Philip of Macedonia from northern Greece that honored his family, including his more famous son, Alexander, known as "the Great." The temple built to honor Zeus's wife, Hera, came next. It predated that built for Zeus, and in it, one of the more famous statues of antiquity, the Hermes of Praxiteles, had been found. Martha often went to the archaeological museum of Olympia just to stand before that mighty work of art and gaze at it.

Beyond Hera's temple was the arched entranceway to the ancient stadium. Martha walked around the stadium practically every time she visited the site. While doing so, she liked to think about all the people throughout time who had participated in races there as well as those like her who walked, or ran, its course during modern times for their own personal reasons. The prototype of all stadiums in the world today, it was another of her thinking spots.

Looking to their west was the square-shaped palaestra—the building that had been both the wrestling school and living quarters for the athletes. Pine trees now grew where that magnificent edifice had stood. Standing, stoic columns in straight lines marked where its porches had been. Martha wondered if it was as enchanting when it had actually been a building as it was now.

They were heading up the section of the path flanked by trees when Leo asked, "So do you?"

She frowned and looked up at him. Had she missed something? "Do I what?"

"Do you have a lot of Mary in you? Do you like to study at the feet of Jesus?" he repeated the question he'd asked while still at the site of the church. She couldn't help but hear the hopeful quality in his voice.

Martha nodded. "My father is a Greek Orthodox priest, and he long ago taught me the love of studying the Bible."

"Really? An Orthodox priest? I have such a huge respect for that ancient tradition. It's so misunderstood by many people, mostly for lack of knowledge. And, most amazing of all, it's the trunk of Christianity forming a direct line back to Pentecost."

A smile touched the corners of her mouth "Your knowledge is surprising."

He shrugged. "My wife was an avid history lover. And especially church history. She made sure I learned." He smiled. "I'd like to meet your father someday. He sounds like an interesting man."

"He is."

"And I can even speak to him in Greek." Using careful diction, he said, *"Milao Elinika*—I speak Greek."

Martha stopped walking and swiveled to look directly at him. She knew that her mouth had dropped open. "You speak Greek?" How rare was that? Much of the English language might have been derived from Greek, but it was still unusual for an American to tackle the Greek alphabet. Ancient Greek for scholarly reasons maybe, but rarely did people try to learn modern Greek. The expression "It's all Greek to me" wasn't coined because of Greek's simplicity.

He nodded, and she could tell that he was proud to admit that he did. "When I realized, six years ago—shortly after my wife died—that God was leading me to Ancient Olympia to make my home, I started learning it."

"That would have been about the same time that I started studying English formally and"—she looked at him, and that connection she had sensed between them seemed to sizzle faster—"when I, too, was being led to Ancient Olympia."

"Amazing to think that God was moving in our hearts about this place at the same time."

Chapter 4

But as Martha continued to walk down the path with Leo at her side, she didn't think that *amazing* was the word. More like *miraculous*, especially when she considered her father's longtime prayer for her: that someday a wonderful man would come into her life with whom she would experience the joys of marriage.

Could this be the man? Could Leo Jones be the one God has marked out for me since the beginning of time?

With the same surety that had made her certain that no man had been "hers" before, she was almost certain that Leo was that man now. It was all very strange. It made her feel almost out of control. What was it her father had said? To let God lead her down the new path her life was taking, even if the steps seemed uneven at times? She couldn't ever remember her steps feeling more uneven.

Martha believed in the power of prayer—especially her father's prayers—and she didn't believe in coincidence. Ever since her father had told her his prayer for her life, she somehow knew that God would bring a special man into it. Like a treasured secret, it was something she almost expected.

But now that the man her father had been praying for seemed to be before her—next to her!—she wasn't quite sure what to do about it, about her feelings for him. She had always thought she would jump at the chance to marry the right man. But now she didn't know if she really wanted such a change in her life, something especially strange since she was so attracted to this man.

Martha didn't like conflict. Her life ran smoothly and that was the way she liked it. A romance would be nice—especially with this handsome, articulate man—but she would have to think very carefully about anything more. She would only take a further step if she was certain that it came from God, that she could join her life with Leo's without creating problems in either of their lives by doing so.

She slightly shook her head. Her thoughts were moving in her mind like a runaway horse on a racetrack. She had only just started talking to the man an hour ago. But because of her father's strange confession two months earlier, she was already thinking in terms of marriage. That was too quick. Even for her.

"How long have you lived here?" she asked, wanting to rein in her thoughts and get them back on track.

"Only about two months."

She looked at him. "Same as me, then." Her voice was little more than a whisper. "And are you going to live here indefinitely?" She wasn't sure where that question had come from, but Martha didn't want to live anywhere other than Ancient Olympia. If he didn't plan on living here forever, then that would put an end to any relationship they might have even before it started.

"God willing."

Yes, God willing. She looked straight ahead. In the end that's what everything came down to. She had to remember that. And trust. Trust God. "Where did you live in America?" she asked, wanting to get away from her deeper, confusing thoughts.

"Olympia."

Her brows shot up like Baba's did when he was confounded.

"Olympia, Washington. It's the state's capital city," he explained.

Martha shook her head. "I had no idea that there was a city named Olympia in America."

"You'd be surprised at the number of 'Greek' cities to be found there," he said, flashing her that full smile of his. "We even have an Athens in the state of Georgia." He grimaced. "Unfortunately the reproduction of the Parthenon is located in another state, in Tennessee. But my Olympia"—he patted his chest—"was named for the Olympic mountain range that runs along the Pacific coast to the north of the city. I assume that those majestic mountains were in turn named for Mount Olympus in northern Greece, which is how this area"—he waved his arms out—"received its name, too, in honor of the mythological gods who lived on Mount Olympus. At least that's what my mother always told me, which was nice to think about. It always reminded us of where at least part of our family's heritage came from."

His family's heritage? Now she better understood his choice of Ancient Olympia as his home. "From here?"

He nodded. "My grandfather on my mother's side."

She touched her fingers to her lips. "My mother's family, too."

"Are you serious? You mean, we"—he moved his hand back and forth between them—"could be relatives?"

She waved her hand in a circular motion, which in Greek indicated the passing of time or an event. "Way back."

"Yes, way back," he agreed just as they arrived at the exit to the ancient site, and they stopped walking and turned to face one another. "Well, Martha—"

"Martha-Mary," she informed him.

"What?"

"Since you like Lazarus's sisters so much, I think I should tell you that my entire Christian name is Martha-Mary. My parents wanted me to embody the characteristics of both those famous Bible women, so they gave me both of their names."

He shook his head. "Have you heard about the book *What's in a Name?*"

Had she heard about it? Since Noel, Natalia's husband, was its author, she had an autographed copy sitting on the shelf behind the cash register in her shop. She even sold the book. But Leo was too new an acquaintance to let him know about her famous brother-in-law, or her sister, for that matter. "Yes."

"Then you will know that the writer shows how important it is to find the correct name for a person. Your father did that for you."

"Do you really think you know me well enough to conclude that?" she couldn't help asking. Forthrightness had always been her way.

"Well. . ." He surprised her by taking her hands in his and looking down at them. She was astonished with herself for letting him and even more at how perfect it seemed. "From your hands, which have the look of your having used them well during your life, I know that you are not idle." Her face grew hot, and she would have snatched her hands back, but from the timbre in his voice, she knew that he hadn't meant his words unkindly.

"Beautiful hands," he whispered, justifying her thoughts. "Helping hands of character, of love." He rubbed his fingertips over her shaped, but shortly cut, nails and up her fingers, past her knuckles, to the backs of her hands. He didn't let go of them when his gaze returned to her face. "And from seeing you sitting on a bench beside a church building that was built in late antiquity reading your Bible, I know that you are definitely a Mary."

In spite of her reservations, her heart was beating to its new romantic tune even as she quickly spoke. "The truth is, until recently the Martha side of me was stronger than the Mary side." Even with a shop to run, coming to Olympia had freed a great deal of time for Martha to be Mary. She had quickly learned that running a home for a family was much more work than taking care of a business. The business had working hours. A home didn't.

The sun had lowered in the sky, and in the light of its red rays, she watched as a slow, very manly, very sweet smile spread across Leo's face. "Martha-Mary, you are a woman I hope to meet often in my travels around Olympia. Both the ancient site and the modern town."

She couldn't move her gaze away from his. She didn't even want to. For this man, this most remarkable and attractive man, was looking at her just as she had seen Noel look at Natalia, Baba at her mother, Stavros at Allie, and so many other men at their mates in Kastro, in New York, in churches everywhere, and while shopping in her store. Martha had never been envious of any of them. But having felt that special emotion of having a man think she was so unique as to warrant that valued look, Martha knew that she could never go back to not wanting it, not needing it.

Dear Lord, is this the one my father has been praying would come into my life? He's like. . .a fairy prince. And even though I don't know how far I really want our relationship to go, I know right now that just as I must draw breath into my lungs and my heart must beat, I must get to know him. But how? Show me the correct way, Lord.

"Where can we next meet?" she heard him ask and blinked at how he seemed to answer her prayer with his question.

"Once Upon A Time. . ." The name of her shop automatically passed over her lips.

His smile deepened and his fingers softly stroked the backs of her hands. With the happy sounds of tourists that surrounded them fading into the background, and with a blackbird chirping out a sweet tune in the plane tree beside them, he spoke softly, affectionately, in a dreamy sort of way. "Once upon a time. . .in a land far, far away. . .that time had almost forgotten. . .there lived a lovely woman full of grace and beauty named Martha-Mary—"

She giggled, breaking the spell, and when he stopped speaking, she could have kicked herself.

But when the slow, secure smile of a man who didn't embarrass easily spread across his face, she knew that everything was all right. "I'm sorry." She licked her lips. "I like how your story goes, but—"

"Our story," he corrected her, and she almost forgot to breathe, as the world seemed to stop revolving on its axis and stand still. Her world, anyway.

" 'Our story'?" she squeaked out.

"The story I hope might be ours," he returned, and her heart pounded against her chest with the force of thunder in the sky, but she had never felt better. "You interrupted me before I got to that part."

"I'd like that," she admitted and felt just like the heroine in a romance novel, but an inspirational one now, where the heroine wasn't fighting the normal progression of a love plotted out by God. "But to have our own story, in order for our story not to end here, we must, as you said, be sure to meet again. Soon."

"Soon. Now that's something I like."

Martha was glad that he obviously liked to do things as rapidly as she. Once she made up her mind about something, that was it. And she had made up her mind that in spite of any reservations she might harbor about unwanted changes and conflicts he might bring to her life, wanted to know Leo Jones better. She had never thought in terms of romance as going fast, but she knew that to go slow wasn't in her makeup, evidently not even where romance was concerned. Then again, she had lived for nearly fifty-seven years on God's planet without a close relationship with a man. How slow was that? She just wouldn't tell Natalia how quickly she let a man into her heart, not after all her own warnings to her sister. "I was just telling you the name of my shop, where we might meet next time." At his confused look, she explained. "Once Upon A Time—that's its name."

As if a light flipped on inside him, his eyes widened. "That store on the main street of Olympia that is always filled to overflowing with women is your shop?"

She nodded. "Once Upon A Time. . ." She giggled. Giggled again. She hadn't giggled—ever. But neither had she ever had such a conversation with a man as she had shared with this one for the past hour or so. "You must always come by when my needlepoint ladies are there."

"Needlepoint ladies?"

She nodded and explained. "Three times a week a group of ladies come with whatever handiwork they are doing, and we all work together. Since needlepoint is my specialty, that's what the gathering first started out as. But many of the ladies are masters at other crafts. Some crochet, others knit, others carve, while still others paint. One woman hand paints beads, while an octogenarian even paints authentic Byzantine icons. And if the ladies so desire, Once Upon A Time sells what they make. For some, it has become a good source of much-needed income."

A whistle passed his lips. "And you have only lived here for two months?" he asked rhetorically and squeezed her hands, reminding her only then that he still held them firmly in his grasp. It had felt so right, so normal, so comfortable even, that she hadn't noticed. "I've often passed your shop and thought that it must be one of the oldest, most established in town. It's always full. You must have quite a good head for business."

She had to suppress the pleased smile that wanted to erupt at his praise. It delighted her in a way no one else's had. "That has come as a bit of a shock to me, too." Once Upon A Time was doing so well that she knew that she had to look for someone to help her run it during the busy summer months. She closed every Sunday—the reason she was able to be out now—but she was finding that keeping store hours six days a week was a bit restrictive and too much for one person to handle. Especially since the shop was often busy.

"What's your secret?"

Giving his hands a light squeeze, she let go of them, and crossing the country road, walked over to the bus stop on the opposite side. He followed beside her. "Well, I only sell the best quality of handmade folk art and crafts that I can find. But mostly, I treat the shop like it's my home and welcome all who walk in as if they are my honored guests. Because they are. I feel as if everyone who comes into the shop is coming to spend a few minutes of his or her life with me. That's special."

"No, Martha-Mary, I think you're the special one," he muttered thickly.

She didn't know what to say. To have him look at her as if he thought she were the most wonderful, most unique, woman in the world was one thing. But for him to say it was something entirely different. It brought everything onto a level that she wasn't sure she was prepared to reach. They might have seen one another for the previous two months, but they had only just met. To cover her confusion, she fiddled with the straps of her purse and was relieved when the bus pulled up. "Are you riding back to town?" she asked and heard a breathless quality to her voice that almost made her cringe.

"No. I have my bike." He motioned in the direction of the fancy bike on which she had often seen him riding. It was chained to a tree. He smiled, obviously not put off by the change in her manner. "I will drop by Once Upon A Time tomorrow if that is okay with you."

She nodded and smiled but really felt like yipping for joy. By then she should have control of the emotions that were bouncing around in her like Ping-Pong balls in perpetual movement. "Tomorrow," she agreed, and as she climbed the three steps onto the bus and sat down, she only hoped that it was a promise.

She closed her eyes. Her blood sang through her veins as she remembered his words. *"Once upon a time. . .in a land far, far away. . .that time had almost forgotten. . . there lived a lovely woman full of grace and beauty named Martha-Mary."*

She opened her eyes and looked out over the historic valley as the bus wended its way down the road. She wondered how their story might end.

A part of her hoped it might be "And they lived happily ever after in a land far, far away."

But another part of her was still confused, and she didn't know what she hoped for—strange for a woman who was normally so well acquainted with her own mind. Even though her father had been praying for a mate for her, and even though a part of her thrilled to the idea, she knew that at this point in her life, to join her world with that of a man's was a major life change. Everything would have to be perfect in order for her to do so.

But oh, how she liked that tall, slender man. She placed her hand upon her chest, and as she took a deep, settling breath, she reminded herself again to do what she had done all her fifty-six years.

As with everything else in her life, she would leave any relationship with Leo Jones up to God. She would follow His leading.

A secret smile played on Martha's lips.

And Leo's leading, of course.

Chapter 5

Leo walked toward the bushes at the side of the road and stood in the protection of a family of blossoming laurel, which hid him from the eyes of the many tourists now exiting the ancient site. He watched as the blue bus drove down the fragrant country road toward the town of Ancient Olympia, its next stop.

"Dear Lord," he whispered out on a breath of yearning. "Is it because of this woman, this very special woman named Martha-Mary, that you have directed my steps here, to this town?" he asked, and a montage of the times he had seen Martha around town immediately flashed through his mind.

The picture of decorum and fine taste, Martha had always been elegantly dressed. But more than her fine clothes and nicely coifed hair that softly brushed her chin, it was the way in which she both held herself and interacted with other people that most captured his attention. She might have lived in Olympia for only two months, but to Leo it seemed as if she had been a pillar of the town for decades.

But more than her outward beauty, it was the beauty of her soul, her spirit, and her intellect that so moved him. She was a salt-of-the-earth woman with sparkling eyes and an intelligence that ran deep. But it was that immortal part of her, which her lovely body housed, that most affected him.

She seemed to personify the verses found in the final chapter of Proverbs. " 'A wife of noble character who can find?' " he softly recited a few lines into the summer's eve. " 'She is worth far more than rubies. . . . She is clothed with strength and dignity. . . . She speaks with wisdom, and faithful instruction is on her tongue.' " He paused and, knowing that Martha-Mary was indeed the reason he had been led to Olympia, breathed out with a thankful heart, "She couldn't be better, Lord. Thank You."

Leo felt the same exhilaration shoot through his system as when he had been a young man of nineteen and in love for the first time. It was an all-encompassing feeling, one that reached to the farthest parts of his body to tingle it with anticipation, and to the innermost part of his being where his spirit and soul danced together at the thought of a mate, a companion, a woman to call his own once again.

Leo was ready for love. He had yearned for another woman—a wife—to share his life with since the day he had let Susan go, about two years after she had died.

It seemed unbelievable that during the first time of really talking to Martha—of speaking more than just a few words of greeting—he should know that she was the one for him. But even more unbelievable was that God should endorse the truth of his feeling within his soul, as God most definitely was doing, in His still, soft way.

But he had been patient.

Leo grimaced at the self-righteous sound of that.

For the most part he had been patient. For the first two years after his wife had passed away, he hadn't dated at all because he hadn't wanted to, hadn't yet thought of himself as being wifeless, as being single again. He had immersed himself in the study of God's Word, church history, and Greek; his work; and sports. In that order. The study of God's Word had been the greatest comfort to him in his loss. He knew from reading the wonderful words of promise and hope that the wife of his youth was safe even if he couldn't have a personal part in taking care of her any longer.

After two years, though, both wanting and needing a special woman with whom to travel through life, he had started dating again. He had gone out with many women. But from the first, he had somehow known that none were for him.

That thought caused a quizzical frown to slice across his face. So maybe it wasn't so incredible to recognize that a woman was the one for him during their first meeting. "Love at first sight?" he questioned himself. "More like love at first conversation."

But it had been the proverbial love at first sight with Susan, his wife. And even though they had wasted many years with the empty living that monetary success often brings to couples, they had, before the end of their journey together, found the Truth that had set them free to be the people they were created to be in Christ Jesus. And then the love they had felt at first sight for one another became something many times more precious. It was one such as that ordained by God for His people, a glorious time of learning together with their spirits tuned to each other's because they were both, first and foremost, tuned to the God of all creation.

Leo took a deep breath and squinted up toward the sky, which was bathed in a summertime palette of orange, red, pink, and yellow. His gaze followed the little fork-tailed swallows that swooped and turned, dipped and dived as they played tag in the foreground, while the sounds of their playing on the soft evening breeze brought delight to his ears.

Was he actually in love with a woman he had only just talked to? He was, he admitted to himself, and with the admission, his spirit felt as light and free as those playful birds. It was soaring along with them.

He laughed, a giant laugh that filled his brain with endorphins. Leaning toward the bush, he inhaled the fragrance that softly perfumed the air around the laurel. He knew that he would forever associate this sweet but mild bouquet with the discovery of his second love. Some might question the validity of his sudden decision as being made on the wings of emotions and, as such, one that shouldn't be trusted.

But Leo didn't.

He had always been quick to make decisions, to come to conclusions. Decisiveness was one of the traits that had made his software company one of the most successful and that had given him the freedom to move halfway around the globe and run his company from wherever he chose.

He only hoped—especially now that he had talked to Martha-Mary and realized how much she meant to him—that he might be able to continue to do so. But there were situations with the company that might need his personal attention. He had always known there was a chance that he might have to move back to Olympia, Washington, and split his time between both Olympias. Until meeting Martha, he hadn't minded the idea. Now he did.

He sighed. He would cross that bridge when he came to it. Leo had learned long ago not to borrow tomorrow's possible problems today.

Leaving his hidden place among the shrubbery, he hummed a favorite tune as he strode over to his bicycle, where he had left it under the watchful eyes of the canteen owner.

He only hoped that he would be as successful with Martha-Mary Pappas as he had been with his business.

Somehow, he felt that he would be.

He strongly believed that God had ordained his steps to meet hers here in Olympia, starting six years earlier. Actually—he corrected his thought as he waved his thanks to the canteen owner and secured the bike chain around its seat—God had ordained their steps to walk together here in Olympia long, long before the original Olympic Games had started in 776 B.C. From the very beginning of time, even...

As he straddled the bike and clipped his helmet strap beneath his chin, he wondered how much more encouragement he needed than that to seek out and pursue, with an eye toward marriage, the lovely woman named Martha-Mary.

None, he thought, as he started cycling down the road, which the bus, holding the woman he loved, had passed over only moments before.

None at all. For when he decided on something, he always achieved his goal. Always. And this was one he was certain God Himself had endorsed.

"'Once upon a time...in a land far, far away...that time had almost forgotten,'" he said, softly reciting the words he had spoken to Martha earlier, "'there lived a lovely woman full of grace and beauty named Martha-Mary. . .' and. . .a man named Leo Jones who loved her. . . ."

He laughed, a laugh unlike any that had sounded from him since his wife had died. Leo was genuinely happy.

And all because of a woman named Martha-Mary.

~~~~~

The intercom buzzed.

Martha sat up in bed and opened her eyes wide all at the same moment. Adrenaline from being awakened from a sound sleep pounded through her system like a wave from a choppy sea hitting the rocky shore. She glanced at Needlepoint. The buzz had only elicited a lazy lifting of one chocolate brown lid. Martha smiled at her blue-eyed feline friend as she placed her hand on her chest to still her own heart's hammering. Throwing back the sheet, she slipped her feet into her seafoam green slippers, grabbed her matching silk robe from the hook on the back of her bedroom door, and padded down the polished plank floor of the hallway to the living area of her apartment.

Her gaze went to the digital clock. 23:37.

By Greek standards, and especially during the summer months when most indulged in afternoon siestas, it wasn't considered too late. But Martha had been unusually tired after returning from her cousins' that evening and had gone straight to bed rather than watching TV while needlepointing, as was her normal custom during the final hours of the day. People who knew her well, though, would know that she was normally awake until past midnight, so she was quite certain that someone close to her must be at her door.

Would Leo, the man who had occupied much of her thoughts during the evening—she had been thinking about him even while carrying on conversations with her cousins—come to her home at this time of night? She hoped not. Since she'd only recently met him, that wouldn't be right. In fact, it would be a major minus against him. And she didn't want any negatives aligned with him.

As if scanning through a movie on her DVD player, she had gone over bits and pieces of their conversation all evening long. She had thought about the way his mouth moved while he talked and how it was always quick to stretch and fill in the smile lines that surrounded it. She had also thought about the way she felt when he had taken her hands in his.

His touch. . . So perfect, as if her hand had been custom-made by the Master Designer to fit into his and none other. There had been nothing strange about it. But that was the most unusual thing of all. Never had it felt right to hold a man's hand. The few times she had dated, she had always been uncomfortably conscious of a man's hand around hers. She hadn't been with Leo. It had been as if it were an extension of her own. . . .

But she knew it wouldn't be Leo at her door. She sensed enough about him to know that he wouldn't come to a woman's home uninvited at this time of night. Especially one he had only talked to for the first time that day.

Martha lifted the receiver to the video intercom, which enabled her to observe and speak with visitors at her downstairs door. She was taken aback to see the young woman whose face filled the screen. "Maria?"

"Yes, it's me, Kyria Martha," the young woman replied, referring to Martha with the respectful feminine title. She turned great big, sad eyes up to the camera. "May I come in, please?"

Even with the imperfect image through the tiny in-house screen, Martha could tell that her young friend was troubled. Very troubled. "Of course, kali mou," she replied as she simultaneously reached for the button to buzz the girl in. But as Martha heard the street-level door being opened, then closed, and heard Maria's soft footsteps on the steep marble stairs, she questioned what could have brought Maria from medical school in Athens to Olympia, rather than to her father's home in Kastro.

Unless—and in spite of the heat of the night, Martha shivered at the thought—she and Dimitri had broken up.

Martha opened the door wide in welcome, and Maria dropped her duffel bag. She immediately fell into Martha's arms, just as she had nine years earlier when Maria had been thirteen and her mother had just passed away. And as then, sobs racked the slender girl's body. Martha was certain, even before Maria got the words out, that her suspicion was correct.

"Dimitri. . .he. . .broke up. . .with me," Maria cried out softly. Maria was never loud even when expressing grief. "I just couldn't return to Kastro for summer holiday. . .where everybody would"—she hiccuped, and Martha knew that silent tears must have been falling from the girl's eyes throughout her long bus trip from Athens—"feel sorry. . .for me." She hiccuped again. "And my father. . ."

She couldn't go on, but she didn't need to. Martha understood. Her father, Petros Petropoulos, had never approved of Maria's relationship with Dimitri. Primarily because he felt it was one his daughter pursued rather than Dimitri.

Martha gently guided the young woman into her living room and over to the floral brocade sofa. "Shh, there, there, you did well in coming here, Maria. You know that you are always welcome in my home for as long as you want to stay."

Maria squeezed Martha's hands in gratitude as the girl sank onto the sofa. She turned her dark, intense eyes up to Martha. "I feel just as I did when my mother. . ." She stopped speaking and patted her chest. "It's as if my heart is being ripped out again."

"No, kali mou." Martha gently took her hands in her own. "It's different." She had to be firm about that. A man not wanting to pursue a relationship with a woman was not anything near as traumatic as a young child losing a parent. And even more, Martha didn't want Maria to let this hurt rule her life as she had with her mother's death nine years before. "I'm sure that Dimitri must have a good reason for deciding as he did." Martha had nothing but the highest respect for Dimitri. She was certain that he wouldn't intentionally hurt Maria. "He probably doesn't think that you have enough in common to live a life together."

"But. . .I love him!" Maria cried softly, with all the lifelong adoration she had felt for the young man in the throbbing sound.

Martha had always felt guilty for wanting Dimitri and her sister Natalia to get together, knowing how this young woman felt about the man. But Martha had agreed with Petros, Maria's father, and never felt that Maria and Dimitri made a good match.

But that wasn't what the heartbroken girl needed to hear right now.

Sitting next to her on the sofa, Martha wrapped her arms around the young woman and cradled her head on her shoulder, just as she knew her mother, Emily, would have done had she still been alive.

Who would know at this moment that this crestfallen young woman was one of the finest physicians in the making? As well as being one of the strongest people Martha knew.

"I thought he was going to ask me to marry him," Maria moaned out after a few minutes. "We had even talked a few weeks earlier about how much we both wanted to have children while we're still young. I had no idea that he didn't mean with me," she said, her voice much weaker than its normal, sure tone. "We never fought," she continued, as if that proved that they were a perfect match.

Martha handed Maria a tissue from the box on the end table. Dimitri and Maria were both too quiet, too much alike. She could imagine them sitting together and studying. But not much else. Dimitri needed someone full of fun and laughter, a get-up-and-enjoy-life kind of girl—someone like Natalia. And Maria needed a man who could show her that life was more than just one responsibility after another.

After Maria's mother had died, the young teenager had taken on the duty of raising her two younger brothers and sister. Not only had she raised them, but she had been their teacher. Their father, full of grief and anger that no one had been able to save his wife and newborn baby, had deserted their nice home in the village and moved his four children to an old woodsmen cabin up on the mountains high above Kastro. Martha was certain that if it hadn't been for Allie, when she was the new doctor in the village, Maria's father probably never would have come down off his mountain. But Allie had proven to him that she was a doctor who cared and made him see that he was risking his children's lives by staying up on the mountain far away from civilization and help. Moving back to the village had been perfect timing for Petros's other children, but Maria's responsible, staid personality had already been formed. And when she saw a grown-up Dimitri—an extremely fine-looking, impressive young man—her childhood attraction had formed, as well.

"I wanted to marry Dimitri. And soon. He would have married me if he had felt about me the way he did Natalia." Martha didn't hear even an iota of rancor in her tone. Maria had never faulted Natalia for Dimitri's love of her, especially since it was unrequited. Besides, Natalia loved Noel, not Dimitri.

"Attraction is a complicated thing," Martha finally replied. She was just beginning to realize that since meeting Leo. That so-called chemistry that makes one person highly attracted to another was fine as long as both parties felt the same way, but misery if only one did. She was so thankful that Leo seemed to find her as nice as she found him.

"I know." Maria's lower lip jutted out just as it had when she had been a young girl. "I just wish I could have proclaimed. . .to the world. . .that Dimitri was *thekos mou andras*—my husband," she finished, as tears dropped from her eyes like rain from a heavy autumn sky.

"I know, kali mou, I know," Martha murmured and held her close.

Martha's heart was breaking for her young friend, and she had to press her eyes tightly shut to keep her own tears from falling. How she wished that things could have been different. If anyone deserved happiness, it was this young woman who had experienced too much pain in her twenty-two years.

Martha hoped and prayed that someone as bright and dazzling as a new and sunny summer day might soon come into Maria's life, someone who would make all the sorrow recede like the tide at the pull of the moon. Someone. . .

Chapter 6

After another hour of tears, talks, and hugs, Maria finally fell asleep in Martha's spare bedroom.

Martha had just finished decorating the guest room the previous Friday. The walls were papered Easter blue, with little sprigs of welcoming jasmine. Fussy priscillas covered the inlaid windows. An antique rosewood dresser topped with an old-fashioned, silver-handled brush and comb set and a cut crystal vase filled with fragrant white roses sat against the large wall opposite the double bed.

It was a room meant to welcome visitors. Martha was glad that Maria had come this week and not the prior one. The sleigh bed had been the last item to go in the room on Friday. Martha had made it up that same evening with eyelet sheets of snowy white, with a hand-crocheted summer throw that one of her needlepoint ladies had custom-made. The blanket was the exact same blue as the walls, and the pillows were Martha's own needlepoint designs of Siamese cats. She had her cat, Needlepoint, to sleep with every night. She wanted her guest to have, if not the comfort and soft, rhythmic breathing of a real cat close by, something similar.

Martha had the room ready in the hopes that she would soon have a visitor. She was glad that Maria was her first guest and that she had the lovely room waiting to offer. Maria needed the psychological security and warmth. Even in her weary and traumatized state, Martha had seen the relief jump into Maria's dark eyes when she had shown it to her. The room was just what the doctor ordered for the broken heart that ailed Maria.

As Martha lay in her own bed thinking about Maria's unexpected appearance, she knew that their midnight reunion had been a time of healing as well as one of decision. They had decided that Maria would spend not just the next few days as Maria had planned before returning to Kastro, but her entire summer break in Ancient Olympia. She would help Martha out at Once Upon A Time, make some money, as well as take the time to sit back and get her bearings, to take stock of her life. Something the girl hadn't done—ever. She had gone from being mother to her brothers and sister to being a medical school student.

She needed a holiday from personal responsibility. She was way past needing it, in Martha's opinion.

Martha reached over to the far side of her bed to pat Needlepoint good night. As she did, she thought about how Maria's life and her own were similar in that they had both cared for their father's family. But in Martha's case, she had been a woman of thirty-two when her mother had become ill and Natalia had joined their family, forty-two when her mother had succumbed to her illness. Maria had only been a child of thirteen, looking forward to a new member of the family joining them. Instead, both her mother and her infant sister had died.

Martha sighed. Leo's baby, like Maria's youngest sister, had died before even having the chance to draw a breath of his own.

She wondered how old Leo's son would have been now, had he lived.

Squeezing her eyes shut, she whispered a prayer for Natalia and Noel's child, whose body was being woven together within the safety of Natalia's body. "Dear Lord, please bless Natalia with a safe and normal pregnancy. Please let her little baby be born healthy and strong." Martha was looking forward to the birth of that new little human with all the hope and excitement that any woman soon to become a grandmother might feel. She couldn't wait to hold Natalia's baby in her arms. She secretly hoped it might be a girl, a little girl who looked just like Natalia.

But for right now, Martha knew as she lay back against her plush pillows to the soft and comforting sound of her cat's contented purr, that she enjoyed the opportunity of having Maria in her home and the chance to act as a surrogate mother to her. She knew that had the situation been reversed, Emily—who had been her dearest friend—would have done the same for Natalia.

Maria's arrival in Olympia couldn't have been better timed, either. Not only was the spare bedroom ready, but now Martha didn't have to search for someone to help her with the shop. Having someone she knew well to rely upon was a huge relief. It would also give her the time to let the Mary part of herself continue to grow strong and to study the Word of God and learn.

But that thought easily reminded her of Leo and how he had brought up the Bible story about the sisters, Martha and Mary, after finding out her name.

Leo.

As she remembered their meeting earlier that day, a smile touched Martha's lips, right before a happy sigh—something similar to the sound her cat made when her purring turned into content breathing.

Martha could hardly wait for the new day to start so that she could see him again.

She glanced at her alarm clock. One thirty.

It was the new day.

She closed her eyes. She wouldn't have much longer to wait. Or to sleep.

But even with the excitement that thoughts about Leo brought to her,

Martha fell asleep with a prayer on her lips for the young and hurting woman in the next room.

"Dear Lord, please heal Maria's heart. And Lord, if it be Your will, please bring a young man full of sunshine and fun into her life—one who will teach her how to live life joyfully. And a man who might help to make the memory of Dimitri fade like a favorite but worn-out old shirt."

The crystal chimes on the back of the shop door jingled late the following afternoon. Martha looked up from explaining the computerized cash register to Maria and into the deep green eyes of the man she had been waiting to see pass through her store's portal all day long.

"Leo," she gasped, not even thinking she should hide her pleasure in finally seeing him again. Her lack of pretense, however, was rewarded with the quick and full smile that she already associated with him as his long, athletic gait took him across the polished plank floor.

Before Martha knew it, her hands were once again encompassed by his—a feeling that she thought most heavenly. Certainly not something she had ever experienced before. "Hello, Martha-Mary. It's been too long." His voice was husky.

She glanced at the antique clock on the wall behind his left shoulder. "Almost twenty-four hours." She could tell from the downward tilt of his head that her concurrence surprised him. "I had thought to see you sooner than this."

His left eyebrow rose slightly. "A complaint, Martha-Mary?"

Her smile grew. "Most definitely."

"Well, if I have to hear a complaint, at least it's one in which I am in complete agreement," he admitted wryly, then, with a serious tone, said, "I would have come sooner," his lowered voice leaving no doubt to the truth behind his words. "Actually, I had intended to be the first one through your door this morning"—his voice returned to normal—"but my housekeeper's sister went into premature labor." It was then that she noticed the strained look in his face. "I wanted to do whatever I could to assist the family."

"Of course." Martha saw the pain of losing his own child in the intensity of his eyes. "How are mother and child?"

"Fine, thankfully; this story has a happy ending."

Unlike the unhappy one when he lost his own little child, Martha thought.

"We managed to get the new mother to Patra before the babe was born. Having the correct facilities for preemies, the doctors there expect the baby to completely recover from the ordeal of being born too early."

Martha could feel the tension leave his body as he spoke the blessed words, their utterance seemingly needed to cement the reality of this new baby's health.

"That's wonderful, Leo. I'm so glad."

He took a deep breath before letting it slowly slide out, and Martha suspected that the whole episode had cost him greatly in terms of personal memories. "Me, too."

"Patra has very good facilities for premature babies." Maria spoke from their side in an encouraging way, and Martha turned to her with a smile.

"Leo, I'd like for you to meet Maria Petropoulos. She's from my village, Kastro, and is the daughter of two of my dearest friends. She's a medical school student, so she speaks with knowledge concerning Patra's hospital. And just last night"—Martha put her arm around the girl's shoulder and gave her a slight squeeze—"Maria agreed to stay with me through the summer to help me run the shop before heading back to med school in the fall."

"That's wonderful." Leo extended his hand. "How do you do, Maria?"

Maria reached for it. "Very well, thank you." She tilted her face toward Martha. "Since coming to stay with Kyria Martha-*Mary*." She put the emphasis on the name Mary, and Martha felt the blood rush to her face. No one but her father had ever called her by both her names. And he did so only on select occasions. Maria knew that, and from the speculative way in which her young friend was regarding her, Martha was sure that she also knew that something was up. Martha would explain everything to her later. Not that there was much to explain—as yet.

Her unexpected feelings for Leo confused Martha and ran the risk of throwing her perfect life into another orbit. But a big part of her—that innate part of every woman that wishes for a mate of her own—admitted to being hopeful that there might soon be more to tell. She was following her decision of the previous day and leaving her relationship with Leo up to God. It was one that had granted her peace beyond understanding.

Maria's next words, though, had her momentarily forgetting her romance with Leo.

"You're not the only one who has a name change, Kyria Martha-Mary," she said, and Martha frowned, wondering what she meant. "As of today—this very moment actually"—she flashed a quick smile that showed off her even teeth—"I have decided to start introducing myself as Stella."

"Stella!" It surprised Martha, but pleasantly so. That had been the name Emily had actually wanted to give her firstborn child. But wanting to follow Greek tradition and give the first female child the paternal grandmother's name, Emily had settled for Stella being her daughter's second name. But Stella was the name Emily had used when talking to her daughter. Stella, "Star" in Latin, had always been Emily's little star. She had always told her daughter to shine like the stars in the universe.

"I've missed my mother always calling me by that name," Maria—Stella—said, echoing Martha's thoughts.

Martha nodded. "Me, too. . .Stella." It wouldn't take long to remember to call her that. It was more her name than Maria had ever been.

"Plus. . .because of. . .everything"—she waved her hand before her in an all-encompassing way that Martha knew meant Dimitri's splitting up with her—"along with spending the summer with you, I'd like to make another major change in my life."

"I think it's a good idea." Martha was surprised at just how much she liked it. Maria's use of her second name might help her to leave the somber Maria persona behind and recapture the happy, carefree girl she had been before her mother passed away.

"Well, Stella," Leo said, "I'm pleased to make your acquaintance, and I'm especially glad to learn you will be helping Kyria Martha-Mary out at Once Upon A Time. That will give her more free time to spend with me."

Martha tilted her head toward him. "I like the way that sounds."

Stella's big brown eyes widened so much that Martha thought her eyeballs might pop from their sockets. Martha laughed and winked at her young friend—an old signal between them that meant she would tell all later—then turned back to Leo. "Do you like the shop?" she asked.

While glancing around, Leo nodded approvingly. "It's one of the most wonderful stores I can ever remember having the pleasure of entering. So homey and yet exquisite, too."

As if seeing it for the first time again, she let her gaze follow his around the various sections of the room—the wooden shelves and tables tastefully arrayed with exquisite handmade crafts as well as selective souvenirs from the ancient Olympic Games; white-washed walls covered with fine artwork; and the back right section of the store with its two cream-colored twill sofas situated around the arched arms of the huge fireplace, the place where she welcomed tired tourists to sit and rest and where her needlepoint ladies gathered. A sense of contentment filled her that she could agree with his assessment.

She listened as he continued. "Everything is set up like a museum piece, but it's approachable." His gaze met hers. "It's truly a 'Once Upon A Time' kind of place. It makes one feel all that is right and good in this world of ours."

"Thank you. That's just what I wanted to do." It pleased her immensely that that was the impression it gave him. "It's the culmination of many dreams of mine come true." She had loved setting the gift shop up, but she loved even more coming down the steps each morning, opening the shutters, and turning the sign on the door to read "Once Upon A Time is opened for all the people of the world who wish to enter."

"I feel as if I have stepped into another era," he commented.

Martha looked around at the beamed ceiling, the deep, recessed windows with their slated shutters, and the tzaki that was the focal point of the living area. All was similar in her apartment upstairs, and she had to agree. "You can't imagine how thrilled I was when I learned that this traditional building, situated right here on the main street of Ancient Olympia, had been put on the market immediately after extensive renovations had been completed. The only thing I had to do was to unlock the door and move in."

"How old is it?"

"It was built in the late 1800s."

"That's pretty old."

She smiled. "By Greek standards, it's really not."

He chuckled. "You've got a point there."

She motioned toward the living area. "Would you like a cup of coffee or a glass of iced tea and maybe a piece of baklava?" She referred to one of the more famous Greek pastries. Made of walnuts and honey and layers of paper-thin pastry dough called philo, it was a sweet for which Martha was well known. One of her specialties.

"May I take a rain check?"

"Of course." Martha spoke the words but couldn't help the cold fingers of embarrassed disappointment that seemed to move over her skin like a cloud over the sun. She hadn't realized until that moment just how much she'd been looking forward to sitting right now and getting to know Leo better. A form of sadness that that didn't seem to be his desire unexpectedly flooded her.

What was wrong with her? She had never imagined such a feeling could be hers from a man speaking such a simple sentence. She didn't seem to know her own mind any longer, a very unusual occurrence. Is that what love did to a person? If it was, she wasn't so sure she wanted it.

Leave it up to God, a voice inside her reminded. *Follow your practice of a lifetime, and leave Leo and your feelings for him and how those feelings might change your life in God's capable hands.*

Yes. That was what she would do. She was glad for the diversion that a large number of happy, carefree tourists entering the store at that moment afforded. She smiled at them to hide her regret and embarrassment.

"What I had hoped—" Leo said, and as she turned her face back to his, she tried not to let the hope she felt at his words be too evident. He motioned out the door at the mellow softness, which the sun riding closer to the horizon cast upon the land. Gone was the brash plunder of its hot draining rays when at its zenith. It was as if the earth sighed at the respite that the sun traveling westward on its daily journey afforded it—a good night's sleep was ahead, but first, a glorious,

Grecian summer's eve. "It's such a splendid evening, I had hoped that you might like to take a stroll with me," he suggested and turned to Stella. "That is, if Stella thinks she can handle the store on her own for a while."

"No problem," Stella said quickly, and Martha smiled at her. Could Stella possibly know how grateful she was for her answer and her presence? Just having the younger woman close at this most unusual and remarkable time in her life was a security Martha hadn't even realized she needed. Until living it. But she knew Someone else did know what she needed. That was another reason why He had sent Stella to her. She—and her confusion—needed Stella just as much as Stella needed her.

"Are you sure, kali mou? This is your first day, after all."

Stella motioned to the cash register. "I've got it down now, but"—she handed the cell phone to Martha—"to ease your mind and mine, take this. If I need anything, I'll call you." She winked as she came from behind the table that served as the shop's counter on her way to help the tourists. "Have a great time."

Chapter 7

Martha and Leo did indeed have a great time—so much so that they started taking evening walks on a daily basis. Sometimes they wandered around the tree-lined streets of the modern town of Ancient Olympia, stopping now and again to enjoy an ice-cream sundae at an outdoor café under the cool, whispering leaves of a reaching plane tree. Other evenings they meandered the fragrant country roads surrounding Olympia. Other times they went into the archaeological site itself and envisioned how it must have looked nearly two and a half millennia earlier at its heyday, when it was one of the greatest places in the world.

Martha decided to enjoy the here and now with Leo and to stop thinking about how their future might unfold. But it was something she had to continually turn over to God. She was too confused by both wanting a future with him and not wanting one that might upset her orderly life. So far there didn't seem to be any major conflicts that might disturb their relationship. But even though the idea of joining her life with a man's was enough for her to consider, she refused to give in to temptation. She continually gave her fears to God and let Him guide her in her relationship with Leo. Totally.

A few days after their first walk, they took a break from roving the ancient site and sat on their favorite fallen column, the one where they had first talked. Leo said, "The ancients didn't consider Olympia a city, rather, a sacred precinct."

Martha nodded her agreement and gazed over the pastoral valley with all its beautiful trees—evergreen oaks, Aleppo pines, planes, poplars, cypresses, and ever-present olive trees—tucked between two rivers, with the conical and green Mount Kronos climbing to the north. "I can well understand how people who hadn't learned about the 'Unknown God' could believe this place to be sacred. I guess they felt close to 'God,' as they perceived supreme beings to be. Especially when considering that verse in Romans and God's invisible qualities."

" 'For since the creation of the world God's invisible qualities—his eternal power and divine nature—have been clearly seen, being understood from what has been made, so that men are without excuse,' " he recited. Shifting his gaze to her, he seemed to watch her expression closely. "Is that the one you mean?"

She nodded.

A frown pulled his dark brows together.

"What?"

He took a deep breath. "Personally, Martha, I think that verse refers to God's general revelation to mankind—that of the creation, the natural world, and its natural law—and should have actually directed the ancient people toward Him, especially considering their historic capacity as a race to think, and not to images made to look like mortal men." He pointed to the right toward the ruins of the temple to Zeus. Only the three-level base and huge, fallen drums of circular-cut stones remained now, but it was still easy to see how massive and grand the structure had been. "Phidias's gold and ivory statue of Zeus sat in there."

"True." She pointed toward what had been the church. "And that's where Phidias sculpted that statue in about 435 B.C.—it was the site of his workshop before the church was built there. In the fifth century A.D., the statue was transferred to Constantinople where it most likely perished in a fire about forty years later. That early Christian church was built on the ruins of Phidias's workshop, and even though the church building itself has suffered at the hands of invading humans and nature and it's in ruins today, too, the message that it brought to this land, unlike the one the temple to Zeus purported, is not.

"The people of the first centuries after Christ who lived here, upon being given God's special revelation—His Word—combined it with His general revelation and left their questioning, pagan ways and built churches to honor the God of Jesus Christ, the God whom they had loosely worshipped before as the Unknown God. Once they understood who He was"—she flashed him a grin—"and it was that delight in reason, in thinking, you mentioned a moment before that assisted the Greeks, they built church buildings, successors to that one there." She nodded toward the brick walls with arched windows and the marble screen of Byzantine workmanship that remained of the structure. "And the church has been in their hearts for much, much longer than that statue of Zeus, made of gold and ivory—elements of God's earth—sat in that temple. It's not something that can ever be burned in a city fire or"—she indicated the entire area that had sat underwater for centuries due to the Alpheos River having changed its course in the Middle Ages—"destroyed by floods, earthquakes, vandals, or thieves."

His chest lifted on a deep breath and slowly went down. "In the fifteenth chapter of John, twenty-second verse, Jesus said to His disciples concerning the nation into which He was born—the Jewish nation—'If I had not come and spoken to them, they would not be guilty of sin. Now, however, they have no excuse for their sin.'" He sighed. "The Jews not only had God's Son with them, but they had received God's special revelation in the Old Testament. And yet so many rejected Jesus. Many didn't—enough to start the infant church—but still, many did."

He paused, and Martha watched as his glance slid over the ruins of the church building and stopped on the crosses, which were cut into the marble screen. "The Greeks didn't reject Christ. Even though they had a culture that was one of the greatest the world had ever seen, or will ever see, they didn't hold on to their own pagan ways, but recognizing a better Way, embraced it."

His gaze left the church and turned to her. Martha's heart seemed to soar with the swallows that played in the wind. How similar in thought she and Leo were! It was a heady experience, almost the same as when they held hands.

She knew that he hadn't agreed with her at first, and yet he had listened and honestly considered her words. He had done that many times during their time together, something very important to any future relationship they might have. The physical attraction that sizzled between them was wonderful, but thoughts, feelings, and beliefs would eventually render that shallow. She had to know that she could always speak her mind with Leo and that he would always carefully consider her feelings. And vice versa. Agreement about everything—except for their belief in Christ—wasn't the issue. Communication was. "That's the way I see it, Leo."

He looked down at her hand and rubbed his thumb across her knuckles before training his gaze back to hers. "You know, when I told my friends at my church in America that I was moving here, to Ancient Olympia, many of them had questions about the Olympic Games and Christianity."

"It's an interesting subject and actually something that I've given a great deal of thought to." She had. Both the ancient and modern games. She knew that some people thought that the games never should have been reinstated. But she had always thought that a little study about it would change most minds. Even devout minds.

"Somehow, I was certain that you had." His lips turned up at the corners. "Tell me," he encouraged.

She loved that he wanted to know. With a quick return smile she nodded, then motioned with her arm toward the historic land around them. "What the ancient Greeks did here with the original Olympic Games was not perfect." The games had been held in honor of Zeus. "But it was something that brought the people together for the promotion of the brotherhood of mankind, and it was a way to take the bellicose nature of man and place it not on a battlefield, but rather in a sports stadium in a movement of peace. They did it for more than a thousand years, practically every four years." She laughed gently. "We people of modern days who have both God's special as well as His general revelation have only held the games for a little over a hundred years. And that includes missing three modern Olympiads due to the two world wars in the twentieth century."

"You have given this subject some thought, haven't you?" he said with a lazy gleam in his deep eyes that made the blood rush to her face.

She held her hands up to her checks. "When I get on the subject of the ancient games compared to the modern ones, not to mention God's involvement in it all, I do tend to go on so."

"No." He lowered her hands from her face, then squeezed them while staring at her in that intense way that made her feel like she was the most special woman in the world. The depth in his eyes held all the sparkling adoration that a woman could ever hope to see in a man's gaze. The multitude of green shades reminded her of this valley. His eyes were peaceful, calm, and intelligent, as if, like this land, they had much to tell. "I like it," he said. "I could listen to you talk all day long." He laughed. "Besides, I asked."

"Are you sure?" She laughed wryly. "Believe me, I have much more to say on the subject. I think it has always appealed to me because one of my ancestors—from all accounts a very strong Christian, too—gave a great deal of support and money toward organizing the first modern Olympics in 1896. She attended them, too."

He whistled between his teeth. "Really? I've never met anyone with a relative who attended the first games."

"I'm not sure if you've noticed, but I have a photo of that ancestor—Sophia—on the mantel at the store."

He nodded. "I wondered who that was. She was a very attractive young woman."

Martha had always admired Sophia and often regretted that her mother's relatives had lost virtually all contact with her after Sophia moved to America. Nodding, she leaned toward him, and in a conspiratorial way, said, "It gets even better. She met her husband at those first games. He was an American from Princeton, New Jersey."

"No kidding?" A smile played with the corners of his mouth. "So others in your family have been brought together by something to do with Olympia and the Olympic Games?"

"Others?" She frowned. "I don't know. But I imagine it's possible. Actually, I think Sophia and Henri's daughter married a man whom she met at the Lake Placid Winter Games in 1932. I don't know for sure, though, because we've lost track of the relatives from that branch of the—"

"No." He interrupted her. "Darling Martha-Mary, by 'others' I mean us." He flicked his pointing finger between them. Just a little gesture, but one that said so much, that they were a couple. Martha's heart experienced that funny little jump it had so often done since meeting Leo.

"Us?" she squeaked, her voice unrecognizable to her ears.

The lines around his mouth filled with his smile. His head lowered toward hers, so close that the musky scent of his fine aftershave mixed with that of his own essence to fill all that was feminine in her. She felt such joy in being in his presence that she thought she must be dreaming. It was a form of intoxication, a good one, that God had decreed right and excellent between a man and a woman.

She closed her eyes to drink in the exotic moment, one serenaded by nature's orchestra—cicadas grinding, pigeons cooing, bees buzzing, and a warm summer breeze that played the leaves of the poplar trees into violins fluttering. But nothing in her life had prepared her for how she felt when Leo's lips—his perfect, sweet, masculine lips—touched lightly, like the wings of a butterfly—upon her own.

She heard a groan.

Was it he or she?

She wasn't sure. All she knew was that this was a moment she had never experienced.

"Darling Martha-Mary," he whispered.

She wished she could contain the small giggle, but she couldn't.

"What?" He chuckled in return, resting his forehead against her own.

"Don't feel bad, and please don't stop calling me by both my names, but. . ."

She paused and chewed on her lower lip. How she wished she hadn't laughed. She would have much preferred to still feel his lips upon her own. Instead, there was the chance that she had offended him.

"Go on," he prompted with laughter in his voice, reassuring her that he hadn't taken offense.

"Well, I always feel. . .a bit. . .like a nun in a movie I once saw—I can't remember its name—when you use both my names."

The glint of humor in his eyes was a match to that in his voice. "Is that how you feel right now?" he challenged. Most people would call his deep, soft voice sexy, but she thought it made her feel like the most cherished woman in the world.

"No, Leo," she hastily assured him. "A nun is the last thing I feel like."

He stared at her deeply, as if he were trying to look past her eyes to see into her soul. His eyes narrowed more until he spoke the words Martha had long since ceased expecting to hear a man say to her. "*S'agapo*, Martha. I love you."

And just as when he had taken her hand in his, and when he'd kissed her, the words seemed natural and right. She didn't allow reason, which might question whether it was right for her life and his; she only whispered her feelings back. "S'agapo, Leo."

"You do?" He blinked as if he hadn't expected that reply, as if it were almost too easy.

She shook her head. "Darling Leo. What's not to love?" That was the truth.

She loved everything about this man. The way he treated her, the way they talked together, laughed together. The way they believed the same things. But mostly, the way he made her feel. Special. Cared for. Loved.

"It's not too fast for you?"

"I like doing things fast. Besides, I'm just telling you that I find you the most wonderful man I have ever met. And you make my heart beat in a way that it has never done before." She put her hand on his forearm, relishing the feel of the muscles beneath his skin, the soft hair beneath her touch. "There's plenty of time for anything more." And she knew that that was the truth, too.

"Martha, I believe that God brought us together so that we might share a future."

She knew he felt that way. She had sensed it from the first day they talked. It was one of the reasons she'd felt apprehensive about her life changing with meeting him.

Oh, it was so confusing.

She both wanted him in her life—embraced the idea of the wonderful change he would bring to her world, one God recommended for men and women—and yet, at the same time, she loved her life just the way it was. She loved living in Ancient Olympia, loved her shop, her apartment, her friends, her church. As much as it depended on her, she didn't want conflict of any sort in her life.

But whether she wanted it or not, it was there, because more than any of the things she loved about her life, she loved having Leo in it now. But in spite of her father's prayer for her, she felt that that very love might conflict with the good life she had made for herself in Ancient Olympia.

"I don't know about any future we might share yet, Leo." She spoke softly, not wanting to hurt him—never that—but knowing that she had to be honest. "But I do know that I'm so glad that God brought you to this land that is so far, far away from the world but so close to me."

"Oh, Martha," he murmured. And just before his lips joined with hers again, he whispered, "Me, too."

Martha wished that life might always be just as it was at this moment, wonderful and, as yet, so free of complications. But something—maybe having lived life for more than half a century—warned her that that would not always be the case.

Chapter 8

A few days later—days of shared joy in their new love for one another—Martha and Leo stood in front of the huge statue of Hermes of Praxiteles at the archaeological museum. Made of Parian marble—the fine, white marble found on the Greek island of Paros—and standing tall above their heads, it was the ideal combination of grace and strength that the sculptor, Praxiteles, had been able to form from an element of God's earth. The Olympian serenity on Hermes' face, as well as its perfect proportions, combined to make it one of the finest pieces of artwork in the world. Its white marble was perfectly offset by the deep red of the walls behind it.

"We have this beautiful piece, and it's the star of the museum," she said as they walked through the cavernous halls of the museum toward the exit. "But it just makes me wonder about all the other works of art that the vulgarities of time have destroyed here at Olympia."

"We wouldn't even have it or all these other statues"—Leo pointed to those that lined the walls of the room they now walked through—"if the Alpheios River hadn't changed course, flooded the site, and hidden them from both the eyes of ravaging humans and other even more destructive elements of nature."

"Amazing to think of a flood protecting something."

"Even more is that a volcano can do that," he said. They passed the modeled reconstruction of the ancient site—which depicted the buildings of the ancient city in all their Hellenic splendor—and exited the museum. "Like what happened at Pompeii in Italy when Vesuvius erupted in A.D. 79."

She nodded her agreement, and threading her arm through his, they started down the tree-lined path toward the main road. Walking arm in arm in companionable silence was one of those nice little unexpected things that had come from her relationship with Leo. It was something she really enjoyed about having him in her life. He was her man to reach out and touch, to hold hands with, to fix down his windblown hair. Those simple things were what made both life and the new love they shared together special and oh, so romantic. No words were necessary to fill empty places, because there were no vacant spots in their time together. Silence was time shared and golden.

As their feet crunched over the stones, the symphony of summer—the cicadas' drone, birds playing in the breeze, the sounds of children and their parents out together to inspect a bit of history—all played around them. Martha's mind wandered.

She had learned some very interesting things about Leo earlier that day. Her needlepoint ladies had met at the shop, and several had told her how Leo was known to fill any need in town he heard about. She knew that he often did handiwork around the homes of the elderly who could no longer do the work themselves, but what she hadn't known was that he would pay plumbers and carpenters if the work was beyond his abilities. And he would do the same for young mothers who needed help. He would not only arrange for babysitters and housekeepers, but pay their salaries, too. Any injured or stranded tourist he heard about was always put up in a nice hotel, again at Leo's expense. He was, in essence, a silent "need meeter" around the town of Ancient Olympia. Although he asked all whom he helped not to tell anyone, Ancient Olympia was too small for it to be kept silent. Many other wonderful additions had come to town since Leo arrived—park benches, playground equipment for the children's park, equipment for the medical station in town.

She knew that he spent several hours every day running his American-based software business from his computer at his home office and that he often said he had business around town to take care of, but she hadn't known the extent of his endeavors until the ladies told her.

They had confirmed her suspicions that Leo's main business was people. Together with the priest in town, and a few others, he filled any and every need that he could. He was a good steward with both his skills and his money.

She squeezed his arm tighter against her own, and when he looked down at her, she smiled up at him. This man was becoming better and better with everything she learned about him.

"Tomorrow is my birthday," he said out of the blue.

Coming to a full and sudden stop, she asked for confirmation that her ears hadn't deceived her. "What did you say?"

"That. . .tomorrow is my birthday." His brows came together, forming a solid line of question. Tilting his head, he asked, "What's so remarkable about that?" He chuckled. "We each have one."

Martha touched her hand to her chest. "Yes, but, Leo, not normally a shared one. You see. . .tomorrow is my birthday, too."

A wide grin split across his face. "Are you serious?"

She laughed. "Believe me, after celebrating fifty-six of them—fifty-seven as of tomorrow—I should know."

He made an amazed sound and ran his fingers through his thick hair before holding up his hand. "Wait a minute. Tomorrow is your fifty-seventh birthday?"

She grimaced. "Did you think I was older or younger?" Most put her about ten years younger, a vanity she admitted to because it had never been important to her. But was it important to Leo? Had he thought her younger, and was he disappointed to learn that she wasn't? Fingers of apprehension slithered up her backbone, and she scrunched her eyes together as the seconds added up.

Seeming to understand how far he had placed his proverbial foot into his mouth by his delay, he quickly replied. "No. No. You look younger. At least ten years younger. But your age isn't consequential to me, nor to my feelings for you."

Relief flooded her. That was the best thing he could have said.

"What I can't believe is that I will be celebrating my fifty-seventh birthday tomorrow, too."

She blinked, then opened her eyes wide. She knew that her father would have told her that her eyeballs were about ready to pop out of their sockets and run off to play basketball. "You mean, we not only share the same date, but we were born the same year, as well?"

"It's seems that way."

She giggled. "I don't believe it. Natalia and Noel share the same day but not the same year. I thought that was incredible. But this is even more so. I feel like a little kid with a secret treasure."

"I was going to ask if you would come out to dinner with me tomorrow night to help me celebrate, but I know that your family probably—"

"I'd love to."

"But what about your family?"

"In Greece birthdays aren't that big of an occasion. It's our name day that is celebrated grandly with relatives and friends."

"That's right," he replied thoughtfully. "The name of the Christian saint in whose remembrance you were named."

She nodded. "I have my choice of either Martha or Mary since they are both Christian names, but because St. Mary's Day—Maria—is a national holiday here on the scale of Thanksgiving in America, I celebrate my name day then, on August fifteenth. That's in a few weeks. My father will be back from America, so he will come here, along with several other friends from Kastro, to celebrate it with me. I hope you will come to my party, too."

"Hmm. . ." He twisted his head as if considering. "To not only meet your father but a good many of your friends at the same time. . ."

"And don't forget my relatives here in Olympia, too." She slanted her eyes at him. "Does it make you nervous?"

He leaned down, drew her close to him, and lightly placed his lips upon hers before whispering, "I think I can handle it."

She had no doubt that he could.

His dark eyes seemed to drink in the essence of her. "But tomorrow you will be all mine." His low voice made her feel as if she were melting on the inside. "I know of a lovely restaurant on the sea where I can order a romantic sunset unlike any you have ever seen. So dress in your finest, and let's go celebrate the day of our birth."

She liked the way that sounded.

⁓⋄⊙⋄⁓

The phone rang at Martha's apartment all morning long with well wishes for her birthday. Natalia and her father had been the first to call, all the way from New York and just before her father had retired for the night: Midnight in New York was 7:00 a.m. in Ancient Olympia. The time difference never failed to amaze her father. He wished her *hronia polla*—many years—and asked her to describe the sunrise over the mountains near his hometown. Martha had gladly obliged, describing it just as Homer did in *The Odyssey*, "rosy fingers" and all. She had just closed the door behind Stella, who was on her way to open the shop, when the phone rang for the umpteenth time.

It was Dimitri. Martha had hoped he would call. She wanted to ask him a few things, needed reassurance about others. After the normal salutations and well wishes, she did so, and his answers proved to her that she was right to think so highly of him.

"What I don't understand, Dimitri, is why you didn't tell Stella months ago, years even, that she wasn't the one for you. It's been very hard for her."

"Stella?"

Martha explained the name change—with which Dimitri wholeheartedly agreed—then he answered her question.

"If a woman loves a man, and the man feels much affection for her, isn't it worth trying to see if love can become a two-way pattern? I feel for Maria—Stella—many forms of love, Kyria Martha. All of those described by Paul in First Corinthians. That's why I tried. I thought that the love of friendship I have always had for her could eventually turn into romantic love. But it hasn't, and I know now that it never will."

Martha could hear the regret in his deep voice. "I just don't love her in the way a man should love a woman whom he wishes to marry," he said. "I know because I have loved in that way."

Martha knew he referred to Natalia, but she didn't say anything.

"It would be unfair of me to offer Stella anything less than that wonderful, romantic, storybook love she both craves and deserves."

"But isn't so-called romantic love the reason so many are divorced today?" *Am I asking for Stella or for myself? I most definitely share a romantic love with Leo.*

"Not if their love is, first and foremost, based on God's love."

My many talks about God-related things with Leo and our prayer time together have proven that Leo and I most definitely share that.

"As long as God is part of their union," Dimitri continued, "then romantic love can move on to the pure love—the agape love—which is the love of God in their lives. And then if all the loves talked about in Corinthians come into play in a relationship, it's the most perfect form of romantic love."

Martha knew that she had always liked Dimitri. Even as a child he had been wise beyond his years. So different from his parents, who had always let their emotions rule their lives. More than ever her heart ached for Stella. She could easily understand why the young woman was so enamored of this man, who was as handsome on the inside as he was on the outside.

"Even though there is a difference between romantic and physical love, it's when people start and stop at those two forms that there are so many divorces in the Western world today," he said. "People have forgotten about the spiritual side of their union and how that must be ordained by God. They have forgotten, too, that once a person gets married, all of the words on love in First Corinthians must be applied to their relationship even more."

"And—if you don't mind my asking—what sort of love do you lack toward Stella? You don't find her attractive?" Martha couldn't believe she was being so bold. But she had to ensure that she was correct in advising Stella in the manner in which she had—to let Dimitri go.

"Maria—Stella, I mean—is a very attractive and desirable woman. To have a physical relationship with her would be a very easy thing to do if she were that sort of woman and I that kind of man. But I want more than that and for Stella, too. I want the romance." He paused. "When I love I want to feel toward a woman like Solomon felt toward his wife. 'Place me like a seal over your heart, like a seal on your arm; for love is as strong as death. . . . It burns like blazing fire, like a mighty flame. Many waters cannot quench love; rivers cannot wash it away.'"

Martha's heart now ached for this intense young man. He had felt all that for Natalia. But Natalia hadn't felt it for him, but rather, for Noel. "I pray, Dimitri," she whispered, "that you will one day soon feel that kind of love for a young woman, one who will return it in kind."

He sighed. "Except that I would love to have a whole house full of kids while I'm young, I don't mind waiting. Like you, Kyria Martha, singleness is not something that rests badly on my shoulders. I do hope to someday find a woman to love, but until then, I will use the time wisely." He let out a deep sigh. "I just want Stella to be happy. I do love her—as a friend—and I hurt when I think of her hurting."

"Someday she'll thank you for caring enough to let her go."

"I hope so, Kyria Martha. I hope so. Because to let go of what she was offering was one of the hardest things I've ever had to do."

That was something Martha, because of her relationship with Leo, could well believe.

Chapter 9

A few minutes later, Martha walked through the back door of the shop and, out of habit, checked to see who was there. The only patron was a young man with sandy blond, reddish-tinted hair, who looked over the hand-painted porcelain beads. Martha had never seen him before. Sensing her gaze, he looked up and smiled warmly, as if he had a jolly laugh ready to erupt. Martha immediately liked the young man.

A smile formed on her lips, and she was about to ask if he needed help with anything when Stella sang out, "Hronia polla, Kyria Martha!" Stella embraced her in a great big hug.

Martha laughed and knew that she had to be beaming from all the love Stella had showered upon her since she awoke that morning. First, three fragrant yellow roses had been placed artistically on her bedside table for her to see upon opening her eyes, then a beautiful breakfast—complete with sterling silver and bone china, homemade bread and jam—set on the veranda awaited. Now this sunny greeting. As she turned to Stella, Martha felt certain that no mother could have felt more love from a daughter than she had from her friend Emily's little Stella, her Star. Even though she had been so unhappy lately, Stella had made a point to be cheery. Martha was very touched.

"Thank you, Stella. It's not even nine-thirty in the morning, but you've already made my birthday so special."

"It's your birthday?" the young man asked from behind her. When she turned and nodded, he immediately said, "Happy birthday!"

"Why, thank you." Martha was touched that a stranger should care enough to wish her birthday greetings. She smiled at Stella but was surprised to see that the girl had lowered her head and seemed to be busy with some papers on the desk. Odd. Stella normally enjoyed talking with the patrons.

"I like birthdays." The young man laughed. "All holidays, actually," he qualified and looked toward Stella's bent head. "Anything that marks a day as being special." He glanced back at Martha. "As indeed every day is."

"I couldn't agree more," Martha replied and slanted her gaze toward Stella, still perplexed that she seemed to deliberately avoid talking to the young man. Martha quickly turned back and asked, "Have you been in Olympia long?"

"About two weeks."

"Really?" That surprised Martha. She had thought he was just a short-term tourist, perhaps a recent high school graduate touring Europe.

He waved his arm in the direction of the ancient site. "I'm an archaeologist researching aspects of the ancient games for my dissertation."

Freckles were sprinkled like grain across his nose, and his fine hair fell straight down his forehead. That and his compact size made him appear hardly old enough to be out of high school, much less in graduate school. "An archaeologist? You're in the right place, then."

That ready smile spread across his face. "Don't I know it. It's great here. Really special."

"I agree." Martha said. She liked this young man more and more the longer she talked to him. And the subject of his dissertation seemed fascinating. "How long will you be here?"

"The rest of the summer."

Stella lifted her head, and his gaze connected with hers. "There's a chance I might be in Athens after that." Martha couldn't help but notice from the gleam of interest shining in his bright eyes that in spite of Stella's quiet manner, the young man was enamored of her.

She wondered if the young man might be exactly the proverbial doctor-prescribed medicine for Stella. What better way for a heart to mend than to have an attractive, personable man show an interest? This young man was the total opposite of Dimitri, which would probably help, too. Where Dimitri was tall, dark, and classically handsome—all the mystery of a deep velvet night—this man was like a field of wheat shining in the summer sun.

The chimes on the door rang. Martha turned, and from behind a bouquet of a dozen red roses, Leo's deep voice said, "Special delivery for Martha Pappas!"

"Leo!" Martha hurried across the room to meet him. Taking the flowers, she cradled them in her arms, while rising on her toes to receive his kiss.

"Happy birthday, birthday girl!"

"Happy birthday back to you, Leo."

"Happy birthday, Leo," Stella sang out.

"Wait a minute," she heard the young man speak from behind them. Martha turned just in time to see Stella lower her eyes again. "It's both of your birthdays today?"

Leo nodded and placed his arm around her waist. Martha reveled in that feeling of belonging as Leo responded, "But it gets even better. We were born the exact same year, too."

"Wow! That's neat!" The young man beamed at them, and Martha could tell he was impressed by the coincidence. "Happy birthday to you both."

"Thanks." Leo smiled down at Martha before turning back to the young man. "You're American?"

"Yep. From Pennsylvania. Philadelphia." He turned back to Stella, and Martha couldn't help but admire his persistence. "The City of Brotherly Love, which was named after one of the seven churches of Revelation."

Stella's eyelids moved slightly up and down as she regarded him, and Martha could tell that his knowledge of both ancient Greek and the Bible impressed her. "That's right."

Leo's eyes met hers briefly. He saw that something was going on between Stella and the stranger. Winking at her conspiratorially, he extended his hand to him. "I'm Leo Jones." He turned to Martha. "This is the owner of Once Upon A Time, Martha Pappas." After the young man's polite nod of greeting to her, Leo turned to Stella. "And this is Stella Petropoulos."

The young man walked toward her with his hand outstretched. Stella had no choice but to take it. "*Stella* means 'star' in Latin, and *Petropoulos,* well, let me see"—he tilted his sandy head and seemed to consider it, all the while holding Stella's hand—"*Petro* is for 'Peter' or 'rock,' while the second part of your name, *opoulos,* means that you come from this area of Greece, the Peloponnese."

"That's right," Stella agreed, and as if suddenly realizing that her hand was still within his, she quickly let go and dipped her head shyly.

Martha and Leo's gazes met briefly before Martha asked, "And you are?"

"Brian." He flashed a self-conscious grin before divulging his last name. "Brian Darling."

Martha returned his smile. Of course he was. He couldn't be named anything other than Darling. She pointed at the autographed copy of Noel's book, *What's In a Name?* and sent a smiling glance at Leo. She had given Leo a copy when she'd told him all about Noel and Natalia. "My brother-in-law wrote that book," she said to Brian Darling. "I think he would like your name."

Brian laughed, exactly the infectious laughter Martha had expected him to have, which made his blue eyes sparkle and dance above the freckles covering his nose. She glanced at Stella. She was looking at him as if she were trying to figure him out. "He certainly would. Especially if he were to meet my sisters. They are so. . .cute. . .and well. . .darling." Martha couldn't help but wonder if he had looked in the mirror lately. But she didn't say that. Most men didn't want to be called "darling," except by the woman they loved.

From the way Brian Darling's eyes returned repeatedly to Stella's face, Martha was sure he wouldn't mind Stella's calling him that way. But in order to have that happen, Stella would have to leave her love of Dimitri behind. She wondered if Brian would be patient enough to wait for that to happen. Martha hoped he would. She wasn't sure, of course—only time would tell—but

Brian seemed to have exactly the personality Stella needed in a man. From the way Brian looked at Stella, Martha suspected that some interesting days were ahead.

Martha wasn't above helping him. She motioned toward the living area of the store and offered Brian a pastry in honor of the day.

"Baklava!" His bright laugher filled the four corners of the large room in answer to Martha's invitation. "Are you kidding? I'd have to be crazy to say no." But Martha could tell that what he liked most was the chance to sit with Stella and get to know her.

Brian, Leo, and she started toward the sitting area, but when Stella's attention returned to the cash register and she claimed she had work to do, the frustration on Brian's face, which was as open in happiness as it was in disappointment, almost hurt. But the three of them had a nice time, even though Brian's gaze frequently wandered toward Stella. After he left, Martha and Leo agreed that he was a fine young man.

While Leo went to put the flowers in a vase, Martha took the chance to question Stella. "Why didn't you come and sit with us? Nothing is so pressing that you couldn't have taken a few minutes. Brian seems like such a nice young man."

"Almost too nice," Stella murmured.

Martha frowned. "What do you mean?"

Stella set down her pen and gave Martha her full attention. "Kyria Martha, I still love Dimitri. It's too soon for me to. . ." She paused and shrugged. "I don't know." A heavy sigh escaped her. "Brian does seem like a very nice man. I'm sorry for that comment. But it's too soon for me to think about. . .anyone else. . .yet," she said, rubbing her fingers over her eyes.

"Where shall I put the vase?" Leo interrupted, and Martha, detecting a bit of moisture in Stella's eyes, walked toward Leo, to give Stella the privacy to control her emotions. She felt bad, though. Her young friend was still hurting so deeply. *Dear Lord,* Martha prayed, *please give me the right words to speak to Stella and the right time to do so.* Martha knew that timing in talking with a young person was just as important as the words. Stella's heart had to be open to any words she might say.

"Oh, Leo, the flowers are beautiful." They were a work of art, God's work. She took a deep sniff of the bouquet. The whole room seemed to fill with their sweetness. "Put them on the table in front of the sofa, I think." She motioned to the large couch where she and Leo had just been sitting adjacent to Brian, who had been on the smaller love seat.

He placed the cut crystal vase, then, coming back to Martha, drew her into an embrace and whispered into her ear the hour that he would pick her up for their date that evening.

"Our date," she answered back and, feeling bold, planted a quick kiss upon his lips. "I like the way that sounds."

"Me, too," he said.

After sending Stella a quick wave, Martha walked with him to the door. She watched him walk down the main street of town until he turned the corner and was out of sight. Then she returned to the cash register and Stella.

"You're so lucky, Kyria Martha," Stella said softly. Martha turned to her in question. What was she lucky about? "To have found such a man," Stella explained, and Martha smiled her agreement. Although she didn't consider herself lucky so much as blessed. "Leo is so romantic and loves you so much." Martha heard the wistful quality in her voice and knew then that what Dimitri had told her on the phone about Stella's need for romance was absolutely correct. She admired Dimitri even more for realizing that he couldn't give it to her.

"You will have a romance someday soon."

"Soon?" Stella asked, turning her head to stare at the wall. But Martha was certain she wasn't seeing the paintings or afghans artfully arrayed below on a vintage truck, but rather the love for which she so yearned. "Do you really think so?"

If the way Brian had looked at Stella was anything to go by, Martha thought it would be a lot sooner than Stella imagined. "Just be open to God's leading, Stella. Be open to whom He might bring into your life."

Stella's shoulders sagged. "That's the problem. I've associated myself with Dimitri for so long that I just can't see myself with anyone else," she said, confirming Martha's thoughts on why her young friend seemed so shy around Brian. He wasn't Dimitri, and any man who showed an interest in her would make her feel uncomfortable because of that.

Martha rubbed her hand between the girl's slender shoulder blades and spoke as softly as she could to take the sting out of her words, "But, Stella, Dimitri isn't yours. And he never will be. If you want marriage someday—"

"I do!"

"Then you have to face that it will not be to Dimitri, but rather to a man who will be much, much better for you. One of God's choosing and not your own."

"God's choosing," Stella repeated, and a smile touched the corners of her lips. With the first flicker of hope Martha had seen in her eyes since she had come to Olympia, she said, "I kind of like the way that sounds."

Chapter 10

Martha left Once Upon A Time earlier than usual to ready herself for her birthday date with Leo. She had made an appointment with her hairdresser to lightly trim, highlight, and style her hair. Its chin-length razor cut now softly swept her cheekbones as she walked home, and when she ran up the twenty-two marble steps to her front door, it bounced—a reflection of Martha's mood. Martha had her hair professionally cared for every week. It was another thing she had started upon moving to Ancient Olympia and a life change that had made her feel good about herself. Special. She never worried about her roots showing or it growing to an awkward length.

Long massaging soaks in her pink, marble Jacuzzi was another luxury she allowed herself after moving into her own home in Olympia. The only structural change to her apartment she made when moving in was to the master bathroom. She had had it designed by the same interior designer responsible for Natalia's well-appointed Fifth Avenue apartment in New York City. Until visiting Natalia in New York, Martha hadn't even realized that bathrooms could be so luxurious. It was her favorite room now. Hanging ferns, a shelf elegantly arrayed with her collection of antique perfume bottles, a skylight, and a stereo system that normally played Vivaldi's *Four Seasons*, helped to make the room with its plush carpet of pink rose so special. After soaking in the apothecary's personal blend of basil and lemon essential oils, and being massaged by the water jets for half an hour, Martha patted herself dry with a thick, soft bath towel. Leaving the bathroom, she went to inspect the contents of her walk-in closet.

Natalia had sent her several outfits from New York the previous week, and Martha knew she would wear one tonight. She wanted something previously unworn for this evening, an outfit that she would forever associate with her first birthday dinner with Leo. And she knew what she wanted when her gaze fell upon the knee-length skirt with a striped diagonal pattern of black and yellow. They would be dining outside at a classy restaurant overlooking the Ionian Sea. The huge, yellow summer sun would give way to the black silky night. The skirt would go well with the ambience of nature, and the fitted, pale yellow, short-sleeved sweater of silk and cashmere blend would in turn go with the skirt. She was certain Natalia had chosen it to be a match.

Martha dressed, then stood in front of her cheval mirror to critically observe what Leo would be looking at all evening, a purely feminine desire to please the man she loved.

She turned to the right, then to the left. Although she was on the short side, her figure hadn't changed much in the last twenty-five years. She was still slim with youthful curves. It had been a bit of a shock when she had started donning designer clothes to discover just how well she could wear them. She pressed her hand against her tummy, sucked it in, then smiled at the reflection of Needlepoint, who yawned from her corner of the bed behind her.

"Hey." Martha turned to the cat. "You don't have to look so bored. I'm not too bad for a fifty-seven-year-old," she said and walked to the cat to scratch her under her chin. A deep, contented purr answered her.

Giving her cat one last pat, Martha returned to her closet and slipped her feet into a pair of black leather thongs. She looked with longing at the Manolo Blahnik, two-inch-heeled sandals that sat beside them. Natalia had sent them to go along with the outfit. But high heels were the only fashion items in which Martha didn't indulge. She was too afraid of falling and breaking a leg. Spraining it, at the very least. And that was something she couldn't afford to do. Not with Once Upon A Time to run. The flat thongs would have to do.

She reached for the thick gold-cuff bracelet—an arrAs jewelry design— Natalia had sent to her in celebration of this day last year and the black, ruched leather clutch. She added money, lipstick, tissues, and a comb inside; snapped it shut; and glanced at her reflection in the mirror now that her ensemble was complete.

She might not be twenty-five, but it sure wasn't visible in the way her pulse beat, her spirit soared, and her face beamed. She was going out on a date with the man she loved. You didn't have to be twenty-five to feel that anticipation, that excitement.

As the doorbell buzzed Leo's arrival, she turned away from the mirror feeling like the most blessed woman in the world.

That feeling only escalated when she opened her front door to Leo and they stood for a minute, unabashedly taking in one another's appearance. Dressed in a tailored linen jacket, matching slacks, and an Italian silk tie with the fleur-de-lis emblem of the city of Florence elegantly printed on it, he looked as if he had just stepped out of a boardroom.

That thought surprised her.

He had always been so casually dressed before, athletically attired or in blue jeans or shorts and a polo shirt, that she had always associated him with being just that—a casual man who, because of the wonders of the computer age, was able to carry out his business from his home here in Greece as easily as he did from the States. But attired this way, it was as if she were seeing another side of him—one similar to the high-powered men in suits who walked the streets of New York—and one that he wore as comfortably as he did casual clothes. He oozed innate power, and she realized that she really didn't know too much about what he had done—about his business in general—before moving to Ancient Olympia. He had said that he had a software company. For the first time she wondered what, exactly, that meant. His lean cheeks were freshly shaven, revealing the natural lines of his features, all angles and strength; there was nothing weak about his face. She somehow knew, too, that that was a reflection of who he was.

But when he smiled, that half smile full of lazy confidence that she was so familiar with, she forgot everything but who he had been to her during the previous weeks—a warm and giving, caring man who made her world shine in a way it had never done before. Because of Leo, getting out of bed in the mornings was an adventure. She counted the moments until he either walked through the doors of Once Upon A Time or called her on the phone with a merry good morning. She wished life could go on like this forever, with nothing to change just what they shared now. She treasured each moment and had to continually give her fear—that something or someone or some situation would eventually alter it—over to God.

She watched as the lazy gleam turned into that of a man who was very pleased by what he beheld. It sent her pulse skyrocketing. And when he pulled a fragrant bouquet of pink roses framed by baby's breath out from behind his back, she instinctively held out her arms for them. "Oh, Leo," she cradled them close to her and closed her eyes as the aroma filled the air around them. "More beautiful flowers for me. Thank you." They were such a lovely birthday present, and along with the ones he had given her that morning in the shop, she would carefully dry each one as a keepsake.

"They aren't half as beautiful as you, my darling," he said, and placing his hands on her shoulders, he leaned toward her and slowly lowered his lips to meet hers. Their smooth warmth moved softly, lovingly, a dance that was like flowers blowing in a spring breeze. "Happy birthday, Martha," he whispered, after a moment, letting his hands slide to her neck and up to cup her face.

"Happy birthday, Leo," she whispered back, and turning her head, she kissed the palm of his hand.

He pulled her close to him and, heedless of the flowers between them, whispered, "You smell so good, feel so perfect. I love you, darling. So much."

"As I. . ." She inhaled the manly musk that clung to his freshly shaven cheeks, and she couldn't speak as a storm of sensations engulfed her—the aroma, the awareness, the essence of him. Their birthday celebration could end right here, and it would still be the best ever.

"As you. . . ," he prompted, after a long moment. With his thumb he traced the exposed column of her neck, sending little shivers of longing coursing through her system. Tilting her head back, she looked into his eyes. They had darkened to the deepness of an olive-tree grove at dusk. But still, as with the underside of an olive leaf, his eyes sparkled and gleamed silvery. The leaves did so when touched by the sun, his eyes from the light that was within his soul.

When she could finally answer, her voice sounded as foreign as the wondrous feeling that had become a part of her since meeting Leo. "As I love you." She didn't know where their love would take them, only that it was the truth. She loved him. Dearly and more and more with each day that passed.

He sighed deeply, satisfied. He held her, giving them both the chance to regain their equilibrium, one that they knew as mature adults and as children of God they must recapture. Then Leo stood back and, using more willpower than he knew he had, moved his gaze away from hers and swept it around her living room before he focused back on her.

"This is the first time I've been in your apartment," he said, glancing around the room once again. She wondered how he saw the parquet floor; lacy curtains fluttering at the windows, tzaki, and the feminine print of her floral sofas.

"It's lovely. So similar in feeling to Once Upon A Time. . ."

She was pleased that he sensed that. Part of her dream had always been to make her shop seem like her home. She reached for her clutch and the decorative bag that contained Leo's birthday present, a needlepoint of the ancient church at the archaeological site, which she had both designed and stitched. Leo opened the door and motioned for her to go out first. He closed the door behind them and held out his arm. She threaded hers through his, finding great pleasure in the feel of his lean strength through the fine linen of his summer jacket. They walked down the steep stairs together.

A whimsical thought went through her brain: With Leo's arm to lean on, she could have worn her high-heeled sandals, after all.

Chapter 11

The Bay of St. Andreas sparkled as though thousands of shining diamonds had been tossed upon it as the setting sun highlighted the softly rolling sea. The wind blew Martha's hair along her neck in a feathery caress that was almost as sweet as Leo's hand upon it had been earlier. A happy sigh escaped her, and Leo chuckled.

"You look like a content cat."

"Well, as you know, I'm partial to cats. I will take that as a compliment."

"And here's another one. You're lovely. As lovely in a human way"—he motioned out to the water—"as that setting sun is upon the bay."

Martha sighed. "You really must love me."

Leo chuckled low in his throat. "Ah. . .there's no doubt about that, darling Martha-Mary. And I hope to be celebrating every one of our birthdays together in the future."

Martha's breath caught. If they were to do that, they would have to go through life together. It was almost too wonderful to consider, but at the same time, too much to consider. Even though she would like to marry Leo, she knew that much needed to be discussed first. This was not something that could be agreed upon lightly. Their romance had been wonderful, but marriage was more than romance. It was also facing the hard realities of life together on a daily basis.

But that wasn't for tonight. Tonight was for fairy tales and fun. "I hope so, too, Leo," she whispered. "Happy birthday." They had exchanged the wish many times during the evening; they were still like children in their wonder of the simultaneous occurrence.

He reached for her hand. "It really is one of the best ever."

"The best ever for me," she specified but didn't mind that he couldn't say the same. He had been married to a woman he'd loved very much, and she would be happy with it being "one of the best." She never wanted to take anything away from his life with Susan. It made her happy somehow to know that he had been happily married before. That meant that he had been a success as a husband, and in a world permeated by divorce and short-term relationships, that was very special.

"I love it here. I think it's one of my favorite places."

She looked at him quizzically. "Do you like it more than Ancient Olympia?"

"No. Ancient Olympia is my very favorite place and where I choose to make my home. But this is definitely beautiful." A lazy smile crossed his face. "Maybe it's because it's connected to Olympia in that it was the ancient port of Pheia, where the ships from around the Hellenic world brought contestants, diplomats, spectators, and others for the ancient games. It's probably the reason I like it more than any other seaside location."

He motioned toward a low-lying home sprawled atop the north bluff of the horseshoe bay. "Now that's quite a location in which to live. I'm sure that the people who call that home think this bay is the best place in the world."

"We do," a woman said from the table behind.

Martha and Leo turned to see an attractive woman taking a squirming infant from her husband's arms. The woman smiled as she bounced the fractious baby on her lap and motioned to the house on the bluff. "I'm sorry to interrupt, but that's our home, and it is the most special place in the world. To us at least."

Her husband smiled over at her. "That it is."

"From here it looks like a Shangri-La," Martha commented.

The woman smiled. "Although not hidden from the world like that imaginary land, it is our utopia." She motioned to her husband and the rest of her family, which included a boy of about eight, a girl of about six, as well as the baby she held in her arms.

"You're American?" Leo asked.

"I am," the woman replied. "My husband was born and raised here in Greece but lived in the States for many years."

"But we all live there now." The husband motioned at the sprawling house. "I'm Luke, and this is my wife, Melissa. And these are our children."

"I'm Leo and this is Martha."

"Nice to meet you both. Would you like to join us for coffee?" Luke offered. He chuckled, tickling the tummy of the infant, who wiggled like a worm. "If you don't mind our little one. She's teething and gets a bit out of sorts around this time of day."

At the encouraging look Martha sent his way, Leo quickly accepted. "That would be wonderful." He motioned toward the squirming baby, who was as cute as she was fussy. "But only if I can have a turn at trying to calm her."

Melissa and Luke turned startled gazes at one another. But their faces didn't begin to compare with how Martha felt.

"You can try, Leo. But she's pretty finicky about who she lets get near her. Especially when teething," Melissa warned.

"I love babies," Leo returned. "And funnily enough, they normally like me, too, and, even better, quiet down when I hold them."

He and Martha pulled their chairs over, and Melissa handed him a cloth diaper to drape over his shoulder. "Let's see if the charm still works," he said, as he placed the baby against his shoulder and, with the tips of two fingers, rubbed her little back in a circular motion.

When she gave one final sputter, then stopped fighting and fidgeting, everyone at the table stared at him with their mouths hanging open.

"She's quiet," the boy, who Martha thought was the image of his father, exclaimed. "She's actually quiet."

Luke chuckled. "You've got to teach me that trick."

Melissa turned to Martha and asked, "How many children do you have?"

Martha felt the blood rush to her face. She quickly waved her hand between Leo and herself. "We're not married."

Seeming to sense how uncomfortable she felt, Leo quickly continued, "I'm a widower, and my wife and I were never blessed to have children. She miscarried our child."

Martha looked at him sharply. He didn't realize it, but this line of conversation troubled her more than the couple thinking they were married. They had talked about the two children that had almost been his several times. But until now, seeing him with this baby and observing just how much he actually adored children, she had never realized just what this might mean to their future relationship. Chilling fingers of apprehension surged up her spine.

Had his wife had a medical problem that prevented them from having children, or did he? Fear crashed around Martha like a tidal wave. He could possibly still father children, could still have a chance to have the babies he loved. Shouldn't he be courting a younger woman—one who could give him children should they marry? It was only yesterday that he thought she was ten years younger than her actual age. Until a few years ago she still would have been able to bear a child.

"I'm sorry," Luke murmured.

Leo nodded. "It was one of our greatest sorrows. We had wanted a whole house full of kids when we married. But when my wife became sick, we understood why she had never been able to—"

He broke off, and Martha felt chilled. It had been because of his wife that he—this man who was so good with babies—hadn't had any of his own. And now he was getting involved with her—another woman who couldn't give them to him, but this time, because of the biological passing of time.

"Well, you may borrow ours whenever you want," Melissa said, relieving the mood. Leo chuckled.

"That's what I do all over the world. It's really not all bad." He scrunched up his nose. "Especially when it's time to hand the baby back to her parents for a change of diapers."

"Oh, no," Melissa groaned, reaching for the little one. "She didn't!"

"Hmm." Leo chuckled. "She did."

"Yep, Mom," the boy confirmed and got up from his seat to place more distance between himself and the smelly baby. "She did."

~~~⊙~~~

Not even plaguing thoughts about children were able to mar the return trip to Olympia. Serenity seemed to grow on the vegetation that the car sped past.

The coastal valley slept in the summer way of peace. As Martha gazed out the window, it seemed to her that the other three seasons of the year existed just for this one. The night was a harmonious synchronization of the physical world that was a special treat to their senses. Martha was glad when Leo abandoned the air-conditioning in favor of the night-scented air. Oregano and thyme mixed with that of the pine and eucalyptus trees that sashayed their scent down upon the earth, causing her to draw deep, rejuvenating breaths. And the flowers, hundreds of different ones, created a bouquet that no perfumer in the world could ever hope to re-create.

The town of Ancient Olympia was mostly asleep when the high-powered engine purred its way down the main road. Martha glanced at the clock on the dashboard. It was past one in the morning. It didn't seem any later than ten.

As Leo pulled the car to a stop in front of Once Upon A Time, her comfortable, content feelings found expression in the soft sigh that escaped her lips.

He turned to her, and his eyes crinkled at the corners in the way she liked. "I agree with that."

She laughed softly. "It was the most wonderful birthday I've ever had," she murmured for at least the hundredth time. Reaching up, she placed her hand against his cheek. "Thank you, Leo."

He caught her fingers and planted a soft kiss into her palm. "No, thank you. Since Susan died, holidays of any sort have been difficult for me. Maybe if we had been blessed to have had those two children who were almost ours. . ." He sighed.

Feelings of inadequacy flooded back in, wiping out all the contentment that the ride home had lent to Martha. She had watched him with Melissa and Luke's children. If any man should be a father, it was this one. He shouldn't be wasting his time with her, a woman past childbearing years. He should be dating a younger woman, one who could give him the children he so obviously desired. Wasn't procreation one of the main reasons for marriage, after all?

Even though she was breaking on the inside and her throat felt like dry toast, she had to agree. "Having those two little loves would have made a big difference, Leo." She licked her lips, unsure as to whether she should go on, the topic being deeply personal. But she knew that she had to. Before they took their relationship any further, this was something they had to discuss. "You're a man and. . .you can still. . .have children. If"—her voice dropped to a whisper—"you have the right woman."

His eyes widened, flickered briefly with an intangible hope, and she knew what he was asking.

She lifted one shoulder in a sad shrug. "We met a few years too late for that."

He leaned across the seat, and his husky voice was like a caress. "And yet I most definitely have the right woman. The only woman. . ."

His warm lips met hers in a touch that was firm and persuasive, not demanding response, rather, giving one of love and reassurance that his feelings for her did not depend in any way on her ability to give him children.

But hope had flickered in his eyes when he'd thought that there might be a possibility that she could still conceive a child.

She had seen it. And she had seen the look of disappointment that had flickered briefly before he had deftly smoothed it away, leaving only the grim set of his jaw to indicate that her reply wasn't the one he had wished to hear. It was an impression she would not soon forget.

She squeezed her eyes shut to keep the tears from sliding out. This was not the moment to express sadness over their future—a future she felt almost certain now they couldn't have.

She had somehow known all along that something would keep them apart. She just hadn't thought that it would be something so insurmountable as her age. She had thought it would be her resistance to the change being married might bring to her perfect life. Now she realized just how surmountable that problem was.

With prayer.

In fact, it came as a bit of a shock to her to realize that, having turned over all her doubts to God about the change that being married could bring, she hadn't actually thought about it much in several days.

Could she do the same with this problem?

She knew that she had no alternative. Other than discussing the situation with Leo, that was the only thing to do.

But she wouldn't talk with him about it tonight. They were still on their birthday celebration.

And he had just told her that it was the first holiday that he had enjoyed since he'd lost his wife. She wouldn't let anything mar it. Any discussions about this could wait for another time.

Any time, other than this one.

And only after much prayer.

Chapter 12

During the days following their birthday, Leo doubted that the ancient winners of the pentathlon could have gone around Olympia feeling any better than he. Even though the earth was at one of its most charming stages, it seemed to take on an even more special glow as his love for Martha grew stronger and deeper. They went everywhere together and talked about everything, both serious and frivolous. And although he sensed that there was something on her mind that she wasn't discussing with him, he had been married long enough to Susan to know that when a woman was ready to talk about something, she would.

Susan had always prayed about serious topics before discussing them with him.

He knew that Martha was the same: a similarity between the two women that was as striking as it was admirable. How many problems among couples—in the world in general—could be prevented if everyone prayed to God before voicing them? He would be patient. He would neither pry nor push. And, as had often happened between Susan and him, the problem—or at least most of it—would probably be resolved through her prayer time with God.

They were sitting at a café under a reaching plane tree, enjoying the sweet, natural air-conditioning the ancient deciduous afforded, when he asked something he thought she might enjoy, "How about a bike ride this evening?"

Clink! Her demitasse met its saucer too quickly. He thought it was a testimony to the quality of the porcelain that neither the cup nor saucer broke.

"A. . .bike ride?" she choked out. It was not the response he had expected.

He frowned. "You have ridden before, haven't you?" Cycling was such a large part of his life that he couldn't imagine anyone not doing so.

She laughed, a self-depreciating sound that made him instantly regret his insensitively put question. "I think it might be better to say that a bike, with the help of a mountain, has ridden me." She grimaced and, holding up her hand to keep his question at bay, quickly explained. "The first—and last—time that I was on a bike was when I was about twelve. My older brothers were determined that I should learn. The contraption had always scared me a bit—all that chrome and metal with parts sticking out in all directions seemed daunting."

He chuckled. "I've never seen a bike quite like that." He had always seen it as a streamlined work of engineering.

"Well, my moments on the bike proved that my impression was correct." She paused, and even though her eyes were trained on his, he knew that she wasn't looking at him, but rather into the memory of her first and last bike ride.

"Amazingly, after only a few moments, I seemed to have perfect balance on the two-wheeled wonder, so much so that my older brother let go of my seat. I found myself pedaling down the main street of our village without the umbilical cord of his grip on the seat. Those first few moments were like a dream."

She sat back, and he could tell that she was reliving the perfect sense of freedom while bike riding. It was one he knew well. "I was going so fast, my waist-length hair flew behind me like a cape, and I felt so"—she shook her head—"I don't know, free."

"Ahh. . .now that's definitely what riding a bike is all about."

Her face instantly clouded. "But the dream soon turned into a nightmare. I found myself at the end of the village, where the road dipped sharply on its meandering trip to the valley far below. It was then that I realized that I didn't know how to do two very important things." She laughed sourly. "I didn't know how to turn the bike, but even more, I didn't know how to stop the contraption."

"Oh no."

"Oh yes," she replied. "I could hear my brothers and all the children of the village running behind me, shouting instructions. But I was too terrified to decipher their words, and the cacophony of their voices just added to the out-of-control feeling of my headlong flight. My front wheel hit a rut in the road, which made the bike turn to the right. The next thing I knew, I was no longer on the paved road but flying through a field on the steepest, most direct, and fastest way down the mountain."

"I guess you were about to set a world record for speed," he commented wryly.

She laughed. "It sure felt that way. I probably would have if the front wheel hadn't then hit a rock, and I learned one way in which to stop a bike. Fast."

He winced. "You didn't."

"I did. But, hey, it wasn't all bad," she laughed. "Other than getting to see how it was to ride a bike, I also got a lesson in flying. I flew about ten feet through the air—but at the time it seemed more like ten miles—before landing on my left shoulder and severely cutting both my knees."

"Ouch."

She kneaded her left shoulder. " 'Ouch' doesn't begin to describe how my dislocated arm felt. Nor the burning skin on my knees. But the physical pain wasn't anything compared to the damage done to my pride that day. It was a mortifying experience, one in which I have no desire to put myself again."

"But, Martha, haven't you ever heard the saying, 'When you fall off a horse you've got to get right back on and ride again'?"

"If it had been a horse," she countered with all the logic of a person raised in the country, "I would have gotten back on, dislocated shoulder and all. A horse is a living, breathing creature, and I wouldn't want to hurt its feelings nor have it think it had bettered me."

That wasn't exactly Leo's point. "The idea is that you shouldn't let something like a fall defeat you. Not when you are giving up something as wonderful as riding a bike." He flashed her the most endearing grin he could muster. "Especially, darling, when riding a bike through the countryside around Olympia with me."

~~~~~

"Darling?"

As with each time he called her by that endearment, the part of her heart that had been without a love of her own for so many years jumped within her. A fog of swirling, happy feelings inundated her.

"How about if I teach you to ride?" he asked, and—*poof*—the fog disappeared. His offer had caught her off guard. She hadn't expected it. Hadn't really wanted it, either.

"I don't know, Leo. . ." To have fallen and made a fool of herself when she was a girl of twelve was one thing. To chance doing the same thing now was an entirely different situation.

He leaned back in his chair and eyed her thoughtfully. "Please, Martha. I love cycling, but to have you by my side, as we ride the country lanes together, would be perfect."

"By my side. . .together. . ." Those words had the same effect on her as an endearment or whenever he told her he loved her. It made her melt inside. To ride a bike with Leo by her side seemed like a very pleasant thing to do. And since cycling was so important to him, shouldn't she at least try to ride again?

"We live in a valley, so you don't have to worry about a mad dash down a mountain," he pointed out.

"That's true."

"I want you to experience the wonder of riding a bike, Martha." He spoke with passion. "It's something so simple, and yet one of life's greatest pleasures. To my way of thinking, anyway. The exhilaration of knowing that the speed you are going is one your legs, along with kinetic energy, make and of feeling the wind in your face—"

"I feel plenty of wind just walking around here during the blustery season," she pointed out.

A throaty chuckle emanated from him.

With patience he said, "You know it's not the same thing." His voice dipped to that low timbre, a cross between a growl and a gentle caress, and she wondered how any woman could ever resist its charm. She knew she couldn't.

"I know," she admitted.

He reached across the table for her hand. "I promise, darling, that we won't go any faster than you want to."

Looking at him, while feeling his thumb run in a one-way motion across the back of her fingers, she couldn't help but wonder if he were speaking on two levels.

Was he referring to more than just riding a bicycle?

To their relationship perhaps?

Somehow she thought that he was. And the idea filled her with warmth. She so wished that their relationship never had to change from what it was right now. Staying as they were meant that she would never have to face other issues: most important, that of not being able to give him a child. She continually gave that conflict over to God, but other than indefinitely remaining a romantic, dating couple, she didn't see any way around it.

She wanted to talk to Leo about the problem again. But until she resolved the issue in her own mind, until she prayed it through thoroughly and felt peace from God about it—something she knew from experience would eventually, one way or another, be hers—she wouldn't.

"What would my first lesson be?"

A big smile filled the lines around his mouth while a complementary twinkle flashed in his dark eyes. "How to stop, of course."

Martha didn't attempt to hide her smile. "Of course." She paused. "I really would like to learn, Leo. Not much has ever defeated me, and it goes against my core to be afraid of something, especially something little children do so easily."

"That's the spirit."

"It's always looked fun to me. I've always been particularly fond of pink bikes with white wicker baskets. I think I might look for one like that. Imagine riding to the farmer's market and filling up a basket with flowers. . ."

She could tell from the way a smile played around his mouth that that wasn't quite what he had in mind for their cycling ventures. But he didn't seem to mind. "You're adorable, you know that?"

She guffawed. "A woman my age cannot be described as adorable, Leo," she challenged. *Especially not with the confused thoughts I have.*

"I disagree," he returned. "What has age got to do with the concept? To be adorable means one of two things: Either you are worthy of adoration—and that is reserved for Christ alone—or you are delightful and/or charming. That, my dear, brave Martha-Mary, describes you perfectly." He looked at her with that special gleam in his eye. "You are the most delightful and charming woman I know."

As his dark eyes focused on her lips, a faint tremor quivered through her. "You flatter me."

"Ah, Martha-Mary. But don't you know I would much prefer to be kissing you?"

Martha knew because that was what she wanted, too. "Would you settle for teaching me to ride a bike?"

"For now," he returned, his voice low and soft, just as she liked it. "For now."

Chapter 13

Martha knew now that although having the love of a man like Leo might make her world a bit more complex and confusing, it definitely made it nicer, too.

And it was because of her love for Leo that she could better empathize with Stella's pain at the loss of Dimitri. Her heart went out to her young friend.

Stella put on a brave face by day, but Martha was often awakened by the soft sound of Stella's sorrow finding expression during the deep hours of the night. It was more a feeling than a sound actually, a motherly intuition, a change in the atmosphere of the house, that told Martha tears fell from her young friend's eyes. Knowing Stella as well as she did, Martha knew that it was better to uphold the girl in prayer rather than offering an embrace, as her arms ached to do.

But after several nights, Martha felt certain that her prayer for the right opportunity to talk to Stella was being answered. Slipping her feet into her seafoam green slippers, she donned her light summer robe and went to the girl's room. Deep in mourning for her lost love, Stella didn't hear her until she spoke. "Stella, would you please join me on the veranda for a cup of chamomile tea?"

Startled, Stella hastily swiped at the tears that glistened in the moonlight on her cheeks. She reached for her travel clock and, seeing the late hour, offered, "It's the middle of the night, Kyria Martha."

"The best time for a heart-to-heart, I'd say."

"But—"

"No buts. I've sensed your pain every night. I've prayed for you until I knew that sleep had given you release from your distress. But tonight the air is sweet, the stars are shining down upon us, the crickets are singing, and God has placed within my heart a few words to share with you. Words that only a woman who has lived for more than half a century without the love of a man has the right to tell a young woman such as you." She paused and softly finished with, "Will you please join me?"

Kicking aside the eyelet sheet, Stella pulled a tissue from the nearly empty box on the night table and, sitting up, nodded. "To be honest, I think I would like that."

Martha smiled. Of course Stella would. God knew what was in the young woman's heart. "I'll put the kettle on," she said and went toward the kitchen.

When Stella emerged a few minutes later, Martha couldn't help smiling. Dressed in a long T-shirt with a smiling kangaroo on it, she looked like a young teenager. But Martha knew that her appearance was deceiving. The heart of a woman beat fast and true. And some man one day would be very blessed to have all the love this special young woman had to give and wanted so desperately to give.

Martha had already opened the French doors that led to the vine-laden veranda off the kitchen. Picking up the wooden tray arrayed with her tea service and fresh butter cookies, she motioned Stella outside.

The young woman stood for a moment at the railing, looking out over the sleeping village of Ancient Olympia. Martha watched as she took a deep breath, then another, before turning her ever-observant eyes up toward the heavens. The Big Dipper could easily be picked out, but it was the earth's own galaxy, the Milky Way, cutting across the zenith, a long cloud of snowy light, that drew Stella's attention. "Such a big world," she murmured.

"Yes, kali mou, it most certainly is," Martha agreed as she poured the tea into the teacups. She had always liked the soothing sound the liquid made, like a softly flowing brook, as it was transferred from pot to cups, but now, during the deep of the night, even more. "And it's from the God, the Creator of that wonderful sky filled with stars and other worlds, that we who are blessed to be called His children should derive our happiness. Not from any other relationship."

Stella's slender shoulders sagged. "You're talking about Dimitri." Her voice had a deflated sound.

"No, kali mou. I'm talking about any relationship. Our worth shouldn't be derived from which town or country we hail or which church or school we attend or whose daughter we might be or our bank balance or even"—she paused to let the last have added weight—"which man might love us. Our worth comes from our relationship with the One who created that expansive night sky and"—she held her hand up to her ear to indicate the multitude of insects that were singing all around them—"the littlest creature that crawls upon the earth."

Stella's chin dropped to her chest, and Martha knew she was trying hard not to cry. "My head knows that you're right, Kyria Martha," she replied softly. "But my heart—"

She balled up her hands and, holding them against her chest, bent over, as if she had been struck. "My heart just doesn't want to listen to reason. I miss. . . Dimitri. . .so. . .much. If only. . ."

Placing the teapot on the table, Martha wrapped her arms around Stella and gently pulled her up so that she stood straight. She wished she could wave a magic wand and take this hurt away from her. If any woman in the world deserved happiness, it was this one. But Martha knew that people often didn't know the difference between what they wanted and what they needed.

"If only. . ."

But Martha wouldn't let her dwell on what would never be, a treacherous route to take. "There are no 'if onlys' in life, Stella. If onlys are as fleeting as the foam on the sea. If onlys are deciding we need something rather than allowing God to decide if that is how our life is to go. If onlys kill contentment in our life faster than weed killers do the weeds in our gardens. And worse, they kill the knowledge of knowing that we are living in God's will even if an answer to a prayer is not the one we had hoped and wished for, like children wishing upon the first star they see in the night sky."

"But. . .I hurt. . .so badly." she choked out, and Martha could feel the tension take over the muscles in her slender body. "Physically." She placed the heel of her hand against her forehead. "Mentally. . ."

"I know, dear, I know," Martha massaged her tense back muscles. "But right now is the time when you must let your spirit draw its strength, its courage, its counsel, from God's very own. His Holy Spirit will uphold you through this as He did nine years ago when your mother passed away. Remember what the Lord said in the Gospel of John about the Comforter, the Counselor." *Dear Lord, help me remember the words. Please.* She so seldom could recite verses, but she so desperately hoped she could now.

And she did. They just seemed to flow from her mouth. "'And I will ask the Father, and he will give you another Counselor to be with you forever—the Spirit of truth. The world cannot accept him, because it neither sees him nor knows him. But you—'"

Stella raised her hands, and Martha panicked that not even those words of the Lord's—the very ones that had most strengthened Stella all those years ago—would help her sorrow this time. But when Stella turned her gaze to the infinite sky, even though tears still glistened on her lashes like drops of morning dew upon pine, Martha could see the faint flicker of hope. "'But you know him, for he lives with you and will be in you. I will not leave you as orphans; I will come to you.'"

"I knew you would remember," Martha murmured. "Rather than allowing pain and its debilitating consequences to rule you, let God's courage take ahold of your heart. But most of all, kali mou, be courageous and strong and ask yourself if you should accept Dimitri not loving you as coming from God."

"I don't have the courage to ask that," she answered faintly, casting her gaze downward again. "Not yet."

Martha placed the palms of her hands on either side of Stella's small face until the young woman looked up. "Listen to me, Stella." Her throat was tight with welling emotions. She loved this girl—the daughter of her best friend—so very much. "You are the most courageous person I know. Even when facing the death of your mother and infant sister, as well as the despair of your father, you kept your family together. You were indeed your mother's *stella*, her star, who made sure that the children she loved more than life itself were safe. You and your courage did that for your father, your brothers and sister, and for your mother, who relied on her little Stella."

"This is different."

"Yes, it is different," Martha agreed, shocking a response from Stella as evidenced in the widening of her eyes. "This is easy compared to what you, a girl of thirteen, did then. This is understanding with a woman's heart that a man, realizing something is missing in the way he is supposed to love you, breaks off your relationship. And it's trusting that God probably has someone else picked out for you, someone who will give you what Dimitri cannot give, is unable to give because"—she ran her hand gently down Stella's cheek, trying to impart comfort—"he is not the man for you."

Tears spilled from Stella's eyes again. "But I'm not like you, Kyria Martha. I want to be married. I yearn for it."

Martha stood back. Her concern turned to shock. It reverberated through her. "And who said I don't?"

"But. . .you've never married. And from what you just said about a person's worth coming from God—"

"My worth will come from God whether I remain single all my life or not. I'm not waiting for a man to give me my worth, and neither should a man wait for me to give him his. Marriage has nothing to do with that. Marriage is about companionship; it was designed by God to be the closest and best of all human relationships. God made man and woman to complement one another physically, emotionally, socially, and, most important of all, spiritually."

Stella swiped at her tears and looked at her in the direct way that, in spite of the disquieting turn of their conversation, warmed Martha's heart. This was the Stella she knew, a young woman with bright, inquisitive eyes. Not downcast, anguished ones. "Has that man come into your life? Is it Leo?"

Martha answered carefully. "Our relationship hasn't reached the point yet where we've discussed a future that includes marriage." They had alluded to it but never talked about it. "And even though you and Dimitri dated for years, neither did you reach that point with him. And that's the reason—for your own peace of mind and to make room in that big heart of yours for the man God does have in His mind for you to marry—that you must let Dimitri go."

Anger jumped into Stella's eyes. "But I don't want to let him go," she grated out, her voice militant. "I won't."

"You must," Martha returned.

Stella's eyes hardened. "Could you, Kyria Martha?" she shot back with equal candor. Her eyes were like shiny hard jet, but there was no malice in them. Just pain. "Could you let go of Leo, should you have to?"

Martha took a step back as if she had been slapped. She felt the full force of Stella's ache then. It wasn't just an ache but an agony. The very thought of losing Leo made Martha feel as if something had poked through her skin, her muscles, the bone of her chest, and pierced, with just its tip, her heart. And she knew at that moment that she could never let anything as juvenile as fearing the changes to her life that marriage to Leo might bring come between him and her. There was really only the issue of a child to consider. . . . It was quite a revelation. And a freeing one.

Leaving Stella's side, she walked to the railing and let her gaze roam the sleeping world. It was peaceful, perfect, a starry summer night. And she drew strength from it to answer Stella's question, as she knew she must.

"If for some reason Leo had to leave me or he decided that he didn't love me"—*or because I am barren and he decides that he really desires children*—"I would let him go, Stella. My heart would hurt, but it wouldn't break, for I would continue to live my life as I always have." She turned back to Stella. "I would live it in the knowledge that my relationship with a man does not define who I am." She touched her hand to the beating of her heart. "I'll admit that I've learned these last few weeks that to have a man—to have Leo—in my life is a wonderful thing, a tremendous blessing, something much greater than any of my fanciful daydreaming even thought it to be."

Her confession drew a small smile from Stella's sad face.

"But the greatest blessing is in knowing that I stand approved by God with or without Leo Jones in my life. And it's God who sustains me, not my relationship with any man. Even the one I love."

Stella nodded. "I appreciate your honesty, Kyria Martha. It's not fair of me to come into your home and be so unhappy while you should be basking in having the gift of such a love. And after so many years of patience. Patience I know I wouldn't have. And you are right. I must—"

She broke off, squeezing her eyelids shut to stay the tears that were always close by. But she couldn't. They dropped like liquid weights.

Martha went to her and wrapped her in her arms again. Placing her head against her shoulder, Stella whispered the words that Martha knew were some of the hardest she had ever said. "I must. . .finally. . .let Dimitri. . .go. And trust God to choose a man for me."

Martha breathed out a silent prayer of thanks. This was a major breakthrough in Stella's recovery, and Martha knew that the strength and determination of her young friend, and her faith, would indeed help her to let go of the man she had loved forever.

Planting a kiss on the top of her head, she whispered, "Yes, kali mou, you must."

Chapter 14

That their late night talk seemed to have done some good was evident in the days that followed.

True to her declaration, Stella made an effort to let Dimitri go, as she seemed to will thoughts of him as far apart from her as he was physically. Although there were still moments when shadows would cross Stella's sweet face, Martha felt sure that her young friend's healing was progressing with a rapidity that only God could have brought to her hurting soul.

When Petros, Stella's father, called a few days later to check up on his daughter, Martha was relieved to be able to tell him that Stella was on the mend. Even though Petros had never considered Dimitri and Stella a good match, he had always feared that his daughter would never let go of the man. Martha was glad to hear the relief in his voice. Even after nine years, Petros was still mourning the loss of his wife, Emily, and there was only so much a man could bear. Guilt that he had wronged his eldest child after Emily's death weighed heavily on his mind.

~~~❦~~~

Casting a glance around the shop as she always did on first entering each morning, Martha gasped. Her gaze immediately zoomed in on the shiny new bicycle with the big pink bow that sat beside the fireplace in the living area.

"Happy late birthday," Leo said as Stella stood by his side clapping her hands and laughing in delight.

"Leo?" She skipped over to the bike and ran her hands over the smoothness of the shiny chrome. "It's beautiful." It was pink and white, the bike of every girl's dream for Christmas morning. "I don't know what to say. It's perfect and—" She giggled when her eyes spied the white wicker basket in front of the handlebars. It was overflowing with a bouquet of flowers. "A basket!" she lowered her face to the flowers and inhaled. "I see you have already gone to the farmer's market!"

"No. Not without you. Those were bought at a florist's."

"Leo, I don't know what to say." She put her hand on the bike's soft seat, which was a little bit higher than her thigh. The seat of the bike she had ridden in the village many years past had come up to her waist at least, maybe even her chest. "It even fits me."

"Of course it fits you," he said, as he came to stand by her side. "It was specially ordered from a shop in Athens just for you. And see"—he pointed to various aspects of the bike—"it has suspension, twenty gears for ease of pedaling, and it's made of titanium, which means it's light but strong. All the things a proper mountain bike needs to traverse the bumpy roads of Greece."

He was so excited that she almost didn't want to say anything to burst the happy bubble he seemed to ride. But she knew that she had to. "Leo, it's wonderful. But when I told you I don't know how to ride, I mean. . .I. . .really. . .don't. . . know how," she said, emphasizing each word. Maybe she hadn't made that totally clear the other day when they'd discussed her previous bike-riding endeavor. Did he know what he was in for?

"But didn't we already agree that I would teach you?" His dark eyes focused their attention on her lips, and a faint tremor quivered through her. "I'll teach you everything you need to know," he said, and she wondered, as his warm lips touched upon her own, if he was only talking about teaching her to ride a bike.

But her senses were soon so overwhelmed by the sensation of his nearness, her mind no longer questioned anything—whether she was right for him in spite of her inability to bear children or anything else. She relished the feeling of being adored by a man. By this man. When the kiss ended, she knew that she had never felt more womanly than she did at this moment. Nothing—not her pretty clothes, not the weekly hairdresser appointments, not even her luxurious baths—gave her that sense of fulfillment from being in his arms. It was a gift for which she thanked God—especially since it was something she had never expected to experience.

"May I?"

Her eyes narrowed. "May you. . .?" What was he asking?

"Teach you to ride this little bike."

Of course. The bike. She nodded. "I'd like that. But I feel so bad. All I gave you for a birthday present is a needlepoint."

"All?" His brows came together, cutting a straight line across his forehead. "Darling Martha, that needlepoint of our spot at the ancient church ruins is so much more than just a bike. It's something you created, a work of your hands." He took them in his own and touched each finger. "Something of you had to go into each stitch to make it so beautiful. I'll cherish it forever. And not only me, but generations long after we are both gone will, too."

But to have generations, there must be children.

There are children, Martha. A calm voice of reason returned. *Natalia's little baby will be as your grandchild, and because of Leo's and your love, that child will be Leo's grandchild, too.*

She took a deep breath. That was what she had to remember, what she had to focus on.

"Your needlepoint is real and good." He kissed the tip of her nose. "And next to your love, it's the most wonderful gift you could have given to me."

Children would have been the most wonderful gift.

But again willing away that nagging thought, she brought her arms up and around Leo and hugged him close. "I love you, Leo."

He rubbed his cheek and jaw against the top of her head, and she felt a slight tremor go through him as he whispered back, "And I love you, Martha."

"Okay, you two," Stella said and laughed, making both Martha and Leo grimace at one another self-consciously. "Enough of that. Go teach Kyria Martha to ride a bike, why don't you?"

"I'd like that," Leo said, reaching for Martha's hand. "But I can't." He twisted his wrist and glanced at his watch.

"Already trying to get out of the lessons?" Martha bantered.

"You wish," he said and tweaked her nose. Then, on a serious note, one that sent alarm through Martha's system, he said, "A situation has come up with my company, one that requires a computer conference. It's to start in about half an hour."

His company. Of course. He kept it so separate from their time together that Martha often forgot that he worked at it from his home each day.

"Isn't it the middle of the night at your home office?" Stella asked.

"It's late, but not the middle of the night. But this conference will take place from several locations around the world, so many of the men and women will be going to their computers at odd times."

"But since you're the boss—"

"I got to choose the time," Leo finished and grinned. "So, Martha, your bike lessons will start this evening."

But Martha's mind really wasn't on her lessons. It was on his company. "I hope nothing too serious has come up with your company, Leo." *Nothing that will take you away from me,* was what she wanted to say.

"Don't worry; this conference should be able to handle it." He kissed her lightly. "The wonders of the computer age." And turning away, he tossed over his shoulder as he walked out the door, "I'm quite partial to it."

⁂

"Wow!" Brian said as he walked into the shop a few hours later and saw Martha's new bicycle. "What a cute bike! I haven't seen one with a wicker basket in years."

"Why, thank you, Brian. Leo gave it to me. A late birthday present."

Brian rubbed his hand over the shiny new handlebars, then sauntered across the room toward the cash register and both Stella and herself.

"Hi, Stella," the young man greeted her.

"Hi." Stella returned and dipped her head slightly. Her shyness around Brian was so acute that Martha was sure that had she been as light in coloring as Brian, her cheeks would be bright red.

Seeming to understand and wanting to relieve her, Brian flashed his smile while turning toward the colorful glass beads that one of Martha's needlepoint ladies had handcrafted and painted. "Do you suppose that you could help me select some of these, Stella?" he asked and turned back to her.

Stella's eyes widened like Needlepoint's when she was frightened. Always before Brian had settled for her monosyllable replies and hadn't asked anything more of her. Martha was glad that he seemed to want to push her out of her shell now.

"Of course." Stella put aside the ledger she had been writing in and walked to the array of baskets with beads. Martha noticed that she still held on to her pencil. From the grip Stella had on it, Martha was afraid she might unwittingly break it in two. "What do you want to make from them?" she asked, slanting her eyes toward him. When he flashed a bright smile, she lowered her eyes back to the beads.

"I don't know exactly," Brian admitted and let his fingers slide through their smooth coolness as Stella looked on.

Looking at the two, Martha thought they made a lovely, if contrasting, couple. Brian's hair was fine and light with red highlights, and he had happy freckles across his face, complementing his extroverted personality. Stella's hair was dark and straight, her skin smooth without even so much as a mole on her cheek, somehow fitting her serious and introverted personality. But even with their differences, they seemed to fit together like two pieces of a jigsaw puzzle. They complemented one another.

"What would you suggest?" he asked, and Martha's mouth quirked. She was certain that Brian didn't need help in selecting beads. Martha hoped he would succeed in bringing out the woman who had obviously captured his fancy. Stella needed a fun-loving man like Brian in her life, even as just a friend.

"It depends on what you want to make, the colors you want to use, and. . . and. . .the amount of money you want to spend," Stella answered softly. But her answer seemed to give Brian hope. Martha suspected that it was the most she had ever said to him.

He turned and looked at Stella directly. Stella had no choice but to look up at him. "A necklace," he said after a moment. "One with green and gold"—his playful gaze roamed Stella's face—"that brings out its natural sparkle."

"I. . .see," Stella answered slowly and turned back to the beads. "Well, we have quite a nice selection of green glass beads in right now and these cloisonné." She held up the round beads of enamel work in which the surface decoration had been formed by thin strips of wire. "You could intersperse spangles on the strand, which should make it pick up light and sparkle quite nicely."

"Good idea. I like sparkle in. . .necklaces."

"Okay," Stella reached for a small plastic bag. "How many ounces do you want?" She picked up the little scoop.

"Ten beads."

"Only ten?" Stella turned to him in confusion. "I thought you were going to string a necklace out of them."

"I am."

"You will need more than just ten."

"I'll come and buy more after I string these first ten." He held up his hands and wiggled his fingers around. "I doubt that these thick fingers of mine will be able to do more than that each day, anyway."

Stella's gaze lowered to his hands, and she frowned. "Your fingers aren't thick. They're slender and—" She clamped her mouth on the rest of her sentence, but Martha was almost certain Stella had nearly said "nice."

"Okay, ten." She counted out a variety of green glazed beads, gold spangles, cloisonné, added a package of thread, and put everything in a bag. After sealing it shut, she handed the bag to Brian and retreated behind the cash register to ring up the sale.

Nodding at the new bike, Brian asked of Stella, "Do you ride?"

Stella glanced at Martha, who could tell her friend wanted to say no. But that would have been a lie. At medical school, Stella used a bike to go everywhere. Not only did she ride, but she was very good at it. Due to traffic, the roads of Athens were not biker friendly. Only the very best dared to brave them.

After a moment she gave a quick nod.

"Would you like to go for a ride sometime?"

"I. . . I don't have my bike here."

Martha looked at her sharply. They both knew that it was arriving by bus later that week. They had discussed only that morning how they could ride together, after lessons.

"A walk, then?" He glanced down. "Your legs are both here."

The chimes rang at the door, and Stella swallowed her reply, looking relieved. She used the distraction as an excuse to ring up the sale at the register.

Martha couldn't help but be pleased, as well, when she saw that it was Leo. He strode toward her, tall and vigorous, a smile splitting his strong face. She moved from behind the table and walked into his arms. "Hello, Martha-Mary," he said, kissing her lightly.

"Leo." She breathed his name. "Is everything okay with your company?" She had been thinking about his conference all day, concerned that something to do with his business—of all things—might take him away from her for good.

"Everything should be fine."

"'Should be'?" If that was meant to reassure her, it didn't. Apprehension slithered up her spine.

"Really, darling. I think we managed to get everything sorted out. It's nothing to worry about." Over her head, Leo smiled a greeting at the other two. "Hey, Brian. Stella. How are things going?"

Martha frowned. Had he turned to them as an excuse to drop the subject? He'd said not to worry. . . .

But more than that, God didn't want her to worry. She would give her fears over to Him and trust both Him and Leo to work out their future. Every aspect of it—her current fear of Leo's work having to take him far from her, her old fear of not being able to give him children. . . She would give everything. . .again . . .continuously. . .through prayer. . .over to God. Or at least she would try very hard to do so.

Brian's infectious laughter returned Martha's attention to the present. He dropped some euros into Stella's hand and held up his beads for Leo to see. "I just wanted something fun to take my mind off scholarly things."

Leo frowned at the little bag. "What's in there?"

"Beads. To make a necklace."

"A necklace for someone special?"

Brian laughed again and tossed the bag a couple of inches in the air as he walked toward the door. "You never know," he threw over his shoulder just as the door closed behind.

Leo beamed. "I really like that guy. He's always so happy."

"He is," Stella whispered, and when both Martha and Leo turned to her, she shrugged shyly. "He seems so uncomplicated, so. . .I don't know, nice."

Leo slanted his eyes toward Martha and smiled. She smiled back. Wisely, neither commented. Martha hoped that Brian wouldn't get tired of trying to draw out the girl. Stella was finally responding.

"Are you ready to start your lessons?" Leo asked, surprising Martha.

Stella smiled. "Go for it, Kyria Martha," she encouraged. "I want you to learn so that we can bike ride together."

"It seems to me"—Martha looked toward the door that Brian had just exited—"that someone else wants to do that with you, too."

A bashful smile flittered across Stella's face. "Maybe when my bike arrives I will go for a ride with Brian," she admitted, making Martha's heart thrill at how healthy it sounded, in terms of Stella's getting out and getting to know a man other than Dimitri.

A Japanese-speaking couple walked through the door, and Stella looked over at them. "Now go learn to ride. I'll hold down the fort," she said, as she moved toward the pair that were looking at a display of ceramic vases, replicas of those found in the archaeological site just down the road.

Leo walked over to the bike, relieved it of its bow, and pushed it toward the door. "Shall we?"

Martha lightly touched her hand to her stomach to still the butterflies that had taken flight. The idea of riding a bike still terrified her. Even such a friendly looking, Martha-sized bike. "Promise you won't let go of the seat until I'm sure of what I'm doing?"

"Scout's honor."

She breathed out deeply and, waving to Stella, preceded him out the door.

She soon found out that her butterflies were there for a reason.

Even though they found a nice quiet spot to learn, and the frame was better proportioned than the one from her childhood; even though Leo ran beside her patiently, giving her instructions and valiantly holding on to the seat of the swiveling bike; and even though it had a white wicker basket filled with flowers, it was still a bicycle. And it took her days of lessons before she felt confident enough to allow Leo to let go of her seat. And several more days until she could do more than ride in a straight line before stopping the bike, getting off, and turning it around in order to go in a straight line down the dirt path again.

Getting up the nerve to turn the bike to the right or to the left was almost as traumatic as allowing Leo to let go of the seat. And she doubted that she ever would have done that if the front wheel hadn't hit a root on the path and twisted the handlebars in her hands so that she either had to go to the right or fall. So then she could ride in a circle, but only in one direction. It took her several more days until she could turn the bike to the left. And several more days after that until she could go to the right, then to the left, at will. But the big day finally came when Leo decreed that she could officially be called a bike rider and that she could actually go out on the quiet streets.

Martha wasn't so sure about that but didn't want to disappoint him. She hoped that her clothes might give her the confidence she lacked, so she dressed for the big adventure in a fitted, cap-sleeved, navy T-shirt; khaki cotton twill pedal pushers; and brown leather sandals with turquoise beads. She donned her pink and white bike helmet, rather than her normal straw hat, and went to meet him.

"Don't you look. . ." He paused, glancing at her ensemble. "Nice."

"What's wrong?" Martha looked down at her clothes.

"Don't you think you should continue to wear your sneakers?"

She lifted her right foot to show him the rubber soles. "These should be fine." She flashed him a smile. "And don't they look much better than sneakers?"

"I like your sneakers."

"But my feet get so hot. Let me try riding with these. If I don't feel comfortable, I'll change."

"Okay, but let's go back to the field so that you can get the hang of cycling with sandals," he said, nodding at her footwear in a none-too-pleased way.

"All that dust!" Martha cried. She had had enough of that field. It might be flat and devoid of traffic, but the *Meltemia*—summer winds similar to the Californian Santa Anas—was late this year, and dust blew everywhere. She had had to soak for nearly an hour in bath-oil beads each evening to feel like a woman again—and not like a prickly porcupine. "No. I'll go slow."

His brows rose in doubt, but he nodded. "Okay. But be careful. People don't realize it, but shoes make a big difference when riding a bike. Your pedaling perception can change with footwear, and it's easy for your foot to slip off the pad."

And that was something she soon found out when, after only thirty feet, her right foot slipped out from under her, got caught in the spokes of the back wheel, and she found herself tumbling to the hard pavement.

"Agh!" Her rump hit the road with a bone-rattling thump. She lost her hold on the handlebars and watched as the bike continued on a teetering, weaving, lumbering gait down the road without her.

"Leo!" she cried. Even though she well remembered the last time she had fallen, she hadn't remembered it hurting quite so much as it did now. Her whole body throbbed.

But then, Leo was by her side. "Martha!" His hands reached for her, cradled her. "Don't move until we find out if anything is broken."

She gave a shaky laugh. "Just my pride," she said, as she saw people come running from every direction. "I should have listened to you. I should have worn sneakers." She looked down at her pretty sandals. They were askew, with the blue turquoise beads scattered all across the road. But it was her right ankle that got her attention. It seemed to be screaming at her and made her forget the bleeding cuts on her left elbow and shoulder and the scratches that seemed everywhere except, thankfully, her head.

"No, darling. I shouldn't have given you a present that you could hurt yourself on. I should have insisted that you wear sneakers—" But he stopped speaking as she bent toward her ankle, and his eyes widened in concern. "What is it?"

"My ankle. . .it hurts. . ." Tears sprang to her eyes at the sharp pain that seemed to pulsate from it. She clutched at his shirtsleeve. "It. . .really. . .hurts, Leo." She couldn't help the groan that came out. The muscles in her foot felt like they were tearing apart.

"Let me see." The ridge of his jaw was grim.

"Do. . .you. . .think I. . .broke it?"

"I don't know, but I think I'd better get you to the hospital to have it X-rayed."

"Oh no," she groaned.

"Let me through!" Stella's competent voice reached Martha's ears. The most Martha could offer the concerned young woman as Stella knelt by her side was a wobbly smile. After a commiserating return smile, Stella was the competent professional. She ran her hands over Martha's body, and Martha knew that she was seeing the side of Stella that would turn her into one of the best of physicians.

"It's her ankle," Leo supplied.

Stella nodded but completed her exam of Martha's more important organs before moving to the ankle. Her touch was light but capable. "Can you move it?" she asked. Even though it hurt to do so, Martha was relieved to see that she could.

"I don't think it's broken. Just badly sprained," Stella pronounced. "But for now—" She spoke to the crowd that had gathered. "The sooner we get ice on it, the better. Can anyone get ice for me?"

"Here." Brian extended his unopened can of icy cola. "Use this until I get an ice pack from the kiosk," he said, then took off for the pack.

Taking it with a grateful nod, Stella applied the cold cola to Martha's ankle right where it was swelling.

"Can she be moved?" Leo asked, concern lacing his voice.

Stella didn't answer him but gave Martha a reassuring smile. "How do you feel, Kyria Martha? Do you hurt anywhere else? Your back, your neck, your hip? Anywhere?"

Martha focused on each of those areas as Stella listed them. Except for the jarring pain of her body having been thrown to the ground, she didn't think anything else hurt too badly. "I don't think so."

"Do you want to try walking?"

"No," Leo interjected. "I'll carry her." Looking at Martha, he asked, "If that's okay with you."

Martha nodded. "I would be grateful. Are you sure I'm not too heavy for you, though?"

Leo chuckled. "You're a lightweight." His eyes darkened with loving concern, the best medicine in the world to Martha. "But even if you weighed as much as a horse," he continued, "I would still be able to carry you."

Brian returned with an ice pack. "The man at the kiosk also gave me a stretch bandage." He looked over at Martha and grimaced. "He said lots of tourists seem to need them."

She smiled her thanks for trying to lessen the blow to her ego, as Stella expertly tied both the bandage and the ice pack around her ankle.

"If you can just wrap your arms around my neck," Leo instructed after a moment. But that was easy for Martha to do. A natural instinct. She felt herself being lifted from the pavement and, for the first time since she was a little girl, carried by a man. She rested her head against his chest and listened to the rhythm of his heart. It worked as a tranquilizer.

But suddenly remembering her bicycle, she swiveled around. "My bike!" It was on its side in the middle of the road, fresh flowers scattered. The white of the wicker was now black in places. The back wheel looked bent and flat, with several spokes sticking out like spiked hair. "Oh, my bike. . ."

"I'll get your bikes," Brian said as Leo started walking back toward the shop. All the people—townspeople and tourists alike—wished her a speedy recovery.

"My beautiful bike. . .that you gave me," she whimpered.

"The bike is the least of our concerns right now. It can be fixed." He spoke through clenched teeth. "Not only did I insist that you learn to ride—something you really didn't want to do—but I gave you the instrument of your torture, too."

"She'll be fine, Leo," Stella said from their side. "I don't think she even broke her ankle. Just sprained it."

"But it was caused by the present I gave to her."

Martha heard his tone, and even though her leg hurt, she knew that his irrational guilt probably pained him more. "Stop that now, Leo," Martha instructed. "Stop it right this minute," she repeated, when he looked down at her. "If I had worn the correct shoes, we would even now be sailing down the country roads. It's my fault. And as soon as my ankle heals, I will get on the bike again and take not just one but many bike rides with you." She grimaced. "But with the correct shoes next time."

He bridged the two inches that separated them and kissed the tip of her nose. "You are quite a woman, Martha-Mary. You know that?"

And with those words Martha suddenly didn't feel even one of the hundreds of screaming nerve endings in her body.

Chapter 15

Martha was relieved that the medical station in Ancient Olympia had an X-ray machine—one of the many presents to the community from Leo. She was grateful that she didn't have to go to the hospital, but even more, that her fall in the street hadn't ended with a broken ankle. It was only sprained, as Stella had thought. She was told to stay off it for several days to give the ligaments around her joint time to heal.

"But how am I going to do that?" she complained to Leo a couple of hours later, after all her cuts and bruises had been tended and her ankle wrapped in a fresh bandage. She was on the long couch in Once Upon A Time, with her leg elevated. "I'm not a 'stay off it' kind of woman, and I have the shop to think about," she grumbled.

"Bah," the deep, rasping voice of her father answered from the doorway, and Martha's shocked gaze flew to meet his. "Stella is a competent young lady, and she will look after your store while I will look after keeping you from getting too bored for the next couple of days."

"Baba!" Martha exclaimed and held out her arms to the slender man as he approached. He leaned down and kissed her on her forehead. As always, his beard tickled her nose. "How did you know? I wasn't expecting you until tomorrow, for my name day."

He winked at Stella, who sent him a conspirator's smile as she rang up an item on the cash register. "A pixie girl told me about your accident."

Martha smiled at Stella. "I'm glad." She squeezed her father's hand.

He rubbed his other hand against her face. "Did you honestly think that we wouldn't come? Especially since I was as close as Kastro? I returned from New York yesterday."

"What do you mean by 'we'?"

The chimes jingled as Allie, Stavros, and their children, as well as Petros, Stella's father, and her younger brothers and sister came flooding in. "Us!" Jeannie Andreas, the oldest of Allie and Stavros's children, shouted out, speaking for them all. Laughing and chattering, everyone gathered around Martha and Stella. All the children had bouquets of flowers from the hillsides of Kastro for Martha.

"Oh, wow," Stella squealed, as she hugged her father, sister, and brothers.

"I can't believe you're all here."

Martha smiled over at the family. She knew how much Stella had been missing them. She had planned to visit them for St. Mary's Day, which was Maria Stella's name day, too. But with Martha's sprain, that wouldn't have been possible.

Martha looked at her father, and tears sprang into her eyes.

He knew her so well. When she had had an appendectomy a few years back, they had learned that the best way for her to forget her pain was to have company all around her. Some people liked quiet. Not Martha. The more people around, the better. But what was she going to do, stuck on the sofa with her foot propped up on pillows?

"Now before you start worrying about looking after us all, we have all checked into the Olympia Hotel, and our needs are all taken care of. The only thing we want is to take your mind off being laid up for the next few days."

"Well, that's not the only thing." Allie spoke from the foot of the sofa. "As your doctor, I want to have a look at that leg," she said, and they all laughed.

Martha's eyes searched out Leo. He had stepped back to let her father and friends gather around her. He was looking at the scene with that of wonder mixed with a poignancy Martha didn't really understand.

"Leo." She extended her arm toward him. When he reached her side, she took his hand and said, "I would like for you to meet my father, as well as some very dear friends." To her father she said, "Baba, this is Leo Jones." She winked at him. "You might remember, the man you told me about last May. . ." At his quizzical frown, she continued. "You know, the one you said you have been praying about for many years."

Martha had always thought that there wasn't anything that could surprise her father. But she knew then that she had found the one thing.

In the quick way she had inherited from him, her father swiveled around to face Leo. He looked at Leo from above his glasses, a mannerism he used when studying something of much interest or importance. Then he nodded. "Yes, Martha-Mary, I can see that he is," he said, sizing up Leo in the way eighty-five years of living and making people his business had taught him to do. Extending his arm in greeting, he offered. *"Heiro poli,* Leo."

Leo returned the salutation meaning "nice to meet you" in perfect Greek. "Heiro poli, Papouli."

Baba's eyebrows rose higher at the perfectly spoken greeting before falling again below the rim of his glasses. Martha had told Leo in the past how everyone, with the exception of her brothers and sisters, referred to her father as Papouli—grandfatherly priest. She was pleased that he had remembered. "You speak Greek. But you aren't Greek, are you?" Papouli asked.

"No, sir," Leo replied, again in Greek. "I'm American."

"Ha!" Papouli exclaimed. "So is Natalia's husband."

"So Martha-Mary told me."

The older man raised one eyebrow at the use of the double name. "Do you live in America?"

"No, Baba. Leo lives here. In Ancient Olympia."

"Ahh." Between his beard and mustache, a smile lit the old man's features. "Of course you do. Your Greek is superb." Turning to Martha, he said, "I'm glad for you, kali mou. Even though Natalia visits Greece often and has a lovely home in America, I know that it's hard for her to be so far away."

Her father already had her married to Leo! It was time to change the direction of the conversation. Motioning to Brian, who was standing next to Stella, she said, "Brian is American, too." Introductions went all around, and when everyone quieted down again, Martha asked her father, "Did you have a nice time in America, Baba, while visiting Natalia and Noel?"

"A wonderful time. Natalia and Noel are so adorable together and so looking forward to the birth of their baby."

Martha sent a hesitant glanced up at Leo. Natalia could give Noel a child—several children, even. She couldn't do the same for this man. She looked for something in his face that might show that it troubled him. But there was nothing.

To her father she said, "You must tell me all about it."

"I will," he assured, then looked at her with the concern of a father in his eyes. "But you look very tired now. I think you should get some rest. We'll all come back later tonight after you have had a nap."

"I agree," Allie spoke, her doctor persona fully in place. She was holding Martha's X-rays up to the window to get a better look at what the picture showed. "You were very blessed, Martha. I agree with the doctor in town," she said and flicked her French braid behind her shoulder. "Nothing is broken. It's just a sprain that should heal well if you give it the proper amount of time to rest." She handed the X-rays to Stavros and lightly touched Martha's ankle to examine how it was bandaged. "It doesn't feel too tight?"

"No, it's fine. It doesn't hurt too much if I don't move it."

"It's very black-and-blue," Leo commented.

Allie nodded. "That's to be expected."

"Do you want to see it?" Martha asked.

"No, no. That's not necessary." Allie looked at Stella. "Were you able to apply ice to it for the first half hour or so?"

"Yes." Stella glanced at Brian and smiled, a real smile, Martha noticed. One that wasn't overridden with a bashful tilt of her head. "Brian made sure that I had plenty of ice. And fast."

Allie nodded at him. "Good job. That's probably why there isn't too much swelling." Then she turned to Martha. "Just keep it elevated for the next twenty-four hours and try not to walk on it. We'll bring you a pair of crutches to use this evening."

"But how are you going to get up the stairs to your apartment?" Baba asked, concern covering the lines of his face.

Martha knew that the only disadvantage to her refurbished traditional home was its lack of an elevator. She had already decided that she would sleep on the shop's sofa for the next few days. She wasn't sure how well she would rest, but she really didn't know what else to do.

Before she could answer, Leo said, "I'll carry her up and down the stairs for as long as she needs, Papouli."

"Leo." She looked at him in surprise, delighted at the prospect. One nice thing that had come from her fall—along with her father's and friends' unexpected arrival had been those few minutes spent in Leo's arms when he carried her back to the shop. He had done so effortlessly. "You don't have to do that," she demurred. "I'll stay down here for the next few days."

"No, Martha. You can't rest here. You need your own bed to recover quickly." He looked at Allie. "Isn't that right, Doctor?"

"Absolutely," Allie returned. But a slight twitch around her mouth and a quick glance at her husband gave away her obvious delight in Leo's concern for Martha.

Martha scanned the faces all around her. She could tell that they were all very interested in learning more about Leo. She would gladly tell them. Soon. "But I'm too heavy for you to be carrying me up and down those stairs." Because the building was so old, the stairs were very steep. There was a big difference between carrying her down a flat road and up those steps.

Leo's smile connected with those of the other men in the group in a male way before he turned to her. "Like I said earlier, you're a lightweight. Believe me. Susan was as tall as the doctor here."

He looked at Allie and smiled, and from her peripheral vision, Martha saw Baba's eyes widen in interest. She knew that she would be called upon to do some explaining about Susan soon. "And Susan weighed much more than you do," he continued. "Even at the end. For the last three months of her life, I carried her all over our house. I want to help as much as I can. After all, I gave you the bike."

"But I wore those silly shoes," she countered. "They were beautiful, though," she sighed.

"Shoes." Baba laughed, the deep throaty one of a man pleased about something. "Don't worry about your shoes, kali mou. "I have a whole suitcase—a big one—filled with clothes and shoes and accessories for you from Natalia."

"Really?" Martha couldn't help how much that pleased her. She enjoyed clothes, but mostly the ones Natalia picked out for her. It was only a hobby for her, though, because her worth wasn't connected to her pretty clothes. She could be without all her lovely clothes tomorrow, and it really wouldn't make much of a difference to her at all. The Lord's words about seeking first His kingdom and His righteousness were words Martha lived by. Her fashionable wardrobe was just a gift she accepted from the Lord, much like a child who accepts a good gift from her father.

"Now if that doesn't make you feel better, what will?" Stella said, and everyone laughed in understanding. "So it's settled," Stella said, continuing the decisive tone that Martha was glad to hear. Since her breakup with Dimitri, she'd been anything but resolute. Martha couldn't help but wonder if having Brian by her side had something to do with it. Even through her pain, Martha noticed how they had been working in accord since her fall. First concerning the ice and the bikes, and now, over at the cash register as Brian helped her with the many patrons who were in the store. Her accident wouldn't be too bad if it helped to bring these two closer together, even if only as friends. "Leo will carry you back and forth from your apartment to here so that your foot will heal as quickly as possible."

"Yes. So you can wear all the new shoes Natalia sent to you," Baba said, bringing titters from the young girls, who recognized a good bribe when they heard one.

Martha held out her hands in defeat. But it was one she was happy to concede. "Thank you, all." Her eyes touched on everyone before weariness assailed her, nearly closing her heavy lids. "My own bed does sound very good right about now."

Leo squeezed her hand before turning to Allie. "What do you say, Doctor? Shall I start my duty right now?"

"Absolutely."

Stella turned to Brian. "Can you mind the store for a few minutes while Yatrinna, that means a 'female doctor' "—she referred to Allie—"and I go and fix Martha's room and get her settled?"

"Sure," Brian was quick to agree. Martha could tell from the way his mouth curved and his light eyes twinkled that he was pleased Stella had asked him, too.

"Stavros and I are going to take this group to the sea to swim." Baba motioned at the children, who were wandering quietly around the shop looking at all its treasures. "We'll come back with dinner this evening and keep you company on your veranda. How does that sound?"

"Wonderful," Martha murmured. "I'll rest much better knowing you will all be returning. Thanks so much for surprising me a day early for my name day. Somehow, something that could have been so bad"—she motioned to her ankle—"has ended up being quite. . .nice." *Really nice, actually.*

"Remember, kali mou, 'with God all things are possible,'" Baba said, repeating the same verse he had told her to apply to her life the day she told him about her desire to move to Olympia. "He can even take something as nasty as a spill from your bike and use it to bring about good."

"Amen," Allie agreed, and Martha smiled over at her dear friend. She knew that that was a promise Allie had held tightly to when she had first come to Greece.

After kisses and well wishes, everyone filed out, leaving only Brian and Leo alone with Martha and a few tourists who were admiring the Byzantine icons one of the needlepoint ladies had painted. Allie and Stella had gone upstairs to the apartment to fix up Martha's room.

Leo pulled up a chair and sat next to Martha while Brian busied himself with retrieving a ladder to dust the highest shelves in the room.

"How are you doing?" Leo asked, as his fingers lightly traced her cheekbone.

She reached up for his hand. "It's funny. I should be sad because of my fall and my ankle." She lifted her elbow and grimaced. The deep scrape on it hurt more than her ankle at the moment. "But the only emotion I have right now is gratitude. I feel so loved. By you, by my father, my friends. . ." She motioned upward. "My God."

"Darling Martha-Mary. You are loved. And your father and friends seem so special."

"You seemed almost. . .sad, though, at one point."

He didn't deny it. "No, not sad. Wistful. My parents are long gone. My wife, for the last six years. I didn't have any brothers or sisters, so there's only me."

"No cousins?"

"Not close ones."

And no children, either, that taunting refrain went through her brain. But she pushed it aside and rubbed her hand against his cheek. "Leo, you have family now. Not only mine, whom I will gladly share with you, but everyone in Olympia who loves you."

Shouldn't that be enough? Were children necessary when one was blessed with so much love? Dear Lord, please help me overcome my doubts about this.

"I thank God for bringing me here."

"Me, too, Leo." She rubbed her face against his hand much like her cat might. "Me, too."

～～～

Allie and Stella settled Martha into her bed, helping her change into her most comfortable summer sleepwear, a cotton gown of soft pale pink, and rearranged the pillows until her leg felt comfortable. Through the slats in the closed shutters, the curtains danced to the strong beat of the dry wind; the cicadas ground out their deep, hot-weather tune; the happy sounds of tourists wafted up from the street. To these much-loved summertime melodies, Martha slept like a baby. She slept safe in the knowledge that her baba and friends were close by and that the man she loved was in the next room, ready to take care of most all her needs.

And that was a trend that was to continue for the next several days. She was never left alone. Since Stella was needed in the shop and Leo had computer work to do, he brought his laptop and, more often than not, sat in the shade of the vine-covered kitchen veranda working while Martha slept each afternoon. And when Martha awoke, he traded places with Stella and kept an eye on the shop while Stella helped Martha with her toiletries and dress.

Her name day celebration had been, despite her injuries, one of the best— and the first that she had not prepared from start to finish on her own. Allie, Stella, and her needlepoint ladies had insisted on taking care of everything. The shop was closed for the day since the feast day celebrating the assumption of Jesus' mother, Mary, was a national holiday. Except for the *torta*—torte—and cake, they had the entire party catered by a local *taverna*—restaurant, and Martha sat like a princess among her cushions while all her many friends as well as her relatives in Ancient Olympia came to her home to wish her hronia polla. Souvlaki and gyros; fried zucchini and eggplant; ten different cheeses including the snow-white goat's cheese, feta; five different salads; and bowls of fresh fruit—figs, peaches, plums, melons, and grapes—were offered to all, as well as large servings of torta and Allie's famous American-styled chocolate cake.

But what Martha enjoyed most was watching Leo interact with everyone. He and Baba had become the best of friends. They spent much time together talking about things ranging from the Olympic Games—both ancient and modern—to the latest computer software Leo's company was developing, to Baba's research for his book on the early fathers of the church.

But when Leo wasn't with her father, he was with the children. Stella's youngest brother, Vassili, a young teenager whose voice broke endearingly every now and then, had grown into a computer whiz. He and Leo seemed to talk another language as they discussed the world of computers. But Leo was equally at ease with bouncing Allie and Stavros's youngest child on his shoulders. It was bittersweet, watching him with the children. They seemed to be drawn to Leo as if he were St. Nicholas himself. And seeing him with them only reinforced those prickling fears that Leo deserved the chance to have children of his own. It was the only sadness to touch her during the early days of her convalescence and one that she had to continually give over to the Lord in prayer. She knew that when the time was right, she would talk to Leo about it once again. She only wanted to devote more prayer time to it before she did so.

By the time her family and friends returned to Kastro two days after her name day, Martha's ankle was feeling much better, even though Allie insisted that she still stay off it for the next several days. Since her injured tendon seemed to scream whenever she moved it the wrong way or applied pressure, those were doctor's orders that Martha didn't have difficulty following. Especially since she had Leo, Stella, and even Brian to help her with the shop.

Martha sat on the sofa in the shop the afternoon after the Kastro contingent of friends and family had left, her current needlepoint project in her lap—one that she had created of the ancient stadium, a very popular item with the tourists. Leo sat on the other sofa reading a newspaper. Martha sent covert glances above her half glasses toward the cash register, as Brian tried to entice Stella out for a bike ride. Her bicycle had arrived the previous day.

"I can't leave the shop, Brian."

"I'll watch it," Leo interjected, looking above the newspaper at the young couple.

"Are you sure, Leo?" Stella asked, and the hopeful expression in her eyes made Martha's heart rejoice. "The cash register can be kind of tricky."

"I know." He had used it several times. "But I've got it down now." He walked to the register, reached for the cell phone, and handed it to Stella—just as Stella had once done to encourage them to go for a walk together. "To ease your mind—and mine—take this, and if I need anything, I'll call you." He gave an exaggerated wink as he went around the table. "Have a great time."

Stella laughed. Brian beamed.

And Martha didn't think she could love a man more than she did the giving one named Leo Jones.

Chapter 16

A little over a week later, Leo walked into the store one morning. Martha looked up from where she stood. . .without her crutches.

"What's this?" That he was shocked to see her in the shop alone and standing without aid was evident in his tone. "How did you get down the stairs?"

"Believe it or not, I walked." She held up her hand to stay his ready protest. "I almost hate to tell you, but Allie came by late last night and declared that my ankle is nearly healed. As long as I keep it bound in a stretch bandage and don't overdo it, it should be fine for normal activities." She laughed. "But she warned me, no bike riding—or attempting to do so—for another month."

He chuckled. "I certainly won't rush that." He frowned. "It's wonderful news, but why did you say that you hate to tell me?"

"Because I'm going to miss not having you around so many hours every day, Leo," she replied without pause. She wanted him to know the truth. She didn't want to go back to just seeing him every now and again and in the evenings. She liked seeing him first thing every morning and then for several hours afterward.

"Darling Martha." He ran his hand down her cheek and smiled that lazy half smile that made her sing on the inside. "Don't you know that nothing could keep me from coming here every single morning now?" His gaze lifted to the apartment above them. "Actually, I wouldn't mind living there with you."

She knew that her own eyes had to have become as wide as saucers.

"As your husband," he said, and the world seemed to stand still.

"What?"

He laughed, that mighty, soft rumble that she rejoiced in hearing, especially since she knew that she was the one who had brought it out in him. "Don't you know how much I love you and that I want to spend the rest of my life with you?"

Tears gathered in her eyes. Happy tears just like her father's when glad emotion ran through his system. She tried to blink them away. But Leo wouldn't let her.

Lowering his head to hers, he gently kissed first her right eyelid, then her left. Martha felt as if the world had not only started moving again, but that it was now spinning out of control.

"I love you, and I want to marry you," he said, wrapping his arms around her shoulders to pull her close. With a sound beyond words, he captured her lips with his own. Martha felt the fireworks that she had always heard people talk about.

"I love you, too, Leo," she whispered back. She rested her nose against his neck, savoring the manly scent of him. Had he actually said that he wanted to marry her? Even though their relationship had been moving in that direction from the very first, she almost couldn't trust her ears. And she learned at that moment that thinking about changing her life by marrying and actually being offered the opportunity by a man she loved and who loved her were two entirely different things. Emotions totally supplanted questioning thoughts now, but in a healthy way, a good way—the right way.

" 'A wife of noble character who can find?' " he said softly with loving emotion, quoting from the final chapter of Proverbs.

He took a half step back so that their gazes could meet. " 'She is worth far more than rubies. . . . She sets about her work vigorously; her arms are strong for her tasks. She sees that her trading is profitable, and her lamp does not go out at night,' " he said, indicating her shop with a slight twist of his head. " 'She is clothed in fine linen and purple.' " He ran his hand over her fitted sleeveless shirt, which happened to be purple linen, and chuckled. " 'Her husband' "—he smiled the way a woman hopes a man will smile at her—"the man I want to be to you, Martha," he qualified, " 'is respected at the city gate, where he takes his seat among the elders of the land.' "

"Oh, Leo." The fact that he believed her to have all the makings of a such a wife made her feel deeply blessed. She had never thought that a man would feel that way about her.

"Wait." He touched his finger to her lips. "There's more. 'She is clothed with strength and dignity; she can laugh at the days to come. She speaks with wisdom, and faithful instruction is on her tongue.' As has your wisdom and faithful instruction been toward Stella all summer long."

"Leo, I don't know what to say—"

"Shh," he smiled and continued. " 'Many women do noble things, but you,' dear Martha, 'surpass them all. Charm is deceptive, and beauty is fleeting; but a woman who fears the Lord is to be praised. Give her the reward she has earned, and let her works bring her praise at the city gate.' " And please, please, dear Martha, marry me and make me the happiest man alive."

She gasped. There it was, clear and sure and perfect. The question she had thought never to hear and yet, since meeting Leo, somehow had always known she would be asked. And with it, all the uncertainty she had felt about marriage—the conflicts she had been afraid might come into the perfect life she had made for herself by joining her life to his, his business taking him away from her, and even, the greatest of all, her lack of being able to give him a child—seemed to fade away as the peace of God that transcended all understanding finally, after so many prayers, prevailed within her. She knew then that to marry Leo Jones was most definitely God's will for her life and what she wanted more than anything else in the world. Leo was the man her father had been praying would enter her life.

Without allowing even a heartbeat more to pass, she wrapped her arms around his neck and didn't hesitate in answering. "Yes! Yes!" she shouted, and as his strong arms went around her, he lifted and twirled her round and round. She couldn't stop laughing, couldn't ever remember being happier.

"Thank you, darling. Thank you," he whispered in her ear as he held her close to him. "I promise to make you happy. I promise to be the husband you deserve."

"Oh, Leo," she said, as her feet touched the floor once again. "I only hope you are happy with me. After all, I've never been a wife before. And you have already proven that you make a good husband."

Holding her face between his hands, he looked straight into her eyes. With emotion deepening his voice, he said, "You are an answer to many of my prayers. And one even—" He swallowed, and she watched his Adam's apple move up and down. "One even that Susan made before she passed on."

She reached up and touched his face. "She wanted you to remarry?"

He nodded. "She knew. . .how much I need the companionship of. . .a special woman in my life. She often admonished me to be open to recognizing that woman when God led me to her. You, dear Martha, are she. I knew it the first afternoon that we talked."

Nodding, remembering that she had felt it even then, she took his hand and led him over to the cream-colored sofa. Sitting, she said, "Tell me about Susan and your life together. Even with our marrying, I don't want you to ever think you have to forget her or your love, or feel as if you shouldn't talk about her. This might sound strange, but I love her for loving you as much as she did and caring for you when I couldn't."

He shook his head and softly, like a feather touch, cupped his left hand over her right cheek. "No, not strange for you, darling Martha-Mary. Normal for you."

Turning her face to kiss his hand, she then took his hand in her own and prompted again, "Tell me about her and your life together." She had often wanted to ask him but had felt that it was too personal. But with his proposal and her acceptance, everything had changed. Nothing was too private to discuss between them now. Nothing.

"When we married, we weren't Christians. Oh, we were traditional ones, having been raised in the tradition of Christianity and not anything else, but we had never made a conscious choice to follow Jesus Christ and to let the Spirit of God rule in our lives."

"I understand what you mean." She did. Many people called themselves Christians without really understanding what joys and wonders that declaration should bring to their lives—and what a commitment it was on their part, too.

"I made a lot of money doing something I loved—designing software—and Susan and I, well, we were very good at spending it. Houses around the world, luxury cars, vacations at the most renowned resorts on earth—"

"Wait. Are you still that wealthy?" She knew that to help others as much as he did, and the community of Olympia in general, that he had to be comfortable, but she had had no idea that he was that well off—not "houses around the world" wealthy. His own home was nice but not spectacular, certainly with nothing to show off such exceptional wealth. But would she expect anything less from him?

He nodded, but with a funny little twist to his eyebrows. "Even more now," he admitted. "But, Martha, my greatest wealth is that which belongs to all believers, the richness of knowing Jesus as my Savior. That's true wealth. The fact that I also have money means that God has entrusted me with a great responsibility, one that I am to use to help as many people as I can. It's a privilege but also a tremendous responsibility," he said, and she knew that the accountability he felt over the use of his monetary assets was great. "One much bigger than the running of my company has ever been. To give away money goes against the nature of man. I should know. For years it went against my own."

Because of what Natalia and Noel had told her—who were both wealthy, too—she understood what he was saying. But unlike Leo, Natalia had given of her money from the first. "Wealth doesn't impress me, Leo," she assured him. "Except maybe in terms of how it's used to help others."

He nodded. "I was sure that it wouldn't. Not with your sister being famous and wealthy."

"Natalia is quite well off, but she's not the reason I'm this way. Baba is. And it's the same for Natalia."

He grinned. "Now why doesn't that surprise me?"

She returned his smile. "He might only be a village priest, yet he's the richest man I know. He doesn't have a portfolio declaring his material worth, rather a portfolio of good works that declares his relationship with Christ. My father's faith has expressed itself in love and obedience his entire life."

She grinned. "He doesn't have monetary wealth, even though Natalia and Noel are constantly trying to change that. But that has never stopped him from giving all that he has."

" 'Silver or gold I do not have, but what I have I give you. In the name of

Jesus Christ of Nazareth, walk.'"

As it always did, that verse from the third chapter of Acts, where Peter healed the crippled beggar, made goose bumps rise on Martha's arms. "Precisely."

"Susan and I learned the hard way that wealth didn't make us happy. There was actually no comfort in it at all."

"My father has often said that it rarely brings comfort. On the contrary, it brings problems unless it's used correctly."

"So we learned. It actually turned me into a monster of sorts. Susan, too. I felt as if I could rely on my wealth and myself for everything, that I didn't need anything else. Not even God, really."

He paused, but when he spoke again, his voice had the sound of a judge's gavel being struck on a desk. "Then Susan became ill." Deep sorrow crossed over the planes of his face. "And we learned the hard way what was important in life. In spite of the years in which we had lived for ourselves—only for ourselves, not for God, and certainly not for His people—we were blessed. God granted us several years of living together as Christians in all the wonderful, miraculous meanings of the word. And we really lived life then, lived life as it is supposed to be lived, with God as the King of our lives.

"Money can be such an insidious thing, Martha. It can make people believe that they are strong. But it's really nothing. Faith, hope, and love, the love that came in the form of the incarnate Christ—that's everything. That is riches beyond comparison."

"You're such a wise man," she murmured, and she was glad that she had asked him about his life with Susan. He was telling her much more than she had expected.

"Only because of the grace of God and only after having lived very foolishly for many years. I wouldn't go back to my thirties or forties for anything."

"Not even to see your wife?"

"I will see her again one day, and then it won't be with pain in her eyes."

She smiled. "And that's what makes you one of the wisest men I know. Almost as wise as my baba."

"Now there's a compliment." But then, with deep seriousness, he took her hands in his and said, "Martha, from the day we marry and on, you will be my wife. God has brought you into my life now for that purpose."

She understood what he was saying. And she loved him for it. "The Lord said, 'At the resurrection people will neither marry nor be given in marriage; they will be like the angels in heaven.'"

He nodded. "That's right. It's only here and now that we marry, that we need a helper. In heaven the relationship of marriage is not in existence. Susan is not waiting for me there as her husband, only as her brother in the Lord."

"And that will be a grand reunion."

"It certainly will."

"But, Leo, what about children?" She had to hear from his lips, just one more time, that he really didn't mind that she was too old to give him a child. "Are you sure you don't mind—"

He held up his hand and looked at her as if a piece of a puzzle had just fallen into place. "Is this what's been on your mind all these weeks?"

She knew that her mouth had dropped open. She closed it. "You knew?" How had he known? Having wanted to pray about it, she was sure that she hadn't said anything about it except for that time on their birthday.

"I sensed that you were wrestling with something. I just had no idea it was this. If I had—" He stopped speaking, then, squeezing her hands for emphasis, said, "If I had, I would have told you, Martha, that this is not something that you need to dwell on. It's not an issue with me."

"But I saw that look that passed over your face on our birthday when you thought that I might still be able to bear a child. You were thrilled with the idea."

He shook his head. "If we were ten or twenty years younger, then I would have loved to have had a child with you, Martha. But that has nothing to do with now."

A week ago, she wouldn't have been able to understand what he was saying. In fact, she would have totally misunderstood him. But she didn't now. The power of prayer. . .how she thanked God for His constant presence in her life. So many problems were being avoided by her having gone to God about this situation first. "God has made that clear to me. But, Leo, I have to ask you this question, just one more time—"

"You can ask me anything, as many times as you want, Martha. Anything. Always. Whenever." He assured her.

She nodded. "Leo, you are a man, and you can still have children if you were with the right wom—"

"As I told you on our birthday, you are the right woman for me, Martha. The only woman."

"But you love children, Leo."

"Of course I love children. What's not to love? But I love Formula One racing cars, zebras, and clipper ships, too. That doesn't mean I have to have my own."

"Leo, a child is not like any of those things."

"No, of course not, but the point is the same, Martha. I long ago found peace about this issue. I'll be honest; it was one that plagued both Susan and me for years. That's why we decided to adopt the little girl, our little girl."

"Leo." An amazing thought popped into her head. "Why don't you try to find that girl now?"

The way he looked at her, as if she had just told him he won a billion dollars, made her heart beat even faster.

"Martha, I don't know if you will believe me, but even as I spoke the words 'our little girl,' that was exactly the thought that came into my head, too."

"Of course I believe you, Leo." Oh, how she believed him! God and His amazing ways!

He stood up and ran his hand through his hair. She could tell that the idea thrilled him. "Do you really think it's possible? Do you really think that we might be able to find her?"

We. He immediately put them together in this. That little girl, who was now a young woman, was to be both of theirs to search for, to love. . . It touched her deeply. "With God all things are possible, Leo," she said, her voice husky with tears of glad emotion. "And if He wants us to find her—and something tells me that's exactly what He wants—then we will."

"We didn't give her up, you know, Susan and I. We just wanted her to have a home with both a father and a mother. Susan only lived for three years longer."

"I know, Leo. That's what makes your searching for her even more special. You and Susan went out looking for her all those years ago because you wanted her in your life. And now you and I are doing the same thing because we want her. At least to let her know that there is a couple in a land far, far away who loves her. If nothing else."

"You really wouldn't mind?"

"Mind?" Martha stood. "Leo, what's to mind?"

He gave a short laugh. "And she's eighteen now. That's good, because I honestly don't think, at this point in my life, that I would like getting up during the middle of the night to care for a hungry baby." He chuckled. "God does have a reason for that biological clock."

"Ah. . .now wait a minute, Leo. Are you forgetting that we might just be doing that soon?"

He frowned. "What do you mean?"

"There's Natalia's baby to think about. Since I'm practically the baby's *yiayia*—grandmother—that means that upon marrying me, you will become its *papou*—grandfather. We will be sharing in midnight feedings upon occasion."

"Ah. . .see dear, sweet, adorable Martha"—he smiled, a slow smile of wonder—"you are giving me a baby, after all."

Feeling like the heroine in her very own love story, she whispered, "I love you, Leo. Thank you for loving me."

"Thank you back, Martha-Mary. Thank you and. . .for giving me a family."

Chapter 17

When Brian and Stella walked into the shop a few minutes later, the young couple might not have been surprised to see the older couple sitting on the sofa enjoying one another's company, but Leo and Martha were definitely taken aback when Brian leaned over and gave Stella a slow but sweet kiss on her lips. Brian acknowledged his audience with a happy smile and a good-natured wave before he turned and disappeared out the door. Martha saw that there was an extra spring to his steps that hadn't been there before. And that was saying something, because Brian's walk had always had a bounce to it.

Stella nearly floated over toward them, with the look of a woman in love written across her face. Martha noticed that she was fingering a bright, sparkly necklace that hung from around her slender neck.

Martha's and Leo's eyes met. "I think that romance is in the air," Martha said, and Stella giggled.

"It is," she agreed and two-stepped between the displays of the discus thrower and the Byzantine icons, which made her skirt twirl around her legs like an open umbrella.

"Well, well, well," Leo said.

"Tell, tell, tell," Martha trilled, patting the sofa beside her.

Stella skipped over to her side and threw her arms around Martha's neck. Stella was so different from that night at the beginning of the summer when she had arrived at Martha's door, a sad and heartbroken young woman. There was energy in this hug, the thrill of life radiating through her body. And fun.

"Oh, Kyria Martha, you were right," Stella sang. "You told me that if I were to marry someday, that it would be to a man of God's choosing and not my own."

Martha blinked. "Wait a minute." She waved toward the door. "Are you saying that you and Brian—?"

Stella laughed the way she had years ago, before her mother had died and responsibility ruled her. "No, no. Not yet, anyway. But since your accident, Brian and I have become very close. Look," she said, pulling at the beaded necklace. It was green and gold and looked as if it had been fashioned expressly for Stella.

Martha frowned. She recognized the beads. They were the ones they sold. "Wait a minute. Those aren't the beads that Brian—?"

"Yes! Yes! Can you believe it? Brian was buying the beads for me." She patted her hand against her chest. "He wanted to make me a necklace! Have you ever heard of anything so romantic?"

"Well, I'll be," Leo said and chuckled from the other side of Martha. He leaned across Martha to get a better look at the necklace. "Nice job, too. I always said I liked that young man."

"You were right." Stella sat back and sighed. "You both were." Her lips turned up at their corners. She sighed a contented, dreamy breath. "He's wonderful. So full of life and fun." Sadness shadowed her eyes, and her voice lowered. "Even though he's suffered gravely." She swallowed; then, looking down at the hardwood plank floor, she explained. "A week after his eighteenth birthday, his parents and twin brother were killed in a small plane crash."

Martha's hand covered her mouth. "Oh no."

Leo clicked his tongue against his cheek. "That poor boy."

Stella nodded. "Because he had just legally become an adult, though, he was able to become guardian to his twin sisters, who are a year and a half younger than he." She paused again to swallow down emotion that threatened her with tears. "Because of that he was able to keep his family together." She turned her eyes to Martha. "He didn't even have his father to help him as I did. Except for his sisters, who were devastated, he had only himself and. . .his amazing faith in God. He said that that was what got him through." Her voice lowered. "And still does."

"Other than seeing him in church each Sunday, I thought I saw the stamp of Christianity on him," Leo murmured.

Stella nodded. "He has a fantastic working faith. One that is much stronger than mine."

"Don't say that, kali mou," Martha admonished. "You were only thirteen when your mother died."

Stella shook her head. "No, not that. Lately. With Dimitri, I mean. Thank God, Dimitri is an honorable man. I shudder to think what might have happened to me if his scruples weren't so high."

"Call him sometime and tell him that you understand now why he broke up with you. He's been very worried about you."

Her eyes widened. "He's called and asked about me?"

"Of course. He loves you. . .as a friend," Martha was careful to qualify.

Stella nodded. "As I do him. I will call him. Soon." A bright smile lit her face. "I only hope that a fun-loving and joyful woman might soon come into his life. He needs someone like that as much as I need Brian."

"I hope so, too," Martha murmured. Dimitri was still one of Martha's favorite people. "But what's going to happen now that summer is almost over? Is Brian returning to Philadelphia?"

Stella beamed up at her. "No! That's why I'm so happy today. He just told me that he's going to definitely be working at the American School of Classical Studies in Athens this year. That will give us the time to really get to know one another and see if we are meant to be together as we both feel we are."

"I'm so glad, Stella." Martha hugged her young friend close. "Your mother would be so proud of you, as I know your father is already."

"I'm glad, too." Leo interjected and, with a conspirator's wink at Martha, said, "Glad to hear that Brian will be in the country this year, because I'd really like him to be at our wedding."

Except for her eyes, which swiveled back and forth between Martha and Leo like windshield wipers on a car, Stella's whole body seemed to freeze. But only for a moment.

"*Zito!*" she shouted, the Greek equivalent of *yippee* and flew up off the sofa and into their arms. "I'm so happy for you! So happy." After hugs and kisses, she ran to the phone. "We have to call everybody! Oh! Natalia! Natalia is going to be so happy! And Yatrinna—Allie—and your baba*!*" She put the phone down. "But first I have to tell Brian." She ran toward the door, then ran back to Martha and, throwing her arms around her again, squeezed her so tightly that Martha could hardly breathe. "Oh, Kyria Martha, the whole world is going to be happy for you!"

When she left, Leo wrapped his arm around Martha's shoulder and pulled her close to him. "I don't know about the whole world, but I certainly am happy."

"Umm. . .me, too," Martha murmured.

"You don't mind changing your whole life for me? Sharing your world with me?"

She looked up at him sharply. Did he know how that thought had plagued her before? She couldn't be anything but truthful with him. "To be honest, Leo, in the beginning I wasn't so sure about wanting such a change. I wanted you but"—she motioned to her store, which represented the life she had made for herself, with God's help—"I wanted this, too."

"And now?"

She smiled. "Now I know that my life here will be enriched by having you in it. But more than that, you are more important to me than any of this. I love it here, but I love you more. All of this could go away, or I could move away from it." That was something she would never have considered before the remarkable events of this day. But she knew now that it was the truth. Suddenly, even this lovely little spot on earth wasn't important to her when compared to her love for Leo. "But I wouldn't want to go anywhere without you, agapi mou."

"Thank you, Martha. That means so much to me." He kissed her forehead.

Then, chuckling, he asked, "Were there any other conflicts going on in that lovely head of yours that I should know about?"

"Well," she giggled and admitted, "I was afraid. . .for a time. . .of your work taking you away from me."

He laughed. "Believe me, Martha. That will never happen. I would sell my company before letting it."

"Sell it? Leo, no." She was appalled. "I would never ask you to do something like that. Like I said a moment ago, I can even move with you to Olympia, Washington, if you needed to go because of your company." She was flabbergasted to realize that she really could.

"And leave Once Upon A Time. . .?"

"If it came to a choice between Once Upon A Time and you, Leo, there is nothing to choose from. Once Upon A Time is just a shop. You are the man I love. The man God has, after fifty-seven years, brought into my life to be my companion, my helper, my love."

"Ah. . .Martha. You are worth far more than rubies. . . and diamonds. . .and platinum. . .and gold. . ." He kissed her nose, then sat up straight. "To be truthful, agapi mou, my work isn't even a question anymore. After much prayer and careful consideration, I have actually decided to sell my company."

"Leo, no!" She swiveled to look at him. "Tell me this isn't because of me?"

"No." He tweaked her nose. "It's for me, for us. I feel it's the direction God wants my life to go. I'm ready for a change. And I love this little town. It's where I want to live, and for the first time since I was nineteen, I will be free of the responsibility of running a rather large company. At the moment I just want to stay and help you run Once Upon A Time, where people representing the whole world seem to come to us."

She snuggled down against his shoulder. She believed him. She wouldn't question his decision about his company. She actually felt like it was the correct one, too. "Umm. . .and if we don't want the whole world. . .?"

"We have only to close our door. . ."

"To be alone. . ."

"Together. . ."

She tilted her head up to look at him. "In our land far, far away. . ."

He leaned down, but just before his lips met hers, he whispered, "From the rest of the world. . ."

Epilogue

Five Years Later—Kastro

Hugging the mountainside as gracefully as only very old towns can, Kastro, with its sparkling white houses and red-tiled roofs, gleamed like a necklace of rubies and pearls in the light of the setting sun. But it was the people of the village, who walked and laughed among its little streets and alleyways as they made their way to the square, that were the village's greatest charm, its greatest treasure.

That was something that Papouli, who sat in the seat of honor at the front table in the square, knew very well. It was his ninetieth birthday, and friends and family had come from near and far to help him—the village priest—celebrate both having lived nine decades on God's earth and the publication of his book.

Lanterns and streamers hung from the centuries-old plane tree with long, flower-bedecked tables set up under it for the festivities soon to begin. Papouli trained his eyes upward toward the castle. It sat a stalwart friend to him all these years. He remembered playing among its walls when he was just a young boy, courting his dear wife, Tacia, there before they married, and taking his children up there when they were all still too young to climb up alone. A smile formed between his beard and his moustache.

His children.

All six of them were now happily married with children—and some even with grandchildren—of their own.

Even Martha.

His eyes searched out that dear, dear daughter. They crinkled at the corners when he found her right where he had expected her to be: in the hubbub of all the preparations for the feast that was soon to begin.

His Martha-Mary.

His eyes went to the man who stood beside her, helping her, being her loving companion, just as he had been every day of the four years that they had been married. Leo was the perfect answer to his prayer for a mate for Martha. And then some.

Papouli's eyes went to his newest granddaughter, Helen, who was near her new mother and father, Martha and Leo. He could tell from Helen's animated

348

movements that she was reveling in all the love, not only from her new parents, but also that which the extended family wanted to share with her.

It had taken several years, but Leo and Martha had finally managed to track down the little girl Leo and his first wife had almost adopted so many years earlier. And Papouli knew that that had been a part of God's plan, too. Helen, twenty-three years old now, had once again found herself all alone in the world when the couple who had adopted her—parents Helen had loved very much—had gone to heaven within months of each other.

Leo and Martha had arrived in her life within weeks of that sorrow, and now she was their daughter, both emotionally, and as of a few days previously, legally.

Papouli's gaze slid over to his Natalia.

He knew from Natalia how wonderful adopting a child could be.

Natalia was playing not only with her own little golden-haired daughter, but with all the children who came anywhere near her reaching, welcoming arms. And there was Stella and her husband, Brian, playing right along with them. Brian had one of his and Stella's twin sons on his shoulders while Stavros held the other. Dimitri and his wife swung their youngest child—a little boy of Indian background—in the air between them. He squealed out in the delighted way of babies secure in their world.

Ahh. . .the happy sounds, Papouli thought as he lifted his gaze up toward the cross that sat atop the dome of the Byzantine church that had been his place of worship for all of his ninety years. The sounds of his friends and family laughing and talking and playing were glorious.

He closed his eyes.

It was like a symphony.

The symphony of life.

Or else it was like one of his daughter's and Yatrinna's much-loved fairy tales: Happily-ever-afters sent straight from God had come to all his children and friends.

And with tears of joy glistening in his fine old eyes, Papouli said the simplest but most heartfelt prayer of all. "Thank You, Lord. Thank You."

A Letter to Our Readers

Dear Readers:

In order that we might better contribute to your reading enjoyment, we would appreciate your taking a few minutes to respond to the following questions. When completed, please return to the following: Fiction Editor, Barbour Publishing, Inc., P.O. Box 719, Uhrichsville, OH 44683.

1. Did you enjoy reading *Love from Greece* by Melanie Karis Panagiotopoulos?
   ❑ Very much—I would like to see more books like this.
   ❑ Moderately—I would have enjoyed it more if _____
   _____
   _____

2. What influenced your decision to purchase this book?
   (Check those that apply.)
   ❑ Cover   ❑ Back cover copy   ❑ Title   ❑ Price
   ❑ Friends   ❑ Publicity   ❑ Other

3. Which story was your favorite?
   ❑ *Happily Ever After*   ❑ *A Land Far, Far Away*
   ❑ *Fairy-Tale Romance*

4. Please check your age range:
   ❑ Under 18   ❑ 18–24   ❑ 25–34
   ❑ 35–45   ❑ 46–55   ❑ Over 55

5. How many hours per week do you read? _____

Name _____

Occupation _____

Address _____

City_____ State_____ Zip_____

E-mail_____

HEARTSONG
PRESENTS

If you love Christian romance...

$10.⁹⁹

You'll love Heartsong Presents' inspiring and faith-filled romances by today's very best Christian authors. . .DiAnn Mills, Wanda E. Brunstetter, and Yvonne Lehman, to mention a few!

When you join Heartsong Presents, you'll enjoy four brand-new, mass market, 176-page books—two contemporary and two historical—that will build you up in your faith when you discover God's role in every relationship you read about!

Imagine. . .four new romances every four weeks—with men and women like you who long to meet the one God has chosen as the love of their lives. . .all for the low price of $10.99 postpaid.

To join, simply visit www.heartsongpresents.com or complete the coupon below and mail it to the address provided.

Mass Market, 176 Pages

✄ -